EVEN THE DARKEST STARS

EVEN THE DARKEST STARS

HEATHER FAWCETT

BALZER + BRAY
An Imprint of HarperCollins*Publishers*

For all those who wander

ISBN 978-0-06-246338-8

Typography by Sarah Nichole Kaufman
17 18 19 20 21   PC/LSCH   10 9 8 7 6 5 4 3 2 1
❖
First Edition

PART I
AZMIRI

ONE

I STRETCHED MY hands over the dragon eggs, focusing all my concentration on their indigo shells, and murmured the incantation. The air rippled and shimmered.

I can do this. The thought was born of desperation rather than confidence. My fingers were frozen, my stomach growled, and my legs ached from hours sitting cross-legged. Behind me, the sheer slopes of Mount Azmiri, draped with cobweb clouds, rose to greet the gray sky. Beyond the narrow ledge I crouched on, the mountainside fell away as if hewn by an ax. The forest far below was hidden under waves of mist, with only a few treetops floating above the surface like skeletal ships. The wind stirred my hair and slid its long fingers down the collar of my *chuba*. I shivered. The faint light gathering over the eggs flickered and died.

Chirri smacked me on the back of my head, causing me to drop my talisman, a string of ravensbone beads. "Foolish girl! Don't break your concentration. You'll never get it right that way."

"I'll never get it right *any* way," I muttered.

She smacked me again. Perhaps she thought I would do better if my brains were rearranged. "This is the simplest resurrection spell I can teach you at your level. Do. It. Again."

I made a noise halfway between a sigh and a growl. The incense burning beside the clutch of lifeless eggs tickled my nose, and I pressed my lips together. If I sneezed, Chirri would make us go inside, into her cramped, airless hut, with its smell of burned herbs and its shelves lined with poorly cleaned animal skulls. Sending a silent prayer to the spirits, I looped the talisman around my hands, shook the beads over the eggs, and began the incantation again.

After several moments, Chirri let out an exasperated cry. "Are you speaking the words correctly?"

"Yes, Chirri," I said, straining to keep the anger from my voice. "I'm speaking the words correctly. I'm focusing my mind. I'm doing everything right, and I'm still a completely useless apprentice."

"You are wasting time with this obstinacy, Kamzin."

"We've been here since dawn," I snapped, losing my temper at last. "Trust me, the last thing I want to do is waste time."

The old woman smiled, the folds of her many wrinkles deepening, and I cursed my foolishness. Chirri was never angry, not truly—she merely used it as a ploy to make others reveal their weaknesses.

"You will stay here," she said slowly, "until every egg has

hatched. Or until the glaciers rise up and cover the village, or the witches return to the mountains in search of human souls."

Chortling at my expression, Chirri untucked her legs and drew herself to her feet, arranging her many shawls with exaggerated care. Then she retreated toward her hut, which perched higher up the mountainside on an even more precarious ledge. From there, she would watch me until I did as I was told.

Or froze to death.

I glared at the eggs, as if my incompetence was their fault. With a growl, I stretched my aching limbs, then settled in to try again. A bead of sweat trickled down my neck.

"*Hshhh*," came a low voice behind me. "Is she gone?"

I whirled. "Tem!"

To my astonishment, my best friend's head poked up over the side of the ledge. He must have climbed sideways from the terraces, finding footholds and handholds in the weathered granite of the mountainside.

"Er—Kamzin?" he said. "Could you give me a hand? My fingers are numb."

Bracing my foot against a rock, I hauled him onto the ledge. He collapsed on the ground, panting.

"How long were you down there?"

"Only since your fiftieth try," he said. I tried to punch him, but he rolled away, laughing. His handsome face was flushed with cold, and his hair, which usually hung low over his forehead, obscuring half his features, stuck out every which way. I couldn't help laughing too. I had never been happier to see him in my life.

5

"You look like a rooster," I said.

He blushed, running his hands through his hair so it would curtain his face again.

"You'd better hurry," I said, glancing over my shoulder. The clouds were advancing up the slope, sweeping over us in lacy bands. Chirri had vanished, as had her hut. "This weather won't hold."

He gazed at me uncomprehendingly. "What are you talking about?"

"You know what—you have to help me with these eggs."

"I can't." His face went white. "Chirri will know."

"She won't. She won't even know you were here."

He glanced from me to the eggs, then back at me again. "But she'll never believe—"

I grabbed his shoulder. "It doesn't matter if she believes it or not. It just has to *happen*, so I can get out of here. Please, Tem. I'm going crazy."

He glanced from me to the eggs. I could see him weighing his fear of Chirri against his desire to help me. "All right," he said finally. "But Chirri can't know I can do this. Or my father."

I nodded. Tem's father worked for my own father, as his head herdsman. He was a dour, sharp-tempered man who was gentler with a misbehaving yak than he was with his son. Tem was supposed to follow in his footsteps, and his father wouldn't be pleased to learn that his true talent lay in shamanism, not husbandry.

Tem took the talisman, winding the beads around his fingers, and began to chant. He seemed to change, in that moment—something in his bearing and demeanor shifted slightly, and he became almost a stranger.

I shivered. I had watched Tem work spells before—he often helped me practice, in secret—but I had never entirely grown used to it. He murmured the incantation in the shamanic language confidently, absently, with none of his usual self-consciousness, and I could feel the power gather like a storm. The ravensbone made a shivery sound that seemed to vibrate the air.

The eggs glowed. The glow turned to flickering, like sunlight through branches. Cracks appeared in the shells, and then, suddenly, they burst apart.

The baby dragons were the size of sparrows, with long, snake-like bodies supported by six squat legs. They began chittering almost immediately, shaking their damp wings in the breeze. The little lights they carried in their bellies flickered on and off. These were thin and colorless when the dragons were young; as they aged, they would gradually darken and take on color—commonly, an iridescent blue or green.

"Stand back," Tem said. He murmured again to the largest dragon, which let out a questioning chirp. As one, the dragons spread their wings and took flight. They swirled around us in a tumult of wind and feathery scales, making me shriek and laugh. Then they zoomed away like a glittering arrow, their lights bouncing through the clouds.

"Where are they going?" I said.

"I sent them to Chirri."

I doubled over with laughter, imagining Chirri's reaction when the baby dragons swarmed her hut, hungry for milk and teething on her furniture.

"Why aren't you here in my place?" I said, shaking my head. "You should be Chirri's apprentice. You're as powerful as her."

"Because my father isn't the elder," Tem said. "And no, I'm not as powerful as Chirri."

"Near enough," I said lightly, sensing the mood shift. My apprenticeship to Chirri had always been a sore point between us. The truth was, Tem would have made a far better shaman for our village than me. But Azmiri's shaman was always a relation of the elder, usually a child or younger sibling—a way of consolidating power, which would surely backfire spectacularly with me. Tem, as gifted as he was, was a herdsman's son. It was unheard-of for someone like him to assume such an important position in the village.

"Come on," I said, grabbing his hand. "Let's go find some breakfast."

We flew down the rubbly slope of the mountain, leaping over boulders and grassy knolls with practiced ease. As we came within view of the village, the cloud lifted, revealing huts of bone-white stone huddled against the mountainside, threaded with steep, narrow lanes. The southern half of the village was newer and more uniform than the rest, the huts less eroded and roofed with pale terra-cotta tiles. They had been constructed two centuries ago, replacing those destroyed by the terrible fires that had swept through Azmiri.

We took a shortcut through the orchard, and I leaped up to

snatch an apple from one of the boughs. It wasn't the season yet, and the flesh was painfully tart, but I didn't care. I was hungry enough to eat my own boots.

The terrain rose again, and I scrambled up the hill. The earth fell away on one side. Across the valley, the mountains Biru and Karranak shoved their snowy heads into the clouds. A familiar feeling welled up inside me—the feeling that I could leap across the valley and come to rest lightly on one of those other peaks. As if I could dig my toes and fingers into the wind and scale it as I had scaled so many earthbound things.

I was ahead of Tem, and didn't at first hear him yelling. I turned, laughing breathlessly, running backward now.

"What did you—" I began, then let out a cry. I stumbled over a rock and landed hard on my elbows.

All I could see was color. A cacophony of color, green and red and purple and blue. It filled the sky like a monstrous cloud. But as I opened my mouth to scream, the thing resolved itself into a shape—a balloon.

A hot air balloon, sweeping silently over the mountainside. I could make out several small figures silhouetted on the deck, gazing down at me like haughty ravens. The balloon's shadow passed over me, and I shivered.

Tem reached my side. "You all right?"

I nodded, and he helped me to my feet. We watched the vessel drift over the village, slowly descending until the deck came to rest on one of the barley terraces. The massive balloon sagged to the ground, obscuring our view of the occupants.

"Spirits!" was all I could say.

Tem made a dismissive noise. "River Shara travels in style. He's probably full of enough hot air to power that balloon himself."

I stared at him. "River Shara?"

"Ye—"

"*The* River Shara? You're telling me that was the *Royal Explorer*?"

"I think so. I—"

"The greatest explorer in the history of the Empire?"

"Well, I don't know if he's—"

I grabbed his arm, excitement flooding me. "Why didn't you tell me he was coming?"

"I only heard of it yesterday, from one of the traders. You should have known, anyway—why didn't Lusha tell you?"

"Oh, of course," I said, with exaggerated understanding. "I forgot that you haven't met my sister."

Tem rolled his eyes. "All right. But I'm sure she and Elder have known about this for weeks."

"Of course they have." I kicked at the top of a tree poking over the edge of the cliff. Somewhere below, a vulture let out an angry squawk. "They wouldn't think to tell me. What in the world would the Royal Explorer be doing here?"

Emperor Lozong had many explorers in his employ—men and women, mostly of noble blood, charged with mapping his vast and mountainous empire, spying on the barbarian tribes that threatened his southern and western borders, and charting safe paths for his armies. As his territory expanded, the emperor relied increasingly on explorers to provide him with vital information, not only about the lands he possessed, but also those he wished to conquer. My mother, Insia, had been one of them, though her connection to the nobility was so distant that it would have counted for little at court. River Shara, on the other hand, belonged to one of the oldest noble families, one with close blood ties to the emperor himself. He had earned the official title of Royal Explorer—the most powerful position at court, rivaling even the General of the First Army—after leading a harrowing expedition beyond the Drakkar Mountains in the farthest reaches of the Empire, scaling mountains and glaciers and cheating death countless times. Though many men and women had occupied the position of Royal Explorer, few were spoken of with the same reverence as River Shara.

Tem was shaking his head. "Maybe the emperor sent him to make sure we're still here, and if not, to update the maps."

I snorted. It wasn't an unlikely idea. High in the Arya Mountains at the eastern border of the emperor's lands, we rarely received visitors from the distant Three Cities. When we did, it was the talk of the village. Even a band of cloth merchants was cause for a banquet.

And this was no mere merchant.

My heart pounded. "I have to meet him. I have to talk to him."

Tem had been speaking—about what, I didn't know, for I hadn't been listening. He fell silent, his expression troubled. "Kamzin—"

"This could be my chance." I didn't have to explain what I meant—from the look he wore, he understood well enough. He knew how I jumped at the opportunity to join my father's men on their hunting trips in Bengarek Forest. How I spent my free days climbing the neighboring mountains. How, when my mother was alive, I had begged her to take me along on her expeditions, and how I still spent many evenings poring over her maps of strange and distant lands, tracing the faded lines of ink with my fingers. I wanted to be an explorer more than anything in the world. I wanted to traverse glaciers and map wilderness and sleep under a roof of stars. I wanted to push against the world and feel it push back.

"So what are you going to do?" Tem said. "Walk up to the Royal Explorer and ask him to please bring you along on his next expedition? Offer to carry his pack or massage his feet?"

"I don't know what I'm going to do." I twisted my fingers through my braid. It smelled like Chirri's incense. "I have to think."

"What you should be thinking about is your lessons with Chirri," Tem said. "Not impressing some noble from the Three Cities."

"And where will that get me?" I felt my temper rise. "Tem, I'm seventeen years old, and I'm still only a junior apprentice. Chirri refuses to make me her assistant, and you know what? I don't blame her. I hate magic—I'm terrible at it. You know I can't do this for the rest of my life, no matter what my father says."

"You're terrible at magic because you don't try," Tem said, giving me an exasperated look. "Anyone can do magic. You get better the more you work at it. It's like any skill—weaving, or running, or anything else."

What Tem said was true enough, to a point. Anyone could do magic, provided they had the right talismans and knew the incantations. But there were some who, for whatever reason, took to it more naturally than others. Who possessed an affinity no amount of training could match. That was Tem—it would never be me.

"You know I'm no good at running," I pointed out. "My legs are too short. I always finished last when we used to race each other. It's like that with magic—there's a part of me that's too short, or too small, and nothing is ever going to change that."

"You've improved since I started helping—"

I turned away. "You're not listening."

"I always listen to you," he said. "I doubt you'll be able to say the same for River Shara. He's known for many things, but listening isn't one of them."

I scowled. I knew River Shara's dark reputation—everyone did. Stories of his merciless assassinations of barbarian chieftains, his intolerance of weakness in his traveling companions. He was said to have stranded men and women who had proven too weak to keep up with him, and not all of them made it back to the Three Cities.

I also knew that most stories were like the shadows painted by the late-afternoon sun: deceptive and exaggerated. I wasn't going to be afraid of stories.

Tem gazed at me for a long moment. Then he sighed. "What do you want me to do?"

I leaped into his arms, wrapping him in a tight hug. "I knew I could count on you."

13

He pushed me away, trying and failing to hide the blush spreading across his cheeks. "Have I ever told you how crazy you are?"

"A few times," I said. "Look on the bright side—if I become a famous explorer, I'll take you on my expeditions."

"So I can traipse around in the wilderness, sleeping on rocks and roots and half freezing to death?" Tem snorted. "I'd rather herd yaks."

"No, you'd rather be Chirri's apprentice." I regretted it instantly. A shadow crossed Tem's face, and he ducked behind his curtain of hair.

"Anyway," I said, "I'm going to talk to Lusha. Maybe she'll know what this is about."

"She's Lusha," Tem said. "She knows everything. Whether she'll be in a sharing mood is another question."

TWO

"OF COURSE I knew River was coming," Lusha said. "He sets out for the North in two days. I'm going with him."

I stared at my sister. She ignored me, calmly tapping the excess ink from her brush. She bowed her head again over the star chart, which was so long and wide it needed eight stones to pin it to the table. I glared at the side of Lusha's head, contemplating grabbing one of the inksticks and grinding it into her careful drawings. Biter, one of Lusha's ravens, gave me a warning *crrrk* from his perch on the windowsill.

"You're going with him," I repeated.

Lusha made no reply. The paper rustled as she shifted position.

"You didn't say a word to me." I kept my tone even through sheer force of will.

"There was no reason to."

I shot Tem a look, but he only shook his head. He was hovering by the open door frame of the observatory, as if ready to dart away at a moment's notice.

My sister glanced at me, her large eyes narrowing, as if she couldn't comprehend what I was still doing here. Lusha wasn't beautiful in the traditional sense, or even particularly pretty, with her thin face and ears that stuck out like the handles of a vase. But she was tall, with limbs like willow boughs, and eyes that flashed when she smiled. Her thick hair swirled to her shoulders like liquid night, appearing to be in motion even when there was no wind to stir it. Every week it seemed there was a new man falling tragically in love with her. Tragic for them—Lusha never seemed to take much notice of anything apart from astronomy. Plotting the courses of the moon and stars, tracking the constellations, and predicting future events based on their movements—it was a rare gift, more intuition than power. She had been even more obsessive about it recently, sometimes staying up all night and appearing late at the breakfast table with shadowed eyes and ink-stained hands. Whenever I remarked on her behavior, I was just met with a blank look, or, more commonly, a pointed comment about my own indulgent sleeping habits.

I wrapped my arms around my body, chilled even in my heavy *chuba*. The seer's observatory, perched high above the village, beyond even the goatherds' huts, was lined with windows with neither curtains nor shutters. There was a large square hole at the highest point in the roof, through which the wind whistled perpetually. The salt candleholders lining the table somehow only increased the feeling of cold as their small flames shivered in the breeze, permeating the air with a sharp, briny taste.

"Why would he need you?" The question just slipped out, harsher than I meant it.

Lusha gave me a stern look. She was only two years older than me, but it often felt like more.

"Because I can help him," she said.

"With what?"

She seemed not to hear me. "I was honored that he would seek my assistance. We should all be honored. If the expedition goes well, Azmiri will win favor with the emperor."

"Well, *you* will, anyway," I muttered. It was typical of Lusha to assume that her own triumphs would somehow improve the world. Perhaps knowing from birth that you were destined to become an elder had something to do with it.

I edged closer, trying to get a glimpse of her worktable. But I saw no maps there, nothing that could give me a clue about this mysterious expedition. Only endless star charts—piles and piles of them. There were more scattered around the observatory, furled and leaning against walls, or hanging from nails hammered between the stonework.

"What are you doing?" I said. "Counting every star in the sky?"

Lusha's brow furrowed as she traced a constellation with an inky finger. "I'm trying to work something out," she muttered into the table.

I blew out my breath. I was used to my sister's vagueness, but this was too much. "Lusha, why is River here? What does he want with you?"

She was quiet for so long I thought she was not going to answer. "I'm going to lead him to Mount Raksha."

There was a loud clatter. Tem had knocked over one of Lusha's wooden telescope stands. He stared at her, his eyes round as coins. I knew that my own expression was a mirror of his.

"Raksha?" I could barely get the word out. "He wants to climb Raksha?"

"Yes."

"But why?"

"I don't know. I only know that the emperor places a great deal of importance upon him doing so, and quickly. I'm to lead him there before the winter storms set in. Once we leave Azmiri, we'll stop for nothing."

"But why you?"

She gave me a hard look. "Because I'm one of only two people living who knows the way."

The wind swirled through the observatory, smelling of night and snow. But this wasn't the reason I shivered. The memories were, memories that stirred in my mind like a wind that heralded a storm.

"Are you mad?" I said.

"Not to my knowledge." Lusha turned back to her star charts. "Now, Kamzin, if you could go someplace else? I'm really quite busy."

I stood there, motionless, for a full minute. Lusha did not raise her head or give any sign that she was aware of me. I could have been a wayward comet in a constellation that did not interest her.

Finally, I stormed out, Tem trailing behind me.

Back in my room, I upended one of my clothes chests, spilling scarves and dresses across the already messy floor. I opened my cabinet and rifled through scrolls, tossing several onto the pile.

"Kamzin," Tem said, "what are you doing?"

"I threw another scroll over my shoulder. Ragtooth, sleeping on my pillow, let out a growl. He opened one green eye to gaze at me.

"I can't believe she agreed to this," I raged. "I bet she doesn't remember the way."

"Do *you* remember the way?"

I didn't answer immediately. The memories were old—I had been barely eleven—and I didn't like thinking about them. It had been the first and last time Lusha and I had been allowed to join my mother on one of her expeditions. We'd set out in a large group, accompanied by several shamans and healers. Our goal was to search for new paths through the Arya Mountains—paths that could be taken by the emperor's armies, or his enemies—and it had taken us within sighting distance of Raksha, the highest mountain in the world. *Higher than the stars*, the legends said. On the way back, half our party had been killed in an avalanche. A storm in Winding Pass had claimed more lives. My mother had barely managed to save Lusha and me.

"Yes," I said quietly. "I remember."

After my mother's death, Lusha and I became the only living

survivors of an expedition to that distant place. Yesterday, this hadn't seemed significant.

It was now.

Tem rubbed his face. He looked tired—these last few days, he had been out late into the night, helping his father with the herds. "This isn't like Lusha. She's not usually reckless, and this goes beyond that."

Shaking off the memories, I murmured in vague agreement, tossing another scroll onto the pile. Raksha was said to be unclimbable. Only a single explorer had ever attempted it—a man named Mingma, some fifty years ago. The only two survivors of his expedition—both of whom had died before I was born—wrote of black crevasses hidden beneath the snows, of ferocious storms and blizzards, and of sheer walls of ice hundreds of feet high. The mountain was said to be the abode of monsters, and cursed by spirits as ancient and unyielding as the glaciers. Even to lay eyes upon it was considered bad luck.

I found the scroll I was looking for. The light was fading, and I whistled for one of the house dragons. The beast that nested in the back corner of my room uncoiled himself sleepily and fluttered to my side. I dug the sour apples out of my pocket and placed them on a dish—dragons will eat almost anything—and he set upon them with enthusiastic gnashing and gnawing. Immediately, the faint glow radiating from his belly brightened enough to chase the shadows away. I bent over the scroll again, following the lines with my fingertip.

"Kamzin."

I jumped. Tem was standing behind me, looking over my shoulder.

"What?"

"If you think climbing Raksha is madness, why are you looking at a map of the Nightwood?"

I didn't reply. The witches' forest was a dark stain, with little in the way of labeled features—few explorers had visited it, fewer still had returned. It encroached upon the only viable route to Raksha, a grueling, northward hike through the Arya Mountains' eastern foothills, which lay outside the domain of the Empire.

"Why are you really upset?" Tem's voice held an undercurrent of anger. "Because Lusha is risking her life on a fool's errand? Or because you want to be in her place?"

I let the scroll curl back up, turning to face him. "I thought you understood. You said you would help me."

"That was before I knew what it would mean." There was no hesitation in Tem's voice now, as he met my eyes. "How can you even consider this? You saw what happened to your mother's expedition. You were there."

"I won't make the same mistakes my mother did."

Tem muttered something under his breath.

"What?"

"I said, you're unbelievable." His face was pale. "What do you expect to gain from this?"

"Everything!" I slashed the scroll through the air. "Tem, this is *River Shara*. If I can impress him, I could be leading my own expeditions for the emperor one day. Imagine—me in a tahrskin *chuba*."

Tem didn't need to ask what I meant. All the emperor's explorers—*only* the emperor's explorers—wore *chubas* made from skins of the mountain tahr, a rare and exceptionally difficult beast to hunt. A single skin could fetch enough gold to buy half a village. The tahr were born with coats of sooty brown, which gradually lightened to white as they aged. Hides of each color were stitched together to make a coat as warm as it was lightweight, and two-sided—the dark a perfect camouflage for forest travel, the light allowing the explorer to blend in against the snow. In a tahrskin *chuba*, you became part of the landscape itself.

"You would throw your life away for that?" Tem said.

"I'm not throwing my life away." My own anger was rising. "Are you saying I can't do this?"

"I think you can do anything," he said quietly. "That's what scares me."

"So are you going to help me or not?" I turned away from him and began digging through the heap of clothes. I needed something that would make me look older, and imposing. More like Lusha.

"Tem?"

Silence.

I turned around. "Don't be—"

I stopped. I was talking to a room of dragonlight and dusty scrolls. Tem was gone.

THREE

THE ECHOES OF the dinner bells had long since quieted by the time I entered the banquet hall. I had planned to arrive after Lusha, so as to be the one everybody would stare at when I swept dramatically into the room. But, to my annoyance, my sister wasn't there yet. The few people who glanced up at my arrival soon looked away again, unimpressed.

I gazed around, momentarily overwhelmed. Father had spared no expense in welcoming the Royal Explorer to Azmiri. So many villagers had shown up that they spilled into the yard, where a roaring bonfire provided relief from the mountain cold. Guests lounged on bamboo benches that lined the stone-paved hall, or crowded around the central hearth, drinking *raksi*. The wooden pillars that held up the high, flat roof were adorned with brightly patterned tapestries, which, combined with the murals, gave the room a colorful, chaotic appearance. Dragons threaded their way sinuously through the crowd or perched on stone shelves that lined the walls, suffusing the hall with a shifting glow as they begged alternately for scraps and ear rubs from sympathetic guests. Because they were so costly to breed and maintain, Father liked to have as many dragons around as possible when trying to impress important guests. This, however, was more than I had ever seen in one place. Father must have borrowed some for the occasion from other villagers. Guests waded cautiously through the sea of scales and flickering light, nudging aside the beasts with their feet.

I had never seen anything like it.

A nervous shiver traveled down my spine. For a moment, I wondered what I was doing. River Shara was the most powerful man in the emperor's court, and the hero of so many fireside stories it was sometimes difficult to believe that a living version of him existed. He was known for his ability to climb mountains like a snow leopard, find uncanny routes to safety through enemy lands, and hike for days over grueling terrain without wearying. What he was *not* known for was either patience or sympathy. It was said that when one of his assistants betrayed him, he had hunted the man down, stripped him of his clothes, and left him tied to a tree in a frozen mountain pass.

But I knew I would never have another chance like this. Taking a deep breath, I plunged into the sea of chattering guests.

"Kamzin!" It was Litas, one of the village boys. "Is it true? You met River Shara?"

"I saw him land, but—"

It was the wrong thing to say. Three of Litas's friends pressed close, their eyes wide. "How big was the balloon?" said one.

"Did you speak to him?" another demanded. "Is it true that the barbarians cut off both his earlobes"—the girl pressed her hands against her head, mimicking earlessness—"and now he can hear leaves rustling ten miles away?"

I sighed, reeling off a brief description of what Tem and I had witnessed. The children listened with fascination, pelting me with more questions. How tall was River? Did the balloon bear the emperor's insignia? How many shamans did River have, and had they announced his arrival with lightning and fireworks? It was some time before I was able to satisfy their curiosity enough to escape.

I scanned the room. Scattered among the crowd, mostly in small groups, were men and women who could only be members of River Shara's entourage. They all had the same Three Cities look—as if a dye shop had thrown up on them, as I had once sneeringly remarked to Tem. I had never been to the Three Cities or the emperor's magnificent court, with its glittering pagodas and fragrant gardens—nor had most villagers, given that it was a weeks-long journey along a winding trade road favored by bandits—and I had no desire to, judging by the people who lived there. Blue hair seemed to be the fashion now, and they wore theirs curled and woven with silver charms that looked as though they would be an awful trial to remove. Instead of *chubas*, they were draped in wispy cloaks of dark green.

I had no idea what River looked like, but it wasn't a stretch to

25

assume he would be the center of attention. Soon enough, I found him.

He was as handsome as the stories said, with a wide mouth, tousled hair, and broad shoulders. He stood several inches above the tallest man in the room, but even without this, there was something about him that drew the eye. An odd, uneven scar extended from the edge of his temple across the bridge of his nose, halving his face. He wore the same elaborate costume as the other Three Cities guests, but his hair was undyed. Consequently, it was easy to see that he was graying at the temples. Deep furrows extended from the corners of his eyes, though he was far from an old man— perhaps thirty or so.

That gave me pause. Given River Shara's reputation and accomplishments, I had expected someone close to Father's age. Still, there was no mistaking the curious crowd of villagers gathered around him, listening intently as he spoke. He had an expressive manner, moving his hands as if painting his story in the air.

I smoothed my dress, which was dark blue with fox-fur trim. It was the finest I owned—or rather, the finest Lusha owned. She never bothered with the luxurious clothes her suitors bought for her, and I doubted she would even notice it was missing. I had altered it, of course, from her narrow measurements to my stouter ones. Around my neck I wore my whitest silk scarf, edged with gold stitches, and beaded earrings hung past my shoulders, clinking softly when I moved my head. The outfit felt strange, almost like a costume—my lessons with Chirri were usually outdoors, and involved messiness in some form, so I spent most of my days in plain tunics and sheepskin trousers. But I knew I had to do something to make up for my otherwise unfortunate appearance. My bronze skin was burned from the fierce sunlight that had beat down while I crouched over the dragon eggs, and my hands were scaly with a rash I had acquired helping Chirri prepare a healing salve. I hadn't had time to exorcise all the tangles from my waist-length dark hair, and during my frenzied brushing I had broken several of the tines of my comb, which I was certain were now lodged somewhere behind my head.

Tem wasn't there. He must have been angry enough to risk insulting my family by not attending the welcome banquet. Either that, or his father had ordered him to tend to the herds, not an uncommon occurrence. I tried to ignore the twinge of disappointment. Although I was still angry with him, his familiar presence would have been a comfort.

River had come to the end of his story, and seemed to be excusing himself from the hangers-on. He began making his way to the barrel of *raksi*.

I glanced over my shoulder. Where was Father? It was the height of rudeness to allow a guest, particularly one of River's stature, to serve himself.

An idea slid into place.

I flew across the room, dodging elderly aunts and uncles and neighbors. More than one greeting was tossed at me, and I did my best to mumble and smile my way through them. I made it to the barrel a heartbeat before River did.

"More *raksi*?" I said breathlessly.

He paused, taking in my flustered appearance. Then, with a smoothness that reminded me of pulling on an old cloak, he flashed me a broad, wolfish smile.

"You read my mind," he said, handing me his bowl.

I smiled back, quaking with nervousness while I maneuvered the bowl under the spout. I turned the spigot too hard, and wine splashed to the floor, spattering him.

"I'm so sorry—" I stammered, horrified.

"No matter," he said, grasping my shoulder as I bent to brush at the stains. It was a rather firm squeeze, though he smiled still.

I refilled his bowl with shaking hands, cursing myself. "Forgive me, *dyonpo* Shara, I didn't—"

He gave me a sharp look. "I'm afraid you've mistaken me. My name is Mara."

"Oh." I thought I would faint with relief. "I'm sorry, I shouldn't have assumed—"

"That's all right. He gave me that grin again. His teeth were very long and white. "An honest mistake. I'm not nobility, so you needn't call me '*dyonpo*.'"

I nodded. All the nobility had two names—the second announced their lineage. I couldn't help noticing how Mara's smile had tightened slightly as he spoke, so I added hurriedly, "I'm Kamzin, Elder's second daughter. Are you with River Shara's expedition?"

"Yes. I'm his official chronicler."

"His chronicler?" It sounded important. "So you write down everything he does?"

An irritated look flitted across his face, quickly swallowed up by another white-toothed smile. "In a manner of speaking. I make notes, sketches, maps; take measurements; and draft official accounts. It can be dull stuff, but it is important. In the past, the Royal Explorer never traveled with fewer than three chroniclers. River insists on only one."

I shook my head at this. The idea of being followed around by chroniclers documenting your every move! It would inflate the ego of the humblest person in the world.

Mara's gaze darted over the room. I could see he considered our conversation over. Most guests came to this decision quickly. I was the younger child of a village elder—that warranted polite small talk, and rarely anything else. I knew I had only a second or two before he made his excuses and moved on to someone more interesting.

"How long have you served as chronicler?"

"These past three years. Since River was named Royal Explorer."

"I'm sure you've faced your share of danger," I said in a flattering tone. "No doubt come close to death yourself."

Mara's brow furrowed. His expression went curiously blank for a moment, as if an invisible hand had scrubbed some thought out of existence, and then he turned his attention back to the room. It happened so quickly that I thought I must have imagined it.

"Naturally," he said dismissively. "As have most explorers."

"You must know *dyonpo* Shara well," I tried again.

Mara was still staring over my head. "As well as one can."

I wasn't sure what to make of this, but pushed on. "Would you

29

be able to introduce me? As I've been to Raksha, I thought—"

"Of course." He fixed me with another smile that told me he hadn't heard a word I said. "If you'll excuse me, Tamzin, there's someone I must speak with."

He strode back into the crowd, leaving me staring at his back. Muttering darkly to myself, I filled another bowl to the brim and downed the *raksi* in a single draft. I grimaced as it burned its way down my throat.

"That didn't go very well, did it?" said a voice behind me.

I turned. A young man was perched on the window alcove, half in shadow, gazing at me with a faint smile that seemed a shade less than mocking. He could only be one of the courtiers. He was just as richly—and impractically—attired as his companions, his dark, gauzy cloak spilling down the wall like the world's most useless curtain. His unkempt hair, which stuck up on one side as if he frequently scrubbed his hand through it, was vividly blue, and his fingers were crowded with jeweled rings that flashed in the light.

"I don't know what you mean," I said, filling my bowl again. A dragon snuffled up to the barrel and began lapping up the spilled wine. I aimed a kick in its direction, and it darted away, somewhat unsteadily. "We were just talking."

"*He* was talking." The young man waved his hand, and I realized that he was at least partly drunk. "You were drooling. I feel I must inform you that Mara is neither as clever as he thinks he is nor as interesting as *you* think he is."

I stared at him, openmouthed.

"Yes, that's it," he said. "That's exactly how you looked a moment ago."

I felt myself redden with anger. "How is it any of your business? Is eavesdropping on private conversations how all nobles behave in the Three Cities?"

"I only eavesdrop on people who interest me." He dropped to the floor with unexpected grace. "It's a compliment."

I snorted into my wine. "You think a lot of yourself. Where did you come from, anyway?"

"Where did I come from?" For some reason, he seemed to find this hilarious. "Oh—I've been here all along. You might've noticed, if you hadn't been so busy flirting with Mara."

"I was not flirting," I snarled. "For your information, I have more important things on my mind."

"Do you? That's very mysterious." The young man maneuvered his bowl under the wine spout. When nothing came out, he pounded on the barrel until wine gushed out in a great torrent, overflowing the bowl.

I couldn't help laughing at him as he stared in dismay at his wine-stained sleeve. He began to laugh too, leaning against the barrel for support.

My amusement faded as I noticed that all the villagers in the vicinity were staring at us. A few almost looked afraid—probably concerned that I was irreparably harming the dignity of Azmiri, I thought, with a mixture of guilt and irritation.

I sized up the courtier. He was a little older than me, perhaps, but not much. I thought he might be handsome, underneath the blue hair and the jewels, though his eyes were unsettling. They were the strangest eyes I had ever seen—one was a warm golden brown that reminded me of the floor of a sunlit forest, while the other was so dark it appeared black. His gaze left me flustered, torn between a desire to stare and a desire to look away.

He seemed to be sizing me up too, his eyes smiling at the corners. Underneath that, though, I sensed a sharp focus. "Was that true, what you said to Mara? You've been to Raksha?"

"Maybe." I raised my chin. "Why do you care?"

"I have my reasons."

"That's very mysterious."

He laughed again. It was an appealing sound, ragged at the edges, as if he wasn't quite in control of it. In spite of myself, I felt my heartbeat speed up. I shook my head. What was I doing? Laughing and drinking with some strange boy, when I was supposed to be looking for River Shara. The thought brought my nervousness back, and I hastily swallowed the rest of my wine.

"Easy," he said, and suddenly I was holding empty air. I blinked stupidly at my hand for a moment—he had my bowl, and was spinning it idly in his palm. He had moved so quickly I hadn't even seen it.

"What do you think—"

"You've had enough, Kamzin."

"*I've* had enough?" I glared at him, searching for a retort. But my thoughts were all muddled. Involuntarily, my gaze drifted to his hand—there was something wrong with it. He was missing the tips of two fingers, the fourth and fifth.

My eyes narrowed. I had seen the result of frostbite before—but never on the hand of a pampered courtier. His brown skin was as dark as mine, as if he too spent most of his days outdoors in the mountain sun. Something nagged at me.

"Kamzin!" It was Zhiba, one of my cousins. She bowed to the young man and touched my arm gently, as if to draw me away. "Chirri has been looking for you. Come."

I squinted at her. Chirri was never looking for me. "What are you talking about?"

Zhiba glanced over her shoulder. I realized a knot of people had formed nearby, all gazing at me and muttering. Most wore looks ranging from worry to disapproval. Others—my younger cousins in particular—pressed their hands over their mouths, as if to muffle their laughter. I stared at them, annoyed and confused. Clearly, I was the butt of some private joke, the meaning of which I could not comprehend.

"Kamzin," Zhiba said, her voice low, "how much have you had to drink?"

"Is that what this is about?" I shook her arm off. "First him, and now you. Leave me alone, Zhiba."

"But—"

"*I'm fine.*" All the frustrations of the day—my disastrous lesson with Chirri, my argument with Lusha, the embarrassing encounter with Mara—seemed to come bubbling to the surface. I raised my voice. "And you can tell the others to stop staring. Do you want our guests to think we have no manners at all?"

Zhiba fell back, a pained look on her face. One of my cousins let out a muffled snort.

"Everything all right?" the courtier said.

"Yes," I muttered. Then I started. "Oh no."

My sister had just entered the room. Predictably, every head turned toward her.

"Who's that?"

"Take a guess," I said dourly. Lusha wore a simple gray robe, and her long hair was pinned back from her face with a silver clasp. A raven perched on each of her shoulders, eyeing the gathering with beady eyes.

"Ah, the great Lusha of Azmiri," the young man said. "You don't look much alike, do you?"

His tone was musing rather than snide, but I still bristled with a familiar irritation. It was true that Lusha took after our tall, slender mother, while my stoutness was all Elder's. Growing up, I had been teased about my size by the other children, and reduced to tears more than once. Whenever Lusha found out, she dealt with the offenders with her customary decisiveness—usually with a punch in the nose. The more resolute bullies would be treated to recitations of dire fortunes filled with suffering and calamity, delivered in such ominous tones that they had difficulty sleeping at night. The children, awed by Lusha, learned to leave me alone.

The courtier gazed at my sister with cool appraisal. "She would be far more impressive without those creatures hovering around her. I've never understood you mountain people and your fondness for pets."

"They aren't pets," I said. "They're familiars. It's rare enough

34

to have even one, you know. Lusha and I are the only people in Azmiri who have them."

"That's fortunate for the people of Azmiri. I for one wouldn't want a flock of ravens following me about. I doubt I'd be very popular at parties."

"A familiar is a mark of the spirits' favor," I said. "And they're useful, even if they are only animals. Lusha has had ravens watching over her since she was a baby. They fetch things, carry messages, alert her to danger—they look out for her, no matter what. People who have that sort of bond with an animal are respected in the mountain villages. Well," I added in a mutter, "*most* of them are respected."

He regarded me blankly. "So I should be impressed?"

"*River* should be impressed." I chugged the rest of my wine. "She doesn't care what you think, whoever you are."

He laughed. I let out a giggle, hiccupping, which only made us laugh harder. We leaned against each other, trying unsuccessfully to muffle the sound. Heads turned in our direction—it seemed as if the entire room was staring at us now.

"I think," I said between gasps, "you've had too much wine."

Half choking, I straightened up, using his arm as a support. It was a good one, strong and solid, with more lean muscle than I would have expected. Somehow, the exertion had cleared my head, and I wondered again what in the name of the spirits I was doing, talking and carrying on with this strange Three Cities boy who hadn't even given me his name.

I stopped. My laughter died as suddenly as a thunderclap.

"What is it?" He was still panting, his strange eyes alight with merriment.

I took a step back. My gaze drifted from the tip of his hair to the hem of his cloak. There was nothing in what I saw to prove my suspicion, and yet I knew. *I knew.*

"Who are you?" I demanded.

"Uh-oh." He held up his hands in a warding gesture. "You got there, did you?"

I stared at him, my mouth hanging open. Half my brain refused to comprehend what the other half was telling it. *Please, no. It can't be.*

"You're doing it again, Kamzin," he said. "The drooling."

Father appeared suddenly, Lusha at his side, and clapped the young man's shoulder with his massive hand. "There you are, River! Lusha has been looking for you."

My sister nodded politely, though it was clear from the look on her face that she had been doing no such thing. I began to sway. I wondered if I would faint.

"I've been having a very interesting chat with your charming daughter," River Shara said, threading my arm through his and pinning me solidly to his side. The smell of wildflowers and wine and something faintly smoky filled my nose. "Did you know the spotted orchid can be brewed as a tea for snow blindness?"

"I didn't realize Kamzin was so knowledgeable about healing," Elder said, an edge in his voice as he surveyed me. I was in the way. And I was drunk.

"Yes, she's a very impressive girl," River said.

There was a confused silence. I doubted either Lusha or Father had ever heard that word applied to me by anyone. Biter, on Lusha's left shoulder, croaked a warning. He was looking at River, and the expression in his eyes was not a friendly one. Lurker took notice of him too, and began to croak deep in her throat. Lusha muttered something, and they fluttered away, up to the thatching in the roof. There they continued their jawing.

"I apologize, River," Elder said. "We didn't mean to leave you alone for so long. Only you disappeared so suddenly, and—"

"I wasn't alone," River said. He was still gripping my arm, though I had been surreptitiously trying to pull it free since he had taken it. I pinched him, and he let out a muffled yelp. Father's confused look deepened to bafflement.

"*Dyonpo*, perhaps you would like a tour of the house before dinner." Lusha had to raise her voice, as the ravens continued to squawk at River with a ferocity they usually reserved for the village cats.

"I think not," River said, rubbing his arm. "I have—ah—something to attend to." He wandered away without another word, his dark cloak drifting behind him. People bowed to him as he passed, some so hastily they spilled their drinks. River seemed to take no notice.

"What did I say, Lusha?" Father muttered. "Half-mad, if not more."

"What were you talking to him about, Kamzin?" Lusha said, her eyes narrowed.

I swallowed. Something was rising in my throat.

"Kamzin? What's the matter?" Father said.

"I—" The words died on my lips. Clapping my hand over my mouth, I pushed past Lusha. The door was a mile away. I shoved my way through the crowd, bumping into guests and knocking bowls out of their hands. I finally reached the door, and there was Mara.

He placed a hand on my shoulder, stopping me from advancing farther. "What in the name of—"

I couldn't hold it any longer. I sagged to the ground and emptied my stomach onto his boots.

FOUR

THE EVENING WAS a haze after that. I couldn't be absent
from a dinner of such importance, and so I sat at the table, green
with nausea, as the dishes were passed around. Everything was of
the finest quality, but I didn't touch a morsel. Lusha sat on my
right, her legs crossed gracefully beneath her, while Father knelt
beside her. Mara sat across from Lusha, a smile hovering on his
lips. He looked as if he couldn't believe his luck.

River did not come to dinner. His absence was a tremendous
slight, and consequently no one even spoke his name. The expedition to Raksha, though, was the main topic of conversation, which
led to awkward pauses and veiled hints as guests struggled not to
speak about the man who was the reason for the party.

"Well, Mara," Father said, "I imagine you've seen a lot, as
chronicler to the Royal Explorer."

"You could say that." Mara tried to catch Lusha's eye. She was feeding her ravens scraps of *balep* from her plate.

Lusha glanced at him, possibly for the first time since they had been introduced, her expression cool and appraising. Mara, taking this as a sign of encouragement, launched into an animated story about a narrow escape from a pack of silver jackals. Given that he was sitting before us, quite alive and with all his limbs, I found it difficult to stay interested, and sank back into my private misery. Lusha's attention seemed to wander too, and she went back to feeding Biter.

"Lusha, I understand you've discovered two new stars in the dragon catcher's net," Mara said, naming one of the constellations that hung low over the mountains in summer. "I would be interested in seeing your sketches."

I stifled a groan. How Mara had learned of my sister's sketches, I didn't know, and I didn't care to.

Lusha smiled at him. It lit her eyes and made her bony face less severe. "Perhaps you will. Why not tomorrow?"

Mara smiled back. He was completely under the spell of Lusha's charm, and, like most men, assumed it was conjured specifically for him. I knew, though, that Lusha would forget her offer by morning. "I would like that. If you won't be too busy?"

Father stiffened at the oblique reference to River. "Mara, were you fortunate enough to stop in Lhotang on your way here? The elder is an old friend of mine." Father was friends with everyone. He could name every village elder, along with their wife or husband and all their children, from here to the Three Cities.

"We did," Mara said. "A charming village—I would have been sorry to miss it. Though I heard some disturbing tales from the villagers. They spoke of powerful storms brewing in the North, and sightings of the *fiangul*."

"The *fiangul*?" Father frowned. Those sitting nearby looked up at the word, and I felt my body tense. The *fiangul*, or bird people, appeared sporadically in the history of Azmiri. They were human—or at least, they had once been—travelers who became lost in a blizzard or squall while traversing the Aryas, and were possessed by the winged spirits who haunted the snows. They were slowly driven mad, and transformed into terrifying monsters. Their only goal was to lead others to the same fate they had suffered. Or, failing that, to kill them.

"I find that difficult to believe," Father said. "The *fiangul* have never been known to stray this far south. I doubt such talk is more than rumor."

The conversation shifted to a discussion of Lhotang's weavers, and I stopped paying attention. My drunkenness was wearing off, leaving only shame and a pounding headache in its wake. It was all I could do not to lean over and rest my forehead against the cool stone of the table.

"Drink, you idiot," Lusha muttered at me. She filled my bowl with tea, her smile in place the whole while. "You'll feel better."

"Liar."

Slowly, the bowls and platters emptied. My aunt Behe passed around a cup of spiced beer, so dark and thick that it had to be scooped with a spoon. I pretended to drink, gagging at the smell, and then handed the cup to Lusha. Once the cup was emptied four times, it would signal the end of the meal, and I would be able to crawl away to bed. I watched each of the guests as they drank, silently cursing those who took dainty mouthfuls.

Raised voices from one of the back rooms cut through the murmur of conversation. The red-and-blue curtain was pushed aside, and Tem's father, Metok, strode in. His breath was ragged, his beard speckled with snow. Though it was summer, snow was not unusual in Azmiri, nor was it strange that Metok would be out in it. During calving season, Metok and the other herdsmen were busy at all hours of the day and night.

Metok came to Father's side and murmured in his ear. Elder stiffened, but did not reply. He merely nodded, dismissing Metok. The herdsman's face was a strange, pale hue, and his hands shook as he left the hall. I had never known Tem's father to be anything but brusque and unpleasant. My confusion was heightened when Father stood, bowed to Mara, and departed. Lusha followed close behind. What was going on?

It was some time before I found out. Finally, the cup was emptied for the fourth time, and the guests began to trickle out of the hall. Aunt Behe swept in to pester Mara with more tea and sweet cakes. He politely refused.

"What was that about with Metok?" I said to no one in particular.

Mara gave me a penetrating, dismissive stare, which might have been upsetting if I were in a different mood. I wished I could dislike him, because it would ease my humiliation, but I still found him intimidating and far too handsome. "Something I'm sure Elder and Lusha will have no trouble resolving," he said.

"Oh, give it a rest," I grumbled. "Lusha can't hear you. And she's not interested, by the way. Don't flatter yourself."

Mara's expression hardened. He stood. "I don't know what you mean."

"Fine." I rubbed my head. I knew I would get in trouble if I was caught speaking this way to a guest, but fortunately there were no nosy relatives within earshot. "Did you hear what Metok said or not?"

Mara was turning to leave, but he stopped. His ego was too large for him to resist the urge to be the bigger person. "Someone took a tumble off the rocks, trying to recover a calf. The herdsman's son."

I flew to my feet. *"What?"*

The remaining guests stared at me. Biter, who had been left to peck at the scraps in Lusha's bowl, took fright and sailed out the window. I followed by a more circuitous route, through the kitchen and out the back door that led to Aunt Behe's house. I turned right, off the path and onto the open mountainside. I

I soon slowed. I didn't know where Tem was, and I wasn't wearing my *chuba* or heavy boots. Snowflakes, sparse and fragile, swirled around me, but there was a chill in the wind that hinted at worse to come.

An echoing caw in the distance. Ignoring my lurching stomach, I ran toward the sound, skirting the stone wall that lined the farmer's fields at the edge of the village. As I rounded the western flank of the mountain and began running uphill, the wind hit me in the face. It was bitterly cold, and sent me staggering back a step. I thought about retreating home, at least to retrieve my *chuba*.

Tem.

I lowered my head and ran on. Three ravens flew past, heading for home. Lusha, Metok, and Father were not far behind. A group of house dragons trotted alongside them, their lights throwing misshapen shadows everywhere. Father shouted and grabbed my shoulder.

"Kamzin! What are you doing here?"

I wrenched away. "Where's Tem?"

"Metok saw him fall from Kunigai Spur, but he can't find the spot again in this weather."

"We're going to the village to gather a search party," Lusha shouted in my ear.

"What?" I stared at her. "You can't leave Tem alone out here!"

Lusha made an angry noise. "Don't be ridiculous. This storm is—"

"Leave the dragons," I said. "Leave them and go. I'll keep looking."

Metok and Father were already retreating, assuming, as any sane person would, that Lusha and I would follow. A wisp of cloud fluttered over us like a wet sheet. I grabbed two dragons by the scruffs of their necks as they ran past me.

"Go!" I yelled at Lusha. "Bring help. I'm not leaving him."

Lusha's face was a dark fury, but she didn't argue with me further. With one smooth motion, she swept off her fur-lined *chuba* and settled it on my shoulders.

"Lurker will stay with you," she said. The raven alighted on a rock by my feet. "She'll lead us back to you, if anything happens."

I nodded. "Thank—"

But Lusha was already gone, leaping lightly down the slope.

I shrugged on the *chuba*, immediately grateful for its warmth. Only my face was still cold. I tugged the collar up and carried on, whistling for the dragons. I didn't pay Lurker any heed—she would track me more easily than I could track her.

It was only a short climb to Kunigai Spur, which jutted out over the valley separating the village from Nalash, one of the mountain's lower peaks. Only my own knowledge of the terrain told me that, however; Nalash was completely obscured by the clouds. Beyond the spur, the ground fell away steeply, a curve of slippery rock that ended in a sheer drop to the valley floor.

I squinted, trying to see through both the darkness and the pain of my pounding headache. My stomach roiled as if trying to compete with the fury of the wind. I swallowed, forcing myself to ignore the sensation, to focus on the only thing that mattered.

Normally, there were sentries stationed nearby, but I wasn't surprised they had decided to seek shelter indoors. On clear nights, this side of the mountain afforded a good view of the darkly forested lands to the east—the edge of the Nightwood, the witches' forest. It had been a long time since the witches had attacked Azmiri, but nevertheless, Elder liked to keep a watch out, particularly given the village's position. If the witches invaded the Empire, they would almost surely travel through the Amarin

45

Valley between Azmiri and its neighboring mountain, Biru. At one time, the emperor had stationed soldiers here to maintain a constant watch on the enemy. But the witches were broken and beaten, and those soldiers had more important tasks now.

I passed the crumbling half walls that the sentries used as lookouts. These had been proper structures once, destroyed by the dark, unnatural fire that swept the village more than two centuries ago. It had been witches who had set that fire. They had always hated us—or rather, they hated the emperor and his ever-expanding territory. They had sought to destroy the village, and very nearly succeeded. The stone the fire touched remained warm to this day, steam ghosting off its surface as the snow melted.

Shouting Tem's name, I walked the length of the cliff. The snow was falling heavily now, and soon my feet were soaked in my flimsy sandals.

I let out a cry of frustration. I wasn't going to find Tem this way. No, the only option was to climb down that sheer face to see if Tem had come to rest on a ledge. I didn't think about the other possibility—that he was resting far below in that dark valley, beyond anyone's aid.

Just below the spur was a shallow depression that folded into the cliffside. I lowered myself into it, digging my fingers into the rocky soil. The dragons chirped at me, wondering if they should follow. The wind was too strong for them to fly safely, and though they were stout climbers, I didn't want to take the chance that they would fall and leave me completely in the dark.

"Stay there," I said, shooing them away from the edge.

I crabbed sideways over a boulder that stuck out from the slope like a knuckle. I could just make out the tips of the pine trees that crowned the lower slopes of Azmiri—trees that eventually, many miles away, darkened and deepened, and became the witches' forest.

The height didn't bother me, but the visibility did. My eyes and nose were streaming, and snowflakes kept collecting on my lashes, blotting my view. I wiped my face on the sleeve of Lusha's *chuba* and lowered myself down the cliff, one foothold at a time. Once I was out of the shadow of the overhang, I paused. Numerous ledges jutted out from the mountainside, and here and there a gnarled tree that Tem could have caught hold of. But it was so dark—I couldn't tell a rock from a motionless body.

"Tem!" I hollered.

My voice echoed back at me. I strained my ears trying to hear over the howl of the wind. I thought I heard someone reply, but I couldn't be certain.

"Tem!"

"Need a hand?"

I started, casting my gaze around for the source of the voice. It came to rest on none other than River Shara.

He crouched on the ledge above me, looking perfectly at ease. One of the dragons was sitting on his head. Its blue glow only intensified the color of his hair—it was as if his whole head was alight.

I let out an incoherent noise. He smiled, seeming pleased by my shock.

"Now, Kamzin," he said, "you don't really plan to climb down there without a belay, do you?"

"Yes, I do," I said, once I had recovered myself. "I've climbed this peak before. I don't need a belay."

"On a night like this, you do." He reached behind him, gathering up a length of rope. Attached to one end was a leather harness. "Come on, Elder's daughter. I may be half-mad or more, as your father put it, but you have to admit, you're not acting particularly sane yourself at the moment."

My already red face grew even redder. Rather than reply, I snatched up the harness when he lowered it to me. It was awkward pulling it on at that angle, but I managed it, sliding first one leg through the loop, then the other.

"There we go." He drew an iron nail from his pocket and pounded it into the side of the mountain with a rock, then looped the rope through it. Finally, he tied the end of the rope around his waist using a rat's-eye knot. He did all this within a few seconds, moving with practiced ease. I couldn't help staring.

"Carry on," he said, making an elaborate motion with his arm.

Shaking my head, I lowered myself down another foot. There were plenty of handholds in the cliff face, though many were deceptive—large rocks that seemed solid, but were dry and cracked from the cold, and would fragment under too much weight. I chose each movement carefully, sometimes pausing for as long as a minute to select my next step.

I could hear River's voice as I went—fragments of it, jumbled by the wind. It sounded like half a conversation, but who could he be talking to? Himself, I supposed. Wasn't that what mad people did? The sound died as I put more distance between us. Now I could no longer see the glow of the dragons.

"Tem!"

I heard something in response, again from my right. It didn't sound like a voice, exactly—I wasn't sure what it was. I craned my neck, trying to see. It was then that the rock I was standing on gave way.

Immediately, I punched my feet back into the crumbly mountainside. One of my hands slipped, but I held on with the other. The cliffside was impenetrable; I couldn't find a spot to wedge my feet in. Grunting, I slowly, shakily, lowered myself down the cliff, supporting myself with only my arms. Finally, I found a solid crevice to rest on.

My entire body shook. Suddenly I was immensely grateful for the harness River had given me.

A flutter of movement out of the corner of my eye. There—a narrow ledge with a broken tree leaning over it. Beneath the tree was a dark shape, motionless. At the lip of the ledge, a small, pale blot paced back and forth, shaking the snow from its coat. A yak.

Fighting the urge to hurry, I inched myself down to the ledge. Once I had tested it with my weight, I released my handholds and scrambled over to the body that lay crumpled against the cliff face.

The yak, which couldn't have been more than a month old, nosed up to me as I crouched by Tem's side, seeking warmth or food or some combination of both. I ignored it, and examined my best friend.

He was alive—I almost cried with relief. From the branches crushed under his body, I guessed that the tree had broken his fall.

I ran my hands over his body, but I couldn't find any sign of broken bones. When I placed my hand on his face, he muttered something, half opening his eyes.

"Tem," I said, fighting back tears. "It's all right, I'm here."

There was a gash on his head—my hand came away sticky with blood—but I couldn't tell how bad it was. I pulled off my harness and slid it up his body.

I gave the rope three short yanks, wondering if River would know what that meant. If he didn't, I was going to have to haul Tem up the mountainside myself, and I didn't like my odds with that. But, after a moment, the rope tensed three times in quick succession, and then there was one longer tug. Tem slowly began to rise up the cliff. River was a few yards away horizontally, so there was some awkward bumping and jostling as Tem's body drifted slowly sideways as it ascended. I grimaced as his shoulder hit a rock jutting out of the cliff.

I watched until Tem was out of sight. I didn't like the idea of following him up that dark slope after my near-fall but I didn't have much choice.

The calf grunted. I turned and found it watching me with large brown eyes.

"No," I said sternly. "I'm sorry, but no."

The calf grunted again. The wind gusted over the ledge, and the beast pressed itself against the shelter of the mountainside, shivering.

With a ferocious curse, I snatched up the calf—more anxious grunting—and slung it over my shoulders. The animal didn't weigh much, but it was enough to throw me off balance. I pressed my face and chest into the mountain as I climbed. If I leaned even slightly in the wrong direction, the calf's weight would pull me inexorably into the vast emptiness at my back.

Fortunately, the calf didn't struggle. It was exhausted, and content to simply enjoy the warmth of my body. The yak's long hair soon had me blinking sweat in addition to melting snow from my eyes. My shoulders burned.

Of course, climbing blind is always a dangerous last resort, and I was soon confronted by a problem: a sharp overhang in the rock directly above me. I could have scaled it alone, but as it was, I would have to find a route around. I made my way sideways for a while, over a slick wall of granite with few handholds, before starting up again. After a few desperate minutes of scrabbling up a wet, grassy slope more treacherous than anything before it, I found myself standing on solid ground, at the crest of Kunigai Spur.

The yak had fallen asleep. It started awake when I placed it on the ground, then followed at my heels.

A green light bobbed ahead. I whistled, and the dragon trotted toward me. It was snowing only lightly now, but a chill cloud had descended on the mountain. I couldn't see past a few feet, and so when I stumbled upon Tem and River, I was so startled that I yelped.

Tem was sitting up, drinking from a flask that River must have given him. The blood running down the side of his head seemed to be drying, and apart from that, he looked unhurt. He let out a joyous cry at the sight of me.

"Kamzin! River was about to climb down for you. We both thought—"

"I'm all right," I assured him. "I was carrying some extra weight. Slowed me down."

Tem rubbed the calf's ears. "Look at this idiot. I almost killed myself running after him when he escaped his pen, and now he thinks he's going to get a treat."

"How do you feel?" I examined his head in the wavering light.

He brushed my question aside, gazing at me as if we hadn't seen each other in months. "Kamzin, you never should have gone after me alone."

I made a dismissive noise. "Come on. Kunigai is no match for me, even in this weather. There was never any danger."

He gave me an exasperated look. "I'm just glad River was here."

"*Tsh*. We would have been fine." It was, of course, a blatant lie. Looking back, I was astonished at my own foolishness. What would have happened if River hadn't shown up? I would still be on that ledge with Tem, both of us growing colder and wetter by the minute, with no way of getting him back up the mountain, or even signaling for help.

I stood and found River staring at me. For once, there was no amusement in his gaze. His eyes were narrowed, coolly scrutinizing.

"How did you do that?" he said.

"Do what?"

He made no reply. He took a step toward me, and I had to resist the urge to move back. He seemed to have become a different person.

I glanced down at the calf, just for an excuse to break eye contact. "He wasn't very heavy. And I've climbed this part of the mountain before."

River just stared at me, as if at any moment he expected me to sprout feathers or burst into flames.

"Kamzin!" It was a disembodied cry, carried on the wind. Lurker soared into view, then circled us, cawing. Several dark shapes were approaching, which soon solidified into Lusha, Father, and three men from the village.

"What happened?" Lusha demanded. Her eyes drifted to River, who turned away slightly, as if to gaze at the view.

"We're fine, thanks," I said. One of the men helped Tem to his feet; another roped the calf and dragged it off toward my father's pens.

Father turned to River. "Was this your doing?"

River made an elegant gesture. "There's no need to thank me. It was nothing."

Elder glanced down at the leather harness. "You've rescued not only one of my best herdsmen, but my daughter as well. If you hadn't been here, I'm sure she would have done something foolish."

I opened my mouth, but River cut in smoothly, "It was my pleasure. Please don't be too hard on Kamzin. She was a great help."

I stared at him, so outraged I couldn't speak.

"*Dyonpo*, let's return to the house," Lusha said smoothly. "Perhaps you would like some butter tea?"

They strode on ahead, leaving me and one of the men to assist Tem. I felt an odd pang as I gazed at their retreating silhouettes—tall and graceful, striding confidently down the uneven mountainside. There was a sort of symmetry between them. Lusha turned her head to speak to River, and then the clouds swallowed them up.

Father glowered at me. "I don't know what you were thinking," he said, pushing me ahead of him. "Going after Tem by yourself. You and I will have a talk when we get home."

I would have started shouting then and there, had not Tem grabbed my arm on the pretext of supporting himself. Moving slowly, we followed the others down the mountainside.

"Thanks for defending me," I muttered.

Tem looked at me, surprised. "I thought all you cared about was impressing River."

"No." My anger drained away, leaving behind exhaustion and little else. I was cold, and wet, and my head was pounding again. "I don't care about impressing anyone."

We were on the lee side of the mountain now, and the wind dropped to a murmur. The storm was clearing—clouds snagged against Azmiri and began to fray, revealing little patches of starry sky. I tightened my hold on Tem and guided him toward the lights of the village.

FIVE

I AWOKE WITH a weight pressing against my chest. Ragtooth was curled on top of me, his bushy tail tickling my chin.

"Get off, you hairy lump." I pushed at the fox, but he only nipped my hand. "Ouch! Why do I even let you in here?"

Ragtooth stretched and yawned, treating me to a good view of his long, sharp teeth. Then he hopped onto the floor.

Sunlight streamed through the cracks in the shutters. It seemed brighter than usual, and only intensified the pounding in my head. I let out a long groan. Judging by the direction of the light, it was nearing midday, which meant I had missed my morning lesson with Chirri. Why had no one come to wake me?

After a few halfhearted attempts, I dragged myself out of bed. As usual, my room was a mess. My toe collided painfully with an ornate sheepskin drum Chirri had given me to practice incantations—it was buried under a pile of robes, and smelled funny from the wine I had spilled on it months ago. My shelves were crowded with other shamanic talismans, all in similar states—some merely gathering dust, others broken and then hidden behind something else in the hopes that Chirri wouldn't ask after them. Much more interesting objects lined my windowsills—colored stones, feathers, and pressed flowers I had collected when I went with Father to visit other villages, or explored the neighboring mountains with Tem. I liked having a souvenir from each place I traveled to. I could remember the origin of each item, down to the precise mountain shelf or streambank.

I stumbled over another pile of clothes, cursing. The state of my room had only deteriorated since Lusha and I stopped sharing several years ago, but I certainly had no wish to go back to that arrangement. Few people knew how terrible Lusha's temper was on the rare occasions she became angry, and she had been a tyrant when it came to my mess. One day, after repeated lectures had failed to have any effect on me, I had woken to find our room virtually empty. All my belongings were gone. Lusha serenely refused to answer any questions about their whereabouts. Days later, I found them—scattered across the ground below the nearest cliff.

I poured water into the stone basin on my dressing table. It was cold, and the cold felt good against my aching head. I plunged my face into the water, shivering from both the chill and the relief it brought.

Once I was washed and dressed, I made my way to Lusha's

room. The heavy door, ornately carved with intricate knots and openmouthed skulls, was closed. I considered knocking but decided against it.

"Lusha?" I said, stepping inside.

My sister wasn't there, though her presence—strong enough to draw all eyes in a crowded room—lingered like scent. The blue shutters were drawn back and neatly tied to the walls. Lusha's bed was made, and the scrolls and star charts that usually cluttered the low table by the window were rolled up and sorted into their shelves. Her room always felt empty; Lusha had few nonfunctional possessions, apart from two that had belonged to our mother—an ornate jade comb, and a chipped cosmetics box inlaid with gold. But today it felt especially barren.

She was probably in the observatory. Or, more likely, with River, helping to organize their supplies for the journey. The thought made my stomach twist, but not as much as I would have expected.

As I was turning to go, however, something caught my eye. Lusha's shrine.

It was a finely carved wooden chest painted in bright reds and blues, lined with niches for ceramic statues representing generations of ancestors. Most of the little doors were closed, but one was ajar, revealing an empty shelf.

I knelt before the shrine and opened the first door, my fingers brushing against the patterns of overlapping knots carved into the wood. The statue behind it was old—so old that the clay was discolored and crumbling. The statues were not made to be recognizable, however; they were always rough, only vaguely human in shape, and meant to decay over time. I traced the character carved into the base—my great-great-grandmother's name. I carefully returned the statue to its niche and examined the other shelves.

The statue that was missing was my mother's.

A shiver traveled down my back. I checked the table, the floor, though I didn't believe for one second that Lusha would have been clumsy with the statue. Frowning, I closed the little door.

I examined the room more closely, trying to determine if anything else was gone. An empty spot on the far wall gave me pause. It took me a moment to remember (I didn't often visit Lusha's room, and when I did I was generally ordered out again)—Lusha's bow, and her quiver of arrows. The bow was common enough—most households had at least one, to guard against the snow leopards that made nightly forays into the village. But Lusha's arrows were the most expensive kind—tipped with obsidian, the only material that could kill a witch. Back in the days when the witches had threatened the village, all arrows had been made this way. Witches were shape-shifters, capable of assuming the form of any animal they chose, which meant they could be anywhere, at any time—among the flock of choughs circling the fields, behind the eyes of the marmot creeping through the grass. The arrows were a poor defense against creatures of such power, but they were better than none at all.

Ragtooth brushed his mangy back against my leg. He knew that when I got out of bed, breakfast would follow, and he would pester me until he got it. Shaking off my apprehension, I followed him from Lusha's room.

When we didn't have guests, my family ate in a small nook next to the kitchen, which faced the farmers' terraces that stepped down Mount Azmiri on its southern and western slopes. From there, I could see the place where River's balloon had landed.

The memory made me uneasy. So did the breakfast dishes that hadn't been cleared away, and the empty kitchen. Where was everyone? My appetite fading, I picked at someone's half-eaten bowl of buttered *balep* and stewed apples, while Ragtooth nibbled at some sweet curds. The house was too silent. When Aunt Behe entered the room, I felt like leaping over the table and hugging her.

"Kamzin! I didn't expect to find you here."

"What's going on?" I said. "Where's Lusha?"

Aunt Behe stared at me. "Did you sleep through all that commotion, child? Lusha's gone."

I stared at her.

"Such a mess she's made." Aunt Behe pushed her sleeves back over her shoulders and began stacking up the bowls and plates, her movements methodical and unhurried. I had often thought that Lusha had inherited a good deal from Aunt Behe. "The entire village will talk of nothing else for months. I'm sure the Royal Explorer is furious. He can't have expected this betrayal."

"Betrayal?" The nagging fear I had felt in Lusha's room was back. "How was he betrayed?"

"Oh, child." Aunt Behe set the plates down and looked at me properly for the first time. "You did sleep through everything, didn't you? Lusha left this morning, long before anyone was stirring, with one of River Shara's men. That tall, smiling one—the storyteller."

"*What?*"

"A merchant saw them heading north—toward Winding Pass. They made off with the better part of River Shara's supplies—rope, tools, blankets. It seems they may be planning to beat him to that mountain."

I gazed out the window without seeing anything. My head still pounded insistently, but I no longer noticed it. This made no sense. None at all.

"Has anyone gone after her?"

"Your father has had men scouring the foothills since Mara was discovered missing. But by the time they learned which direction she had taken, it was too late. Your sister can move like the wind when she wants to, and she had a head start."

"Why?" My voice was almost a whisper. "Why would she do this?"

My aunt gave me a long look. Shaking her head, she said, "If you don't know the answer to that, Kamzin, then it's doubtful anyone else would."

I found River at the edge of the village, bartering with one of the farmers. His hair stood out a mile away, a blueberry splotch against the muted greens and grays. The fog was thinning, but its ghost still clung to Azmiri's lower slopes, so that the world below seemed to fade slowly into nothingness.

"What's going on?" I demanded as soon as I reached him. "What did you say to Lusha? Did you frighten her somehow, or threaten her? Because if you did, I don't care if you *are* the Royal Explorer, I'll—"

"Good morning, Kamzin." River barely glanced up from the basket of *sampa* he was examining. "You seem recovered from last night—though do keep your voice down, please; I have a nasty headache." He was dressed all in black, and seemed taller, somehow, than he had before. His fog-thin cloak, embroidered with a complex, whorled pattern, was tossed casually over one shoulder. It was the most expensive garment I had ever seen, yet he wore it with the carelessness of someone who had a hundred more.

He brushed the barley grains from his hands and nodded at the farmer, who was gazing at me in horror. "Yes, this looks satisfactory. We'll need a full crate from your stores, if you can spare it."

"Yes, *dyonpo*," the man said, bowing low, and almost ran away.

"What happened?" I said, as he turned to face me. "Lusha wouldn't do this without a good reason."

"I'm sure you're right," River said. "She seemed a mulish sort of person. But I know as much as you do, Kamzin. Less, probably."

I shook my head. "Yet you don't seem surprised."

"Oh, I wouldn't say that." River's expression darkened. "Though I've always known Mara had it in him to do something like this."

"But why?" I said. "What would he gain?"

"The title of Royal Explorer, of course."

I blinked. "But—"

"Yes." He waved a hand. "I hold the title. But the emperor has been displeased with me lately. These past months, he has become obsessed with discovering the location of a rare talisman. He has sent me from one end of the Empire to the other in search of it. As I've not been successful, he has announced that whoever discovers the talisman will be named Royal Explorer."

"A contest," I said, feeling an odd shiver of excitement.

"Of a sort. A dozen explorers are already scattering throughout the Empire, searching other locations. Little good it will do them."

"Then you believe this talisman is on Raksha?"

"There is nowhere else it could be. I've ruled out the other possibilities."

"But what is it?" I said. What sort of talisman would be hidden in such a remote place?

"I can't tell you that," he said. "I'm sorry. The emperor has ordered me to secrecy."

"Mara knows."

"Of course." River sighed. "Mara should have been first in line for the title of Royal Explorer when I won it three years ago. He has resented me ever since."

"Why was Mara passed over?"

"Because I was better," River said simply. "Because he makes mistakes. The emperor doesn't much trouble himself over loss of life, but Mara's mistakes added up to something even he couldn't ignore. The man doesn't think, and people die because of it. I've seen it myself—I lost two assistants because of him. One fell from a rope he neglected to secure, and the other was swept away while we forded a river—all because Mara ordered her to swim after a scroll he dropped."

An image of Mara's wolfish smile flashed through my mind. I felt cold imagining my sister traveling with a man like that. "None of this explains why Lusha would agree to help him."

"Mara comes from a very wealthy family. He has more gold than most of the nobility. I'm sure he was convincing."

I narrowed my eyes. "You don't know Lusha at all if you think she would be motivated by gold. It doesn't matter to her."

"You're right. I don't know your sister." River shrugged. "But I do know that even the noblest souls can be swayed by material considerations."

"And you?" I crossed my arms.

He smiled. "I have many motivations."

I gave him a long look. In the morning light, I could see the faint dusting of freckles across his nose, making him look even younger than last night. What sort of man was he, I wondered, that he had accomplished so much already? Conquered so many dangers?

River held my gaze, the smile hovering around his mouth. He seemed to be scrutinizing me in turn. Whatever conclusion he was forming, though, was impossible to decipher.

A dark thought occurred to me. "What will you do if you catch Mara?" I said. "Take off his clothes and leave him tied to a tree?"

River stared, then burst out laughing.

"That's an unappealing thought," he said. "The first part, anyway. What made you think of it?"

"It's a story I heard," I said. "People say that's what you did to a man who betrayed you."

"People say a lot of things about me. I didn't take the man's clothes. I only took his cloak."

I stared at him. "Is there a difference?"

"I suppose not," he said, in an absent tone that sent another shiver down my back. What was I doing, speaking to River Shara this way? Last night, I had felt strangely at ease in his presence. And I still did, in a way—but now it was as if there was a second version of him, overlaying the first like shadow. I wasn't sure which was real and which was air.

"I'm sorry," I said, after a small silence. "Lusha made you a promise, and she broke it."

He waved a hand. "You don't have anything to apologize for."

"All the same, if there's anything I can do—"

"I was hoping you'd say that."

I stopped. His strange eyes glinted in the sunlight.

"What do you mean?"

"I must get to Raksha, and quickly," he said. "It won't be long until the snows arrive, and this is not a mission that can be put off for another year. To have any real chance of success, I need a guide, a skilled one. I have it on good authority that Lusha isn't the only one who knows the way."

It took me a moment to process what he was saying. "I—"

"Ah—Norbu," River's gaze slid past me. I turned, and found a very tall, very skinny man approaching along the path. He was perhaps fifty, and dignified in a tired, worn-out way, as if he had not merely aged but weathered, like a rock face subjected to too many storms. His hair was almost entirely white, with only a few black strands here and there, and he wore an old sheepskin *chuba*, which, while not cut in the mountain style, was at least a recognizably practical piece of clothing.

The man bowed to me. It was an odd thing to do, given the disapproval on his face, but he managed it. I knew I didn't look at all deferential in the presence of the Royal Explorer, standing there with my arms crossed, frowning at River, in the stained *chuba* I usually wore to my lessons with Chirri.

"Kamzin, this is Norbu," River said. "My personal shaman, and one of the greatest in the Three Cities. Norbu, this is the Kamzin I told you about."

Norbu's disapproval faded slightly, and he nodded to me. I didn't nod back—I was still looking at River. Who was the Kamzin he had told Norbu about? The drunken Kamzin, who had embarrassed herself in front of the entire village? The Kamzin known only as Insia's *other* daughter? The Kamzin who had, with River's help, rescued her best friend from almost certain death?

"*Dyonpo*, the village shaman has been uncooperative," Norbu said. "No matter what I offer, she refuses to part with any of her healing herbs."

I snorted. "Chirri is always uncooperative. And she only trades with people she knows."

They both looked at me, Norbu with a sort of confused surprise, as if a dragon had spoken, River with a smile.

"Norbu," he said, "it sounds like Kamzin is offering to assist.

You can leave this matter to her."

"What? I didn't—"

But before I could get another word out, River seized my arm and began pulling me along the path. "That's enough talking. We have a lot to do."

"We?"

"I'm putting you in charge of the supplies," he said. "That was Mara's job—he was hopeless at it, so don't be too concerned about my expectations."

"River—"

"And I'd like you to speak to the herdsman about borrowing another yak. I don't like the looks of the one your father offered. The way it stares at me, it's as if it's plotting something. I don't travel with plotters. Thieves, liars, cheats, that's all right, but I can't stand plotters. What else?" He snapped his fingers. "Oh yes. I'll need you to hire two stout-hearted villagers to assist us at camp."

"But, I—wait. Two? You'd need at least four, for—"

"No. Two. I travel light. That goes for supplies and assistants. Finally, see if you can find me a good ice ax. I lost mine."

I stared at him. An ice ax was one of the most important—and personal—things in an explorer's pack. My mother's had been beautiful—intricately carved, its bone handle grooved from the pressure of her fingers, and the blade narrowed from years of sharpening. "You *lost* your—"

"A yak trampled it on my last expedition. Snapped it in two. Did you hear what I said about choosing your yak carefully?"

We came to the shed where the men had stored River's balloon. I could just see the brightly colored fabric buried beneath a heap of what looked at first like rubble, but what I soon realized was the entirety of River's supplies. Packets of tea and dried foodstuffs, some of which spilled out onto the dirt floor, a jumbled pile of knives and whetstones, a satchel of healing herbs tied in loose bundles, and a dozen mysterious wooden chests of varying sizes stacked in several teetering columns.

"I'll leave you to it," he said. "Let me know what your sister has left us with."

"But—"

He was already walking away. Steeling myself, I called, "I never said I would go with you."

He stopped and turned slowly to face me. In the breeze, his cloak floated behind him like a rippling shadow.

"You never said you wouldn't." His gaze was cool again.

I stared him down. There was a part of me—the far more rational part—that questioned my own sanity for doing so, but I would not let him order me around, or dismiss me as he would some fawning courtier. I wouldn't let myself be that—no matter what he offered me.

He held my gaze for another moment, and then, slowly, he began to smile. I breathed a silent sigh of relief.

"Kamzin," he said, "will you come with me? Will you show me the way to the mountain?"

"Yes," I said, trying to keep my voice even as excitement pulsed through me. "On one condition."

He seemed to find this amusing. I realized that he could not be used to people challenging him. "Name it."

"I want to know what we're looking for," I said. "Why this talisman is so important to the emperor. What properties it has."

He looked regretful. "I wish I could tell you, truly I do."

"How am I supposed to trust you if you won't answer any of my questions?"

"Trust me?" He shook his head, bemused. "You're worrying about the wrong thing. Trusting me is not something I recommend to anyone."

And with that, he was gone.

I bit my lip, staring at his retreating back. My thoughts seemed to be spinning in a hundred different directions.

The supplies were a mess. Lusha—or Mara, perhaps—had evidently ransacked them with abandon, and much of the foodstuffs were trampled and ruined. I began piling the crates up, running over the last few days in my mind.

It made no sense that Lusha would abandon her promise to River and sneak off with a man she had just met—a man who, as evidenced last night, she found about as compelling as our great-grandfather Tashi after his third bowl of wine. Yet as I considered everything, sweat beading on my forehead as I shifted the heavy supplies, surprise was not what I felt—it was anger.

Anger at Lusha for keeping secrets. Anger at her for risking her life like this. And anger at how, once again, she was the center around which everything, and everyone else, revolved.

Lusha knew that I wanted to escape Azmiri. She knew that I

would have given anything to prove myself to River—and what had she done? Shown up not only me but the Royal Explorer himself. If they beat us to Raksha, and found the talisman, Mara would win the title of Royal Explorer, and become the second-most-powerful man in the Empire. And Lusha would share in the glory.

If they beat us to Raksha. I stabbed at a teetering pile of crates with my foot, steadying them. As highly as Lusha thought of herself, she was no match for me when it came to applying stupid, brute strength to physical obstacles. She could hunt, and read maps, and hike difficult terrain—but I could navigate an icefall on a moonless night, and stick to mountains like sap. It was the one way I had always bested Lusha. She couldn't climb Raksha, I knew that in my bones. And she had convinced herself—convinced River, convinced Mara—that she could.

I kicked at a whetstone so hard it flew into the air. I didn't know if I wanted to stop my sister from getting herself killed, or kill her myself.

Ragtooth showed up a few minutes later, nosing around in the box of dried plums. I shooed him out, but he only drew his ears back and hissed at me like a cat.

"Don't even think about stowing away," I warned. "You're not coming."

Once I set my mind to the task, it didn't take me long. I wrapped the spring hooks, pitons, and the rest of the climbing gear carefully in oilcloth to prevent rust, and I counted and measured every length of rope I could find. Everything else I organized into piles and tucked away in packs, tallying the items that were missing and would need to be borrowed or bought from the villagers.

"Kamzin?"

It was Tem. He looked paler than usual, and I could just make out the line of the cut through his hair, but he seemed otherwise recovered from last night. His trousers were muddy, and strands of yak hair clung to his *chuba*. His father must have commanded him to tend to the herds that morning, in spite of his injury. Or, knowing Metok, because of it.

"What are you doing?" he said. "Did Lusha—?"

"Lusha's gone." I explained quickly. Tem's expression grew more and more confused.

"But that doesn't make any sense," he said. "Why would she betray River Shara? She wouldn't care about a rivalry between two rich nobles."

"River thinks it was gold."

Tem made a skeptical noise. "You believe that?"

"I don't know." Lusha certainly wasn't interested in profit for her own sake. But for the village?

Though she wasn't the elder yet, Lusha had always seen herself in that light, much to my annoyance. She cared more for Azmiri than she did for her own life. And the village, isolated as it was and far from the trading routes, was certainly not wealthy. If Mara had offered enough gold to make us prosperous, to make medicine shortages and lean winters a thing of the past, would Lusha have accepted?

I shook my head. "Tem, do you still have your grandfather's

ice ax? River needs one, and I don't think any of Elder's will suit his grip."

"You're going with him." Tem's voice was flat.

I looked at him. "Are you surprised?"

"No. You've always been completely mad."

I turned back to the crates. "You made your opinion clear yesterday. Please, let's not argue anymore. I don't want it to be the last thing we do."

"Neither do I." Tem sighed. "That's why I'm coming with you."

I dropped the crate I was lifting, spilling tea leaves across the floor. "What? You are not!"

"I'm your friend. And I'm not letting you do this by yourself."

"River will never allow it."

"I bet he will, if you ask him."

I let out a snort of laughter. "Right. The Royal Explorer will do exactly as I say."

"I'm coming with you." Tem's voice shook slightly, but his gaze was firm. "I'll follow alone if I have to."

"Your father will never forgive you." My voice was low.

He looked away. "Well, that's nothing new, is it?"

I felt a familiar stab of sympathy. Tem's father was as cruel as he was handsome—and this had been even more true in his youth. Metok traveled frequently to other villages to trade his animals, often leaving heartbroken young women in his wake. After one gave birth to a child, she had been so ashamed that she had traveled to Azmiri and abandoned him on Metok's doorstep.

Metok claimed he didn't know her name, and given his reputation most villagers took him at his word. He had decided to raise Tem himself, instead of surrendering him to the emperor's army, the most common destination for unwanted orphans, only because he thought it would be useful to have a son to help with his herds—a fact he hadn't kept secret from anyone, including Tem.

"Tem, I—"

"Don't." He looked awkward again. "Just tell me what you need."

I studied him. I knew I would never change his mind—Tem was impossibly stubborn. He *would* follow me, unless I tied him up or placed a spell on him. And, knowing Tem, it would take him all of five seconds to break any spell of mine.

I let out a long sigh. "All right. Let's start by finding that ax."

SIX

THE OBSERVATORY FELT even colder than usual. Though the candles had been put out, their presence hung in the air, a taste like tears. The village below shone against the dark mountainside, lit by dragonlight that wavered and traveled, revealing glimpses of color from the drawn shutters. I felt closer to the sky at this lofty height than I did to the human realm. The square hole in the roof framed cloudy gatherings of stars, occasionally disturbed by the trail of a comet.

I whistled for the dragon I had brought with me. He hopped onto the table, preening. I scratched his chin absently while I examined the sheaves of paper that Lusha, in her haste, had left scattered over the drawing table. The wind that whispered through the observatory had stolen several pages; I had found two snagged in the grass outside.

I flipped through the papers. Most were careful maps of the constellations with calculations of azimuths and meridians. I was soon completely lost. I had never liked astronomy; there was too much fiddly detail and guesswork in it for me. Although Lusha had successfully predicted several events in our village, such as an early birthing season for Elder's yaks and an avalanche that had destroyed one of the buckwheat terraces, there were many things neither she nor the seer had foreseen. There seemed to be little rhyme or reason to it.

I squinted at her notes, which were nearly illegible, interspersed with sketches of the constellations.

I'm trying to work something out, Lusha had said yesterday.

The more I thought about it, the more I wondered if she had seen something in the stars. Something that had driven her to abandon her promise to River and throw her lot in with his rival.

"Where is it, Lusha?" I muttered into the table.

But I could make out only a few words, and these were of little help—mostly astronomical babble like "apogee," "nadir," and "lunation." My name was there in three places, underlined, but I also saw Father's name, and other family members'. Even "Tem" appeared once. Everything was such a jumble, and some of the sheaves were dated months ago. I couldn't be sure if they had any relevance to what I was looking for.

I froze. At the very bottom of a pile of star charts, almost as if it had been buried there on purpose, was a page titled "Shara."

I moved the page closer to the dragon's light. It showed a long list of names, together with notations indicating specific stars. I recognized several—River was not the only famous member of his famous family, which had included another Royal Explorer, several Generals of the First Army, a shaman who had single-handedly defeated an entire barbarian army, and the architect who had built the emperor's palace.

I frowned, puzzled. What interest could Lusha have in River's family tree?

"Looking for something?"

I jumped, dropping the scroll. But it was only the seer, Yonden, who stood in the doorway.

"Yes." I glanced back at the papers. "But I don't seem to be having any luck."

Yonden was silent. He may have been thinking over what I said, or waiting for me to speak again—it was often impossible to tell with him. Yonden was young to be village seer—only a few years older than Lusha, his apprentice. But his talent was such that people from other villages would travel all the way to Azmiri to consult with him. Thin and already balding, he was not impressive to look at. His gaze, however, was intelligent, and warmed by the slight smile he always seemed to wear.

He was not smiling tonight, however. His face was drawn and serious. There was an indefinable emotion in his gaze, almost as if he had been expecting—or hoping—to find someone else there.

"I'm sorry," I said. "You came here to work—I'm interrupting."

"Not at all." He stepped inside, his expression relaxing into its usual gentle smile. "Lusha thought you might come here." He tucked his hands into his sleeves, studying me. Yonden did not look at people so much as *peer* at them, as if they were spread across a distance like a mountain range.

"You spoke to her before she left?" I said.

"Yes." Yonden's tone became opaque. I thought I could guess why. Lusha hadn't bothered with good-byes—except, it seemed, for Yonden.

I regarded him curiously. I had always suspected there was something going on between him and Lusha, though I had never fully believed it. Yonden was the most talented seer Azmiri had seen in generations; he would be risking his livelihood by entertaining a relationship with anyone. It was forbidden for seers to marry—even friendships were frowned upon. Their abilities, it was believed, were diminished by associating too much with other people. Good seers were like the stars themselves—pure, cold, and removed from earthly concerns.

"What else did she say?" I asked. "Yonden—I know Lusha saw something in the stars. Something about the expedition to Raksha. Do you know what it was?"

Yonden gave me a long, thoughtful look, and I smothered a sigh. Seers were impossible. They were free to speak about some things they read in the stars, but not others. Lusha had said once that it depended on whether a coming event was fixed or unstable, whatever that meant.

After a moment, Yonden said, "We see many things. Truths, possibilities, events both past and future. Some things cannot be read, for they are always shrouded, or in endless motion."

I bit back my frustration. "But is there anything you *can* tell me?"

Yonden paused again. "I can say that there is great instability surrounding this expedition. Almost all the signs are contradictory. Some are very, very strange."

It was like talking to a wall of mist. "So that's it?"

Yonden turned to one of the windows and adjusted the telescope. "There is the matter of the fire demon."

I froze. "The what?"

"You will meet a fire demon on your journey. I advise you not to befriend it."

"Why would I befriend a fire demon?"

"Others have done so, or tried. Nevertheless, you should keep your distance."

My heart had begun to pound. A *fire demon*. This was terrible news. Worse than being told that I would be caught in a rock slide, or confronted by a family of hungry bears. Fire demons were strange creatures—ancient, elemental spirits who mostly avoided humans, and about whom little was known. But of that little, none was positive. Shamans summoned them, sometimes, to work difficult spells, but only at great cost. A fire demon did not grant favors or forgive debts. They were greedy, hungry things. I had never seen one myself—few people had—and I hoped I never would.

Yonden shuffled across the room and bent over a stone in the floor. It lifted easily, revealing a dark cavity that I had never seen before. I heard papers rustling, and a few mysterious *clink-clink* sounds, before he finally retrieved a single scroll, which was gray with age.

"Here," he said, passing it to me. "Handle it with care. It's very old."

I stared. I was gazing at a topographical map of an enormous mountain—but not just any mountain. I recognized its sharp, distinctive contours, how the ridge leading to its summit jutted like a protruding spine. I unfurled the map more, revealing different angles of the same subject, along with detailed drawings of key features.

Raksha.

I whistled for the dragon, and he flew to my shoulder. The map was indeed old and faded, but still legible.

"I didn't know it had been mapped," I breathed. There were even notes along the side, written in a firm, spiky hand.

"It's Mingma's," Yonden said. "The survivors of his expedition managed to retrieve it and bring it back to the emperor. Your mother borrowed it before her own journey north. It's not complete—Mingma never had a chance to finish it."

I nodded. Mingma was a legendary figure, one of the first to hold the title of Royal Explorer. No one knew if he had actually made it to the summit of Raksha fifty years ago. If he had, he had not lived to tell of it.

"Lusha has a copy," he said. "She wanted me to keep the original safe. But I think you can make more use of it than I."

"Thank you," I murmured.

Yonden smiled. Retrieving a drawing board and a sheaf of

paper, he sank to the ground before the telescope. His pencil scratched against the wood. I was clearly not expected to stay any longer.

"Is there anything else you can tell me?" My voice seemed very small, suddenly.

Yonden's pencil paused, but he did not speak for a long moment.

"Yes," he said finally, pinning me with one last, deep gaze. There was a shadow on his face, but it didn't conceal the quiet sadness there. "Look out for your sister. But do not forget to look out for yourself."

PART II
WINDING PASS

SEVEN

WE LEFT AT dawn.

Or we would have, if River had been on time.

"Probably fixing his hair," Tem said. He stood erect beneath the weight of his pack, resting his arm calmly on his walking stick. Too erect. Too calm. He was doing his best to appear untroubled—and would have succeeded, had I not known him as well as I did. Based on the stiffness of his mouth and the faint tremor in his hands, I guessed he wasn't far from throwing up.

I said nothing, too preoccupied with a dream from last night. I had been running from a fire demon, who stalked me through dark woods. A beautiful woman appeared, half shadow and half flesh— even though I had never seen a witch, I knew she was one. But before she could lay a curse, the fire demon stretched its mouth to a terrifying size and swallowed her whole—then it turned toward me.

It doesn't mean anything, I lectured myself. *Just nerves.* In the morning light, this was somewhat easier to accept.

Even more unpleasant than the dream had been saying goodbye to Father. I had found him sitting by the fire in his reception room before sunrise, his head in his hands. The doors of his shrine were ajar, and a stick of incense burned in the censer, as if he had recently prayed. The scent of jasmine and chani leaves filled the air, cloying in the close little room, which was sparsely furnished with a few woven mats for visiting villagers to sit on. A silk scroll took up an entire wall, depicting the generations of elders who had come before him.

"Papa?"

He started. "Kamzin. I didn't hear you come in."

I went to his side and wrapped my arms around his shoulders. "It's time for me to go. Won't you come and see us off?"

"No—I don't think so."

I could see he had been crying. I went back to the door, closed it, then returned to his side. Father's reputation was as a stern but fair leader, a wise arbiter of disputes who put reason before emotion when coming to decisions. But in truth, he was the most soft-hearted person I knew, more likely to cry at a wedding or birth ceremony than even my great-aunt Yema. He doted on his daughters—Lusha in particular—even more since my mother had died.

"Lusha will be all right," I said, kneeling beside him and taking his hand. "And so will I."

"Kamzin—"

"You don't have to say it," I interrupted. "I know you don't want me to go. But I have to do this."

He let out a sigh, his beard fluttering. It was mostly white now—despite his straight back and keen gaze, Father was not a young man. He had been twice my mother's age when they married, and was now older than some grandfathers.

"When River Shara first wrote to Lusha," he said, gazing into the embers of the fire, "I told her no. But, as Lusha said, how could we deny the Royal Explorer? I'm a village elder, and he's one of the most powerful men in the Empire. And yet I wish with all my heart that Lusha had listened to me. There is a terrible darkness surrounding that mountain."

"That's just superstition, Papa."

"That's what your sister said." He picked up a poker and stirred the embers, releasing a few lurking flames. "Now she's gone. Somehow I can't help feeling that it's my fault."

I touched his shoulder. "Of course it isn't."

He gave the embers another stir, then set the poker aside. "If your mother were here . . ."

My throat clenched. Father used those words often. In serious moments, when a storm or early thaw threatened the village, it was an invocation. Other times, when Lusha and I argued about who would travel with him to the spring markets, it was almost a joke. He never finished his thought. He didn't need to.

If my mother were here, everything would be different.

My mother had rarely taken the dangers she faced seriously, dismissing them with her booming, infectious laugh. She had been *big*—not merely in terms of size, but everything about her. She had always seemed like the sort of person no amount of space could contain. In the end, though, it had been a small thing that had taken her. A fever that hadn't seemed out of the ordinary—little more than an inconvenience—until it suddenly took a turn for the worse. In the space of a night, she was simply gone.

"Kamzin." Father took my hand and drew me in front of him, so that I was looking down into his lined eyes. "You must promise me that you will turn around at the first sign of danger. Don't let River convince you to do something that doesn't feel right. I don't care who he is—your life is more important than the emperor's displeasure."

"Papa, I—"

"No." He was gripping my hands so tightly that I felt my bones creak. "Promise me."

I swallowed. "I promise."

I had felt guilty as I said it. Now, in the cold light of the morning, I felt even worse. Because I didn't think I could keep my promise.

I didn't think I wanted to.

I gazed over the valley and the misty landscape beyond, the towering mountains and sweeping expanses. I felt a familiar pull—to dive into the wilderness, digging my boots into soil no one else had touched. Now, for the first time, I didn't have to ignore that pull. I could let it take me.

The two assistants I had hired, Dargye and Aimo, waited

patiently by our yak. They had already proven their competence that morning—the yak was loaded comfortably but securely with the bulk of our gear, and they had consulted the maps I had brought and provided sound suggestions. Dargye was a heavy man with moody eyes beneath a single brow. He was a low-ranking member of the village council, and his size and strength had made him an obvious asset for an expedition this dangerous. Rumor had it he could fell mountain birches without the help of an ax. Looking at the enormous biceps battling the seams of his shirtsleeves, I didn't doubt it.

I didn't know much about Aimo, a young woman in her early twenties. A year ago, her daughter had escaped her grandparents' care, tottering down the mountain and into the Nightwood. Aimo's husband had followed in search of her. Neither had returned, and no one doubted that they had met a grisly end. It was said that the witches devoured human souls, leaving behind empty bodies that they kept as slaves, or drained of blood for their mysterious spells. After the period of mourning, Aimo had carried on running the family's large farm by herself. With her stoic temperament and reputation for generosity toward her poorer neighbors, she was widely respected in Azmiri.

"Thank you," I said as she repositioned one of my satchels on the animal's back. She nodded, her smile transforming her plain face. It was no wonder, I thought, that she had received three marriage proposals since her husband's death.

"Is everyone ready?" It was Norbu. With him was a slim, handsome boy with a large pack slung over his shoulders.

"We are," I said as they moved to check the yak's load. "Where's River?"

The boy looked up from the strap he was examining. He wore a slight smile that seemed familiar. "Honestly, Kamzin, will I need to introduce myself each time we see each other?"

My jaw dropped. Tem made a low noise that sounded like *woo*. River laughed.

"Come now," he said, making a sweeping motion with his arm. "Surely I don't look *that* different."

But he did. The young man standing before me was as far as possible from the elegant noble I had met at the banquet. His hair was an ordinary dark brown, and while still bird's-nest messy, was cropped shorter than it had been, and no longer woven with expensive charms. The rings and jewels were gone, as were the fine clothes—his trousers and tunic were a plain gray in a weave suited to walking, and his scuffed leather boots looked as if they had traveled many miles in their lifetime. His eyes were the same, though, unsettlingly mismatched in a way that was even more apparent in the morning light, and full of laughter.

"I, um—" I came to a stuttering halt, uncertain how I should address this unfamiliar person. River took little notice. He shook out the *chuba* folded over his arm, then swept it over his shoulders. I had to suppress a gasp. It was the finest tahrskin *chuba* I had ever seen, far finer than my mother's, though made in the customary way—two-sided, one dark and one pale. River's somehow made him seem taller, more sharply defined, and it fit as if it had been made for him. The short black fur gleamed in the sunlight.

"*Dyonpo*, we should make haste," Norbu said. He scanned the horizon, where a line of clouds was gathering. "We should be off the mountain before the rain reaches us."

"I can help with that," Tem piped up. He looked immediately regretful when all eyes trained upon him, but he pushed on. "I've been studying weather spells. I think I could delay the rain, at least for a while."

Norbu stared at him blankly, as if Tem were a species of animal he had never seen before. River grimaced. "What is he doing here?"

I bristled at his tone but managed to keep my temper. "He asked to join the expedition as Norbu's assistant, if that's all right with you. He has a talent for shamanism."

"Does he?" River gave Tem a skeptical look. "I've observed his talent for falling off things, which doesn't exactly recommend him for an expedition like this. And he'll be a nuisance to Norbu."

"I wouldn't mind, *dyonpo*," Norbu said. "I've been missing my assistant."

I held my breath, but River only shrugged. "Kamzin, the map?"

I started. Feeling unexpectedly nervous, I fumbled around in my pack until I extricated the map of the Samyar Plains.

I had sketched out the route to Raksha in charcoal, carefully calculating distances and noting streams and potential campsites. It would take a traveler of average abilities a month or more to reach the mountain from Azmiri—but in a month, summer would be over and the weather on the highest peaks would be unpredictable. My goal, therefore, was to reach it within fifteen days.

I didn't know if it was possible. But we would have to try.

"We can make it to Winding Pass in five days, Riv—um, *dyonpo*," I said, holding the map open so he could see the route. "If we keep up a good pace."

"Five days to the pass?" River said. "Is that the best we can do? I want to close as much distance as possible between us and Mara. He and Lusha have a full day's head start."

"I know this part of the Aryas like I know my own hands," I said. "The other routes may be faster, but they're more dangerous, which could slow us down in unexpected ways."

River nodded as I spoke, peering down at the map. A strand of unkempt hair fell across his forehead. "All right. What are you thinking?"

"We'll travel through the Azmiri foothills. Avoid Bengarek Forest, given how dense the undergrowth can be in summer. It's a thirty-mile hike to Mount Imja—we'll camp beneath it tonight. Tomorrow, we'll push on across the plains toward Winding Pass. I expect we'll catch up to Lusha and Mara there, if not before. They're carrying all their supplies on their backs, after all, and won't be able to move as quickly as us." I unrolled Mingma's map. "It isn't safe to linger in the pass, so we'll have to avoid getting stuck there after dark. Once we're through, we'll be in the Nightwood—the borderlands, anyway." I tried to keep my voice even, as if traveling through the witch lands was something sane people did regularly. "From there, we'll hike north to Raksha."

Dargye, standing behind me, made a small noise.

"Yes?" River glanced at him. "Did you have something to say, ah—"

"Dargye, *dyonpo*," he said. He too seemed nervous, being addressed by River directly. "I can't help wondering why we would avoid Bengarek Forest. The undergrowth isn't as bad as she says, and it's flat ground, unlike the foothills."

"And unlike the foothills, we would have a good chance of being attacked by red-toothed bears," I said, glaring at Dargye. He had agreed to my plan before, when River wasn't there. "Bengarek Forest is infested with them."

Dargye barely seemed to be listening to me. He addressed River again, more confidently this time. "I believe the forest is the wisest choice, *dyonpo*."

River furrowed his brow. "Kamzin, you didn't tell me that Dargye knew the way to Raksha."

"What?" I said. "He doesn't."

"I see." He handed the map back to me, and dumped his pack unceremoniously in Dargye's arms. "All right, everyone, let's make for the foothills."

I couldn't suppress a smile of triumph. Dargye glowered. I thought I saw River wink at me, but he turned away quickly, and I couldn't be certain.

The road that led from the village down to the valley sliced back and forth along the flank of the mountain, following the edge of the terraces. The sun wouldn't touch us for an hour at least, and despite the exertion I was shivering in the chill breeze. It was a crisp, clear day, with only the faintest mist hovering among the forest far below. Despite the early hour, I was full of energy. My feet wanted to move more quickly, and I had to remind myself to take measured steps, to conserve my strength for the long road before me.

River and Norbu walked ahead, their voices occasionally floating back to us, garbled by the wind. I found myself examining River—the profile of his face, as he gestured at something; the stirring of his *chuba* as he strode easily along the path. I still found it hard to reconcile the young man in front of me with my image of River Shara, the man who, in the three short years he had held the title of Royal Explorer, had mapped half the Empire and established himself as one of the emperor's closest confidants. Who fought and killed savage barbarian lords and doomed those who betrayed him to slow, lonely deaths in the wilderness.

I recalled how he had seemed to change suddenly, out on the spur, his capricious manner subsumed by something cold, calculating. I shook my head, feeling oddly out of my depth. I was used to the plain-spoken villagers of Azmiri, whose desires were simple and whose lives were small. River was as different from what I knew as a hawk from a sparrow.

Tem and I walked in the middle of the company, followed by Dargye and Aimo with the yak. Tem was fiddling with a strange talisman—a leather cord strung with bells of different shapes and sizes.

"What's that?" I said.

"Oh—Chirri gave them to me." He blushed. "They're

kinnika—they help ward off misfortune. This one"—he pointed to a small, black bell—"will alert me to the presence of any creature who means to harm us. It won't sound for any other reason. See?" He shook the bell. It made no noise whatsoever. "These two will keep a dark spirit at bay while I speak the incantation. This one—" His brow creased as he gazed at the largest bell, bronze with a reddish patina. "I don't remember what it's for. I wrote it down, though."

"That was good of Chirri," I said. "Something tells me we're going to need all the help we can get."

Tem looked guilty. "She should have given them to you. You're her apprentice."

"*Tsh.* You know me. I would have lost them already, or mixed them up so badly I'd be trying to put out a fire with the bell for banishing ghosts. Chirri chose right."

I had visited Chirri yesterday, to tell her I was leaving. She would have known already, but I had felt it was only right to say good-bye. The old woman's hut, I had been pleased to discover, was still overrun with baby dragons, which had swarmed me like bees when I entered. Chirri herself had seemed irritated by my visit, muttering something about being woken from a particularly sound nap. Her only comment about the expedition was that I should have left long ago, which made little sense. Rather than leaving her hut with words of wisdom or a useful talisman, I had been unceremoniously shooed out with one of the teething dragons, who now perched on the yak's neck, gnawing at her lead.

"I'm glad she trusted you," I added. "I didn't think she

knew—about how powerful you are, I mean."

"I wouldn't put it like that." Tem was the color of an apple now.

"Father would be angry, if he found out she was favoring you," I said, sighing. "He still thinks I'm going to take over from Chirri when she dies. I suppose if I die first, I won't have to worry about it. That's something."

Tem was quiet for a long moment. "Don't joke about that, Kamzin."

"All right, all right." I gave him a playful shove. "Lighten up. I never said I'd die tomorrow. And you know Chirri's going to make it to two hundred, at least."

Tem didn't reply. He stopped to remove a rock in his boot. But he didn't catch up to me again.

When the sunlight oozed over the peak of Azmiri, it grew hot. I removed my *chuba* and looped it through the straps of my pack. The frost on the grasses and rhododendrons was melting fast, a steady *drip-drip-drip* that mingled with the honks of the bar-headed geese passing overhead and the whistling wind. Small creatures stirred among the foliage—warblers searching out their breakfast, or foxes on their way to the village to spy on the chicken coops. I tried to focus on these sounds, and the steady rhythm of my boots against the path, but found it impossible. We caught occasional glimpses of Imja, its snowy, pinnacled summit painted orange by the rising sun. Beyond it, far beyond, was Mount Raksha.

I shivered with mingled excitement and fear. It was as if I could *feel* the mountain out there in the mingled shadow and sunlight of the morning. Now that my feet were set firmly on the path, and moving toward my destination, I realized just how mad my decision was. I had never climbed Mount Raksha.

No one had.

I forced my attention back to my feet. One step at a time. That was all this was: a series of steps. I beat the anxious voice back to a dark corner of my mind, and prayed it would stay there—at least for now.

We stopped that night in the shadow of Mount Imja, at a spring that bubbled from between two enormous boulders crowned with juniper trees. The spray from the water as it tumbled down the rock was cool against my face. I removed my boots and waded into the spring, crouching to cup the icy water in my hands and splash it across my sweaty brow.

I surveyed the terrain, pleased with myself. We had reached our destination with time to spare—there was still an hour of daylight to make camp. I couldn't help gloating at Dargye, who seemed to be avoiding my eyes.

"Let's set up the tents here," I said to Aimo, gesturing. "Dargye, build the fire against that rock."

"It's too wet," the man said shortly, barely breaking his stride. He dropped an armful of firewood on the ground, too close to the tents for my liking. The wind would surely blow the smoke into our shelters as we slept.

I opened my mouth to protest, but Dargye began noisily breaking the scraps of wood into smaller pieces with his bare hands, his enormous muscles straining. Muttering, I turned away.

"Don't let him do that," Tem said quietly.

I sighed. "It doesn't matter. It's just a campfire."

"I don't think so." Tem turned back to his pack. "You're in charge, Kamzin."

I chewed my lip. I was annoyed at both of them now. After a second's thought, I called out, "Dargye."

The man looked up, glowering. A small flame flickered among the moss he cupped between his hands. "What?"

I walked up to the fire calmly, and then, just as calmly, snuffed out the flame with my bare foot—one quick stomp. The large man almost fell over backward in surprise.

"The fire," I said, "will go over there."

Then I walked away. When I snuck a glance some moments later, Dargye was hunched by the patch of earth I had indicated, rebuilding the fire.

I allowed myself a smile of triumph while surreptitiously pressing my foot into the cold sand of the streambank. It didn't hurt—much. My soles were as tough as leather after so many summer evenings spent roaming the mountainside barefoot.

Aimo was watching me from behind the yak. I wondered if she would be angry at me, for her brother's sake, but there was a quiet amusement in her eyes.

"Is he always like that?" I muttered.

Her smile grew. "Yes," she said in her typical matter-of-fact tone.

I laughed. She did too, a pleasant, rumbling sound.

"I wonder why he decided to join this expedition, as he hates taking direction," I said, helping Aimo untie one of the satchels.

The woman smiled again, rolling her eyes slightly. "For me," she said. "He wants to protect me."

"To protect you?" I repeated. "Then it was your idea?" I had assumed, when Dargye volunteered to join the expedition, offering his sister as an additional assistant, that it had been the other way around.

Aimo nodded, bending her head over our supplies.

"Why?"

Her eyes drifted away, and she flushed slightly. Tem reappeared at my side then, and began noisily unloading the layers of oilcloth and wooden stakes that would serve as our tents. Dargye called to his sister, and she moved away.

The dragons soared toward us, skimming the pool of water before coming to rest on the bank. We had brought five. All day they had alternated between sleeping among the yak's satchels and flying above us. A plump one nosed up to me, pawing my leg with its front feet. I winced at the pinch of its talons. Fortunately, Tem distracted it with a handful of dried chickpeas from his pocket.

"Ouch!" He laughed as the dragon devoured the snack. "That was my finger."

I laughed along with him, relieved to feel some of the tension drain away. Tem and I had not spoken since morning. Once the dragon finished the snack, though, Tem went to help Norbu with his satchels. I felt a pang as I watched him go. There was still a distance between us, and I didn't know how to close it.

Dinner was a plain meal of rice and mung beans. We ate seated on the grass around the fire, enjoying the warmth it brought to the cooling twilight air. Aimo caught fish from the pool, but they were so small that they only amounted to a mouthful or two for each of us. I eyed the water moodily as my stomach gave a growl, wondering why I had thought the rations I'd brought would be sufficient. Tem often teased me about my appetite, claiming I could devour as much as fifty dragons in a single sitting. He probably wasn't far off.

Everyone else seemed content with their meals, however. Norbu selected a talisman from the tangled mass he wore around his neck, closed his eyes, and began muttering to himself. Dargye and Aimo murmured together on the other side of the fire—or, rather, Dargye murmured; Aimo listened with a long-suffering expression on her face. River sprawled across the grass, watching the stars appear and chatting easily with Tem about the geological differences between the Arya and the Drakkar Mountains. River was certainly not the haughty, ill-tempered explorer his reputation suggested—he had talked so much through the day that I wondered how he had enough breath to keep up with us—but unlike Mara, little of his conversation involved bragging. When one of his famous exploits came up—his expedition into barbarian territory, for example, where he'd spent weeks spying undetected on their rough camps, or the time he'd rescued twelve soldiers patrolling the northern reaches of the Empire from an avalanche—he shrugged it off, as if bored by the subject. I found myself biting my tongue to keep from asking questions about the deeds he referred to so casually, many of which had already become legend. For some reason, I didn't want him to know I was listening.

Despite the growing chill, River seemed comfortable in his shirtsleeves, and used his magnificent *chuba* as a pillow. I had to suppress an urge to yank the garment out from beneath his head. If the emperor ever honored me with a tahrskin *chuba*, I told myself, I would never treat it with such disrespect.

Absently, I rubbed my shoulders, which burned from the chafing straps of my pack. As River spoke, his face became animated. I had seen explorers who had been marred by their profession—noses lost to frostbite, cheeks carved with deep furrows by the elements. River was nothing like them. Everything about him was sharp and beautiful—an unexpected sort of beauty. It wasn't just the strangeness of his eyes, it was how he held himself, with a loping, lazy grace that put me in mind of a leopard or lynx more than a boy my own age. All the boys I knew were like Tem—awkward and gangly, all bony limbs and overlarge feet that always seemed to be in the way of each other.

But why was I comparing him to Tem? River's gaze met mine, and a smile flickered on his face. I looked away so quickly my neck hurt.

I unrolled Mingma's map of the Northern Aryas, tucking one edge beneath the tail of a sleeping dragon. The explorer had been an accomplished artist—though the mountains were drawn with quick, almost careless strokes, they were more accurate than most other maps I had seen. Raksha—featured among the Arya range and then, in a series of separate panels, by itself—was particularly vivid. I could almost feel the chill of the wind that roared across its slopes, the great and terrible shadow it cast.

I traced the lines of it, picturing Mingma's pen flying gracefully over the canvas, his head bent over his work. He had been young when he died, I knew. I wondered again what had happened to him.

Gathering my *chuba* around my legs, I let my gaze drift to the mountains. Their white peaks were knife-sharp against the darkening sky. Though the western slopes of the Aryas were less treacherous than the east, given the risk of witches, places like this were far from safe. The red-toothed bears of Bengarek Forest were aggressive, and there were also snow leopards and wolf packs to contend with. We would have to cast our warding spells carefully every night, and assign a lookout during the day.

While part of me made note of these things carefully, another, larger part could hardly believe my situation. I was really *here*. Marching into the wilderness with the Royal Explorer, staring down unknown dangers. My hated lessons with Chirri, the weight of my family's disappointment—it was all gone. And if I did well on the expedition, well enough to impress River, it could be gone forever.

A shiver of excitement traced its way down my spine.

I wondered if we would come across any evidence of Lusha and Mara tomorrow. We had passed the remains of a small campfire a few miles back, but there was no way to be certain it was theirs. Hunting parties from Azmiri sometimes ventured this far afield.

I gazed at the rising moon—Lusha could be looking at it too, also with a pile of maps unfurled before her. She couldn't be far away. We would catch up to her—I knew we would.

Suddenly, something was on my shoulder, digging sharp claws into my skin. Something hairy, with a cold, wet nose that brushed against my cheek. I yelped.

"Kamzin, what—" Tem stopped. He let out a disbelieving laugh. "What is he doing here?"

I yanked Ragtooth off me. "You little rat! I told you not to follow me!"

Ragtooth bared his teeth, looking all too pleased with himself. When I released him, he gave a large yawn, stretched his back, and began to groom himself, as if he were settling into his customary place by the hearth back home. I couldn't help laughing.

"What is *that*?" River said. He was propped up on his elbows, staring.

"He's Kamzin's familiar," Tem said.

"I gathered that. I mean, what is he?"

"What do you think he is?" I lifted Ragtooth around his pudgy belly and transferred him to my lap. "A fox."

"Are you sure? Looks more like a hairball with teeth."

"He has some mange," I said with dignity. "There's no need to be rude about it."

River and Norbu exchanged a look. The shaman appeared baffled. "Is it some form of weasel?"

"How many weasels have fangs like that?" River said.

"Stop it," I said. "You're being ridiculous."

"Don't get her started," Tem said to River. "She won't listen to reason about that creature. He's been hovering around her since she was a baby. Her father tried chasing him away, but he came back every time. He gives everybody the creeps."

River looked bemused. "Why couldn't you have ravens, Kamzin, like your sister? Much more useful than—well, whatever that is."

"Still," Norbu said somewhat dubiously, "it is interesting that the girl should have a familiar. I understand it's a rare honor."

"It is," Tem said, while I stewed. "Some say they're sent by the spirit world to watch over those they favor."

"Then these familiars have special abilities?" Norbu said.

"Well, not exactly," Tem said, with an apologetic glance at me. "They're ordinary animals, though the bond they share with their master can be quite useful."

"It's said that the shaman Bansi had a hawk." The look on Norbu's face indicated how I ranked in comparison to the shaman Bansi. I smothered a sigh. Most people reacted with disbelief when they discovered I had a familiar—I was used to it by now. Lusha and I were the only ones in Azmiri to have them, though the elder of a neighboring village had a monkey. Familiars were common among shamans and great heroes, the kinds of people that stories were written about—people like Lusha. Not like me. Clearly, as I had often said to Tem, even the spirits could make mistakes.

Ragtooth bared his teeth at Norbu, and the shaman inched away.

"Drop it," I muttered, poking him. The fox snapped at my finger.

River shook his head. "The spirits have an interesting sense of humor, don't they?"

"Ragtooth and I are going to bed," I said, raising my chin. As obnoxious as the fox could be, I would not sit there and let them insult him. "Good night."

Lifting the beast by the scruff of the neck, I walked over to my tent and pulled the flaps securely shut behind us.

"Don't listen to them," I whispered. "You can't help it if you were born a little different."

The fox gazed at me with his green eyes, which gleamed like polished jade. I tossed my boots on the ground, then—after glancing at Tem's neatly arranged belongings—picked them up again guiltily and tucked them into the corner of the tent. I settled into my blankets, shivering at their cold touch, and Ragtooth curled his body into a pillow of warmth against my head.

I must have slept for two hours, maybe three—when I woke, it was deep night, a darkness that could only exist in the valleys between great mountains. Tem snored on the other side of the tent.

I shifted restlessly. Something had woken me, I was sure of it. As I lay there, listening, the noise came again.

A skittering, snuffling sound.

It was coming from somewhere outside the tent. It seemed to rise and fall, as if whatever was making the noise was moving closer, then away, then closer again.

"Ragtooth?" I whispered. I looked around the tent and met the fox's glittering gaze. Ragtooth's ears were pricked, and though he didn't appear fearful, there was a watchfulness about him.

I lifted myself up onto my elbows. I could see no blue glow through the walls of the tent, and in any case, it didn't sound like a dragon. It was too large.

My heart began to pound, and my mind leaped to an image of a snow leopard, creeping through the darkness on enormous paws, drawn by the scent of human flesh.

The skittering grew louder. Again I heard something breathing in rough, animal pants. It seemed to be right outside the tent now. Terror froze me in place. Behind me, Ragtooth was equally motionless. We waited, barely breathing, until the thing moved away. The noises grew fainter and fainter, and then they were gone.

I fell back against my blankets, cold sweat bathing my brow. Tem gave a snort and rolled onto his side.

"Some comfort you are," I muttered. Ragtooth nosed up to me and licked my forehead. I pulled him to my chest. His heartbeat was faint but steady, and he still gave no sign of fear, though his ears remained pricked long after the sounds died away.

I lay awake for another hour at least, straining to hear. But all was still and quiet, apart from the trickle of the spring and the wind brushing through the trees. Finally, I fell asleep, the fox a warm, soft weight against my chest.

EIGHT

I WOKE AT first light. A crow was squawking somewhere in the distance, fracturing the peace of the morning. I had been dreaming of one of Chirri's lessons—I was hunched over an enormous basket, separating ripe winterberries from green ones. The task would have been easier had I been able to master the spell Chirri had given me—the ripe berries should have risen to the top of the basket, but instead, they flew up and pelted me in the face. While I wiped the stinging juice from my eyes, Chirri harangued me for my incompetence, her voice growing sharper and sharper until it made my ears ache.

As my eyes adjusted to my surroundings, I remembered that Chirri was miles away, and I had no lessons to attend. Muttering a prayer of thankfulness, I staggered to my feet, stripping off my old clothes and swapping them for clean ones from my pack. I moved as quickly and quietly as I could, trying to ignore the feeling of awkwardness. I was used to having Tem nearby when I slept—during his father's drinking bouts, he would often spend the night on a pile of mats in my bedroom. But sharing a small shelter in the wilderness, with no privacy to be sought anywhere, was an entirely different experience, and I found myself wishing we had been able to bring separate tents.

Ragtooth was gone, which didn't surprise me. He always appeared and disappeared at will. He would no doubt follow us when he felt like it, though I half hoped, for his sake, that he had gone home to Azmiri.

There were no sounds of movement from the others. I breathed a small sigh of relief—I wanted to be the first to rise. I had decided that I would make every effort, every day, to impress River with my skill and determination. I would be the first to wake and the last to bed. I would not complain, even if my shoulders burned from the weight of my pack and my feet felt ready to fall off. I would be the image of a daring explorer. I would be *formidable*.

My head nodded as I bent over my boots. Cursing, I forced myself to stand, dashing the sleep from my eyes. This part of my plan would take some getting used to. I was not accustomed to getting up early.

My hair was hopelessly knotted again, but I didn't bother to wrestle with it. Tossing my *chuba* over my shoulders, I stepped out into the chill morning air.

There I froze. In the faint light of dawn, I could make out a line of tracks leading from the scraggly brush at the base of

Mount Imja past my tent.

I bent down, brushing my fingers over the markings. They were like nothing I had seen before. It was as if their maker had half stepped, half glided through our camp. My heart in my throat, I followed the trail past Norbu's tent, and over a little rise in the ground, where it stopped.

Directly outside River's tent.

"River?" I called quietly. No response. "River!"

The tent parted, and River poked his head out. His hair stuck up like an angry cat's. "What?"

I let out a sigh of relief. "I thought the bear had eaten you."

"What bear?" Dargye shuffled out of his tent, looking nervous. "When did you see a bear?"

"I heard it, last night."

"Don't worry, Dargye," River said. "There was no bear. Norbu cast his warding spells carefully."

"I certainly did." Norbu emerged from his own tent. He was still tying his *chuba*, but was otherwise fully dressed. "I have never before allowed such a creature to enter our camp. Any bear that came within smelling distance of us would have become disoriented and turned around."

"Then it was something else," I persisted. "What do you make of these tracks?"

Norbu and Dargye bent to examine them. River had disappeared back into his tent.

"Curious." The lines in Norbu's brow deepened. "It looks like the trail of a snake."

"It was definitely not a snake. I heard it."

"River and I have encountered beasts of all shapes and sizes in our travels," Norbu said. "As the personal shaman of the Royal Explorer, I have some experience—"

"I heard it *snuffling*," I said slowly. "Was it a snake with a cold?"

The shaman shrugged, seeming to lose interest. His gaze wandered to the fire Aimo was waking from the embers. "As I said, my warding spells have never failed. I'm sure it was nothing to worry about." He moved away, Dargye trailing in his wake. I stared after him, speechless.

River emerged, running a hand through his hair. The green of his tunic made his gold-brown eye gleam, while the other seemed blacker by comparison.

"I have all my toes," he announced. "I counted. Nothing took a nibble in the night."

"Is Norbu really the greatest shaman in the Three Cities?" I said.

"Well . . ." River paused. "Why do you ask?"

"For one, Tem said he was having trouble with a basic wayfinding spell yesterday. And those talismans he wears are ridiculous. Gilded monkey teeth? Polished emeralds? They're useless."

River was gazing up at the sky, hands in his pockets, as if checking the weather. "Are they?"

"Yes." My voice hardened. "Chirri taught me that much." Shamanic magic required talismans, which channeled the shaman's power into spells. Most shamans brought a supply of talismans wherever they went, as different talismans were conducive to different spells. Bone talismans tended to suit healing spells, while copper and iron were for warding or protective spells. Talismans carved from wood could influence or even control the elements— some could summon fire, for example. Not all talismans were equal in strength, though, and all weakened with age. Some were fakes—sold by unscrupulous merchants to wealthy villagers for appearances rather than power. These were usually made of gold or precious stones, which seemed to make up the bulk of Norbu's supply.

"Greatness is overrated," River said. "Norbu is one of my oldest friends. He's a trustworthy man."

"As in we can trust him to protect us, or we can trust him to lead us over a cliff?"

River let out a short laugh. "Shall we leave cliff navigation to *your* shaman, Kamzin?"

"I'm going to get Tem to look at these tracks," I said, turning. "He'll know a spell that can identify them."

"What tracks?" River said, and then, before I could stop him, scuffed them rapidly with his boot.

"River!" I cried, grabbing his arm. But it was too late—all traces of the mysterious markings had been obliterated.

"You worry too much," he said. "You'll never make a good explorer if you're always troubling yourself over things that don't matter. Though I have to admit, I'm flattered by your concern. What would you have done if I *had* been eaten by a wild animal?"

I glared at him. I was still holding his arm, and released it hurriedly. "After I finished celebrating, you mean?"

He began to laugh. I left him to it and went to collect my breakfast. I hunched over my bowl, muttering to myself. Tem appeared moments later, and gave me a strange look.

"What's wrong now?"

"Oh, just River," I said, taking a vicious chomp out of a piece of dried yak meat. "I think he's trying to drive me as mad as he is."

Tem, for some reason, looked irritated at this. "Right. I'm sure that's what he's doing."

I finished my breakfast and stared mournfully into the empty bowl. "I can't believe I thought these rations would be enough."

Tem, who had barely taken a bite of his *sampa* cake, handed it to me. "Here."

I pushed it away. "You need to keep up your strength." Tem still looked tired from yesterday's hike. I hoped and prayed that his body would adjust to the demands of the journey.

He shook his head, coughing. "I don't like how Dargye makes it. Too salty."

"I think at this point I would eat dirt if it wouldn't make me sick."

We were packed and ready to depart within the hour. I gave the yak one final inspection, checking that her straps were secure but not too tight, and that her hooves were in good condition. If the beast were to sustain an injury, it would be disastrous. I rubbed the base of her horns, and she grunted with pleasure.

"Did *you* see anything strange last night?" I murmured, stroking her hair, which had a silky texture and smelled like summer grass. She gazed at me with her large, mournful brown eyes, as if she knew the answer to my question, and it was very dark indeed. The shadows were deep around us, and would remain so until midday, in this land of sharp valleys and snowy peaks that scraped the sky. Shaking off my apprehension, I gave the yak's lead a tug and we set out, the others falling into step behind us.

"Dare you to jump in," Tem said after dinner the next night, our third since leaving Azmiri. We sat side by side, dipping our feet in the pool of glacial meltwater beside the rocky meadow that would be our campsite. We had made good time again, reaching our destination several hours before sunset. We could have pushed on toward tomorrow's campsite, but I knew the opportunity for rest was more important. Not that I needed it—apart from a blister or two, I could have kept going all night—but the others did, particularly Tem.

I watched as he leaned forward to splash water across his bare chest. The droplets glinted against his skin, slipping between the planes of muscle and bone. I remembered who I was looking at, and glanced away, feeling vaguely guilty. It wasn't that Tem lacked strength—he could lift a year-old calf without breaking a sweat, and I suspected that his already-muscular build would one day rival Dargye's—but he wasn't built for endurance. When we were ten, I convinced him to hike to Nila Lake, a glittering blue pool fed by the Karranak glacier. It was a six-hour, uphill journey, and halfway there Tem had one of his breathing attacks, so bad his lips turned gray. There had always been something wrong with his lungs, even when he was a baby. He took medicine now that Chirri prepared for him, and submitted himself weekly to her healing chants. It seemed to keep the attacks at bay, but he still tired more easily than other boys his age.

"Come on," Tem said. "I bet you can't touch the bottom."

I shrugged, watching the water swirl and ripple around my feet, the chill soothing the blister forming on my left heel.

Tem bumped his shoulder against mine. "You've been distracted all day. What's wrong? Is it Lusha?"

I gazed over the mountains, the here-and-there patches of melting snow, the meadow grass speckled with clover and blue poppies. "I thought we'd catch them by now."

"They're moving fast," Tem said. "It makes sense. Mara wants to stay ahead of River and reach Raksha first."

I glowered at those words. Lusha would *not* reach Raksha first. Every hour that passed made me more determined to catch up to them. I still didn't know what I would do when we did—either hug her or shout at her, or grab her by the shoulders and shake her until her teeth rattled and she agreed to turn around.

I supposed I could do all three.

I dragged a stick across the damp soil. "I feel like I'm missing something."

Tem nodded slowly. "I feel the same. It's hard to believe Lusha would do something like this for gold, no matter how much Mara offered."

I thought about the charts I had found in the observatory, Lusha's mysterious notes. *I'm trying to work something out.*

"Mara wants River's position," I said. "Maybe he offered her something more than gold."

"Like what?"

I shook my head, frustrated. "I don't know."

"So what do you want to do?"

Laughter floated toward us from the campfire, where the others were gathered. I gazed at them, and an idea occurred to me.

"I want to learn more about this mysterious talisman," I said.

I rose, and Tem followed. But before he could take a step, he suddenly doubled over, coughing.

I touched his arm. "Are you all right?"

He nodded, clearing his throat. "Fine."

"You don't sound fine. Have you been taking Chirri's medicine?"

"Yes." He brushed me away. "Don't worry, Kamzin, it's nothing I haven't dealt with before. What's your plan?"

I frowned, unconvinced, but the look on Tem's face told me that further argument would get us nowhere. I squinted at the sheer wall of rock that towered over the meadow. It was glacial stone, layered and crumbly. Rhododendrons poked up here and there from narrow shelves. A smile spread across my face.

"Kamzin?" Tem said warily.

I pulled my boots back on, ignoring the bits of grass stuck to my wet feet. Then I marched back to the fire.

He was sitting with his back to the flames, drinking butter tea and talking—of course talking—to Norbu in a low voice. His hair was damp from washing, and fell loosely against his forehead. He glanced up and smiled as he saw me approaching—a sudden, unguarded smile that struck me unexpectedly like a physical thing, making my steps falter.

"Kamzin," River said, "would you like to join us?"

"No thanks," I said. "Actually, I'm feeling restless. I thought that, since we're nearing the Nightwood, I'd survey the area before dark. You can't be too careful."

"If you like," he said. "But you shouldn't go alone. I'll come with you."

That was too easy. I suppressed a smile.

"Thank you, River," I said. Norbu winced. He didn't like it when I used River's name, but he couldn't very well protest, if River didn't. Norbu wasn't a snob, I had decided, but he did like things to be done a certain way. He had a wife back in the Three Cities, a noblewoman, and usually that "certain way" of doing things was her way. He had already spent considerable breath instructing Aimo on the precise ratio of flour to water for making *sampa* cakes, and had twice dropped heavy hints in my presence regarding the correct way of addressing nobles, a subject on which his wife was apparently an expert. I doubted that Norbu saw his wife as often as he would like, given how much time he spent tramping around in the wilderness with River, and his comments would almost be endearing if they weren't so frequent—or so frequently aimed at me.

"We'll need to find higher ground," I said. "You can't see much from here."

River raised an eyebrow. "What do you suggest?"

I glanced over my shoulder at the sheer mountain face.

"Kamzin," Tem muttered.

I shot him a look. I needed to get River away from the others, where I could interrogate him without being interrupted. Also, he was less intimidating when we were alone—the others, particularly Norbu and Dargye, acted as if he were the emperor himself, scrambling to fetch him things and hanging on his every word. Even though I found their behavior ridiculous, it was catching.

"What do you say?" There was a dare in my voice. River's smile took on a wicked quality.

"I say let's go."

"*Dyonpo*," Norbu began, "are you certain that—"

"We won't be gone long, my friend," River said.

Norbu bowed his head, frowning slightly in my direction. River shrugged on his tahrskin *chuba* and followed me to the base of the rock face. The others had fallen silent. I could feel their eyes on us. I could also feel Tem's glare boring into my back.

"Would you like to go first?" River said. He gazed up at the mountainside with a calculating look on his face. It was a look I understood well. I felt a shiver of anticipation.

"Why don't I shadow you?" I said.

His gaze met mine. "Is that a challenge?"

"Maybe."

He laughed, and I couldn't suppress a grin.

"All right," he said. "Challenge accepted. You copy me on the way up, and I follow you on the way down."

"Deal," I said. I was almost hopping up and down with excitement, my worries all but forgotten. I knew I was going to win the game.

115

River cocked his head to one side, considering. Then, smoothly, he grabbed hold of a crack in the rock face, dug his toe into a root, and pulled himself onto a ledge.

I watched him closely, memorizing every move he made. It was clear almost immediately that River was like no one else I had climbed with. He climbed as easily as most people walked, moving with an almost bored grace. I found myself almost forgetting to note the route he took—merely watching him, my mouth half-open.

He paused perhaps twenty feet above the ground. Hooking his arm around a rock, he leaned back and called, "Coming?"

I started. Taking a deep breath, I stepped up to the rock face, and began to climb.

We moved swiftly up the mountainside. River paused several times to ensure I was keeping pace. In fact, I could have climbed much faster. I wondered if he was taking it easy to test me. The route he had chosen was straightforward enough, at least for me, though some of the moves he made were tricky, surprising. Creeping sideways along a narrow ledge, holding on with only your fingertips. Navigating an overhang upside down, your feet above your head.

As we climbed, I gradually became aware of the sound of rushing water. There were falls nearby, I was certain of it—somewhere beyond the curve of the mountainside, where I could make out a narrow chasm filled with boulders and trees. River climbed sideways along the mountain until he reached it. He paused, and I caught up quickly.

The chasm wasn't overly deep—we were only halfway level with the pines rising from the mountain rubble below—but it was wide, several times the span of my reach. The other side was a slippery mess, coated with moss wet from the spray of the hidden waterfall. It floated toward us in icy clouds, dampening my face. Through the spray, I could just make out a narrow ledge on the wall opposite, slightly higher up the rock face.

River glanced over his shoulder. I couldn't read his expression, but thought I saw the flash of a smile. I smiled back, because I knew that he was stuck, and I had won. I shifted position slightly, preparing to make way when he began to lower himself down the ridge.

Instead, he turned away from me and *leaped*.

Leaped across the impossible gap, or perhaps flew—I could see little difference. He grabbed hold of a knuckle of stone, wedged his foot against the rock, and pulled himself onto the narrow ledge in a single movement as fluid as a cat's.

I stared at him. He called something, but the crashing of the water winnowed it to "Care—hold—ice—zin." He sidestepped along the rock face and disappeared into the fine mist beyond. There was no doubt in his mind, apparently, that I would follow.

"River!" I shouted.

I climbed to where he had been standing and squinted across the chasm. Now that I was closer, I could see there were, in fact, several decent handholds—narrow, but nothing I couldn't handle.

Did he say "ice"? I saw no sign of it, but that didn't mean anything in this deep shade. I gritted my teeth. Normally, I wouldn't have bothered to attempt what River had just done; I would have climbed down into the chasm, and then up the other side. Or, more likely, turned back. But if I did either of those things, River would win.

I would *not* let River win.

I took a long, slow breath and took my hands off the rock face, lowering my body into a crouch. A stillness settled over me, a feeling that was like hovering at the edge of sleep, but also its opposite, for everything was heightened. Then I sprang into the air.

I caught the handhold. But my gasp of relief was cut short—my hands began to slide slowly, painfully, down the rock.

He said "ice."

Somehow, I managed to jam my fingertips into a crack. Shaken by the near miss, I pushed myself up to the ledge somewhat less gracefully than River, and then stood there for a long moment, my breath hissing against the rock.

Once I had caught my breath, I brushed my hair back from my face and composed my features into a nonchalant expression. The ledge broadened up ahead as the sound of the waterfall intensified. I could feel it reverberate through the mountain and up my legs as I walked. Where was River? The chill mist was sharp against my skin. Then the rock ahead folded back, and I stopped.

The waterfall thundered down, down, down, into a pool clutched between rock walls. The water was blue, glacial, half-frozen. Impossibly long icicles hung down from the mountainside, glinting in the sunlight, and rainbows draped themselves across the water like cobwebs. I stared in awe.

River, crouched at the edge of the cliff, turned his head slightly and tapped a finger against his lips. It was too late—at the sound of my approaching footsteps, the dragons he had been watching spread their wings and took flight. They were feral, I knew immediately. Feral dragons are smaller than domestic ones, barely the size of my two fists stuck together, and their lights were usually colorless. It was a family—two adults and four offspring. The baby dragons bobbed clumsily a few times, chirping, as they followed their parents up the waterfall to settle on some distant ledge.

A cloud of mist rose between me and River. I stepped through it, blinking, and he grabbed my hand.

"Careful," he said. "There's a lot of—"

"Ice," I snapped.

He laughed. I laughed too, surprising myself. It felt like a reflex. I was still amazed. It wasn't that I had never done anything as difficult, or dangerous. But I had never climbed with someone like River, who seemed to understand the mountain on an intuitive level that went beyond ordinary senses. The way I understood it.

We made our way along the ledge to the nearest fall of water, where we washed the dirt from our hands and took turns tilting our heads back to drink. We kept hold of each other, for safety, though River never seemed to put a foot wrong, and his eyesight in that world of mist and shadow seemed sharper than mine. I nudged him slightly as he drank, and he stumbled, the water trickling over his head and plastering his hair down on one side. He gave me another wicked smile. He tugged my arm as we clambered over a boulder, so that I had to stab my foot into a tiny crevice to arrest my fall. I half scowled, half grinned at him. A challenge hung between us like electricity.

My left hand was cold from the waterfall, but my right, pressed against River's, was warm, almost hot. His palm was as rough and callused as mine. He did not attempt to hold me with his left hand, the one with the missing fingertips, as if he thought it would bother me. To show him that it didn't, I made a point of reaching for it myself.

We settled on a ledge overlooking the meadow and the valley, with the waterfall at our backs. I could see the others—small, blobby dots far below—but I didn't think they could see us.

I gazed over the landscape, exultant. I had traveled farther in the last two days than many villagers had in their lifetimes. The days had been grueling, certainly—but they had also brought moments of exquisite wonder unlike anything I had ever experienced, a wonder so complete I felt like an ember stoked to life by a gust of wind.

This is what being a real explorer would feel like. Every day would be like this.

"I'm not easily surprised," River said, "but you keep surprising me."

I swung my legs back and forth, equal parts tired and content. "*I* surprise *you*?"

"I never thought someone like you could exist." He watched me with a half smile on his face. "A girl from a tiny village many explorers have never even heard of, with greater skill than most of them will ever possess."

I flushed. Something in his gaze made my heart speed up and froze my tongue.

Get a grip, I lectured myself. Did I want River to think I was some delicate child, overcome by a compliment?

"I'm sure you've met girls like me," I said, keeping my voice light. "You've traveled from one end of the Empire to the other."

"Yes, I have," he said, in a tone of quiet wonderment that clearly negated my first statement and deepened the color in my cheeks. We were still holding hands—*for safety*, I repeated in my head. An impulsive urge to move closer to him battled with an urge to pull away, and ended in a stalemate. I stayed put.

This is River Shara, I lectured myself. *Not some village boy you can flirt with on Kunigai Lookout.* It didn't matter what he looked like. It didn't matter that I felt strangely comfortable in his presence—more comfortable, in a way, than I did even with Tem. He was the Royal Explorer, and second in power to the emperor himself. I dropped his hand.

River, to my relief, seemed unaware of my confusion. He leaned against the rock. "Perhaps I shouldn't be so surprised, given your mother's reputation. Did you come here with her?"

I flinched. "No. We—we traveled through the forest."

As I said it, a memory flitted through my mind. Lusha and me, racing each other through the trees. I had been all knees and elbows then, tripping over my own feet at every opportunity. Our mother laughing her booming laugh—the mountains seemed alive with it.

"I'm sorry," he said.

"It's all right."

He looked away, his eyes hooded as he gazed over the mountains. "My mother died a year ago."

It was the first time I had heard River speak of his family. He spoke of other subjects freely enough, and perhaps that was why I hadn't noticed.

"What was she like?" I said. "Noble and elegant, I suppose."

For some reason, River laughed at this. He seemed to consider. "She was . . . respected."

I examined him. He met my gaze, and the invisible thread that had been forming between us since the night of the banquet gave a thrum. I looked away, feeling almost drunk. I forced myself to focus.

"River," I said quietly, "what is this expedition about? And please don't tell me the emperor commanded you to keep silent. I find it hard to believe you care about following orders."

He smiled. "Everyone at court cares about following orders. The emperor doesn't generally issue requests."

"Well, we're not at court, are we? And the emperor is hundreds of miles away."

He seemed to consider me. "What do you know about the witches?"

"The witches?" I blinked in surprise. "The usual stories. They devour human hearts and steal children from their beds. They cast spells to make crops wither and animals sicken, solely for their own amusement. They move like shadow and are hungry as fire." *Hearts of shadow, eyes of flame*, the old rhyme went. *None escape who witches claim.*

"I'm not talking about stories," he said, plucking at stalks of grass. "What do you know to be fact?"

I frowned. "They attacked Azmiri once—burned half the village to the ground. They attacked other villages too, and summoned floods to the farmlands of the delta. They wanted to starve the emperor's armies."

"Do you know why?"

"Everyone knows why," I said, annoyed by his tone—clearly River thought the people of Azmiri knew nothing of the wider world. The witches despised the emperor. He and his ancestors had expanded the Empire far beyond the southern delta, building cities out of villages and villages from barren foothills. The witches, either out of spite or fear, took every chance to attack the emperor's soldiers. Dozens of patrols disappeared, as if snuffed out in the night, leaving no trace that they had ever been. Terror of the witches spread through the Empire until, finally, the emperor acted. His shamans bound the witches' powers, trapped them in their human forms, and drove them beyond the Arya Mountains into the dark forests of the Nightwood.

"A lot of people don't know," River said, "that the emperor himself cast the binding spell. He holds great power, though these days he primarily uses it to stave off his own mortality. He recently celebrated his two hundred and thirty-first birthday. Not bad for a man who doesn't look a day over twenty."

I furrowed my brow. "Father says that's just a tale told to frighten the emperor's enemies. That all the emperors since Lozong the First have merely taken his name when they assumed power."

123

River let out a short laugh. "Azmiri is a very long way from the Three Cities, isn't it? I assure you, it's the truth—I was at the party."

"So what?" I said, disliking the reminder of how little I knew about River's world. "What do the witches have to do with any of this?"

"Everything. Many centuries ago, long before the Empire, the witches lived in a great city that they built in the sky. A beautiful and terrible place, inaccessible to ordinary people. No one knows exactly where this city was—it's possible even the witches have forgotten."

My heart thudded in my ears as I understood the significance of his words.

"Raksha," I whispered. "You think it's on Raksha."

River rolled several pebbles in his hand, tossing them one after another over the edge. "I believe so. I've looked everywhere else. It's said that this city is where the witches left a powerful talisman. The emperor needs that talisman."

"Why?"

He tossed another pebble. Far below, I saw a branch shiver. "Because the binding spell has begun to weaken."

"To weaken?" My voice trailed off as I thought back to my lessons with Chirri. There was one truth about magic that formed the foundation of everything she taught me, so fundamental that it was rarely mentioned, rarely thought about. Like everything else in the world, magic decayed. It was why Chirri had to recast the spells holding up the stone fences on the south side of Azmiri every few years. I had never thought about the binding spell that way—like an old fence that would crumble if ignored.

River nodded. He rubbed a hand absently through his hair, which only exaggerated the part that was always sticking out. "All spells weaken. Even the most powerful. And if the binding spell fails—"

He didn't finish his sentence. He didn't have to. The witches had terrorized Azmiri and the other villages for years before the emperor put a stop to it. What revenge would they take when they regained their powers?

"So the emperor wants this talisman to repair the spell?" I said. "Do the witches know?"

River shrugged. "They may know of the talisman's existence, but they would have no way of knowing the emperor's plans."

"They must realize he would do anything to prevent them from getting their powers back," I said. "If they find us—if they capture us—"

"They won't."

"We're walking straight into their lands," I said. "How can you be so certain we'll be safe?"

"I didn't say I was certain." River looked at me. "I'm never certain of anything."

I opened my mouth to argue, but stopped myself. I was shaking—the sweat from the climb had dried on my skin, and in the twilight shadow of the mountain, the chill was sharp. I watched the tents far below, the flickering glow of the fire Dargye and Aimo had built. Was it safe for us to keep the fire going? I wondered suddenly. We weren't in the witches' lands yet, but that didn't mean they weren't watching from the shadows, or some hidden ledge high above.

"Should I not have told you the truth?" River said.

I drew my *chuba* tighter around me. "Yes. I—I'm glad I know."

But as the sky darkened and the wind began to moan over the peaks, I wasn't so sure. What River had said was almost too big to comprehend. Could the safety of the Empire—its very existence—truly hinge on this expedition? And if so, that meant that Azmiri would also be in grave danger if we didn't succeed.

My fear grew, deepening like the shadow that surrounded us. Yet within the fear was a flicker of something else. A fierce determination. I wouldn't let the witches threaten Azmiri. If I could help River reach the summit, I could save the village, and the Empire with it.

My heart began to pound. I saw myself returning triumphant, and telling Father what I had done. I pictured his face—along with the faces of all my relatives—when they realized that I had helped the Royal Explorer defeat the greatest threat they had ever known.

"You understand, now, why this mission is so important," River said. "More important than glory. More important than a title."

His words brought me back to the present. "Then you don't care if Mara reaches Raksha first?"

River launched another pebble. For a moment, I thought he wasn't going to answer.

"Mara won't get there first," he said. "I will."

I didn't know what to make of this. For a long moment, we sat in silence. I knew that we should go—soon it would be too dark to see. But I made no move to rise, and neither did River.

"Can I ask *you* a question?" he said.

I breathed into my hands. My heart was still beating too quickly. "All right."

"Who is Tem?"

It was such an unexpected question that I was startled into silence. I gazed at him, but his expression revealed only mild curiosity. "What do you mean? You know who he is."

"He seems very important to you."

"Well . . ." I was strangely tongue-tied. "He's my best friend."

"Is that all?"

"Yes." I paused. "I mean—yes. Why do you want to know?"

He wasn't looking at me. "I don't. I was just curious."

His voice was light, but something in it belied his words. I opened my mouth, then closed it again. I looked away too, and we both stared at opposite ends of the mountain.

"We should go," I said, as the silence continued to hover awkwardly between us. "It's getting dark."

It felt strange taking River's hand again, but there wasn't much choice. Ice was forming on the rocks, and it was difficult to see the way back. I wished we had thought to bring one of the dragons. They were too far away to hear my whistle.

We came to the ledge where we had jumped. The gap seemed narrower from this side, less intimidating, but perhaps that was only a trick of the light. River's hand tightened around mine, his knuckles brushing my hip. He was close enough that I could smell the campfire smoke on his skin, entwined with his own clean scent, which reminded me of a forest plant I couldn't place—something that bloomed after nightfall, when the rest of the world slumbered. For some reason, I said, "We were."

"What?"

"Tem and I. We were. We tried being—together, for a while. It didn't work."

"Why not?"

I shrugged. I didn't really know the answer—or at least, I didn't know how to put it into words. I never had. "We're just better this way. As friends."

River gazed into the chasm. He may have been calculating the distance, or lost in thought—in the darkness, I couldn't see his face. He released my hand, and I saw his smile flash like a spark.

"Your turn," he said.

NINE

"WHO WON?" TEM said as I approached the campfire the next morning. He had fallen asleep waiting for me—it was long past sunset when River and I returned. Now he was hunched over the stream, washing his socks.

"It was a draw," I said. And it had been. No matter what I did, no matter how impossible the move or narrow the handhold, River had matched me, fumbling only once or twice before catching himself. He clung to the mountain like a spider. Still, all the agility in the world wouldn't make up for his natural impatience, which sometimes led him to make thoughtless moves, overextending his reach or forcing himself into awkward positions. I had watched as the muscles in his arms clenched and strained during the final descent, certain that at any moment he would admit defeat. He hadn't, infuriatingly, but I was certain I could beat him next time. If there was a next time.

We would reach Winding Pass tomorrow.

Tem raised his eyebrows. "That's a first."

I toyed with my breakfast, half lost in thought. I had woken at dawn to examine the maps for the hundredth time. I felt better with them spread out before me, the journey ahead reduced to a series of tidy black lines and labeled features. They helped quell my sense of foreboding.

The feeling grew the closer we moved to Winding Pass. Though our campsite that night was pleasant enough—a patch of springy saxifrage sheltered by two glacial boulders—I could not sleep.

I remembered little of the return journey through the pass with my mother's expedition. We had been caught in a storm; everything was dark and confused. I remembered shouting, Lusha's hand squeezing mine like a vise. Strange shapes woven through the darkness, reaching for us with spectral limbs. I thought something grabbed my shoulder, its fingers cold and thin and sharp—Lusha had yanked me free. Had it been my imagination? Nothing made sense in that swirling void.

I rolled onto my side, rubbing my shoulder—sometimes, it was as if I could still feel that strangely shaped hand. The others hadn't made it out of the pass. Their cries, the shamans' shouted incantations, had faded into the darkness behind us, as my mother half led, half dragged me and Lusha through the storm. Only her iron will and almost superhuman energy had protected us.

The terror I had felt in those moments threatened to envelop me again, but I beat it back—barely. I watched the flap of the tent as it moved in the breeze, gently rustling. My mother was gone. My sister was out there somewhere, but out of reach. This time, there would be no one to protect me if something went wrong. The thought brought with it a surge of loneliness, but also hard determination.

I rolled over again and began going over the maps in my head.

Norbu approached me the next morning, as I washed our breakfast dishes in a half-frozen stream. "This weather won't hold."

I followed his gaze, wiping a wet hand across my forehead. To the north, dark clouds were massing among the peaks.

"The last storm swung east," I said, ignoring a stab of anxiety.

Norbu fingered one of his talismans. "Nevertheless, I should begin the weather chants."

"Tem can help with—"

"The Royal Explorer trusts me to protect his expeditions," Norbu said, a cold note entering his voice. "River and I have endured many such storms."

I'm sure you have. Norbu's abilities had not become any more impressive over the last few days. After the others had gone to bed, Tem had told me in a low voice how he had broken Norbu's warding spells simply by waving his hand through them. He had recast them, of course, properly, but it made me shake my head in amazement. How had River survived so long without a proper shaman?

We set off, and I tried to ignore the darkness gathering in the skies ahead. The wind picked up, cooling my sweaty brow. The dragons took flight and coasted above us, riding the gusts and chirruping at each other.

Where is Lusha?

We should have caught up to them by now, given the pace I had set. They must have been traveling into the night, to stay so far ahead.

Or—something had gone wrong. I tried not to think about what that could be—there were any number of possibilities. Surely Lusha would be cautious, and not take any unnecessary risks. But if Mara protested, would she give in?

I had no idea. I had no idea of anything—what had driven her to sneak off with Mara, what she hoped to gain by betraying one of the most powerful men in the Empire.

I still wanted to catch Lusha, to beat her to the mountain. To see her face when I sauntered into her camp, the dawning realization that I had bested her. But as I gazed at the storm, I also felt something else. A nagging worry, hovering at the edge of my thoughts.

The terrain was difficult, uneven and strewn with rubble cast down from the mountain, and there was a risk of turning an ankle at every step. It was a tiring hike, and as the day wore on, we moved more and more slowly. Tem paused every few steps to cough, while Dargye, his large frame not built for balance, had torn a gash in his knee. Even I was out of breath, and frustrated with my own lagging pace.

Soon the wind was too strong for the dragons—they landed on the yak, burrowing in between our gear, their lights flickering chaotically. At my side, Tem began muttering incantations. He held the string of *kinnika* in his hands, allowing the wind to brush through them. The music they made was gentle but discordant, and formed an eerie backdrop to the worsening weather.

"Can I help?" I said. "Chirri taught me all the weather spells."

Tem glanced up. It took him a moment to focus on me.

"That's all right," he said carefully. "You have enough to do."

I smothered a sigh.

"Kamzin?" River called. "Are you sure this is right?"

I stopped, brushing the hair from my sweaty face. The landscape of broken scree sloped up and up to the snow-streaked mountains, which hovered in the sky like locked doors. There was no sign whatsoever of a way through. And yet, somehow, I knew it was there.

"I'm sure of it," I said, meeting his gaze. I didn't know how to make him believe me. I didn't know if I believed myself.

"What does Mingma's map say?" Dargye said.

"It doesn't," I replied. Mingma's only note about Winding Pass was "inadvisable." By now, I was becoming used to the dead explorer's dry understatements. He had similarly labeled a cluster of caves inhabited by ravenous bears as "nuisance—avoid."

"You can trust her," Tem said. "Kamzin's the best navigator in the village. She sees past the obvious, notices details that others miss."

"We should turn back, *dyonpo*," Dargye said, and I had to resist the now-familiar urge to smack him. "We passed the mouth of a valley, I'm sure of it—"

"No," I said. "That's a dead end. Look, everyone thought my mother was lost when she led us here, but she wasn't. There's something about this place—it's like you can only find it if you already know the way."

"Some strange magic at work?" Norbu said. "Yet I sense nothing unusual in the air."

Tem and I exchanged looks.

"Kamzin," River said with a slight smile, as if this were a debate over dinner settings, "lead the way."

I swallowed. The others gazed at me with varying degrees of skepticism and worry on their faces.

All right, I thought. *I can do this.*

The landscape rose steadily, alternating between short, steep slopes and gradual inclines. The terrain offered a buffer from the wind, which was still rising. Another hour's walk brought us to a crest of land, and suddenly there was Winding Pass, right in front of us—a narrow channel of snowy terrain that flowed like a river, broken with jagged boulders that reared up out of the ice, between two towering mountains. Songri's twin peaks gleamed in the sunlight, framed by blue sky and a few tendrils of cloud. But Mount Zerza was lost in the storm.

"Oh," I murmured.

Lightning darted from the swelling darkness like the flick of a viper's tongue. The clouds did not seem to be advancing so much as *roiling*, like shapeless entities engaged in a violent dance.

"Good job, Kamzin," River said as he caught up to me. "You were right—some magic conceals this place from anyone who doesn't already know the way. As you stepped over that rise, I saw it blink into existence. I could never have found my way without your help."

"River—" I began, but he was already walking away.

"Guess I owe you an apology," Dargye said.

"What?"

"About the pass," he said slowly, as if I were stupid.

I was barely listening to him. "We need to turn around."

"Why?" He glanced at the sky. "It's just a summer storm. We can take shelter if it moves our way."

"It's not just a storm," I murmured. "I've seen this before."

Dargye gave me an odd look and tugged the yak's lead. I let him, Norbu, and Aimo pass me, and waited for Tem. He had been lagging behind all day, red-faced and breathing hard. He smiled when he saw me waiting, but I could see that behind it, he was hurting. I felt a pang of guilt for the punishing pace I was setting.

"Can you do anything about the storm?" I said, my voice low.

"I was trying. Norbu ordered me to stop. He said I was disrupting his incantations."

"Forget about Norbu," I said. "Keep trying. Please, Tem. And keep an eye on that black bell. If it so much as whispers . . ."

He gazed at me, my own thoughts reflected in his eyes. If Chirri was right, the black bell would only sound in the presence of someone who wished to harm us. "It's bad, isn't it?"

I swallowed. I heard my mother shouting at me through the chaos of the storm, heard the shamans' screams, felt the scratch of inhuman fingers against my shoulder. "I don't know."

Tem reached into his pocket and pulled out the *kinnika*. "I'll do my best."

As we neared the pass, it began to snow. Lightly at first—small flakes that eddied around us like insects. The wind picked up, blasting us with a chill that took my breath away. River, walking ahead, held his arm up to block the onslaught.

"Tem?" I said.

"I'm shielding us as much as I can," he replied, his voice low and distant. "But there's something strange about this storm. It's like it's—fighting me. I've never felt anything like this."

He removed one of the bells and rang it sharply four times. The sound, deep as a gong, echoed off the mountains. The snow lessened, and the wind dropped. I could still hear it howling, but it was as if it was separated from us by a wall.

Tem folded forward, pressing his hands against his knees as another coughing fit overtook him. "I don't know," he said between coughs, "how much longer I can do this."

"Just a little longer—please." We were in the pass now, but I hadn't seen any sign of the caves indicated on the maps. I clambered up an enormous boulder, squinting into the distance. But I could barely see twenty yards away—beyond that point, Tem's shield weakened, and the world was hail and wind and darkness.

"Kamzin?" It was River. He stood at the base of the boulder, his expression inscrutable. His tahrskin *chuba* was white today, and he could have been part of the snow. "What are you doing?"

"Looking for somewhere we can wait out this storm." I almost had to shout to be heard over the wind.

"We're not stopping." He held out a hand. "Come down."

There was something in his tone that forbade argument. I took his hand and let him help me off the rock. But I gripped it, hard, when he moved away.

"River, please listen to me," I said, meeting his eyes. His face was only inches from mine; I could count the snowflakes tangled in his lashes. "This is no ordinary storm—I've seen it before. We have to turn back."

"That would give Mara the advantage," he said. "They already have a head start."

I stared at him. I couldn't believe that he was worrying about Mara at a time like this. "River, please listen to me."

River held my gaze. I couldn't tell if he was considering what I had said or lost in his own thoughts. Then he stepped away, pulling up his hood so that his face was shrouded. He turned and strode back into the snow. Norbu followed, and then Dargye and Aimo with the yak.

I felt close to tears. Biting them back, I turned to Tem. His shoulders shook with another fit. "Are you all right?"

He nodded tersely, wiping his mouth on his sleeve. His lips moved silently through the incantations, his hand clutching the *kinnika*. I looped my arm through his, and led him on.

We continued for an indeterminate time—it was still day, but the pass was so dark and turbulent that it was impossible to guess the hour. Tem grew quieter and quieter, his mouth barely moving as he murmured the incantations. We followed the dragonlight. The others were barely visible.

My legs burned. I realized, suddenly, that Tem and I were climbing. The dragons' lights were off to the left, now, and we were moving up a steep incline. How had that happened?

"Wait," I cried, confused. I pulled Tem to a stop, but as I did, I felt his footing slip.

"Tem!" I shouted, grabbing at his arm. But I couldn't find my footing on the icy rock. Tem's weight propelled me after him, into the void.

I fell face-first into a mound of snow, and surfaced coughing but unhurt. We had fallen into the lee side of an enormous granite slab, which had been half-submerged in snow. We must have been climbing up the snow-covered side without even realizing it.

I helped Tem to his feet. "All right?"

He nodded, coughing. He fumbled around in the snow, finally unearthing the *kinnika*.

"River!" I shouted. The wind took my voice and tossed it away. I squinted into the darkness. The dragons' lights were gone.

I pushed my hood back, feeling for the direction of the wind. But it was constantly shifting, and I couldn't be certain which direction we were facing now. Or in which direction the others had gone.

"River!" I shouted again. "Norbu! Dargye!"

There was no response save for the howl of the storm.

How had I not noticed we were climbing up the side of a boulder? How had the others advanced so far ahead of us? I shook my head as if to clear it. The storm was fierce, disorienting. But there was more going on than that, I was certain of it.

"This is just how it happened before," I murmured.

One by one, we had been separated from each other. One by one, the others had faded into the storm, until only my mother and Lusha were left.

Oh, Spirits.

"We should wait here," Tem said, raising his voice to be heard. "They'll double back once they realize we're missing."

"No," I said. No, I wasn't going to wait there like a sitting duck. Surveying the vague terrain, I took Tem's arm and began to walk.

"Kamzin," he protested, "you don't know where you're going."

"Oh yes, I do." I had not spent hours poring over the maps of this part of the Aryas for nothing. I had been counting every boulder we passed, as well as every step I took. I knew where we were, roughly, in spite of the wind's games. I just needed confirmation.

A moment later, I had it. A towering pinnacle of rock, eroding into a mound of broken stone shaped like jagged teeth, loomed before us. I let out a whoop. I had my bearings now. Gripping Tem's hand, I led him slowly but confidently in the right direction, the direction that—I hoped—the others had also taken.

And then—something began to chime. Not the bell in Tem's hand, which he used to battle the storm.

The small, black one that hung next to his heart.

We froze, staring at each other. The bell was silent for a long moment.

Then it jangled again. A small, shrill sound that cut through the moan of the wind.

"Are you moving it?" I said.

"It wouldn't matter if I was." In spite of the cold, Tem's face was dewed with sweat. "That's not how it works."

Tem and I stood still, breathless, waiting. The black bell did not sound again.

"Let's keep going," I said, pushing against the rising panic. We began walking again, clutching each other's arms. The black bell gave a shiver of a chime every now and again, but that was all.

Something moved out of the corner of my eye. I turned my head, blinking against the snowflakes. And screamed.

It was a human figure, tall and skeletal. But in place of a human head, it had that of a bird, with the curved beak of a vulture. Its shoulders hunched, and below the rags it wore its bony legs bent the wrong way.

And then it was gone, as if it had never been. But I knew the truth—I knew what I had seen, knew it with a certainty that chilled me to the marrow of my bones.

"What is it?" Tem gripped my shoulders. The black bell began to chime loudly—a sharp, dolorous sound. "What did you see?"

"They're here," I cried. "They've come for us!"

"What? What's come for us?"

The fiangul. My mouth formed the words, but I couldn't get them out. I seized Tem's hand and began to run.

"River!" I shouted. "Norbu! Dargye!"

I was running so fast, my head lowered against the snow and wind, that I didn't see the shape looming before me.

"Ah!" I cried, as my head hit something warm and soft. I bounced and fell backward into a snowdrift. The yak let out a startled grunt, turning to look at what had collided with her rear end.

Tem helped me to my feet. Aimo was close behind. She brushed the snow from my hood and back, and then wrapped me in a hug.

"Thank you," I gasped. Aimo's lips moved, but I couldn't make out her reply amidst the chaos of the storm. She rested her hand on my arm, an absently sympathetic gesture. I was so relieved to see them that I could have cried.

"What happened to you two?" Dargye said. "I thought you were right behind me."

"Where's River?" Norbu said. "He went to search for you."

"Oh no." It was possible that we had passed River in the blizzard—likely, in fact, given the chaos around us.

I seized one of the dragons, which were huddled beneath a blanket for warmth. "I'll find him."

"Kamzin." Tem's grip on my hand was suddenly very firm. *Ching, ching, ching*, went the black bell.

I turned. Looming out of the swirling darkness were three figures—tall, painfully thin. Little else about them could be made out. But there was clearly a *wrongness* there, something that chilled me deep inside, as if a frost was creeping over my heart.

Norbu held up his hand. In the other he grasped one of his talismans. He took a step toward the creatures, muttering an incantation.

"Norbu, don't." I lunged after him, but Tem dragged me back. He fumbled with one of the bells, a small one with intricate carvings, and sounded it slowly. He began to chant, and a warmth

141

emanated from the place where he stood. The snow falling around us turned to gentle rain.

Norbu was still moving toward the creatures, his arm outstretched as if to banish them back. His outline blurred as the snow grew thicker. The incantation became garbled and broken, and I thought I heard a cry. The snow swirled between us, and Norbu and the creatures were gone.

"Norbu!" I shouted. Suddenly, something passed through the air overhead with a terrible scream, half human and half *other*. Tem and I dove, but the creature circled back, its beak clicking hungrily. Its eyes were the round, black dots of a bird, shimmering white with reflected snow.

Tem raised his hand, and something like heat haze pulsed toward the creature. It jerked back as if struck, and screamed again.

"Stay down," Tem said, shoving me to the ground.

"Let me help you!" I struggled to my feet. Tem did not look at me; he muttered a word, and some invisible force knocked me back again.

Another creature dove toward us, veering off at the last second. Tem rang and rang the bell, almost shouting the incantation now. It was as if the sound of the bell and his voice were gaining form and weight; a glowing mist took shape around us, and spread outward. It reminded me of a cloud of fireflies.

"Spirits protect us!" Dargye cried, diving behind the yak. I didn't blame him—I had never seen Tem work a spell like this. It was at once beautiful and terrifying.

Just beyond the range of Tem's shield, one of the *fiangul* drifted slowly to the ground. There it seemed to multiply, other dark shapes coalescing from the swirl of snow and darkness.

There are too many of them. I struggled to stand, but Tem's spell still had me pinned to the ground. I shouted at him, but he ignored me. His eyes were narrowed, his jaw set. His self-consciousness had melted away, leaving behind a person I barely recognized.

Tem lifted his hand again, and the shimmering mist darted toward the *fiangul.* They screamed and fell back. But they were also fanning out, forming a ring around us that tightened, tightened. How long could Tem hold them back?

"Damn you, Tem," I cried. I flailed my arms helplessly like a beetle on its back. "Let me help!"

Suddenly, the *fiangul* fell silent. A shudder seemed to pass through them, and they cocked their heads, as if listening for something. And then—

A few yards from where I lay, the snow began to move. Something was rising out of it, something with an enormous belly, round head, and an absence of limbs.

A *snowman.*

Ten feet tall at least, with the girth of several men, the snowman was lopsided and faceless, a nightmare brought to life. It leaped on the nearest *fiangul,* or rather *rolled,* gathering snow and height as it went. Other snowmen rose up out of the drifts that surrounded us. The *fiangul* squawked and began their counterattack, rending the snowmen with beaks and talons. But as soon as one fell, another took its place. Feathers floated through the air.

I screamed as the snow rose up beside me, but it fell apart almost as quickly, and River stepped out from the broken mound. I stared at him, stupefied.

"That's all right, Tem," he said, placing a hand on his shoulder. "I can take it from here."

"River!" I shouted. One of the *fiangul* had made it past both Tem's shield and the snowmen, which stood like guards before us. It glided closer, its nightmarish eyes fixed on mine.

"No, you don't, you overgrown vulture," River cried, summoning another snowman and sending it careening in the creature's direction. "Back to the wastes with you! Or rather, back to a *different* waste. This one's taken."

The snowman collided with the creature and broke apart, burying it. The wind lifted the loose flakes into the air, and all that remained of the *fiangul* was a few feathers.

The rest of the creatures vanished, melting back into the blizzard. The remaining snowmen glided forward a few feet before coming to a halt, lifeless.

Tem sank to the ground. The mist subsided, and the weight that had been pressing me down vanished. River was there in a heartbeat, hauling me to my feet.

"What are you doing here, Kamzin?" His eyes, to my amazement, were sparkling with laughter. "I thought surely I would have to dig you out of a snowbank a mile away, and yet here you are, exactly where you're supposed to be. You're full of surprises."

"What did you do?" I demanded shakily, pushing him off. "I've never seen magic like that before."

River shrugged. "I've picked up a few tricks during my travels. Tem!" He pulled him up as well. "Nicely done. I wish there were shamans like you in the Three Cities, rather than these useless mumblers. Speaking of which, where is Norbu?"

"They got him." Tem looked close to collapsing again. "He was trying to protect us."

"Fool. He should know better than to try to protect anyone," River said. He brushed at the snow that still clung to his *chuba*, looking completely composed. "Dargye? Aimo?"

Two heads poked out from beneath the yak. They were red-faced and covered in snow, but seemed unharmed.

"*Dyonpo*, we were just—"

"Doing the sensible thing, and staying out of the way," River said. "Good for you. All right, I'll fetch Norbu." With that, he strode off into the maelstrom.

Tem sagged against the yak's flank, coughing. The beast grunted. Her back was covered with snow mixed with feathers. I brushed it off, only half-conscious of what I was doing. My hands were shaking.

"It's a miracle she didn't run," I said. My voice was too high.

Tem made a vague gesture. "I placed a sleep charm on her. My spell would only protect us if we all stayed within the circle. I didn't realize I could—"

His voice grew muffled as I wrapped him in a hug.

"Kamzin?" He struggled against my grip. "I can't breathe."

"Sorry." I released him, stepping back. His face was pale—the long, straight eyebrows I had always admired were like slashes of ink against his skin. I brushed his hair back from his face and kissed his cheek. "Thank you."

That brought the color back. He pushed me away, hiding behind his hair again. "Don't be stupid."

"Found him!" River strode back into our midst, somewhat out of breath. He was dragging something behind him—something wearing a gray *chuba*, with long, snow-coated hair.

I rushed to Norbu's side. He was breathing, and did not appear hurt, though his skin was as cold as the snow falling around us. His eyelids fluttered, but he didn't wake.

"Is he all right?" I said.

River gazed down at Norbu, frowning. "I think so. He didn't get far."

There came a distant rumble, like thunder but deeper, and the ground trembled. It came from Songri, or possibly Zerza. It was impossible to tell in that echoing valley.

"Oh." River squinted at the mountainside. "I may have destabilized something with my spell. I always forget to be careful of that."

"You may have *what*?" I shouted.

There was another ominous rumble. River lifted Norbu and tossed him over the yak like a bag of grain.

"Come on, come on," he said, beckoning. "Keep up this time, will you? Let's have no more dramatics until we're clear of this forsaken place."

"Dramatics?"

"What about the *fiangul*?" Tem said. "Will they follow us?"

146

"I doubt it. Not after being so badly beaten." He shrugged. "Mind you, they do have terribly short memories. Kamzin?"

I shook my head. "This way!" My arm threaded firmly through Tem's, we half stumbled, half ran through the snow, leading the others. The blizzard roared around us, and the mountains trembled, but they did not cast their snowy blankets down upon us. And then, so gradually that I didn't notice at first, the storm grew quieter and quieter, the snow less and less, until finally it stopped altogether.

TEN

WE EMERGED FROM Winding Pass just as the sun was setting behind the mountains, stepping into the early twilight. The clouds that clung to the horizon, dark and threatening, had split like ice into smaller fragments, which were stained now with orange and gold.

I gazed across the landscape before us. I had never been east of the Arya Mountains—there were few who had. It was a world of foothills and valleys, dark and impenetrable, and beyond that the unexplored lowlands, where there lurked a vast expanse of trees as dark as pitch.

The Nightwood.

I shuddered. Even here, miles away, the witches' forest stretched its tendrils toward the mountains. Rue pines, stout at this altitude, jabbed up from the rocky ground. I brushed my hand against a bough, coming away with a handful of needles. Though they looked black at a distance, they were in fact darkest green—a green that seemed to drink in the growing shadows around it.

"Kamzin," River called, "we need to set up camp."

I looked around. We were still at a considerable elevation, almost at the snow line, and the terrain around us was uneven with till and knifelike grasses. I recognized the place—at least, I thought I did.

"Just a little farther," I said, even though my entire body ached with weariness. "There should be a stream up ahead."

Sure enough, we soon came upon a hollow where a stream trickled down from a waterfall. We removed our packs and dropped them on the bank. Dargye and Aimo helped Norbu down from the yak, while Tem fetched water. Norbu was barely conscious. I spoke to him quietly, but he seemed unable to focus on me, and muttered something about the cold. Blood trickled from a wound above his collarbone, a sharp, circular tear with a bluish cast. Even after I cleaned it with snow, and bandaged it, the wound continued to ooze. I had never seen anything like it.

"Can you set the warding spells?" I murmured to Tem. I hated asking, for he looked so exhausted. His palms, I noticed, were riddled with cuts from gripping the sharp-edged *kinnika* so tightly. But he only nodded silently, took out the bells, and set to work.

When dinner was ready, Aimo helped Norbu with his food. A cup of tea and an hour next to a warm fire had given the shaman some of his strength back, though he still seemed out of sorts. He kept glancing over his shoulder, a puzzled look on his face, as if concerned someone was sneaking about in the shadows.

"He's still cold," Aimo said. Dargye seemed to edge back slightly, as if she had said he was contagious. The big man seemed nervous around Norbu, and kept wandering off to gather more firewood, though we had a healthy pile already. Whenever he looked at him, his hand returned to the single talisman he wore around his neck, a copper pendant of a type popular in Azmiri. His sister, by contrast, quietly kept Norbu's tea brimming and hot, and even periodically attempted to rub feeling into his hands. I couldn't help admiring Aimo's fearlessness.

I touched the shaman's arm, and found that Aimo was right. Despite the blazing fire and the blankets, he was trembling.

"Tem, try that spell you used on me that time I fell through the ice in Gau Lake. Remember?"

Tem shook his head, his forehead creased in a worried frown. "I don't think it would help."

"How is he?" River said, and we all started, as if a stranger had appeared in our midst. Sweeping his *chuba* out of the way, he crouched before the shaman and took his hand. "Norbu? Can you hear me?"

"He's barely spoken since we left the pass," I said. "And his wound is still weeping."

"Perhaps you know a spell that could help him, River," Tem said in an odd, quiet sort of voice.

"I'm afraid not," River said, unnervingly calm. Several *fiangul* feathers were tangled in his hair. The wind caught one and sent it tumbling away.

"We can't carry on with Norbu like this," I said.

"Well, we can't linger here," Dargye said, combing his beard nervously. "This is witch territory. The edge of the Nightwood. I can see that foul forest from here."

"It's witch territory from here to Raksha," Tem said. "We're no safer carrying on than we are staying put."

"How can you be certain of that?" Dargye snapped.

"There's no way to be certain of anything," River said. "Least of all witches. But we must push on. Mara is too far ahead. At this rate, he'll beat us to the mountain for sure."

I stared at him. Did he truly care more about besting his rival than the life of his traveling companion? I opened my mouth to retort, but fortunately, Tem cut in.

"Norbu needs rest," he said. "We all do." Dargye murmured agreement. His knee was bleeding again after another bad stumble while fleeing the pass, and the wound would need to be spelled with healing charms to prevent infection. With a soft gasp of pain, Aimo removed one of her boots, revealing skin covered in blisters and ugly, dark bruises.

"What Norbu needs is a proper healer," I said. "We should go to Jangsa."

The others stared at me.

"Jangsa?" Aimo's brow knitted. "I heard it was abandoned."

I shook my head. "My father knows the elder—he met him once, years ago, when they were both boys. They still exchange letters sometimes, using Lusha's ravens. Father says he's a good man, if a little odd. I think he would help us."

Dargye made a skeptical noise. I didn't blame him—Jangsa, the northernmost village in the Aryas, was situated in the foothills of Mount Zerza at the edge of the witch lands. The inhabitants were a mistrustful, superstitious people who never strayed from their village or sought contact with outsiders. While the southern villages were ruled by the emperor, Jangsa was outside his domain—protected by its isolation, the village stood alone, for better or for worse. Because of this, or perhaps some flinty quality they were born with, the villagers were known for a self-reliance that bordered on fanatical.

"We have no idea what will happen," Dargye said. His hand was at his talisman again, as if merely speaking of Jangsa required warding magic. "They might capture us. Kill us. The people of Jangsa obey no emperor or lord. They answer to no one."

"It's our only option."

Dargye opened his mouth again, but Aimo put her hand on his arm. To my surprise, he heaved a sigh, then fell silent.

"I can adjust our route to compensate for lost time," I said.

River was quiet for a long moment. He gazed at Norbu, his brow furrowed. The shaman's eyes remained fixed on a spot just beyond his shoulder.

"How far to the mountain?" he said.

"We're on schedule," I said. "It took five days to reach Winding Pass. It's another ten to Raksha, twelve at most."

"Not good enough," River said, standing. "With this delay we'll have to move faster. We'll draw up a plan tomorrow."

Dargye opened his mouth to argue, but River was already gone, and Dargye didn't have the nerve to follow him. Norbu began to cough, and Aimo hurried to bring him more tea.

"Thank you," I said. Dargye muttered something to his sister, but she waved his words aside. He let out a long sigh, then removed his talisman and placed it around her neck. She barely seemed to notice the gesture. I found myself gazing at them almost hungrily as they hunched together by the fire. They had each other, out here in the wilderness. In a way, they were home. A shiver of loneliness traced down my spine as I turned back to the darkness.

Had Lusha also faced the *fiangul*? If so, was she all right? Was she out here somewhere—perhaps nearby—as injured and afraid as we were?

I made my way to my tent, half-blind from staring so long into the fire, and so tired I could barely walk straight. I almost collided with Tem, who was tightening the tent ropes by the light of a single dragon.

"Look who just showed up," Tem said, gesturing to a small lump in the shadows. The lump stretched, yawned, and wandered into the light.

"Ragtooth!" I lifted the fox, squeezing him against my chest. He nipped at my hand and let out an intimidating growl that I knew, from experience, was his way of expressing affection. "Where did you come from, you little monster?"

Tem secured a string of bronze beads over the entrance to the tent and glanced over his shoulder. When he spoke again, his voice was low. "You have to be careful of River."

"I know," I said. "He's reckless, even more than I realized. If we had taken shelter instead of—"

"That's not what I mean," Tem said, so quietly I could barely hear him. "That spell he cast—I've never felt anything like it."

"Neither have I," I said, putting Ragtooth down before he could sink his teeth into me again. "Though some of the stories do say he has a strange gift for magic."

"'Strange' isn't the word I would use," Tem said. "It's unnatural. Uncanny. Did you see a talisman?"

I frowned. "I didn't notice—I was too busy trying to avoid being clawed to bits by the *fiangul*. For a snow spell like that, it must have been wood—bamboo, maybe, or ebony."

"It wasn't ebony. It wasn't anything. He didn't use one."

I let out a short laugh. "That's impossible." And it was—everyone knew that. Even the strongest shamans could not pull spells from the air.

"It should be."

"It *is*. What you're saying doesn't make any sense. In all my lessons with Chirri, she never spoke of the sort of magic you're describing."

"Kamzin, you hardly ever pay attention to your lessons with Chirri." There was a disapproving note in his voice, and suddenly, I felt combative.

"What did you mean before?" I said. "That *I* have to be careful? Don't we all have to be careful of River?"

"You especially," Tem said. "I've seen the way you look at him."

I glared at him, furious. Though a small part of me was glad that the darkness concealed my blush.

"I don't know what you're talking about," I said, "but I have half a mind to tell Ragtooth to bite you right now."

"I'm sorry. But I just don't think you're seeing reason where River is concerned."

"I am seeing reason," I protested. "That's why we're going to Jangsa."

Tem turned away. "If you were seeing reason, we'd be on our way back to Azmiri."

"Azmiri?" I stared at him.

"Don't you understand what happened back there?" Tem gestured south, toward the now-invisible pass. "We nearly died. Didn't you see what we're up against?"

"I saw," I snapped. "Lusha is facing the same dangers. Am I supposed to abandon her? Am I supposed to abandon the *Empire*?"

"Is that really what you're worried about?" Tem said. "Or impressing the Royal Explorer?"

My face reddened, this time with anger. But underneath it, I felt a stab of some other emotion—something close to shame.

Something tinkled faintly, somewhere just behind me. I turned. Tem had hung the *kinnika* from one of the tent poles. The moonlight gleamed off the bells, illuminating the flicker of movement.

We were still for a long moment.

"Which one was that?" I murmured.

Tem looked uneasy. "I don't know."

I let out my breath. "Great. Now I'm going to jump out of my skin every time they make a sound."

But Tem didn't reply. He was staring at something just past my shoulder. "What's that?"

"Where?"

"Up there, in that tree."

I followed his gaze and saw something dangling from one of the branches that hung over the stream. It was pale in the moonlight, and gossamer thin. The starlight shone right through it.

I splashed through the shallow water and snatched at the garment. It was snagged on the branch, and tore slightly as I pulled.

I had known what it was before I even touched it. But when I held it in my hands, it was undeniable.

It was one of Lusha's scarves. Woven from yak wool, it was soft and warm, with a line of tiny red and blue stitches along the edge. I remembered she had worn it at the autumn bonfires last year—when she saw me shivering she had tied it around my neck, quietly chiding me for forgetting my *chuba*.

Tem touched my arm. "Are you all right?"

I nodded. To my surprise, my eyes were wet with tears. I brushed the back of my hand across them.

"Hey." Tem touched my face. "This is good. It means they made it through the pass."

I nodded, the tears blurring my vision. I couldn't stop staring at the scarf. For a moment, all thoughts of Raksha dissolved. I just wanted Lusha to be there in front of me, even if it was with a quip on her lips about my melodramatic tendencies or disheveled appearance. To know that she was all right.

Tem sighed. Then he kissed me gently, beside my mouth. "Come on. Let's get some sleep."

We set off the next morning just as the horizon began to blush with light. Tem kept the *kinnika* ready, and there was little conversation—even Dargye seemed to lack the energy to register his usual complaints.

My dreams had been dark, plagued by faceless specters that chased me through a howling storm. From the looks on the others' faces, their sleep had been similarly troubled. Something had changed since the *fiangul* attack—a shadow lay over us that couldn't be explained entirely by Norbu's strange illness. Though I tried to shake the unease, it clung to me like dew, prickling my skin.

I had thought I understood the dangers we faced. I knew now that the journey before us was bigger than I had imagined, the dangers darker and stranger. The *fiangul* we had fought in Winding Pass were no longer shadows in the night, stories told by a fire. The monsters were real, and we could face them again.

Or worse.

I glanced at Tem. He seemed more alert this morning, scanning the terrain, his hand absently brushing the bells looped through his belt. After Winding Pass, he seemed changed in some indefinable way. Was it only my perception? While I had always known of Tem's power, it had never been tested in Azmiri—as a lowly herdsman's son, he had never had much reason to use it, except to keep his animals healthy. The spell he had cast in Winding Pass went beyond what I suspected even Chirri was capable of—though I could tell that, in his thoughtless modesty, Tem was untroubled by any reflections of this nature.

I kicked at a pebble, watching it skitter over snow and grass before tumbling over a ridge and vanishing from sight. Who would Tem be, when our journey was over? Who would *I* be?

River walked behind us, his strange eyes narrowed as he scanned the landscape. He too was quieter this morning, whether from weariness or concern for his friend, or something else entirely. We had sat together by the fire that morning, our knees touching as we bent our heads over Mingma's map. Despite Tem's warnings and my own disquiet, when River and I were alone I often found myself forgetting everything beyond the tenor of his voice and the movement of his strong, sun-darkened hands as he traced the lines of the map.

By midafternoon we had reached the terraced farms that stretched out from Jangsa. The landscape was lush but rocky, boulders jutting up from the dark green grasses, painted with moss. Drizzle began to fall as we passed a spirit shrine cut into the slope of the mountainside. Dozens of bronze music bowls lined the roughly built shelves. The rain pooled inside them, creating a strange, watery melody that seeped through the air, and could be heard long after we left the shrine behind.

Soon we began passing people. A man drawing two yaks behind him; a child watching from the hillside; a woman with a jug of water strapped to her back. Each stared at us as we went by. Tem called out greetings at first, but soon stopped. The villagers' clothing was composed of simple shifts and trousers, mostly undyed. They were all thin, even the children, and pale, and there was a hardness in their expressions that made me shrink instinctively from their eyes.

Norbu, trailing behind with Aimo, stumbled and nearly fell. Two men watching us made a warding gesture, pressing the tips of their fingers together, and retreated into one of the huts. Their door did not open again.

Finally, the hills parted to reveal the village, which crept along the base of Mount Zerza. It was an eerie sight. Easily half the stone structures were little more than ruins. These lay mostly against the lower slopes of the village, but there were some higher up, closer to what was certainly the elder's walled home, that were roofless and crumbling, overgrown with vegetation.

"What happened here?" Tem said.

I shivered. "The witches. Father said they used to raid the village for livestock, or sometimes just for amusement. They laid curses on the houses of those who fought them—most had to be destroyed. When Father visited Jangsa years ago, he said they still hadn't recovered from those times. I guess that hasn't changed."

"They say some of the villagers have witch blood themselves." Tem cast a nervous glance at a woman lurking in the shadows of another hut, who darted back inside as their eyes met. "I wonder if there's any truth to it?"

"I don't know. But I won't be sorry if we don't linger here."

The dirt path broadened as we entered the village. The stone houses lining the streets were unpainted and weathered with age.

They had the appearance of dissolving back into the mountainside, returning to the earth from which they had been hewn. As we climbed, villagers stopped what they were doing, emerging from their homes to watch our progress. A small crowd formed ahead, enough to stop us from advancing farther. Their expressions were not friendly.

River was suddenly at my side. "Perhaps this would be a good time to introduce yourself," he muttered in my ear.

I turned to the villagers. "I'm Kamzin of Azmiri, daughter of Elder Thaken. I'm here to ask for your help."

Silence. The villagers regarded me as if I had spoken a different language. I swallowed, unable to read past their blank stares.

"We don't want to intrude," I said, "but our friend is injured. We are on an expedition to Mount Raksha, but we were ambushed in Winding Pass. This is River Shara. He—"

There was muttering at that. River groaned under his breath.

"What?" I hissed at him.

River only rolled his eyes. A woman approached suddenly and wrapped a welcoming scarf around River's neck. She was followed by another, and another. Soon River was engulfed in so much fabric he appeared to be drowning in it.

He waved another woman back, yanking away the white squares. "Thank you, thank you. That's not necessary—really."

I shook my head in astonishment. Even in a place as isolated as this, people had heard of River Shara.

A man stepped forward. He was tall, nearing middle age, and dressed in a green-and-blue *chuba* that formed a stark contrast to the villagers' plain clothes. Apart from this, though, he wore no signs of rank or ornamentation.

"I am Chonjor, the Elder of Jangsa," the man said. "You are truly the Royal Explorer?"

River extricated himself from another scarf and gave me a look. "Yes."

The man took half a step forward. A strange look flitted across his face, something more potent than the amazement that shone in the villagers' eyes. But it was gone too quickly to identify.

"You honor us with your visit," the elder said, bowing.

River beckoned Norbu forward. The shaman, leaning heavily on Aimo's arm, looked even paler than he had yesterday. "Can your healers attend to my friend?"

The elder bowed his head. "Of course, *dyonpo*. Follow me."

The crowd parted, and we fell into step behind the man. River stayed back to help Aimo with Norbu. I suspected, however, that he was merely trying to use the shaman to shield him from the curious villagers. Many made warding gestures as they caught sight of Norbu, and seemed little inclined to go anywhere near him.

"Kamzin," the elder said as we mounted a steep path that cut across the mountainside, "you must forgive us for not giving you a warmer welcome. Jangsa rarely receives visitors, and as you probably know, we prefer it that way. But a daughter of Thaken is always welcome here. I have heard of your sister Lusha—I didn't know Thaken had other children."

I suppressed a sigh. "That's all right."

He gave me a sharp look, a smile tugging at his lips. Despite his stern mouth and hawkish features, he had warm eyes, bright and keen. I sensed a quick intelligence behind them, that of a man who observed more than he let on.

"You're following in your mother's footsteps, I see," he said. "And traveling with the Royal Explorer himself."

"Yes," I said, "but this is no mapmaking expedition. The emperor has sent us to find something very important to him. To the Empire."

"I see." He nodded, as if this vague explanation made all the sense in the world. "It's a dangerous path you're following."

I gave a short laugh. "There are no safe ones, where we're going."

He gave me another look. "But that doesn't trouble you, does it?"

"I—" My voice faltered. He smiled at me.

"Forgive me, child," he said. "I don't mean to put you on the spot. When you get to be as old as me, you start to recognize certain kinds of people."

"Kinds of people?" I repeated, nonplussed. "What *kind* of person am I?"

"The kind that seeks out danger." His tone was matter-of-fact. "The kind that laughs at it. Your mother was just the same, or so your father told me. I'm sorry to say I never met her."

I stared at the back of his head. I could not think of a response to this. I felt suddenly exposed—as if in the space of a few seconds, this strange man had seen right through me.

We wound our way through the village along roads that were little more than dirt tracks, in some places washed by the rains to a precarious thinness, passing villagers bearing lanterns. A shaman paced back and forth across a square, his head bowed over a censer of incense. Anticipation hung thick in the air.

"What's going on?" I said, eager to turn the conversation away from myself.

"The Ghost March," the elder replied. "We're just beginning the preparations. Tonight there will be dancing and music. You're welcome to attend, if you wish."

"The Ghost March?" I stared at him. "But that was weeks ago. You celebrate it now?"

"We celebrate it every month, on the ninth day," the man said. He seemed to notice my surprise, and added, "we have more spirits to appease than you southerners, you see."

We passed a row of ruins, tall and skeletal, and a shiver traveled down my spine as their shadows fell across me.

"Your ancestors suffered greatly because of the witches," I said.

"Our ancestors were foolish," the elder said, in the same off-hand way in which he had appraised my motivations. He caught my stunned expression and gave a small shrug. "It's true. Yes, the witches stole from us, and worked their dark magic on those who crossed them. But it was the Elder of Jangsa at the time who turned all this into a war. He ordered us to shoot upon sight any witch or wild creature who strayed near our village. The witches retaliated, of course. Our village was very nearly destroyed."

"By the *witches*," I said, emphasizing the last word. "They were the ones who tried to destroy you—you can't possibly believe that was your elder's fault? For protecting you?"

The man laughed shortly. "Protecting us? Yes, I suppose he was protecting us. You can see the results for yourself. Violence leads to one thing only, and that is more violence."

We passed a temple—little more than the foundation and part of a wall, with an array of talismans draped across it.

"But it must be better," I persisted, "now that the witches have lost their powers."

"In a way," he said musingly, and again I couldn't help staring at him. I had never met anyone who didn't speak reverently of the spell that had bound the witches' powers.

"It is easier, of course," the elder added. "Though there are few among us who do not gaze out at that forest and wonder. The witches are not entirely powerless. Nor are their memories short."

I swallowed. Glancing over my shoulder, I could see the outskirts of the dark forest looming on the horizon.

The rain was letting up, a few sunbeams shafting through the clouds. At last, we arrived at the elder's house, which was long and squat, huddled against the mountain. Though it looked in need of repairs, like all the houses in the village, the shutters had been painted in bright reds and blues, and there was a well-tended garden along one side. The door was an even brighter red, with a colorful tassel dangling from the handle.

We left the yak to graze on a patch of grass, and followed the elder inside. Beyond the doors was a small reception room—a fire burned in the hearth, and woven mats had been laid on the floor for guests. Everything was finely made—from the mats to the painted scenes on the walls to the row of wooden spirit wheels, but also worn and faded, as if belonging to another era. A woman greeted us as we entered. The elder spoke to her in a low voice.

"We will send for our healer," the elder said, turning back to me. "While she sees to your companion, you and the others are welcome to rest and eat, as my guests."

"Thank you," I said. My stomach rumbled at the mention of food—real food, not our tasteless rations. Perhaps Ragtooth sensed a meal too, for he poked his head out of my pack and sniffed the air. The woman started.

"It's all right," I said, trying unsuccessfully to stuff Ragtooth back into the pack, and receiving a bloody thumb for my troubles. "He's harmless. Mostly."

"You have a familiar?" the elder said, his eyebrows disappearing beneath his hair.

"Yes." I stopped wrestling with Ragtooth and allowed him to hop onto the ground. He wandered to a sunbeam and began to groom himself. The elder and the woman stared at me, and I began to feel uncomfortable. I was so used to Ragtooth's presence that I often forgot how rare familiars were.

"Where's River?" Dargye said suddenly.

I turned. Norbu, his face sweaty and pale, was being helped by Aimo and Tem onto a low bench. Dargye stood by the door, as if hesitant to proceed farther. River was nowhere to be seen.

"Some kids surrounded him on the road," Tem said. "All begging for stories of his legendary adventures and grabbing at his *chuba*. I guess news that River Shara is in town travels fast."

I snorted at the image of River being swarmed by runny-nosed children. "And you didn't think to help him, Tem?"

Tem gave an exaggerated shrug. "For some reason, it didn't occur to me."

The healer arrived soon after, a slight, older woman with a guarded smile, who took one look at Norbu and murmured something to the elder. He nodded. Two men appeared and helped Norbu to his feet. They disappeared through another doorway.

"Will Norbu be all right?" I said.

The elder gave me another sharp look. "You didn't tell us about the *fiangul*."

"I—I'm sorry. I didn't—"

"No matter." The elder waved his hand, though his brow was furrowed. "You shouldn't have taken Winding Pass. We avoid the place. The *fiangul* grow stronger, and venture farther afield, with each passing winter. And they are not the only dark things stirring in the mountains again."

"I thought those were just rumors," I said, recalling what Mara had told us about the *fiangul* sightings in Lhotang.

The man turned back to Norbu. "It's fortunate you brought him to us. The healer believes we have caught it in time."

"Caught what in time?" Tem said. But the elder was speaking quietly to the healer, who disappeared after Norbu.

"Do you know how long this will take?" I said, suddenly nervous at the thought of being delayed here for long. The elder was kind, if a little odd, and the people were not as unfriendly as I had feared. But still, there was something about Jangsa—its brokenness, perhaps, or its atmosphere of decay frozen in time—that repelled me.

"Don't worry, Thaken's daughter." The elder's sharp features relaxed into a smile. "There's no healer wiser than Yachen. Now you must eat. You will be hungry, after journeying all the way from Azmiri."

I glanced at Tem. He gave an almost imperceptible shrug.

Smothering my anxiety, I nodded and followed the elder into the house.

ELEVEN

THE GHOST MARCH began at the doorstep of the elder's house, and then moved on—or, rather, spread—from there. I had often attended the Ghost Marches in Azmiri, where a small, orderly procession of villagers bearing food offerings for visiting spirits wove its way through the streets of the village, coming to a stop in the square, where minstrels serenaded them—and any ghosts in attendance—with drums and bells and *kangling*. An hour or two would pass, and then the villagers would go home to bed, leaving the food and the instruments in the square for the spirits to enjoy. Through the night, the wind would move over them, giving the illusion—if illusion it was—of ghostly hands tugging at the strings.

Jangsa's Ghost March was nothing like that.

Bonfires burned at street corners, contorting the shadows of those who passed. Ghosts feared light, so the fires were kept low, providing barely enough to see by, and your eyes played strange tricks with the shifting darkness. Food of every description sat untouched upon offering tables, so much of it that I no longer wondered why the people of Jangsa seemed so thin. People danced in the square just below the elder's house, weaving intricate patterns that I couldn't follow. Some hid their faces behind enormous, skeletal masks. Drummers improvised melodies that bled together, then clashed, then bled together again. Lanterns floated through the air, makeshift and flimsy. Some caught fire as they drifted into the sky, their ascent slowing, slowing, until finally it stopped, and they fell like tiny stars.

"Are you coming?" Tem said.

I turned away from the view out the window. "No."

"Kamzin, how many chances will we have to attend a Ghost March in Jangsa?"

"I'm not sure I care for the living inhabitants of this place, Tem. Now you want me to go dancing with the dead ones?"

"We don't have to dance. We can just watch."

I looked back at the window, indecisive. "I should check on Norbu."

"He's asleep," Tem said. "His wound looks better. The healer cleaned it with some sort of salve—I don't know what it was, but it smelled awful—and then I helped her with a purification chant. She says all he needs now is rest. Besides, River said he would look in on him."

"Who knows if that's true," I muttered. When the elder had invited River to attend the Ghost March, he had merely muttered something about disliking crowds, and disappeared in the direction of the rooms we had been given for the night. I had not seen him since. I wondered if he put as much effort into avoiding gatherings back in the Three Cities.

"What about you?" I said. "Did you tell the healer about your cough?"

"I didn't think of it."

"Tem."

"I'll speak with her later, promise." He tugged at my hand. "Come on."

I gazed at him. His chin-length hair, which normally shielded half his face, was damp from washing. It was brushed back, framing the angular planes of his face and his dark amber eyes, which had an ebony ring around the irises. It was unusual to see him that way, and not for the first time I noticed how handsome he had become. Tem had been short and plump as a boy, with a round, doll-like face, but all that had changed in the last year or two. He was well on his way to becoming a near mirror image of his tall, broad-shouldered father—who, despite being widely disliked, was privately acknowledged by the women of Azmiri as the most attractive man in the village. Though I would never tell Tem any of this—he didn't take kindly to being compared to his father in any respect.

"I really don't think it's a wise idea," I said.

"*You* don't think something is a wise idea?" He smiled again, and I felt something inside me relax. With a sigh, I allowed him to lead me out into the night.

I regretted it almost immediately. The square was a chaotic swirl of dancers—some masked and whirling in tight circles around the fire, so rapidly I was amazed they didn't fall over from dizziness, others dressed in plain clothes with only a few rows of bone beads around their necks. The masked dancers wielded curved swords that flashed as they sliced through the air. Children danced too, on the outskirts of the square. Though there were tables piled with food and drink, none of the villagers touched a morsel. The smell of incense and souring yak milk mingled with the smoke.

"Oh," Tem said. I followed his gaze, and stopped short.

River was dancing with one of the village girls. She had flashing eyes and hair like spun silk, and was almost painfully beautiful. Tem and I were not the only ones watching them—a knot of girls hovered at the edge of the dance, some smiling, others wearing envious frowns. River's expression was difficult to make out. He and the girl wove in and out of the dancers like fish in a stream, appearing and disappearing amidst the swirl of light and shadow, as if they belonged to it. I felt an unexpected twinge of anger.

"What's he doing?" I said.

"You have to ask?" Tem was gazing at the girl in River's arms with a look that only increased my irritation. He shook his head slightly and turned back to me. "Are you all right?"

"Of course I am," I said, a little too quickly. "I just don't understand him, that's all. I don't trust these people, and I thought he didn't either."

Tem's gaze drifted to the girl again. I could see he didn't share my feelings where she was concerned.

"Let's dance," I said, gripping his hand.

"I thought you—"

"I changed my mind."

I dragged him into the square. The dancers followed no discernible pattern, clusters of twos or threes or fours weaving together and stamping their feet in time to the music. The only constant was the gaps they left between each other, which were supposed to be for any ghosts who wished to take part. Tem grasped my arms and we spun around, folding ourselves into the dance.

Almost immediately, I let out a yelp. He had crushed my toes beneath his boot. "Tem!"

"Sorry," he said, his face red. "I didn't know you were going to go that way."

"You're still a terrible dancer," I grumbled, trying to avoid his feet. Staring at the ground meant that I was no longer able to watch where I was going, and it began to seem that every few seconds I was bumping into somebody. Tem tried to lead me along the same looping path that other dancers followed, but we always seemed out of sync somehow—which was saying something, given the random nature of the dance.

Suddenly, we were moving very fast. Tem had drawn me into orbit around the masked dancers at the bonfire. He spun me around, drew me close, and then spun me away, the movements almost too intricate for me to see. I felt like a leaf caught in a storm.

"Tem!" I gasped, reaching out to grasp his shoulders. "What are you—?"

The question died on my lips. River gazed back at me, a smile on his face.

I stared at him. I hadn't even felt Tem pull away from me. "How did you—?"

My question dissolved into a yelp as River spun us around so swiftly that the fire seemed to be surrounding us on all sides.

"Stop that," I said, half gasping and half laughing. "Where's Tem?"

"It doesn't matter." River drew me close, so close I could feel the warmth of his body against mine, and spoke in my ear. "I thought you could use a break from being stepped on."

"You saw that?" I felt my irritation return, even as my heart thudded at his nearness. "I thought your attention was somewhere else."

River laughed softly. "Well, I've learned to see past the obvious—to the details others miss."

I flushed as I recognized Tem's words. To take the focus off me, I said, "Are you calling that girl obvious?"

"I guess so—I hadn't really thought about it."

"No, why would you?" I grumbled. "I'm sure wherever you go, beautiful girls are throwing themselves at you."

"Yes, and it's a terrible burden."

I couldn't help laughing. River drew back, his eyes sparkling. Shadow played across the planes of his handsome face. "Watch this," he said.

I shrieked as River lifted me into the air and spun me around, simultaneously drawing us deeper into the ring of masked dancers.

They swirled around us—the swish of their *chubas* and the whistle of their swords through the air made me shudder. Behind their masks, the dancers' eyes were wild.

"They say the people of Jangsa have witch blood," I said. "I'm starting to believe it."

"You're not afraid, are you?"

"Of course not," I lied. "What are you doing here, anyway? I thought you hated crowds."

"I do. But I like dancing." We spun in a circle, so fast that I shrieked again, gripping River's arms with all my strength. He laughed. My eyes were shut tight—I was certain we would collide with the other dancers, or their swords, or trip and stumble into the fire. But somehow, River darted expertly through the crowd, finding gaps that looked too narrow to fit through, barely brushing even the other dancers' *chubas*. He could have been a ghost himself. As he pulled me close again, I wrapped my arms around his neck to steady myself. I could feel his breath against my ear, warm and soft.

"How does that work, anyway?" I said, trying to conceal the pounding of my heart. I was certain River could hear it. "You can't very well avoid crowds in the Three Cities."

He seemed to think for a moment. "I didn't grow up in the Three Cities. The Shara estate is deep in the countryside to the south. It's a beautiful land—high, grassy plains dotted with countless rivers and turquoise lakes—but isolated. My family rarely ventured as far as the emperor's court. The feasting, the parades, the endless parties—I didn't have any of it as a child. It was a different life."

I considered this. "Do you miss them?" I said. "Your family, I mean."

He was quiet. "Yes," he said finally.

"Me too," I murmured. A sword slashed past my head, but I barely heard it. I was thinking of Father. He would be making his customary nighttime rounds now, striding through the dragonlit village with his long *chuba* trailing behind him, on the lookout for intruders both animal and human. Unlike some village elders, Father took his responsibilities as protector of his people seriously. Sometimes too seriously. I could remember many nights when I had stayed up late, hoping he would come to my room to tell one of his stories, only to fall asleep disappointed. Sometimes, when we weren't fighting, I would curl up with Lusha in her bed, and she would open her window and tell me the story of whatever constellation was framed between the shutters. I still did sometimes, though the times when we weren't fighting were much fewer and further between.

If I became one of the emperor's explorers, I would spend long periods away from Lusha and Father—and Azmiri. The thought brought with it a stab of sadness—but little regret. As much as I loved Azmiri, I didn't fit there. I never had. Life in the village was small and quiet and contained, while I craved noise and excitement and wide-open spaces stretched out before me like a blank scroll upon which I could write my own stories.

Perhaps the Elder of Jangsa had been right. After what I had just been through—the grueling trek, the storm, the *fiangul*—I should have been desperate to return home. But I wasn't. My thoughts were already racing ahead to the next part of our journey, to Raksha. If I could prove myself to River, I wouldn't have to worry about my life back in Azmiri. I could have the life I had always dreamed of but never knew how to achieve.

River spun me around again, interrupting my thoughts. We passed between two masked dancers as one drew his sword back and the other slashed his down behind us, through the air we had just occupied.

I laughed. River lifted me into the air, then took my hand and whirled me in a series of intricate circles, so many that I lost count. Finally I grabbed him, laughing and breathless. He laughed too, his eyes alight, and for one breathless moment, I was certain he was going to kiss me. Only then did I notice that the musicians had fallen silent—had perhaps been silent for a while.

I looked around. River and I were the only ones standing by the fire. The others had fallen back and stared at us from the edge of the square. Even the masked dancers had stopped, and stood with their swords at their side. Some had removed their masks, revealing flushed faces. Tem stood with the girl who had been dancing with River, gaping at me. The girl was staring too, her forehead creased with a frown.

River nodded to me, then turned and melted into the shadows. I stood there a moment longer, blinking back at the staring faces. Then I all but ran from the square.

I didn't return to the elder's house—instead, I fled away from the crowd, along a road I didn't recall passing when we first entered Jangsa. It was little more than a footpath, hugging the mountainside over terrain that undulated and twisted. A lantern floated past, but I ignored it.

I stopped suddenly. The road had ended—before me was another ruin, dark against the night sky. A shrine.

A long row of stone steps, cracked with age and patchy with moss, led to a jumble of broken stone. Only one of the columns still stood; the other three lay on their sides, together with what little remained of the roof. Tall statues leaned sideways, human figures—former elders? I wondered—who were now faceless and handless, their arms stretched out toward a world they could neither see nor touch. A family of birds had made a nest in one, in the crook between neck and shoulder.

I sat down on the steps, letting myself catch my breath at last. It was as if the dizziness I should have felt during my dance with River had finally caught up to me—I felt almost nauseous, and too hot. I gazed out over the village as the lanterns drifted into the sky. Most caught fire and fell, but there was one that survived, pulled up and along the mountainside by the wind. I watched until it grew so small it seemed to disappear.

"Kamzin? Is everything all right?" a voice asked.

I started. But it was only the elder, who had come silently up the road behind me. He held a spirit mask in his hand.

"I'm fine," I said. "The music is lovely, but I just needed to get away."

The man nodded. "I understand. Our customs can be . . . unnerving for outsiders."

He took a seat on the steps, and though he left several feet of space between us, I still felt like moving farther away. It wasn't just the way he looked at me with that odd smile—as if he already had the measure of me, and it was a measure that amused him. It was something else, something I couldn't put my finger on.

"The emperor set River Shara a cruel task," he said. "Even if you succeed in climbing Raksha, you may meet with any number of dangers at the summit. The witches may have abandoned the place, but their presence lingers."

I stared at him. "You spoke to River."

"No." He smiled. "You think we don't know about the sky city? It's said that a great many magical objects were left behind when the witches abandoned it. It only makes sense that the emperor would seek them."

I thought this over. "Has anyone ever seen it?"

"Oh no. No human has set foot there. The witches are shape-shifters—or at least they were, before they lost their powers. They can make their homes anywhere. The canopy of a forest, a cave deep beneath the earth. The summit of the highest mountain, which even the birds fear to fly over. We mortals are not so fortunate."

I peered at him through the darkness. "Are you a seer?"

"No." He motioned absently at the sky, as if to pay his respect. "There are those to whom the stars reveal their secrets, but I am not one of them. I have never had the talent for hearing their voices."

"That's too bad," I said, trying to keep my voice light. "I was hoping you could tell me whether we'll succeed."

"Ah." He nodded. "I don't need the stars to answer that. I believe you will succeed, Kamzin, because that's who you are. Though I wonder if it will be in the way you expect."

The elder's gaze was mellow but unwavering. He had not looked away from me since he sat down, not even to glance at the lanterns that floated by.

"What did you mean before?" I said suddenly. "You said the *fiangul* are growing stronger every year, and that other dark creatures are stirring. Did you mean the witches?"

His gaze, for the first time, flickered from mine. "I would not be the first to draw a connection between the two."

"What do you mean? Are they allies?"

"No," he said, "and yes. In Jangsa, there is a tale that tells of how the witches created the *fiangul*. That once, many generations ago, there was a village in Winding Pass whose inhabitants offended the witches. As punishment, they lay a curse upon them, which transformed them into the creatures you met in the storm."

"I've never heard that."

"It's a very old story," the elder said. "Possibly much twisted with time. There certainly was a village—many of the foundations remain, great stone slabs hidden beneath the drifts. But why it was destroyed, and what became of its people, that is anyone's guess."

I swallowed. "Then if the witches were to regain their powers—the *fiangul* would only grow stronger. Wouldn't they?"

"The world is a dark place," the elder said, as if this were an answer. "It has always been such."

I suppressed a shiver. Again I saw the black eyes of the *fiangul*, boring into mine, felt the brush of air stirred by their wingbeats. I didn't want to be there anymore, pinned under the elder's gaze and contemplating such terrifying possibilities.

"I should get some sleep," I said, rising. "We're leaving in the morning, if Norbu is better."

"I'm sure he will be," the elder said placidly. "Good night, Thaken's daughter."

I forced a smile and walked away. I had taken only a few steps when the elder called, "Kamzin?"

I turned.

"You are always welcome here." Another lantern drifted past, briefly illuminating the broken shrine. "It's something I would say to few outsiders."

"Thank you," I murmured.

He smiled. "You remind me of your father in some ways, and I've always respected him. He has an unusual way of looking at the world. He does not divide everything into tidy halves the way most people do. Right and wrong, good and evil—he sees beyond absolutes, like all great leaders."

I opened and then closed my mouth. The elder seemed to take no notice of my confusion, and finally turned to gaze out over the village. Murmuring a good night, I walked hastily away, and even though I knew he was no longer looking at me, I felt his gaze burning into the back of my head.

TWELVE

"I WON'T FORGET that any time soon," Tem said.

We were setting up our tent for the night, having traveled through the day after leaving Jangsa at first light. Norbu seemed stronger for the healer's ministrations, and barely lagged at all, though I noticed he still glanced over his shoulder sometimes, a puzzled frown on his face. River, anxious to close the distance with Mara, stopped often to hurry us. The delay seemed to have put him on edge; he looked repeatedly at the sun as its movement counted down the hours of daylight.

But if River was eager to be moving again, so was I. We found no new evidence of Lusha and Mara—had they taken a different route, or were they now so far ahead that the elements had erased the telltale signs of their presence? I found myself stamping out my own frustration whenever Tem fell behind. After a punishing hike of fifty miles, we were all relieved to have stopped by a grove of chir trees as dusk neared. The light from the campfire and the gamboling dragons played against their trunks.

"Won't forget what?" I said innocently. "Jangsa? Or dancing with that girl?"

Tem's cheeks turned sunset pink. "I didn't—I mean, that wasn't my idea. I don't know how River did it, but—"

"But you didn't mind, did you?" I said as Tem flushed even deeper. "And neither did she, I bet. You probably had to tear your-self away from her at the end of the night. Or did you? Come to think of it, Tem, I didn't hear you return to your room—"

"Stop it, Kamzin."

I chortled to myself.

Later, though, as we both settled into our blankets, trying to get comfortable on the uneven ground, Tem said, "You really wouldn't care?"

I dragged my eyes open. I was so tired I felt as if I were weighted to the earth. "What?"

He coughed. "If I was interested in someone. It wouldn't bother you?"

I was quiet for a moment. "Are you?"

"No."

I shifted restlessly. "Well, what does it matter, then?"

"You didn't seem to mind dancing with River."

"I don't mind being able to walk today."

"It was more than that, though," Tem persisted. "The way you looked together—"

"Listening to you talk about dancing is like listening to a fish talk about fire-building." I rolled onto my side. "It was just a dance. Can we drop it?"

"I just mean—"

"Tem, if you need me to say it, I'll say it. I wouldn't mind if you were interested in someone. The two of us haven't been together that way in over a year. So I don't mind. All right?"

Tem didn't reply, for which I was grateful. I wasn't entirely sure I had told the truth. The thought of Tem liking another girl made me feel strange. It wasn't jealousy precisely. It was closer to loneliness than anything else. If I didn't have Tem, who did I have?

Sleep did not come easily for me, despite my exhaustion. Though the sound of the waterfall and Tem's quiet snores were soothing, I lapsed in and out of a doze. The music of the Ghost March threaded through my thoughts. Part of me felt as if I were still spinning in circles. As if River's arms were still around me, his breath warm against my ear. Others circled us—the masked dancers, but interspersed among them were the *fiangul*. Their beaks snapped at me as I passed, catching at my hair, my *chuba*, my skin. River melted away, and suddenly, they were everywhere, reaching for my throat with taloned hands—

A noise startled me awake, my heart thundering. I listened, and it came again—a snuffling, scrabbling sound. The same sound I had heard before, at the edge of Bengarek Forest.

I lay very still. It was hard to pinpoint the direction of the noise over the splash of the water—but it seemed close. As quietly as I could, I pushed back my blankets and rose to a crouching position.

Ragtooth, who had been sleeping by my head, gave a low hiss.

"Shut up," I whispered. My hand moved to the tent flap. The creature was just outside. I could hear its snout huffing against the rocky bank. Taking a deep breath, I pulled on the flap.

Ragtooth bit my leg—hard.

"Ouch!" I cried. Tem gave a start and muttered something, but he was not truly awake. He rolled over onto his side with a mumbling groan.

Rubbing my calf, I listened. The sounds had stopped, and all was quiet. It was a different quiet from before, an honest, night-time hush. I knew, somehow, that the creature was gone.

In the morning light, there was no evidence of a trail. The earth was hard-packed, almost frozen. Not even Dargye's footsteps left a trace.

"I *know* it was out here!" I said. "It was the same creature I heard before. Whatever it was, it's been following us."

Tem gave me a skeptical look. The others, preoccupied with breakfast, paid little attention to me.

"It could have been the wind," he offered, releasing the dragon he was holding and reaching for a second. The chill air dried their scales, which needed oiling every few days to keep them in good condition. The dragon's eyes half closed as Tem rubbed heartseed oil between its wings.

"It wasn't the wind," I said. "Please say you believe me. I wasn't imagining it."

"I believe you," he said quickly. "But, Kamzin, I set the warding spells myself last night. If an animal had slipped through them, I would have felt it."

I shook my head. "You don't believe me at all. You could at least have the decency to say it."

"Kamzin . . ."

I stomped over to the fire. Dargye handed me a bowl of *sampa* porridge, lumpy and slightly burned, which did not improve my mood. I stabbed at it with my spoon, trying to saw through the lumps.

"The wind can play strange tricks on your hearing," he said, turning his attention to his own porridge—which, I couldn't help noticing, had fewer blackened grains than mine.

"It wasn't the wind," I said through my teeth.

"Do you recall the storm we had last winter?" Dargye continued, as was his habit, as if I hadn't spoken. "The sound it made against my hut—I thought the witches had come to carry me off. But it was only loose branches hitting the windows."

I mashed the lumps with the back of my spoon. "Shame."

"We should choose our camps more carefully," he said. "We're too exposed. I've said as much to River, but he doesn't listen."

"I can't imagine why not."

Aimo brought a bowl of porridge to Norbu, who sat hunched over his butter tea, rubbing his eyes.

"How is he?" I asked.

Aimo made a *so-so* gesture. Norbu was wearing his heavy fur *chuba*, as opposed to his lightweight traveling one, but still he was shivering. He seemed stronger, but there was a lingering weariness in his movements. I eyed him warily. It wasn't just that I was concerned for his health; I was calculating how much he would slow us down. An ill traveling companion was a danger not just to himself, but to the entire group. Our supplies would run low if we were delayed, and Norbu would be unable to handle difficult terrain, forcing us to take roundabout routes that would use additional resources and expose us to unexpected dangers.

Ragtooth nosed up to me, sniffing at my bowl. I fed him a few porridge lumps and let him stick his snout in my tea.

"At least you believe me," I murmured, scratching his ear. He regarded me silently and allowed me to pet him for several seconds before trying to bite my fingers off.

Despite my worries, we reached the edge of Garamai Forest—the day's goal—by sundown. Sleet fell during the night, pummeling the tents and making sleep difficult, but by the next morning the skies were clear of all but a few skinny clouds, which trailed at the edge of the retreating storm like frayed threads.

Ragtooth stayed with us most of the time, trotting along at my side or even running ahead of us, as if scouting out the path. I was nervous here—we all were—expecting at any moment that a witch would rise up out of the shadows and pounce. But the sight of the fox's tawny tail bobbing up and down brought me back to myself. If Ragtooth, with his fox senses, was not troubled by anything, why should I be?

The forest at this elevation was a scattering of trees that only occasionally thickened into groves. These we had to pick our way

through single file. The ground was a soft carpet of pine needles. There were patches of melting snow here and there, and the
ground was muddy. The long, fluted peak of Mount Chening
loomed over us, and beyond that, glimpsed only occasionally in
the distance, was the peak of Raksha.

Clouds wrapped around it like many-layered shawls, but I
knew it was there. I had never seen anything so enormous—it
seemed higher than the stars themselves. Even a glimpse took my
breath away—and terrified me to the core.

What have I done? Yet with the terror, there was excitement,
which turned the fear into something almost pleasurable. It was
a strange emotion that filled me with jangly energy, and I sometimes jogged ahead of the others, delighting in the simple pleasure
of movement. Some of the darkness that had plagued my dreams
since our battle with the *fiangul* seemed to lift, and I marveled at
how far I had come. Few humans had laid eyes on the landscape
before us. I spun around, taking in every angle, feeling every inch
a daring explorer.

This is it, I thought. *This is all I want.*

It took four days to cross the forest, as we were detoured around
unexpected gullies and deep streams that the yak couldn't ford
("tedious," Mingma had written, in his usual dry tone). We tried
to keep to our northward course as much as possible, but ended
up backtracking repeatedly. Another day was spent traversing a
field of towering boulders that had been deposited, long ago, by a
retreating glacier. That night we pitched our tents at the edge of
a pointed outcropping that overlooked Phaomzu Valley and the

Nightwood beyond it. We were not two weeks out from Azmiri, and yet the village seemed a world away.

We made only a small fire. Our position was too exposed— there was no telling what could be watching us from the valley below. We crowded around the flames—apart from Norbu, who sat by his tent, hunched over his talismans, and River, who had wandered off somewhere. The sunlight drained from the sky, leaving a trail of orange and pink above the towering mountains. The few trees loomed out of the uneven ground, arms outstretched in what seemed like a sinister gesture of welcome.

I hunched as close to the fire as I could get, as if it could protect me against not only the cold, but my own fear. My gaze kept drifting up, up, to the snow-streaked heights. To Raksha. All but the very peak was hidden behind Mount Chening, but some of the clouds had cleared, revealing a snowy triangle that gleamed golden from the sunset.

We were almost there. Another three days, I estimated, and we would be setting up base camp. The thought made me want to whoop with excitement and sob with terror at the same time.

Tem sat beside me, treating his feet with salve. We were all blistered and bruised by now, some worse than others. Aimo needed daily healing charms for her swollen feet. Dargye's toenails were blackened and loose, and when he removed his boots there was an awful squelching sound from the blood that pooled at his toes. Neither made any complaint, but I could see the pain written on their faces at the end of each day.

"It's hard to imagine," Tem said, gazing at the sky, "that there was ever a city up there."

I rubbed my hands over the flames. "If it's even true. How could people survive at that elevation?"

"Witches aren't people," Dargye said. Aimo, sitting beside him, seemed to flinch.

"Actually, according to the shamans, they're half-human," Tem said. "Descendants of an ancient nomadic tribe from beyond the Drakkar Mountains and elemental spirits—cousins of the fire demons. Only these elementals were not shaped from fire, but shadow." He paused. "Darkness itself."

Aimo shivered. I shook my head. Tem's knowledge of shamanic lore far outweighed my own. Part of my apprenticeship to Chirri involved hours poring over the ancient shamanic scrolls held in my father's library. The first time Tem accompanied me there, I had to drag him away. While I bored quickly of ancient history and magical theory, Tem drank it in like a sun-scorched forest does the first autumn rains. As I continued to struggle with magic, Tem took to reading over the passages Chirri assigned to me and relaying the important points in words that made sense. Chirri had seemed suspicious of my suddenly improved comprehension, though she made no comment.

Dargye shrugged. "What difference does it make? They're monsters. They probably don't need to breathe. Or eat, or sleep. Who knows?"

"That's nonsense," I scoffed. "Azmiri fought the witches when they set fire to the village. They can be harmed. They can be killed."

"They can also transform into animals and fold themselves into shadow," Dargye snapped. "How can we know what's impossible for them?"

"I wish I knew more about this lost city," Tem said, stirring the fire with a stick. Little sparks rose from the wood. "What are we going to find when we reach the summit? The scrolls aren't specific."

That Tem would know of the witch city didn't surprise me. "What do they say?"

"That it exists"—he coughed—"though its location is unknown. The ancient shamans called it the 'sky city'—they thought the witches built it in the clouds, far above the human realm, that it floated from place to place."

I pictured a glittering city suspended in the sky. "Why did they abandon it?"

"No one knows. It was a very long time ago—centuries, long before the Empire had even begun to take shape. One scroll suggests that the witches grew interested in humans, and they came down from the sky to spy on us. Another claims that a power struggle between their rulers led to a bloody war, and the survivors fled back to Earth to escape the vengeful spirits who haunted them. Whatever the reason, they never returned to the sky city, choosing to dwell instead in the Nightwood—only it wasn't called that back then."

I nodded. I knew that at one time, the great forest had stretched from the plains east of the Aryas—where it was now confined—all the way to the lands that now held the Three Cities. But the

Empire had cleared great swaths of it, and today only a few stands of trees remained west of the mountains. It was said that the Nightwood had not always been a wasted, fearsome place, but the witches had imbued it with their dark magic in the centuries they dwelled there, and when the emperor bound their powers, some part of the Nightwood had sickened, twisting in on itself. Now it was a place even birds feared.

"The shamans believed the witches left something in the sky city," Tem said. "Some ancient power. Perhaps a talisman." He ran his thumb along his jaw, a gesture he made whenever he was lost in thought. "Did Chirri ever mention anything?"

I thought back. Chirri had spent hours, in the early days of my apprenticeship, instructing me on the history of the Empire and the surrounding lands, and of the creatures, both magical and nonmagical, who dwelled there. It was the role of the village shaman to know such things—they lived long lives and were often called upon to advise the elder. But as my ineptness at magic grew more apparent, Chirri abandoned these efforts, declaring that if I lacked the mental faculties to master spells even children could cast, I couldn't be trusted to advise the elder on any subject. My face burned at the recollection.

"No," I said quietly.

"How are we supposed to find something if we don't know what it looks like?" Dargye said.

Tem began to reply, but Aimo stood suddenly and hurried away. We stared after her, startled.

"Is she all right?" I asked.

Dargye's expression had clouded. Without looking at me, he replied, "She'll be fine."

"She shouldn't go off by herself."

Dargye opened his mouth to argue, but I was already on my feet. After the warmth of the fire, the twilight air was almost painfully cold. My eyes watered from the chill wind that stirred the sparse grasses. I found Aimo standing by a grove of dead trees, leaning against one of the trunks as if drawing support from it.

"Is everything all right?"

Aimo nodded, wiping her face quickly on the back of her hand. Her eyes shone faintly.

"It's your family, isn't it?" I had noticed that, whenever the witches were mentioned, Aimo stiffened, as if steeling herself against some invisible assault. The young woman glanced at me.

"Yesterday was my daughter's birthday," she said. "She would have been five."

"I'm sorry." I felt my own voice drop to match hers. "Is there anything I can do?"

She gazed into the distance. For a moment, I thought she wasn't going to reply.

"You already have," she said. "I feel closer to them here."

"Closer?" I knew that the witches had taken Aimo's husband and child. When it happened, no search parties were launched. No one waited to hold the funeral. I tried to read her shadowed face. "What do you mean? You can't think they're still out there?"

Aimo turned back to me. Her expression was serene. There was no trace of the tears I had seen earlier. "I'm sure of it."

I stared at her. "That's why you came, isn't it?"

She smiled faintly. Her demeanor was unnerving—the calm certainty I had always admired, though not understood, seemed to possess a different quality now. She moved away without replying, following a narrow ridge between two boulders.

"Wait," I called. It wasn't safe to stray too far from the fire. Aside from witches, wild animals often came down from the mountains at night to hunt.

"I'll keep an eye on her," Dargye said, appearing behind me. Barely sparing me a glance, he headed in the direction his sister had taken. The faint light gleamed off the dagger he had tucked into his belt.

"Does she really believe that?" I couldn't help asking. "That her family is still alive, and they're out here in the witch lands somewhere?"

Dargye paused, gazing at me from beneath his thicket of eyebrow. His expression was weary. "Is there a reason she shouldn't?"

"It's impossible," I said. "The witches have no mercy. No one they've ever taken has been found again."

"What would you have her believe instead?" Dargye folded his arms. "Aimo and Jai were friends from childhood. They did everything together, went everywhere together—not unlike you and Tem."

A flush spread across my face. Few villagers, I knew, had been surprised when Aimo and Jai married. Surely people didn't see Tem and me in that light.

"What would you have her believe, Kamzin?" Dargye repeated.

"That the witches captured her family, tortured them, and killed them? That they took their souls and condemned them to slavery? Which of the stories is she supposed to accept? Is it any wonder she chooses to hold on to some small hope, however unlikely?"

I felt lost. "She isn't going to find them."

"Of course she isn't," Dargye said. "That doesn't mean she has to believe it."

With that, he turned, following his sister into the gathering darkness.

THIRTEEN

BY THE TIME I returned to the fire, Tem had left to set the warding spells, while Norbu was in his tent, muttering to himself. Dargye's words still rang in my ears, and the darkness was oppressive. I couldn't stop thinking of Aimo, her calm refusal to accept what had happened to her family. I pictured her by the tree, alone and staring into the darkness with that expectant look on her face. She had joined the expedition on the impossible chance that somewhere, in this vast wilderness, she might find them. Was that love, or madness? Could you love someone so much that it stole your reason?

The wind seemed to have voices in it—witches' voices, or perhaps those of long-forgotten spirits. I shook myself, trying to silence my fanciful thoughts.

I wandered to the edge of the outcrop, where two of the dragons were rolling about, biting each other's ears. Leaning against a rock, his legs dangling over the edge of the cliff, was River.

I stopped short. The view opened up here, away from the foothills, revealing a vast landscape that took my breath away. The bowl of the valley brimmed with shadow. Beyond it, the Northern Aryas faded into the distance beneath a sky brightened by early stars. To the east, the Nightwood was dimly visible, sharp treetops reaching for the sky like claws. River gazed out over the land, a brooding look on his face, looking for all the world like a king surveying his domain. The pale side of his *chuba* melted against the weathered stone as if it were part of it. He would have been invisible if I hadn't chanced to look right at him.

I turned, about to go back. It wasn't that River and I hadn't spoken over the past few days, since leaving Jangsa—we had spoken a great deal. Every morning began with the two of us hunched over the maps, planning the day's journey. River was an expert at reading maps, but he didn't trust them implicitly the way most people did. He listened to my advice, and never questioned me when I suggested we avoid a particular route, or pause to climb up the mountainside to survey the land ahead. We always went together, just the two of us, and though I did not openly challenge him to another game of shadow, it was always understood between us. Climbing with River was a wonderful distraction, because we were so evenly matched. Sometimes I felt as if River truly was my shadow, or I his. I finally beat him one morning, trapping him in a narrow crevice that I had only escaped by hooking my heel around a rock almost level with my head while walking my body up the wall behind me with my hands. River couldn't repeat the move, and so climbed up a different way. I had expected him to be annoyed by his loss, or embarrassed, but he seemed to find it uproariously funny. I doubted that anyone had come close to challenging him before, and he seemed to delight in my ability to do so. I understood the feeling—it was wonderful to be traveling with someone who could match me move for move and step for step, who made me try things I would never dare with Tem or anyone else.

And yet, despite all this, I found myself avoiding River's gaze, or purposely positioning myself so that we weren't walking together. It wasn't because I wanted to avoid him. It was because my desire to impress him was now jumbled up with other, more problematic feelings. I spent far too much time thinking about River Shara these days. I might be clambering over a fallen tree, and suddenly I would be thinking about how he had spun me among the other dancers in Jangsa. I might be examining the clouds, trying to determine the direction of the wind, and then I would be thinking about how he scrubbed his hand through his hair when he was lost in thought.

It was annoying.

I was just sneaking away when River glanced up and caught my eye. He beckoned me to his side.

"Drink?" he said, holding a bottle out.

I settled beside him. "No thanks."

He placed the bottle in my hand as if I hadn't spoken. I sniffed it, then took a swallow. The drink scorched the back of my throat and filled my chest with a sharp warmth. It was spicy and smooth in equal measure; I had never tasted anything like it.

"I didn't realize we brought liquor," I said, handing back the bottle. "Aren't we trying to travel light?"

He held a finger to his lips, as if the explorer in charge of the expedition were lurking nearby, listening, rather than sitting beside me. I couldn't help laughing.

He took another drink, then gave the bottle to me. I took only a single swallow before putting it down on the rock between us.

"That's it," I said. "I'm not letting you get me drunk again. I remember too well what happened the last time."

"I don't remember much *getting* on my part—wasn't I the one prying the bowl from your hands?"

I made a face. "My father was so disappointed in me for embarrassing myself in front of such a famous guest. For embarrassing Azmiri."

"I can't imagine you disappoint him often. So what's the harm?"

I made a noise halfway between a laugh and a snort. "But I do. I'm a constant disappointment to my entire family. When they notice me at all."

"That *is* a sad story." River nudged the bottle toward me again. I swatted his hand away, and he laughed. It echoed off the rocks, and if rocks could laugh, I couldn't imagine a wilder, more suitable sound.

"Let me tell you something." He leaned toward me. "I'm the youngest of four brothers, so I have some expertise on this subject. I love my brothers very much, but I also hate them. Really, truly despise them. They're much better than me at many things, and were forever winning my mother's praise, and I hate them for that. But you know, in a way, it's just as hard for them. They're trying to live up to their own set of expectations, even if they are different from those I face." He lowered his voice, as if speaking half to himself. "In some way, we're all trying to prove ourselves to our families."

I gazed at him, surprised. Was that why he had become an explorer, rather than contenting himself with the lavish parties and grand palaces of the Three Cities? Because he wanted to please his family, to be a good son? It struck me again how young he was.

"How old are you?"

"Nineteen." It had the air of an announcement. He held the bottle up as if toasting the darkness. "It's my birthday."

"Today?" I felt inexplicably annoyed. "Why didn't you tell us?"

He laughed. "I'm sorry. Were you planning on throwing me a party?"

"That's what the box of firecrackers is for," I said. "And the drums, and the floating lanterns—just in case I needed to throw River Shara a birthday party. But now I guess it's too late."

He laughed again, sagging forward slightly. Liquor splashed over the side of the ridge. I pried the bottle out of his hand.

"There is one thing you could give me," he said, when he had caught his breath.

His tone made me suspicious. "No."

"You didn't even—"

"I don't trust you," I said sternly, moving the bottle out of his reach. He made a grab for it, and I snared his hand. "At least, everyone keeps telling me not to."

"Your shaman, you mean." He was smiling at me. His teeth were very straight, except for one at the side, which tilted slightly.

"Stop calling him 'my shaman.'" I forced myself to look at his eyes rather than his mouth. "His name is Tem."

"Yes, yes, whatever. Tell me something. How does someone as clever and talented as you become best friends with someone that dull?"

"Tem is not dull," I said. "You just don't know him."

"No, I don't, because he barely says two words at a time."

"He doesn't trust you. He's like that when he doesn't trust someone. I don't know why you're complaining—you talk enough for a dozen people. But I won't have you insulting Tem." I narrowed my eyes. "You should be glad he's here, otherwise who would be setting the warding spells? Who would we turn to if some dark creature attacked us?"

"Me." River shrugged. "That's the way it's always worked. Every night, Norbu would set the warding spells, and then after he went to bed I would go around and set them properly."

With your invisible talismans, I thought but did not say. To my knowledge, River hadn't used his magic again since he had fought the *fiangul*. Despite this, Tem remained convinced of what he had seen.

"There was one time," River went on, his gaze distant, "when Norbu and I were hiking along the Lake of Dumori in the Southern Aryas, and a water ghost sprang up and dragged me into the depths. Norbu stood on the shore, waving his beads around and yelling his useless head off, while I battled twenty of the wet, nasty things, all of them intent on draining the breath from my lungs and taking my place among the living. I had to freeze the lake just to immobilize them, and then hack my body free with my own ice ax. Norbu couldn't even master a melting spell."

I shook my head. "Why bring Norbu at all?"

"All explorers bring at least one trained shaman on their expeditions. It's just the way it's done."

"But why Norbu? Why not someone capable of casting a warding spell strong enough to repel more than a rabbit?"

"I told you—I can trust Norbu."

I sighed, giving up. Perhaps River's reasoning made sense to him, but it made little to me.

River glanced at me, a faint smile on his face. He turned back to the dark valley and made a small motion with his hand. Out of the night rose a single flower, plucked from the valley floor far below. It was a lily, its pale petals brushed with moonlight. River gestured again, and more flowers drifted up, like ghosts rising out of a primordial void. Roses and orchids and heartleaf—they hovered there, as if rooted in the darkness. A shadow meadow, teeming with flowers.

"Oh," I murmured. I had never seen a summoning spell used this way before. As I was staring, River reached around me and grabbed the bottle.

"Hey!" I tried to wrestle it away from him. "You—you *sneak*!"

"Sneak?" He began laughing again. "That's insubordination."

"What are you going to do about it?" I was laughing too, in spite of myself. "Send me back to Azmiri? Let Dargye guide your expedition?"

"Well, he's not as pretty as you, granted, but he's more tractable. Wait, don't—"

As we were tussling, the bottle, slippery with spilled liquor, slid from his hand. I batted it away before he could make a recovery, and it tumbled down into the darkness. We both froze. Seconds later, there was a distant, echoing *smash*.

I turned to him, grinning triumphantly. "Serves you—"

He kissed me.

I let out a muffled noise. His mouth was warm and tasted slightly salty. Before I even knew what I was doing, I was kissing him back, pressing my face into his. A fierce desire rose inside me, hot and rippling like summer haze, startling in its intensity. I could not have said how long the kiss lasted—a second or a minute; I was oblivious to everything except his lips against mine and his hand as it threaded through my hair.

Finally, we broke apart. River gazed at me for a moment, then he began to smile. My heart was pounding, and I felt light-headed, as if I had drunk as much as he had.

"I told you there was something you could give me," he said. He was still holding my arm. I yanked it away.

"You're drunk."

"Yes, I am." He rose unsteadily to his feet. "But not enough, thanks to you. Good night, Kamzin." Shoving his hands in his pockets, he staggered off, heading vaguely in the direction of his tent.

I stayed where I was, waiting for my heart to stop pounding. It took a long time. Whenever I thought about the feeling of River's mouth on mine, it would speed up again.

The flowers were still floating in midair, only now they seemed adrift, like abandoned ships in a storm. The wind tossed them up and down, pushing them south along the ridge. One, a golden marigold, came within arm's reach. I lunged out and grabbed it.

What am I doing? I thought. I released the marigold, and it drifted away with the others. Suddenly, I wanted nothing to do with flowers, bobbing eerily on the wind. I stood so fast I had to steady myself against the rock until the spots cleared from my vision. I turned my back on the floating meadow and hurried back to my tent.

FOURTEEN

IT DIDN'T MEAN anything.

I kept repeating that to myself as we hiked through the rubbly moraine that bracketed Raksha's enormous glacier. Though we were still miles from the glacier itself, we were in another world. We had left trees behind—all that existed now were rocks so battered and broken they could have fallen from the stars, and reticent tufts of grass speckled with tiny pink flowers. The sun beat down. It was too hot for walking and laboring under a heavy pack, and too chilly to rest for any length of time.

It was nothing. It didn't mean anything. Sometimes I muttered it out loud to myself. The yak grunted, as if agreeing with me. River was far behind, walking with Tem this time, gesticulating every few seconds at some feature of the landscape and talking his head off. I had to keep myself from sneaking glances behind me as their voices drifted on the wind. Occasionally, I caught my own name, but I couldn't make out the thread of the conversation.

He kissed you, but he was drunk. He probably doesn't even remember.

And indeed, River hadn't seemed to remember. He had been his usual self in the morning, making strange comments about how the yak was glaring at him and declaring that he had finally decided, after much consideration, that Ragtooth was in fact a raccoon crossed with a monkey. His only reference to the previous night was to ask, when I passed him a bowl, whether I planned to throw his breakfast over the cliff—but even that seemed offhand. Did he truly not remember kissing me, or was it simply unimportant to him? It made me wonder if I *should* throw his breakfast over the cliff.

"What did River say to you, anyway?" Tem asked that night, as we set up our tent in the shadow of an enormous boulder.

I started. "What do you mean?"

"You've been sniping at him all day. I saw you two talking last night as I was setting the wards. Did you have an argument?"

"No," I said, turning away. "It doesn't matter."

We were quiet for a while, the rustle of oilcloth and the hammering of spikes into the rocky soil the only sounds. We were quick at making camp now—it all came together in a few minutes, which was a relief, because it allowed more time to rest. We were only a day or two from Raksha, and were all paying the price of our grueling pace. My blisters had blisters, and my shins were peppered with bruises and scrapes from clambering up hills and over boulders. I tried not to complain, because I knew Tem was worse off. His chest pained him—more, I suspected, than he would admit. He had thrown up after the last uphill hike. More worryingly, his cough was now a near-constant presence, forcing the entire group to stop and wait during the worst bouts. I urged him to increase the medicine he normally took, but he refused, saying it made him tired. As he already had difficulty keeping up with us, I couldn't bring myself to insist.

"I wanted to give you this," Tem said after we had finished assembling the tent.

He drew something from his pocket: a bunched-up piece of soiled wool. He shook it out, revealing—

"A sock?" I said. "Thanks, Tem. You shouldn't have."

"It's not mine," he said, rolling his eyes. "I found it this afternoon, when we passed through that boulder field."

My heart sped up. Gingerly, I took the sock, pinching as little of the fabric as possible between my thumb and forefinger. "Well, it isn't Lusha's, but—"

"But it looks about the right size for Mara." Tem was smiling. I felt myself smile back. I tossed the sock aside and wrapped Tem in a hug.

"Thanks," I whispered. I had been hunting almost constantly for signs of Lusha's presence, with little success. River believed we were still on their trail, but I was beginning to panic. The terror that had accompanied our encounter with the *fiangul* had faded, but in its wake was a dark dread. I no longer fantasized about beating Lusha to Raksha—now, when I pictured her face, all I felt was fear.

I had never considered—really considered—what would happen if I didn't find Lusha before they reached the mountain. But that possibility had become more likely with each passing day. They could easily be there already—setting up their base camp, or perhaps even starting the ascent.

Lusha can't do this.

My sister had a talent for many things, but climbing wasn't one of them. That wasn't what frightened me, though—not exactly. I knew Lusha, and I knew that "can't" wasn't a word she understood. It was a quality I found equally frustrating and enviable, and it would serve her well when she became Elder—it already did. Lusha thought nothing of inserting herself into heated disputes between villagers, leading hunting expeditions, or devising complex building projects. She never doubted herself, because she had never failed before. If she met an obstacle on Raksha that was beyond her, would she have the sense to turn back? If she came face-to-face with her own limitations for the first time in her life, would she even recognize them?

Raksha wasn't the real danger. Lusha was.

I lay awake long after Tem fell asleep, tossing restlessly. A rock dug into my back, which already throbbed where the straps of my heavy pack had pressed against it. I had been fantasizing about sleep for much of the day, and yet now that it presented itself, I found myself completely unable to relax. There were no owls here, no frogs or crickets. The ordinary nighttime noises had been bleached to lifelessness, like the landscape. All that remained was the sound of the wind sweeping, sweeping. Unease plagued me, and not just because we were at the edge of the Nightwood. I brushed my hand against the *kinnika* draped over Tem's pack, stroking the edge of a skinny one with a tiny, unreadable symbol scratched into the side. It shivered under my touch. The black bell was silent.

That was when I heard it.

A snuffling, scratching sound. Soft at first, then louder. Its owner crept along the side of the tent, pausing every few steps, as if to sniff its way.

I sat up slowly. My heart was pounding, my throat tight. Tem, as usual, did not stir an inch, even as the noises grew closer. Ragtooth wasn't there, having disappeared sometime after dinner, to hunt or prowl or whatever it was he did when he wasn't at my side.

The noises passed the front of the tent just as I drew myself to my feet. For a second, I hesitated.

Then I reached into the pocket of my *chuba*, which lay across my blankets, and drew out my knife.

The witches are not entirely powerless, the Elder of Jangsa had said. *Nor are their memories short.* Was that what was out there? Was that what had been stalking us? I glanced at Tem, thinking about waking him. But no—I didn't want to scare the creature away. I wanted to catch it myself.

Fingers tightening around the knife, I drew back the tent flap and stepped outside.

At first, I saw nothing. The moon had not yet risen, and the rubbly landscape teemed with shadows. But then I saw it— something moved through the darkness.

A loping, four-legged something, about the size of a dog. It crept from rock to rock, its nose to the ground. I snuck along behind it, my heart in my throat and my knife clenched tight in my hand. If I could only get close enough to see what it was—

The beast paused. It had passed Dargye and Aimo's tent, and was now just outside River's. As it tilted its head back, sniffing the air, a shiver crawled down my back. It was a wolf, and yet not a wolf. It seemed ill-defined, as if made from shadow or smoke. Only its pointed snout was sharp, sharp as the tip of the crescent moon. It sniffed the air a moment longer, then trotted into River's tent.

River.

I broke into a sprint, heedless of stealth now. The creature's shaggy tail disappeared behind the tent flap. Any moment, I expected to hear shouting, or screaming, as River woke to discover a monster gnawing at his limbs.

"River!" I yelled.

I shoved back the tent flap and charged in, wielding my dagger. River's tent was large enough for several people. Within, there was light—a single dragon crouched in the corner, worrying a piece of yak meat. River himself sat cross-legged, fully dressed, on his blankets in the other corner. Crouched at his feet was the wolf.

Which was not a wolf at all, but a fire demon.

I knew it was a fire demon the second I laid eyes on it. Its body was half substance and half smoke, like all of its kind, and its eyes were the color of fire, as if a furnace burned inside its skull. Though it was wolflike in shape, with a soft gray coat, a plump tail as long again as its body, and tufted paws, its gaze held a strange, hungry intelligence.

"Kamzin?" River rose to his feet, holding one hand out slightly as if I were a wary animal. "It's all right. Azar-at doesn't mean any harm."

Can I taste her, River? The fire demon's voice was low as a whisper, and slithered in and out of my thoughts. *Just one lick. I'll be good.*

"Be quiet, you bag of fleas," River hissed. "Do you think that's helpful?"

I staggered backward one step, then another, slowly emerging from the tent. I tripped over a rock and landed hard on my backside. It knocked the wind out of me, shocking me back to my senses.

River emerged from the tent and reached down to help me. I shoved his hands away, pulling myself shakily to my feet.

"What kind of game are you playing?" I was half shouting. "That was—that was a—"

"Calm down, Kamzin."

"Calm down? It's a fire demon!"

"Well, I can explain that." River looked vaguely uncomfortable. "It's mine."

"Yours?"

"What's going on?" Tem emerged from our tent, his *chuba* draped over his shoulders and his hair sticking straight up. "I heard yelling."

"That's just Kamzin, being dramatic." River tapped a finger

211

against his lips. "I'd rather not wake everybody else, so please keep it down—"

"I'm not going to keep it down," I bellowed. "There is a *fire demon* in our camp. In your tent!"

Dargye leaned his head out. "Is everything all right, *dyonpo*?"

River heaved a noisy sigh. The fire demon poked its snout through the flaps, and Dargye recoiled.

"Spirits protect us!" He made a warding gesture.

"Stop that," River said. The fire demon slithered out of the tent and stood by his side. Its mouth was half-open, its tongue lolling out. "As I assured Kamzin, Azar-at is harmless."

"It's been following us?" I said. I didn't like looking at the creature. All I could think of was my dream. The witch. The forest. The hungry fire demon, creeping toward me, and no protection to be found anywhere.

"Yes, he always travels with me." River scratched the creature's ears. "I asked him to stay out of sight, of course, but I didn't count on you being such a light sleeper. You've almost stumbled upon him more than once."

"You've bound yourself to him, then?" Tem said. His voice made me jump—I hadn't noticed that he had come to stand beside me. He fixed River with a hard, scrutinizing look.

"He's mine, if that's what you're asking." River's eyes narrowed as he held Tem's gaze. I was suddenly conscious of a heat crackling between them, cooler than anger but more intense. Perhaps it had always been there, just beneath the surface, but I had not noticed it.

"So the answer is yes." Tem's tone was flat. I knew as well as he did what this meant. River had made a contract with a fire demon. It was a rare feat, and an immensely dangerous one. In the old days, some of the more powerful shamans would form such bonds, but I knew of none in recent memory who had risked doing so. A fire demon could amplify a shaman's spells, combine them with its own powers, but the creatures were unpredictable, impulsive. The only way to ensure a fire demon's loyalty was to form a magical contract with it, which bound you together for a fixed length of time. In exchange for power, the shaman would feed it. But a fire demon didn't consume ordinary food. It drew its sustenance from the shaman's soul—or, more specifically, small scraps of it, broken off piecemeal like crumbs of bread.

Who is this one, River? The fire demon was gazing at Tem. *He smells of salt and starlight. Such power for one so young.*

River muttered something, and Azar-at sat back on its haunches. It didn't take its eyes off Tem.

River, on the other hand, was looking at me. "I'm sorry I had to keep this from you. I thought it would be for the best."

"It's fine." I turned. I felt an overwhelming urge to be away from River, as far away as possible. "I'm sorry I ambushed you like that. I thought—well, it doesn't matter."

I thought that you were in danger. It seemed so stupid now, looking back on it. River wasn't in danger.

If anything, the opposite was true.

I glanced back at the fire demon. It panted lightly, its belly moving in and out, its tongue lolling, looking for all the world like a large gray wolf, but for the eerie hunger in its gaze. It was no ordinary, animal hunger. It was something very different.

"Well, since you clearly don't need any help," I said, "I guess I'll go back to bed."

River tried to catch my eye. "Kamzin—"

But I was already walking away. Dargye hovered for a moment, but soon disappeared into his tent. I heard him muttering to Aimo.

Tem watched me as I climbed back under my blankets. He started to speak, but I cut him off.

"You don't have to say it." I rolled onto my back, so that I was staring up at the tent rather than at Tem. "You were right not to trust him. All right?"

"I was a long way from right. I can barely believe it. A *fire demon*—how could he be so stupid?"

"I don't know."

"At least I understand what I felt now, when he cast that spell in Winding Pass." Tem coughed, shaking his head. "Fire demons don't require talismans—their magic is of an entirely different kind. Elemental magic. Wild magic."

I was barely listening to him.

Tem let out his breath. "This changes everything."

"Maybe not," I said. "The fire demon is bound to River. That means it can only do his bidding. It can't hurt us, or disrupt the expedition."

"Unless River wants to disrupt the expedition. Have you

considered that? What if he wants to do something that puts us all in danger?"

"Like what?" I let out a humorless laugh. "We're already in danger."

He muttered something.

"What did you say?"

Tem blew out his breath. "I said, you're still defending him. How long are you going to keep doing that?"

I made no reply. After a moment, I heard Tem settle back into his blankets. There was a pause, longer than usual, and then finally, there came the faint sound of his snores. That was when I allowed the tears to slide down my cheeks.

I wasn't sure why I was crying. So River had lied to me. So he had concealed something so enormous, so frightening, that it would make any sane person recoil from him if they found out. I could understand lying in a situation like that.

But I didn't think I could forgive it.

It wasn't just that he had invited an unpredictable creature of unfathomable power along with us. It was that he *was* the danger. He had made himself that way, by his own choosing. That was the unforgivable part.

I shuddered. How much of his soul had River already given the fire demon? How much more would it take before he went mad? For that was the only outcome I knew of, for people who bound themselves to such creatures. They became powerful—frighteningly powerful—but only for a time. Until the fire demon took everything from them, and left behind something that was not quite human anymore.

My tears had stopped. They had not been many, after all—I was too overwhelmed to cry. My thoughts were in such a jumble that I didn't think I would ever fall asleep. Eventually, I gave up trying, and simply listened to the moan of the wind.

FIFTEEN

I WAS UP early the next morning, lighting the fire and starting breakfast. It wasn't my turn, but I needed something to occupy my thoughts. My sleep had been poor—I kept starting awake, each time convinced I had heard the fire demon lurking outside my tent.

I put spices, *momo*, and dried vegetables into the pot of boiling water. I had seen Aunt Behe make *mothuk* soup often enough, though I'd rarely paid attention to the process. Still, after leaning over to inhale the smell, I thought I'd come close.

Dargye and Aimo rose soon after, their weariness evident in their slouched shoulders and shadowed eyes. As I stirred the soup, Aimo touched me on the shoulder and motioned me away with her kind smile. I grudgingly sat and watched Dargye tend to the yak. He brushed out her long hair with quick, sharp strokes, while the beast grunted with pleasure. A few minutes later, Aimo handed me my breakfast. It was not as good as Aunt Behe's, and had an odd aftertaste resulting from a bad guess on the spices, but it wasn't likely to turn anybody's stomach. I wolfed down the meal in ten seconds. I hadn't lost as much weight as Tem or Aimo, but my clothes were not as snug as they had been. At this rate, by the time I returned to Azmiri, I would be as thin as Lusha.

I squinted down at my broad thighs. Perhaps not *quite* that thin.

Tem sat beside me. "Looks like someone's taken an interest in you," he said, his voice low.

I turned. The fire demon, Azar-at, was crouched by River's tent, tail thumping against the ground. In the morning light, it was barely visible, a plume of wolfish smoke. But its hot-coal eyes glittered like sequins stitched to the wind, and they were fixed on me.

"River isn't asking it to hide anymore," I noted. My voice was flat.

"No need, is there?"

River himself emerged soon after, rubbing his hand through his hair. He muttered something to Azar-at, and the fire demon finally turned its eyes away from me.

"Where's Norbu?" River said. His expression was distracted, and he kept glancing at the horizon, where a line of clouds was massing.

Tem and I regarded him in stony silence. Dargye scurried to fetch his breakfast, moving so quickly he could have been treading on hot coals. Aimo, warming her hands by the fire, not-so-subtly maneuvered herself so she was standing as far from River as possible. River, as usual, seemed oblivious to the effect of his presence on others.

The *kinnika* around Tem's neck gave a whisper. I stared. It was the black bell, I was certain of it—as well as the one closest to it, which was small and cracked with age. The metal was unevenly tarnished, as if by fire.

"What's that?" I said.

"I don't know." Tem coughed, his forehead creasing with nervousness. "But it's not the first time it's sounded. Chirri said she didn't know what it was for."

The bells tinkled again. The fire demon sniffed the air, as if it could smell the notes.

"Music isn't required right now, thank you," River said.

Tem gave him a hard look. "They're not meant for your entertainment. They're meant to warn us of danger."

"If that's the case, they should have been ringing madly since the day we left Azmiri," River said. "Put them away. The only purpose they serve right now is to give me a headache. Dargye, go check on our shaman."

Dargye scurried to do as he said. Tem looked at me, and I gave him a slight nod. He sighed and left, and I was alone with River.

"Kamzin," he said, kneeling before me, close enough for me to count the freckles on his nose. "I'm sorry."

I didn't look at him. "Why? You only lied to me, and put us all in danger."

"I didn't lie to you. I simply didn't tell you everything."

I gave him a stony look. If he was going to use logic like that, there was no way I was going to talk to him.

He let out a long sigh. There was a sadness in his gaze that I had never seen before, and which was startling, it was so foreign to his usual expression. It reminded me, strangely, of one of Yonden's long-distance looks.

"Why did you do it?" I said quietly.

River's eyes drifted away from mine. "It was necessary."

"Necessary? You're borrowing magic from a fire demon."

"Not *borrowing*. That isn't how it works. The power is Azar-at's. But the magic is mine."

"What does that mean?"

He leaned forward, taking my wrist before I could stop him. His fingers brushed the bracelet I always wore, which had been my mother's. "Who made this cord? The worms that spun the silk?"

"No." His fingers brushed my skin, and though I should have recoiled from his touch, I felt a tingling travel into my bones. "The weavers did."

"Ah." He smiled. "Well, think of me as a weaver. Azar-at provides the materials. But I shape them and stitch them together. In a way, the spells I cast are as much mine as they are his."

I gazed at him. His eyes always seemed darkened around the rims, as if with charcoal, but I knew it was just his lashes. I had spent enough time sneaking glances at his face, as we bent our heads together over the maps, to know it well. He held my eyes, and despite my fury at him, I felt that traitorous thrum in the air between us.

"*Dyonpo*, the shaman won't get up," Dargye said, striding back from the tents. "I touched his forehead, and it was hot."

River's brow furrowed. He glanced at the sky again, his hand slipping from mine.

"He'll get up," he said, "if we have to drag him." He followed Dargye to Norbu's tent, watched by the fire demon at every step. I shivered and turned my back.

Within twenty minutes, the yak was loaded and we were ready to go. Tem had given Norbu a tea brewed with healing herbs, and spoken a chant to ward off fever. It seemed to have helped—the shaman was up, and moving around, but he still seemed pale, and there was a sheen of sweat on his brow. He seemed diminished, somehow—not just thinner but *drained*.

"What is it?" I said. "He was fine yesterday."

"I don't know," Tem said. "The healer in Jangsa said he needed rest. I think we've been pushing him too hard."

I shook my head. "Once we reach base camp, he's staying put. He couldn't climb Biru in his condition, let along Raksha."

"We're almost there, aren't we?"

"Yes—according to Mingma's maps."

"Mingma," Tem muttered, shaking his head.

"What?"

"You've been poring over his maps for days," Tem said. "Ever since we left Azmiri. You and River rely on them so strongly."

"Of course we do." Tem's tone made me feel annoyed, as if on Mingma's behalf. The explorer's hand was by now almost as familiar as my own. "He's been accurate so far. His maps are a reliable guide to Raksha."

221

Tem laughed softly, but there was little humor in it. "They're a reliable guide to the grave, Kamzin. Don't you see that? We've been following a dead man's map to his own destruction."

I felt a shiver of trepidation. "We don't know how Mingma died."

"No," he said quietly. "But perhaps we'll find out ourselves."

We set off, moving with a nervous haste. Norbu managed well for the first hour or so, but after that, he began falling behind. River muttered to the fire demon, who paced along at his side, every time we were forced to stop.

The terrain rose and fell around the base of Mount Chening, which thrust its long spine out into the valley. Then, suddenly, there it was.

Raksha.

We had seen it before, in bits and pieces—a sliver glimpsed between two mountains, a shrouded peak looming ahead as we came to the top of a rise. But now it was before us, its monstrous form stark against the sky, as if the world had parted to reveal a glimpse of some dread realm where no beast or human had ever trod.

A cloud was draped over its side; it looked strangely like a crossed arm. The peak was embraced by the mountains Yanri and Ngadi, connected by uneven, bony ridges. Though its neighbors were also massive, much higher than Azmiri, Raksha loomed largest. It was cloaked in disheveled layers of snow, and its sharp peak slanted like a bowed head. There was nothing welcoming about the mountain—quite the opposite. The longer I gazed at it, the more I felt convinced that somehow Raksha did not want us there.

This was a place for spirits and monsters. Not for the likes of us.

We reached the glacier that afternoon. Though much of it was covered with rubble and snow, in some places we were walking directly on the ice, which was as smooth as a river-washed stone and gleamed blue-black. Water could be heard flowing beneath its surface, as faint as a whisper. I felt myself becoming lost in the sound as I trudged along. There was something lulling about it. It was like music from a ghost realm.

Tem placed a hand on my arm, pulling me to a stop. "Kamzin."

I turned, expecting to see that Norbu had fallen behind again. However, Tem's gaze was fixed on the sky. The thin line of clouds River had been eyeing that morning had thickened into something far more troubling. A storm was clearly brewing. It stretched to the ground in long curtains of gray.

"We should look for a place to take shelter," I said. "Somewhere out of the wind where we can set up the tents."

Tem coughed. "River wants to reach the mountain today. He's not going to like that."

"Then River can carry on alone." My voice was hard. "This time, we're doing things my way."

"Don't do anything rash," Tem said. "Let's wait to see if the storm swings west."

I made an exasperated noise, but did not argue. We continued on, our footsteps barely audible over the *shush-shush-shush* of the glacier. I began to hope we would escape the storm, that it would turn to the west, as Tem had suggested, and miss us entirely. River set a punishing pace; even Dargye and I were having trouble keeping up. Norbu walked behind River, no longer struggling, but moving with a strange, stiff gait that made me suspicious—it was so unlike his usual stride. Had River, frustrated by Norbu's sluggishness, put a spell on him to strengthen his body? If so, it was a dangerous thing—Norbu might not feel the strain being placed on him now, but he would later, when the spell wore off. Depending on how ill he still was, such a spell could break him.

Suddenly, my thoughts were interrupted by a crash that shook the ground, followed by a terrible cry.

I whirled. Behind me, the terrain had broken into shards, fissures radiating from the jagged crevasse that had materialized in the glacier. I blinked, unable to make sense of it. Aimo and Dargye had been behind me—now Dargye lay at the edge of the crevasse, where the ice sloped toward the sudden void, shouting and clawing at the ground. And Aimo—where was Aimo? Something inside me shattered, and for a second I could only stare—it was as if the world had frozen, like a nightmarish scene on a silk scroll.

I ran. Dargye slid another foot toward the darkness. One of his gloves had come off. Against the snow was a smear of blood from where the ice had grated against his fingertips. He held on, but barely.

I leaped across the crevasse at its narrowest point, trying not to think about how deep those shadows went. Throwing myself to the ground as close to the opening as I dared, I slammed my ax into the ice and reached for Dargye.

My fingers grasped the sleeve of his chuba just as he slipped farther away, the fabric tearing from my grip. Swearing, I stretched my hand out again, praying that my ax would hold. The crevasse was deep—so deep I could not see the bottom. Dargye gazed up at me, his eyes wide and uncomprehending with terror.

"Climb!" I shouted. Dargye slipped another inch. His hand—the cut one—shook uncontrollably as it gripped the ice.

"Do it, Dargye," I ordered. Ice crystals stung my throat. I couldn't hold on much longer myself—every muscle strained and protested. If he could gather enough energy to raise himself to meet my hand, I thought I had enough strength—just—to pull us both to safety.

Dargye slipped again. His mouth was open, but he made no sound. Tangled in his fingers were strands of torn, tan-colored fabric.

Aimo's *chuba*.

I shouted at Dargye again, my voice so hoarse I barely recognized it, but still the man made no move to heed me. He continued slipping, down, down, down, until he had reached the very edge of the abyss. I could do nothing but stare in horror as his grip began to falter.

A whirl of movement on my left. "Kamzin!"

"Tem!" I almost let go of my ax, I was so startled. He had seemed to step out of the wind itself, appearing in a space he had been nowhere near, just seconds ago. "Tem, I can't—"

"Leave it to me." Sounding the *kinnika*, he shouted a word, some incantation I didn't recognize, and suddenly I was falling uphill—as if the rules that bound the world together had been upended. I tumbled up the slope, my ice ax and Dargye skittering after me. My breath was knocked from my body as the man collided with me, and we sprawled across the snow, coming to a sudden, chaotic stop.

Before I could even catch my breath, Dargye was on his feet again and sprinting back to the crevasse. "Aimo!" he shouted.

But River had reached us, leaping across the crevasse. It was farther than I had thought, but he cleared it as easily as I had. Barely pausing, he grabbed Dargye by the shoulder and forced him back.

"I tried to catch her," Dargye stammered. "I don't know how it happened; it just appeared—"

"Stop, Dargye." River wrenched the large man back again. "It won't do any good."

"Are you all right?" Tem caught my hand and pulled me to face him. He was very pale.

"I'm fine." I kneaded my hand. It was red and tender from gripping my ax, but nothing seemed broken or pulled. "Tem, how did you do that?"

"Do what?"

"You just *appeared*." I touched his arm to reassure myself that he was there, that he was flesh and blood.

His eyebrows knitted together. "I ran. As soon as I heard you shouting."

"But you were so far ahead." I shook my head slowly. I knew what I had seen, and yet it was impossible—not even the most highly trained shamans could materialize out of thin air. "How could you—"

"Let me go!" Dargye shouted. He had broken free of River's grip. "Aimo's down there!"

Tem and I raced to his side, and between the three of us, we managed to wrestle Dargye to the ground. He was still holding the scrap of Aimo's *chuba*.

"She's down there!" Dargye said again, but the fight had gone out of him. Moisture ran from his eyes and nose. He made no move to wipe it away.

I whistled for the dragons. Two stirred from their napping perch on the yak's rump and fluttered to my side.

"Find her," I ordered. The dragons hesitated only a moment before darting into the crevasse. Their little lights were soon swallowed up. The crevasse, though narrow, was even deeper than I had imagined—a darkness thick as ink lay just below the threshold. But there would be ledges, places where Aimo's fall could have been arrested.

"Tem," I said. He nodded, understanding where my thoughts had gone, and extricated a length of rope from his pack. He made a loop on one end and began feeding it into the opening.

"Aimo!" My voice echoed strangely over the *shush-shush* of subterranean waters. "Aimo, if you can hear me, grab the rope! We'll pull you up."

River was still kneeling at Dargye's side, a hand on his shoulder.

227

The man was sobbing openly now, his shoulders heaving.

"River, can you do something?" I said desperately. "A spell, anything that might—"

"There are no spells for this, Kamzin." His voice was quiet.

The dragons fluttered back into view, emitting soft chirrups. I motioned them back into the crevasse, but they ignored me. The larger one landed on my shoulder, his tail coiling around my neck.

River murmured something to Dargye. The man drew himself shakily to his feet and allowed River to lead him to the boulder where the yak had stopped, which formed a buttress against the rising wind. The fire demon, which had been dogging River's steps all day, stayed where it was. It lowered its snout into the crevasse.

I turned to Tem. "I can climb down, but I'll need more light."

"I might be able to do something." Tem took the dragon into his lap, stroking its head. "Give me a minute."

He took out the *kinnika* and bowed his head over the dragon, muttering an incantation. The dragon's light flickered, and slowly, gradually, it began to brighten. I looked away, and my eyes met the fire demon's.

"Are you just going to sit there, staring at me?" I snapped. "You have the power to help us. I know you do."

No help for death, Azar-at said.

"Aimo is not dead." I shook my head. "It's not possible. Not like this."

"Kamzin." Tem held out the dragon. Its blue light shone like a tiny sun, so bright I could barely look at it. The dragon chirped and flapped its wings.

"Let him go."

But when Tem released the dragon, it merely flew in a ragged circle before perching at the edge of the crevasse, next to its companion.

I whistled to get their attention. "Go on, you two. Back to Aimo. Show me where she fell."

But the dragons merely sat there, chirruping softly.

"What's wrong with them?" I turned to Tem. "Why won't they obey?"

Tem's expression was dark. He lowered his face onto his hand and did not reply.

"No." I turned to Azar-at, who was still watching me. "It can't be true. Please, if you can help her—"

No help for death. The creature's eyes glowed with a hungry fire. I became aware, suddenly, of how ancient its gaze was, how unfathomable. *Death hangs in the air, in the darkness. I can smell it, like crushed leaves. Would you bargain for her life, brave one?*

"Bargain?" I repeated. "What do you mean?"

"Don't listen to it, Kamzin." Tem's hand was on my arm. "Fire demons can't bring back the dead. Whatever it's proposing, it's not life."

Fire demons couldn't bring back the dead. Aimo was dead, then. I pictured her face, her kind smile. I would never see her again. I had brought her on this expedition, and now she was dead. And this had happened in a moment, a space of time smaller than a sentence. Smaller than a breath.

I rose to my feet. Tem said my name, but I ignored him.

I walked twenty or thirty paces from all of them, then sank to my knees on the snow. I kneaded my hand again, barely registering what I was doing.

I should go back for my ax, I thought. If I lost it—not a difficult thing in this shifting, glacial terrain—it could be disastrous later. But I made no move to stand.

I saw Aimo again, leaning against the tree, staring into the darkness. Waiting, expecting against all odds for her husband to step out of the shadows and join her.

Aimo is dead. I saw the words in my mind, but that was all they were—words. *Aimo is dead.* I tried to grasp them, to absorb them into myself, but I could not. They hovered there, meaningless, empty.

"Kamzin."

I jumped. River knelt beside me. His fingertips brushed my wrist, at the gap between glove and sleeve.

"I can't," I said.

"You can't what?" River's voice was quiet. I turned to look at him. His strange eyes held an unexpected kindness.

"I can't keep going." My eyes wandered over his face, registering the now-familiar planes and angles as if from a great distance. "Not now. I can't make it to Raksha."

River ran his thumb over my hand, back and forth. "Kamzin—you're already here."

"What?" I looked up, taking in the enormous, curving crescent of the glacier. He was right. Only a short hike away, against the slope of Mount Chening, was a rubbly plateau sheltered from the wind—the very place River and I had planned, from consulting Mingma's maps, to make our base camp.

We were here. At the foot of Mount Raksha. The great mountain had been looming over us, ever closer, throughout the day. We were in its shadow now, and had been for some time. It had watched our approach, it had watched Aimo's fall. I hadn't expected good omens on an expedition to a mountain as haunted by myth and legend as Raksha. But this?

I shuddered. It hardly boded well that our arrival had been greeted with death.

The *kinnika* twitched, making me start. Tem knelt at my other side. He placed his hand against the chain to still the bells. It made no difference—the sound came again, muffled against his skin.

"The storm," Tem said.

I became aware of the chill wind combing my hair, and the darkening sky. Lightning flashed behind the mountains. The storm would be upon us soon.

"We have to set up camp." River rose, his *chuba* billowing around him. "Quickly."

It was rough going, maneuvering the yak over up the rubbly slope. By the time we reached the plateau, snow was falling, and thunder rumbled overhead. We set up the tents as quickly as we could, pounding them into the hard earth with extra nails, weighting the bottoms with supplies. Then we dove inside.

"We should be keeping Aimo's ghost company," I said. "That's what we'd be doing if we were back home."

"If we were back home, Elder would be performing the death

chant, and Chirri would meditate for three days by the body," Tem said. "A lot of things would be different. We just have to accept that. Aimo would understand."

Aimo would understand.

At those words, I felt something inside me break. The tears began to fall then, hot and fast. Tem wrapped his arms around me, and I buried my face into the soft fur of his hood. It hurt too much. I couldn't speak.

The storm raged on. An hour passed, perhaps two. Thunder echoed off the enormous mountains surrounding us, and lightning flashed, transforming the dark interior of the tent into a fleeting world of gray shadow. The dragons had all taken shelter in the other tents, and I cursed myself for not bringing one in with me. The wind was so loud, the flapping of the tent so violent, that they would never hear my whistle now.

Tem and I didn't talk. We simply sat together. I leaned against his chest, and he wrapped his arms around me. The storm, as frightening as it was, felt right somehow. It echoed what I felt at that moment, my desire to rage and shout.

Something crashed outside the tent. I started.

"What was that?"

"I don't know." Tem was tensed too. "A rock falling?"

"That's not a comforting thought."

We sat there, unmoving, for a long moment. There came another crash, followed by a shout.

I was on my feet in a flash. "That was River."

Our tent opened, admitting a swirl of icy wind and snow.

Dargye staggered inside, clutching his arm. His face was ashen, and blood welled beneath his hand.

"Dargye, what—?"

"It's Norbu," he choked out. "He's gone mad. He tore my tent apart with a dagger, and then came at me."

"*What?*"

"He would have killed me, I think, if River hadn't distracted him—"

I shoved my way past Dargye, plunging headfirst into the storm. At first I could make out nothing amidst the chaos of snow and wind. Thunder boomed so loud I felt my bones tremble. Back in the tent, the black *kinnika* was no longer whispering, but ringing out loudly enough to cut through the storm.

As soon as my eyes had adjusted, I realized the wrongness of what I was seeing. There should have been three tents huddled against the mountainside—instead there was only one, River's. The sounds I had taken for the crash of falling rocks must in fact have been the tents being torn from their stakes and blown by the gale against the mountainside.

Lightning flashed, illuminating River standing motionless at the crest of a rise, his hands raised. Norbu was just beyond him, swaying precariously. I couldn't make out what was passing between them, but Dargye's wound was reason enough for me to believe that River was in danger. I sprinted toward him, drawing my own dagger from my pocket.

"What's going on?" I panted when I reached his side.

"Kamzin, stay back," River said in a strange, commanding

233

voice I had never heard before. It stopped me in my tracks, as if my feet had frozen to the ground.

"I don't—"

Norbu let out a ghastly cry, harsh and guttural. And familiar.

The sound came again, but not from Norbu. Somewhere in the distance, lost in the storm, the *fiangul* were calling.

They were calling for Norbu.

The shaman let out another terrible, birdlike scream and lunged toward us. His eyes were black, as black as the *fiangul's*, and wide with madness. I raised my dagger and started forward, but River shoved me backward so hard that I tumbled down the rise. I heard him shouting at Norbu, then the sound of a scuffle. Seconds later, River sailed clear over my head, landing hard against a boulder with an *oof* of pain.

"Dammit," he said as he drew himself shakily to his feet. "I never should have cast that strengthening spell on him."

"*What?*" I almost screamed.

River winced. "It really should have worn off by now. I didn't see the harm in it at the time—I knew the *fiangul* had their talons in him, but it seemed as though the bond was weakening, that he was acting more like himself. I realize now that—"

Norbu let out another cry, and surged forward. He moved with a speed so rapid, so unnatural, that I screamed again. He grabbed River by the shoulders and pulled him into the snow, his hands around his neck. Without pausing to think, I leaped onto Norbu's back, putting him in a headlock with one arm and raising my dagger with the other. He reared up, flailing and screeching.

Wings erupted from his back—black, curving, enormous *wings*—rending his *chuba* and flinging me into a snowbank. I pulled myself up onto my hands and knees, just in time to see him lean over River again.

"Norbu!" I screamed over the raging wind. "Norbu, stop! You know River; you know all of us! Please don't—"

But another sound filled the air. The sound of heavy wing-beats, and distant screeching that filled the air like a smothering fog.

The *fiangul* were here.

"River!" I shouted. I ran forward, lowering my head like a bull. I plowed into Norbu, knocking the shaman to the ground. In the process, I knocked all the breath from my body.

"*Ohhh*," I breathed. River's strengthening spell had made Norbu powerful in more than one way, it seemed. He had the density of a tree.

Norbu was already on his feet, already reaching for me. But River was there, suddenly, grabbing the shaman by the hair and driving his fist into his face.

"River, no," I yelled the moment before his fist connected with a sickening crunch.

River shouted in pain. Swearing, he reeled backward, clutching his injured hand. Norbu barely seemed affected. He spread his wings, and braced himself as if to leap at us.

"That's it." River's jaw was set, his face pinched with pain. "I'm sorry, my old friend, but I have to do this."

He made a sharp gesture, and the shaman sailed backward.

He hit the mountainside and tumbled to the ground, where he lay without moving. At least for a moment. There came a flutter of motion, followed by another. Dark shapes descended on Norbu's motionless body. Thin, spectral shapes borne upon wings of shadow.

"They're taking him!" I shouted.

"He was lost already." River grabbed my arm and pushed me behind him as more of the *fiangul* emerged from the storm. They glided toward us, their wings spread wide, their taloned feet barely caressing the snow.

"Oh, Spirits," I moaned. "They're going to take us too! They're going to make us like them!"

River swore again. "Well, I suppose there's no help for it. Azar-at?"

The fire demon was suddenly at his side. *Are you prepared?* Its voice was low and silky in a way that made my skin crawl.

"Would it matter if I weren't?" River said. "Let's just get this over with."

He raised his arms suddenly, spreading them wide over his head. Something descended from the clouds, a dark and churning column of darkness. It passed over us harmlessly, barely stirring my hair, but the *fiangul* were thrown into a frenzy. The funnel dragged them into its maw, devouring even those that tried to flee. It whipped back and forth over the plain, tearing long gashes in the new-fallen snow and tossing up the rocky earth beneath it. Once it had swallowed the *fiangul* in our vicinity, it raced after the retreating cloud the others had formed. I

236

watched, frozen to the spot. As the *fiangul* fled, so did the storm that bore them. The blizzard softened to a light sleet, and a patch of blue sky pierced the clouds. Everything was quiet and very still.

SIXTEEN

RIVER FELL FORWARD. He pressed his hand against his chest, his expression contorted.

I knelt at his side. "What's wrong?"

"Nothing." He pressed his hand against his head, and then his chest again, as if he was not quite certain of the origin of the pain. "Whenever I use Azar-at to anchor a spell, it takes something out of me. I'll be fine in a moment."

I felt cold. "You mean you had to—"

"I had to give him another piece of my soul, yes. But don't trouble yourself, Kamzin. I barely feel it anymore." He paused thoughtfully. "In fact, it's sort of tingly."

"What happened?" Tem raced toward us. "Dargye collapsed, and by the time I had his wound bandaged you were—"

"It's all right." I helped River to his feet. "We're fine. Can you give me a hand?"

Tem pulled River's arm over his shoulder, and helped him walk back to the two remaining tents. "Where's Norbu?"

I couldn't bring myself to recount what had happened. "The *fiangul*."

We settled River in our tent next to Dargye, who was still moaning and clutching his arm. Tem turned to me.

"It's deep, but I managed to stanch the bleeding with a healing charm," he said, burying a cough in the sleeve of his *chuba*. "I didn't have time to do anything for the pain, though. What happened to River?"

"He'll be all right," I said. "I think. In any case, there's nothing we can do for him. Help Dargye. I'm going to try to get a fire going."

What little wood we had gathered before was covered in snow, and damp. I piled it together nevertheless, hoping that I could put to use what rudimentary magic I had learned from Chirri. As I worked, the dragons fluttered one by one to my side. They had scattered during the *fiangul* attack, and now surrounded me, chirping worriedly. I excavated a few slices of dried apple from my pockets and sprinkled them on the snow. The dragons set to work immediately—they were not difficult creatures to distract. In that moment, I envied them.

Where was the yak? I dimly recalled seeing her charge down the hillside toward the glacier as the storm intensified and the *fiangul* approached. What would we do if she was lost or injured?

I set aside my troubling thoughts and tried to focus on the fire. I had taken one of Tem's talismans, a circlet carved from beech bark that could be worn as a ring or pendant. But no matter how urgently I muttered the incantation Chirri had taught me, all I could summon was a tiny ember.

I cursed. Tears of frustration stung my eyes, and I flung the talisman aside. Something entered my peripheral vision with an eerie gliding motion.

The fire demon settled beside me. *I can help you.*

"Oh, really?" I wiped my hand across my eyes. "And what's that going to cost me?"

Nothing. The fire demon watched me, still as a stone. *Just a sniff. A sniff of your hair.*

I turned my attention back to the ember. "Go away."

Why do you fear me, brave one?

"First, stop calling me that. Second, I don't fear you. I just want to be alone. Please."

But you're always alone. You're brave, like River. You are not like the others, and so you are lonely. The fire demon tilted its snout toward me, nostrils twitching. *Your soul is rich like honeycomb. Like strawberries.*

I inched away from Azar-at, trying to mask the movement by reaching for more twigs. "Thanks, but I would rather you didn't compare my soul to strawberries, if you don't mind."

I can help you. Azar-at's tail wagged. It looked every inch like a dog eager to please, apart from the smoke fur and coal-like eyes.

We could be friends.

I started at the echo in the words. *You will meet a fire demon on your journey,* Yonden had said. *I advise you not to befriend it.*

I tried to keep my voice even. "Like how you're friends with River? No thank you."

Azar-at leaned forward, nosing at the twigs and branches. The wood burst into flame.

I leaped backward. Azar-at moved away, but as it did so, I felt its snout brush against a strand of my hair that had come loose from its knot. I recoiled as if the creature had bitten me.

"Stay away from me," I snapped, moving so that the fire was between us. "Or I'll tell your master what you said. I bet he won't be happy about you offering your services to somebody else."

River is not my master. The fire demon's tail was wagging again. *I have no master.*

Tem emerged from the tent, his face drawn. He cast a dark look at Azar-at.

"Go on, you," he said, swinging a foot in Azar-at's direction. "Get." The fire demon darted away, back to the tent, and to River. I watched its bushy tail disappear inside.

"Are you all right?" Tem touched my shoulder.

"You shouldn't do that," I said, brushing him off. "It may look like a wolf, but it's still a fire demon. You don't want to get on its bad side."

"Fire demons don't have a good side to be on," Tem said. "I don't care about Azar-at. I care about you."

I shook my head. "Aimo's dead. Norbu is lost. Dargye and

241

River are hurt. Everything's fallen apart."

"Hey." He pressed my hand. "We're all right. We survived."

"Barely," I murmured, rubbing my eyes. "We still have to climb Raksha."

"What?" Tem stared at me. "How are we going to do that? We have no supplies. The yak ran off. Even if we find her, do you really want to keep going after all that's happened?"

"What else are we supposed to do?"

"Turn around. Go home. We tried, and no one can blame us for that."

"Go home?" I repeated. "What about Lusha?"

Tem looked regretful. "I didn't want to tell you this, because I knew it would upset you. I've been tracking Lusha—her magic, that is—since we left Azmiri."

I stared at him.

"I didn't know what I was sensing at first," Tem hurried on. "That's why I didn't say anything. I've never done this before— I've used my magic more in the last two weeks than I have in my entire life. I didn't even know it was possible to sense another person's magic. Like us, Lusha and Mara have been setting wards every night, spells that leave a trace behind. Yesterday, for the first time, I couldn't find that trace. I sent my magic out for miles in every direction."

I felt cold. "What does that mean?"

"They've either taken a completely different route, which is unlikely—or they turned around."

Tem didn't meet my eye. He knew as well as I did that there

242

was a third possibility. I pictured the chasm that had swallowed Aimo, the creatures that had taken Norbu. My mind recoiled. "Why would they turn around?"

"For the same reasons we should."

I shook my head. "Even if what you say is true, this isn't just about Lusha. You know what's at stake as well as I do. If the witches get their powers back, they could destroy Azmiri."

"Maybe there's another way to repair the binding spell," Tem argued. "We don't know there isn't."

"You're willing to take that risk?"

"Yes, I am! Because it's a risk, and continuing isn't—it's death. We have no hope of succeeding anymore. If we go on, we'll end up like Mingma."

"Turn around, then." I moved back to the fire, heaping it with more wood, but not before I saw the hurt in his eyes. That was good—I needed to hurt him. Because Tem was right: he couldn't carry on any farther. He needed to understand that. "Go with Dargye. Take the pass through the Amarin Valley. Use your power to avoid the witches."

"You really think I would leave you here?"

"I never asked you to come in the first place," I snapped.

"You're so . . ." Tem seemed to struggle to find words for what I was. "You're selfish, Kamzin."

"Selfish?" I dropped the wet log I was holding, and the fire gave an angry splutter. "How am I selfish? I'm trying to protect the Empire."

Tem's eyes blazed. I had never seen him so angry. "You're doing

243

this to make a name for yourself. Or maybe it's to prove you're better than your sister, I don't know. That talisman isn't what's driving you—admit it."

I was frozen, stunned. Tem turned away. "You're just like River."

"Just like River?" I said, regaining my ability to speak. "What does that mean? River cares about the Empire."

"He cares more about reaching the summit first," Tem said. "If you can't see that, you're blind. He's no different from most powerful men, Kamzin. That's all he cares about—power. Glory."

"And you think I'm the same?" I said quietly.

Tem rubbed his eyes. The anger seemed to drain from him, and he sat down heavily in the snow, his back to the fire.

"I'm sorry," he said. "I didn't mean that."

I shrugged faintly, looking down at my hands. My anger had faded too, leaving a cold, hollow feeling in its place.

"It's fine." I sighed. "You're right about one thing—I didn't join River's expedition to protect the Empire. But now—"

I stopped. I didn't know how I felt now. Yesterday had changed everything. Yesterday I had watched two of my companions die. My desire to beat Lusha, to impress River, to earn the tahrskin *chuba* worn by the emperor's explorers—did any of those things matter anymore?

Aimo's face rose in my mind. I hadn't watched her die. I hadn't even seen her fall. Her death had been silent and swift. Perhaps because of that, it cut deeper, shook me harder, than the horror of the *fiangul*, or anything else we had faced since leaving Azmiri.

Tem touched my arm. "Let's not talk about it now," he murmured. "Let's just make it to the morning, and then we can figure out what comes next."

I nodded, not trusting my voice to reply. The fire was burning low—too low. I hurriedly rearranged the wood that was smothering it. Tem rose to help, and we worked in silence, slowly coaxing the embers back to life.

Daylight faded quickly, as it always did in the mountains. Tem and I prepared tea and a thin *thukpa* soup, trying to be careful with what few supplies the yak hadn't run off with. Tem took some food to River and Dargye. Dargye, he reported, was awake and able to eat, but River was asleep.

"I couldn't wake him," he said. "I tried, but he just muttered something and rolled over."

I wondered at that. Had using his strange powers exhausted River, or was tiredness a by-product of having one's soul worn away bit by bit, like a stone worn by a stream?

I couldn't fall asleep. Each time I found my way to the edge of rest, I was startled away by a stab of fear whose source I could not trace. It didn't help that Tem and I were in River's tent, as we hadn't wanted to disturb River or Dargye by moving them. I had one of River's blankets draped over me. It was woven from some sort of Three Cities wool that felt expensive, paper-thin yet unnaturally warm. It smelled like River, I couldn't help noticing, like campfire smoke mixed with wildflowers. Not sweet, precisely—a kind of wildflower most dismissed as scentless. I tried to pinpoint what it reminded me of, before I realized what I was doing. I rolled onto my back. River's tent was large and drafty, and I shivered.

Tem seemed to be having trouble sleeping too, tossing and turning, his body wracked intermittently with coughing. I shuffled across the floor of the tent until I was lying beside him. I lifted up the edge of his blanket and drew it over me, breathing a sigh of relief from the warmth it brought.

"Can't sleep?" Tem said.

"No." I nestled against him, burrowing deeper into the blankets. After a hesitant moment, he wrapped his arm around me, and I pulled him closer, so his chin was resting against the back of my head.

"That's better," I murmured. It wasn't just the warmth that comforted me; it was his nearness. The darkness around me felt thicker, heavier somehow that night, and I didn't want to be alone in it. Tem kissed me just above my temple. His hand moved to stroke my hair.

I closed my eyes slightly. River had touched me like this when he had kissed me on the ledge. His mouth had tasted like the heady liquor we had drunk, and though his hand against my face had been cool, it had brought a heat to my skin that spread from my face across my entire body.

I turned slightly, my face tilting toward Tem's. His hair brushed against my face, and it brought me back to myself. River's presence was all around me—and, apparently, in my thoughts—but it was Tem lying beside me, Tem leaning in to kiss me. I felt a stab of guilt, and stiffened.

"Sorry," Tem said, drawing back.

"No, I'm sorry." I pressed my fingers against my eyes. "I don't know what I'm doing right now."

Tem let out a long sigh. "This isn't easy, you being this close."

I rolled over, putting several inches of space between us. "I shouldn't have—"

"No—I don't mean this," he said. "I mean all of it. Going to sleep every night with you only a few feet away."

"Tem . . ." I paused. "I know what you mean. But it's because it brings back memories, of when we were together. It's not real."

"I thought that was true," Tem said quietly. His expression was wistful, almost sad. "Now I'm not sure."

I didn't know what to say. I knew how Tem felt about me—and I knew I didn't, and couldn't, feel the same. We had been friends for so long—a friendship that could make me feel at home even here, stranded in a vast and terrifying wilderness. I couldn't bear the thought of risking something like that, of trying to twist it into a shape it would never perfectly fit.

"I'll move," I said after a long silence.

"No." He sighed again. "You're shivering. Come here."

He wrapped the blankets more securely around my shoulders, then folded his arm over them, and me, so that we were still touching, but with a shield of blankets between us. I could feel his breath against my head, but he did not move to kiss me again.

I felt uncomfortable at first. But soon, Tem's breathing turned into snores, dissipating the tension in the air. I closed my eyes and drifted into an uneasy sleep.

SEVENTEEN

I AWOKE TO the piercing call of a goose. I lay still for a moment, listening as the flock passed overhead, my mind a comforting blank. It was nice to lie there in my nest of blankets. Beyond the safety of my tent, there was a world filled with monsters—Norbu was one of those monsters now, a man I had shared food and stories with. And somewhere below our sheltered camp was a crevasse that held Aimo's broken body.

I rolled over. I wished the dawn would hurry up—it was awful lying here in the dark, running over everything that had happened. Now that I had started, I knew I wouldn't be able to stop. I would have woken Tem, but I didn't want to deal with the awkward place where we had left things. Instead, I rose and dressed. I would sit by the fire until sunrise.

Rather than attempt to find dry kindling in the darkness, I

woke the fire by feeding it several pieces of parchment, then gradually added twigs. It smoked ferociously at first, but after some coaxing, I managed to build it into a healthy blaze.

I perched on a rock, shivering. No sound came from the tents—Dargye, River, and Tem were still fast asleep. I could have been alone. I felt alone. Two of my companions were dead. My vision blurred, but I didn't cry. I had no tears left.

I gazed at Raksha. It seemed even larger, somehow, in the darkness. Not merely large—it was an enormity, the idea of largeness given material form. Twenty thousand feet, if Mingma's estimates were to be believed. Now it was only a shape that blocked the sky, a patchwork of shadow and snow. The wind whistled over the glacier, lifting my hair and making my teeth chatter, even with the fire. The same wind had scoured the sky of cloud. Except over Raksha, where a strange apparition had formed. A solitary, domed cloud wrapped itself around the very tip of the mountain like a ghostly net. It was banded and swirling, and lit faintly by the glow of the crescent moon that hid somewhere behind the peak. There were no stars in that part of the sky, as if they, like the witches, had forsaken Raksha.

So little was known about it. The emperor had sent Mingma to climb the mountain decades ago. From that failed attempt, we had a map of Raksha—unfinished—and the disturbing tales of the two men who had survived. They had spoken of monsters lurking deep within the mountain, monsters made of snow or ice that knew everything that set foot there, and after darkness fell, came hunting for them. Stories like that were easily dismissed by those who knew anything about mountaineering—the rumble of an avalanche or the roar of a snow leopard could easily be attributed to some hulking monster, especially by those suffering from dehydration or altitude sickness, which was often accompanied by hallucinations. But the story had spread throughout the Empire, and many now accepted it as truth.

More than forty years after Mingma, there had been my mother's expedition, sent to improve the maps of the region and find a new route through the Northern Aryas, one less perilous than Winding Pass. My mother had revised the maps, but she had been unable to discover the path the emperor sought.

And now there was River. River, who had made a contract with a fire demon, and as a result had a very real chance of succeeding where other explorers had failed. But at what cost?

I rubbed my head, which was beginning to ache. It wasn't just my head, though—it was my shoulders, from the weight of my pack, and my legs, from our grueling march over uneven terrain. My knee had throbbed constantly since I took a fall while clambering after River one afternoon, and was now covered in a black bruise. And yet, in spite of all this, I knew I was in better condition than anyone else, except perhaps River. Though Dargye complained little, he had been limping for several days from an injury he refused to acknowledge. Tem's cough only worsened with each passing day. The healing spells he cast on himself were losing their effectiveness—as any shaman knew, a healing spell was undone if the patient refused to allow it time to work. Tem rested at night, but like the rest of us, his days had been spent clambering over boulders and up hills under the weight of a heavy pack. To heal properly, he needed several days of rest, preferably in a bed beside a warm fire, not shivering on the icy ground.

I tossed a few more twigs onto the fire as slowly, slowly, the sky began to lighten. I was just about to begin preparing breakfast when I caught a flash of movement from the corner of my eye.

A light shone down among the rubble left by the glacier. It flickered gently between the rocks, rising slowly up the hill toward our camp. And with it came the sound of footsteps—heavy ones.

Someone was coming.

I leaped to my feet. My knife was in my pocket, and I drew it out, almost dropping it in my haste. The light was closer now. I glanced back at the fire, cursing my foolishness. Had we not agreed to use fire sparingly? And now here I was, lighting up our campsite like a beacon for the witches to follow.

I considered shouting for Tem, but it was too late. The footsteps were loud now. Whoever it was, they were here. I tightened my grip on the knife.

Then, out of the darkness, there came a muffled curse. I let out my breath, because I recognized that voice.

River stepped into the firelight, pulling the yak behind him, the dark side of his *chuba* barely distinguishable from the dense shadows. A dragon ran in front of them, lighting the way—it snuffled up to me immediately, smelled my empty hands and pockets, then darted away.

"I thought you were still asleep," I said, tucking my knife away. I went to the yak and stroked her neck. She looked exhausted and wild-eyed. "How did you find her?"

"She didn't go far." River dropped the lead and moved hastily away from the beast, rubbing his shoulder.

"Are you all right?"

"She charged me."

I almost laughed. The fat, lumbering creature had never charged anyone. "More likely she walked into you in the darkness."

River let out a long-suffering sigh, waving a hand in resignation. He settled on a rock with his back to the fire, still rubbing his arm.

"Thank the spirits you found her," I said. "I don't know what we would have done without our supplies."

"Nor do I," he said. "I won't get far up that mountain without my ice ax."

I gazed at him. River, in spite of all that had happened, was evidently troubled by no new misgivings about the journey ahead. I found that I was not surprised.

"How are you feeling?" I said, sitting beside him on the rock. The fire was warm against my back. It was now light enough to see his features, but only just.

"I'll have a nasty bruise, I think. But I managed to roll out of the way before she stepped on my head, so that's something."

"I don't mean that," I said. "I mean the spell yesterday."

"Oh." River shrugged. "It hurts less. Each time less than the last time. I suppose I should be concerned about that, but I'm not. It's a great relief. The first time, it felt like—well, it's rather hard to describe. Like being burned alive, but from the inside."

He could have been describing a pulled muscle, his tone was so mild, rather than the feeling of some otherworldly creature devouring pieces of his soul. I scrutinized him in the half-light, expecting to see a difference there. But he was the same River, to my eyes, his handsome face flushed in the firelight, his hair sticking up on one side—which it always did, unless he bothered to comb it, which was rare. His eyes registered faint amusement as he returned my gaze.

"What?" he said.

I sighed, looking down at my hands. "My father knew someone once, a long time ago, who did what you did. I haven't been able to stop thinking of it."

River gazed at me silently.

"She was the shaman of a village in the Southern Aryas," I continued. "She lived with her fire demon for years, and eventually she—I don't know how to describe it, exactly. Father said she became *broken*. She was powerful, so powerful, but she decided that it wasn't enough. She began sacrificing animals to the spirits, praying that they would grant her more power. It didn't work, of course—she was mad to think of it—but still she kept trying. Eventually, she started killing people. She took several lives before the villagers discovered what was happening. When they confronted her, she just laughed. Father said they found the skulls of those she had killed buried beneath the floor of her hut. Perhaps she thought to use them as talismans."

"That's a dark tale," River said. "I'll admit, I've heard similar things about other shamans who have formed contracts with fire demons. The risk seems real enough."

I gazed at him. "Then you've never felt—"

"The desire to start a skull collection? Fortunately not. My guess is this sort of magic doesn't touch everyone the same way." He looked thoughtfully at the fire, and seemed to search for words. "It's more difficult to hold on to feelings, I think, than it used to be. Happiness, fear, grief—it doesn't really matter what. I feel it, I think I do, but then it fades. As if it's muffled somehow." He looked back at me. "Did you think about Aimo last night?"

I swallowed. "Yes."

He sighed slightly. "I didn't. Not once. It wasn't until I was walking past that crevasse again with the yak that I remembered. Really remembered, I mean. It's the same with Norbu—the man has been at my side for three years. I should miss him a great deal more."

I didn't know how to reply to this. The cold wind eddied over the campsite, and I tucked my hands into my sleeves.

There was a rustling sound from the tent I shared with Tem. Then, low and muffled, the sound of his cough.

"I should go," River said, standing. "I don't like good-byes, they're bad luck. Give Dargye my thanks, will you? And Tem. He fought bravely back in the pass. I don't think I ever told him that."

"What?" I said. But he was already walking away, heading toward his tent. He ducked briefly inside, then reemerged carrying his pack. "River!"

"What?" He approached the yak, pausing every few steps as

if trying to anticipate an attack. The beast didn't even raise her head—she seemed to be sound asleep.

I hurried after him. When I caught up, I grabbed his arm and wrenched him around to face me. "What are you doing?"

"You know what I'm doing," he said, looking surprised. "What I came here to do. Fetch the emperor's talisman."

I sputtered. "You can't climb Raksha alone!"

"What do you suggest? I won't ask you to come with me, Kamzin. Not after all that's happened."

I stared at him. "So I'm just supposed to turn around and go home?"

He removed one of the satchels from the yak's load, checked it, then slung it over his shoulder. "Why not? I know why you're here. You want to be an explorer, to have great adventures. Well, you've had a great adventure, haven't you? And I promise that if I ever make it back to the Three Cities, the emperor will know your name. You'll be celebrated at court, with your pick of the best expeditions that will take you to the farthest reaches of the Empire. That's what you want, isn't it?"

I stared at him. He stood before me, offering casually what I had dreamed of my entire life. The breeze stirred his tahrskin *chuba*. I had gazed at it so often, so often imagined wearing one just like it, the feel and movement of it.

It was what I wanted. And yet—

"If anything goes wrong—" I began.

"If anything goes wrong, I have Azar-at. He's very reliable."

I shook my head. I could think of a hundred words for Azar-at, and "reliable" wasn't one of them. The idea of abandoning River to that creature, whether he had asked for it or not, was too awful to contemplate.

"I've warned you before about trusting me," he said, and his voice had no levity in it now. "You see why. I lied to you. I would do it again, to complete the mission. It's the most important thing in the world to me. I must succeed, no matter the cost."

"You think I don't understand that?" I glared at him. "Azmiri overlooks the Amarin Valley, the path to the Nightwood. If the witches get their powers back, what would stop them from attacking my village, my family? Will the emperor's armies be able to defend us against creatures that can take any form, or conceal themselves in a hundred ways? Aimo died because of them—they're the reason she came with us." I lowered my voice, suddenly fierce. "I won't let her die for nothing."

And I won't let you die either.

He gazed into the shadows. I noticed, suddenly, that Azar-at was there, standing just behind him. Had he been there all along, watching us?

"Kamzin." He took my hand, drawing me toward him. "If you're truly determined to come with me, I won't argue with you. I'd lose—I know you well enough by now to realize that. Besides, I—I don't really want to leave you behind. But please consider this carefully."

"I have." I stepped closer, so that my face was only inches from his. "I don't do anything halfway. Besides, I'm the better climber."

He laughed then, a familiar sound, wild and twisting. Somehow, in spite of everything, I felt a stab of excitement. I remembered the Elder of Jangsa's words. He had said I sought danger, even reveled in it. He had also said I would succeed—though not in a way I would expect.

I thought of Aimo. Was that what he had meant? A success shadowed by sorrow and loss? Or something else entirely?

"Get your pack," River said. "Let's begin."

PART III
RAKSHA

EIGHTEEN

THE ICE GROANED beneath my feet, threatening to cleave in two. I regained my balance and continued trudging forward. One step at a time, that was what I needed to focus on. Not the groaning, creaking, shifting icefall.

The icefall—a deadly mass of broken snow and ice that flowed slowly down the side of a mountain—was the only viable route onto Raksha, according to Mingma's maps. I had estimated that it should only take River and me an hour or two to cross it, if we kept up a good pace. I thought we could reach the summit of the mountain, and the sky city, in three or four days.

It was pure guesswork. I had no idea what we were facing.

I hopped across a narrow crevasse, my arms out at both sides for balance. Despite the eeriness of walking over a moving carpet of ice, I couldn't deny that the icefall was beautiful. It was as if some giant had taken an ax and carved the glacier into strange and beautiful shapes. When the sunlight hit the pillars of ice that poked up from the surface, they shone like blue-green glass. Ripples and cracks in the ice reminded me of the rings of a tree stump, only there was no discernible pattern.

I tried to keep my mind off the painful scene that had unfolded with Tem, once he realized I was leaving. I had told him the plan, which was highly sensible—he and Dargye would remain at camp, to rest and stand watch over the bulk of our supplies. When River and I returned with the witch talisman, hopefully in a week or so, they would be ready with spells and medicines and anything else we needed to recover from our journey.

To say Tem wasn't happy with this plan was an understatement.

"How can you say this is sensible?" he had yelled. It was all he managed to get out before his voice dissolved into a wracking cough. I grabbed his shoulder and forced him to sit down by the fire. He leaned against his knees, coughing until he could barely breathe. Finally, he leaned against me, spent.

"Please don't do this," he said, his voice barely a whisper.

I felt a wrenching pain in my chest. "I have to."

"I'm coming with you."

I would have laughed if it weren't so sad. "Tem. You'll be dead before the day is out."

"I have my magic."

"Yes." I leaned back to look at him. "And if you stay here and rest a few days, you might be able to use it to heal yourself and

Dargye. You need to stop worrying about following me."

"Kamzin." Tem gazed at me. His face was so pale that I could have cried, his eyes larger in his thin face. He had lost the most weight out of all of us over the course of our journey. "Kamzin, you're all I have. How can I stop worrying about you?"

I pressed his hand between mine, pushing the tears back. "Because I'll be all right," I said fiercely. "I promise. I'll be back before you know it."

Tem seemed about to say something, but the fight had left him. His gaze dropped to the ground. We sat there for a long moment, and the only sound was the wind whistling over the glacier, and the rustling of oilcloth. Then, Tem rose and ducked inside our tent. When he reemerged, he was carrying the *kinnika*.

"Take them," he said, pressing them into my hand.

"I can't." I tried to give them back. But Tem stepped away, and they fell onto the rock. The black bell made no sound when it hit, but then, of its own accord, it let out a whisper. I paid it no heed—I was used to its errant murmurings by now.

"You need them."

"Not as much as you do." He picked up the *kinnika* and dropped them in my lap. "At least you'll have fair warning if anything attacks you. And you know the protective spells. I know you do."

I stared glumly at the chain of bells. Certainly, they would warn me that some monstrous beast was about to tear me in two, allowing me time to mull over my demise before it arrived. I could say as much to Tem, but I knew he wouldn't listen. Magic came as easily to him as breathing, and so, naturally, he refused to accept that it couldn't be the same for me, if not for my obstinate refusal to apply myself. I gazed into his eyes, and swallowed my arguments. If it would make him happy, I would take the *kinnika*. But that was the only reason.

Half an hour later, I was packed. I gave Tem one final hug good-bye, part of me hating myself as I saw the sorrow in his eyes. I knew he would spend every moment worrying until I returned. I fell into step behind River, and I didn't look back. I didn't want to have that image of my best friend as he grew smaller and smaller burned into my mind.

Unfortunately, my imagination supplied it anyway.

In contrast to my gloomy mood, River was in high spirits, chattering about rappelling techniques and hot-air-balloon maintenance and the last party he had attended in the Three Cities, and a dozen other things—I had a hard time keeping up with it all. He seemed relieved to be moving again, and determined to cover as much ground as possible by sundown. He paused only to hurry Azar-at, who was slithering over the ice some yards away. I wished he wouldn't bother—I was much happier when the fire demon was out of sight.

"Are you sure you want to bring him along?" River said. He was eyeing Ragtooth, whose lithe body was slung half over my shoulder and half across my pack. He had been waiting outside my tent when River and I set off, looking as self-satisfied as it was possible for a fox to look.

"He's coming whether I bring him or not." In truth, I had been relieved to see Ragtooth again, so much that I had almost crushed his ribs hugging him. The fox had struggled mightily, twisting his head this way and that in a futile attempt to bite. I released him before he succeeded, and so he had to content himself with gnawing on my boot.

"There's something unnatural about that creature," River muttered, but he made no further complaint.

The terrain rose steadily as we left the icefall and followed a ridge that ran along the southern face of the mountain. The snow was only ankle-deep, and the going was still easy, but the terrain had steepened. We were climbing now, not hiking.

We were climbing Raksha. The thought made me shudder with a not-unpleasant fear.

Now that we were alone, with no one to wait for, River and I moved quickly. It was a wonderfully freeing feeling—I hadn't realized, before, how much I had been holding myself back, forcing my steps to assume a slower rhythm than was natural. Lusha had once nicknamed me "the plow horse" for my dogged, tireless energy, and even I had to admit it fit. I would never be as graceful as my sister, who often seemed to float, rather than walk, across the landscape like the shadow of a cloud, but I had greater reserves of strength than anyone I knew.

I felt a pang when I thought of Lusha. I trusted Tem when he said that she and Mara had turned back—but why had they done so? Had they decided the mountain was too much for them? Or had something else, an injury perhaps, forced them to retreat?

As the sun rose higher, I estimated that we were nearly halfway to the Ngadi face, a wall of ice that connected the smaller Mount Ngadi to Raksha. Below the feature, Mingma had added a single note:

Tricky.

We stopped for an early lunch atop a knuckle of rock overlooking the glacier below. From this vantage point, it was stunningly enormous—easily a mile across when it reached the valley, a long tongue of ice nestled between Raksha and a neighboring, nameless mountain. The landscape in this part of the Aryas was little explored, and not all of the peaks had names. I felt strangely sorry for the smaller mountain, which, after all, was still much higher than those that surrounded my village.

"We should name it," River said when I mentioned this. "Why not? Most mountains are named by explorers. Go ahead, pick something."

"I don't know." I squinted. "From this angle, it reminds me of a boot. That curve there could be the arch."

"Mount Boot? I think we can do better than that." River dusted the crumbs off his hands, and pointed. "That little band there? Those are the coils of a snake ready to strike. The col is a hand wrapped around the snake's neck—the peak is the head of a man, you can see the nose and a hint of a mouth. It's Belak-ilen—the hero who slayed the serpent of creation before it swallowed the Earth. He strangled it with his bare hands, even as its venom spread through his body, killing him."

I couldn't help smiling. River's face grew animated as he spoke, his cheeks flushed red by the cold. He looked several years younger than he was, and about as far as could be from the fear-some explorer of his reputation.

"Belak-ilen is all right," I said. "Though I've never liked that story. I prefer ones with happy endings."

"Do you have a better idea?"

"Yes." My voice was quiet. "Aimo."

River's expression grew thoughtful. He gazed at the mountain. "There's hardly a happy ending in that. But it is fitting, isn't it?"

We began packing up the remains of lunch. We were traveling as light as possible, and not a single scrap of food could be wasted. We weren't even bringing dragons, in order to avoid having to carry enough to satisfy their voracious appetites.

River glanced back at me often, to make sure I was keeping up, and I smiled at him, delighting in the simple pleasure of move-ment. He smiled back. His face was flushed, but otherwise he seemed about as tired as I was—which, with the warm sun on my face, and the mountainside stretched out before me like a dream, was not much. The foreboding I had felt at the thought of Raksha seemed to have vanished, unexpectedly, now that I was actually climbing it.

It grew warm as the day wore on. The sky was cloudless, the sun seeming to burn hotter the higher we climbed. Fortunately, the wind picked up in the afternoon, drying the sweat on my brow.

I can do this, I thought as we traversed a maze of seracs, boulder-sized lumps of ice and snow that towered over our heads, or leaned heavily against one another like weary giants. I felt better than I had in days. As if I could fly up the mountain, as if it were barely a challenge at all. It was how I often felt back in Azmiri, roaming about with Tem. And really, what was Raksha? A mountain. I had climbed mountains. I would climb Raksha just as I had climbed the others—by putting one foot in front of the other.

"Kamzin!" River shouted.

"What?" I almost laughed at the look on his face, it was so uncharacteristically serious. Something groaned strangely behind us. I felt something brush my pack, light as a bird's wing, as a shadow passed over me. Then, suddenly, I was knocked off my feet by a tremendous impact.

I rolled, and would have rolled farther, if River hadn't raced to my side and seized my arm. I drew myself to my knees, dazed. When I looked behind me, my heart stopped.

A serac had fallen into the space where I had been standing only a heartbeat ago. It was a monstrous size, taller than two men and wider than the widest tree. So heavy that its own impact had cleaved it in three—long, jagged fissures running through the ice like veins.

"Spirits," I whispered. I couldn't stop staring.

River took my chin in his hand. "Are you all right?"

I let him help me to my feet. My knees wobbled, and River grabbed me again. "I'm all right."

Was I?

"I thought you were finished when I saw it start to fall," River said. His expression was strange—he looked almost frightened. I had never known River to be frightened of anything, apart from the yak. He touched my face again, as if to reassure himself. "The spirits are looking out for you."

"Are they?" I said faintly, glancing at the serac again. I could still feel its brush against my back, see its shadow envelop me.

"Let's keep going," I said. "I'm fine, really."

"Are you sure?"

I nodded, though my knees still felt weak. I wanted to put as much distance between us and the seracs as possible. But we had not traveled ten paces before there came another tremendous groan from behind us.

Another serac, perhaps weakened by its neighbor's fall, crashed to the ground, sending up a plume of snow crystals. Another fell across it, cracking in two. Behind that, three more seracs, one after the other, toppled over with a mighty thud. I felt each impact through my boots.

River was still holding me. "Well," he said, as finally the sounds of groaning and splintering melted to echoes, "at least we're through the seracs."

We didn't speak much after that. By silent agreement, we hiked as rapidly as possible, our breath rising in great clouds around us. As the moments passed, and the terrain opened onto a steep but even meadow of snow, I began to feel like myself again. My hands stopped shaking, and I no longer heard the uncanny groan of the serac echo in my mind. But its shadow did not leave me.

We moved more cautiously, even after leaving the seracs behind. Our progress slowed further as we made our way up the side of a small cirque, a bowl-shaped depression in the mountainside. Mingma's map clearly indicated that this was the best route, though it was exhausting—an uphill climb over broken piles of snow and ice. River and I were forced to stop frequently, to navigate the difficult path ahead. My knee throbbed with renewed vigor, slowing my pace and further dampening my mood.

We didn't reach the Ngadi face until late afternoon. The shadow of the land had fallen upon it, and clouds obscured the hopefully flat terrain above. If possible, these things only made it more terrifying. The ice rose up, up, up—impossibly high and unforgivingly sheer. It curved around the mountainside, fading into mist and shadow, but what could be seen was monstrous, bigger than any ice wall I had ever faced. It could have been the edge of the world, a great solid barrier preventing entry to the mysteries beyond. The jagged striations reminded me of tear tracks, as if the ice was weeping.

"I guess this is it." I swallowed. "There's no other way up."

"Mingma didn't think so," River said. "He surveyed this side of the mountain thoroughly, before he disappeared."

It began to snow. The wind whistled around us, a thin, billowing sound. I shivered, trying unsuccessfully to shake off the shadow of unease that had stalked me all day. River tapped his ax against the ice wall, seeming to consider.

"We should make camp," he said. "It's only a couple of hours until sunset. We'll hope for better weather in the morning."

I squinted up at the mountain. "Why don't we give it a try? I bet I can get high enough to see what's above these clouds."

"The winds will only get worse with elevation. And even if we do reach the top, we don't know what sort of terrain we'll be facing—Mingma's notes past this point are unclear. I'm not getting stuck out in this storm."

"All right," I grumbled. River was making sense, and that was what annoyed me. He saw my expression and laughed.

"I *can* be patient sometimes," he said.

We chose a spot that was as sheltered as possible to pitch our tent. Even still, with the rising wind and blowing snow, the tent flapped and shook so loudly that I doubted I would be getting any sleep that night. I found the bell Tem had used to block the winds in Winding Pass, and muttered the incantation. Nothing happened. I tried again, and the wind seemed to abate for a few seconds—though it may have been coincidence.

"You can put those away, Kamzin," River said, smiling slightly. He made a gesture, and a drift of snow settled over the tent like a tea cozy. We dove inside, where it was so dark I could barely see my own hands. After some muttered cursing, River managed to light the lantern, suffusing the tent in a warm glow.

We ate our dinner in silence, cross-legged on our blankets. Once I had finished, and no longer had my hunger to occupy my thoughts, I began to feel awkward. I had known, when we made our plans, that River and I would be sharing his tent—it was impractical to bring two, given the limited weight we could carry. But only now was the realization of what that meant beginning to sink in.

River, for his part, did not seem awkward at all. He unearthed a small comb from his pack and started brushing Azar-at's smoke fur, which had grown tangled during the day's climb. He murmured to the fire demon periodically—I only caught the odd word over the howl of the wind. I suspected that Azar-at was replying, though the creature did not include me in the conversation.

"What are you talking about?" I said, yawning. The warmth of the tent was making me sleepy. Ragtooth had already dozed off in my lap. I scratched his belly, making his back foot twitch.

"Oh, this and that," River said. "Azar-at thinks you climbed well today."

"How nice," I muttered.

River was quiet for a moment. "I'm glad you're here, Kamzin. It's selfish of me—but I'm glad."

I smiled. "Well, someone has to be there to stop you from tumbling off a cliff because you're paying more attention to the path ahead than you are to your feet."

River laughed. It was a welcome sound, a contrast to the lonely moan of the wind. "I can be headstrong, it's true. My brother Sky used to tease me about it. He said I wanted to run before I could walk. I was constantly driving our mother mad. Quite a few of my scars are from those days."

The image of River Shara as a clumsy child, bumbling into things, made me laugh too. I lay down, drawing my blankets around me. "Are you close to your brothers?"

"Closer these days than we were. They're much older than me—the youngest of the three is eight years my elder. I think that, for the most part, they saw me as more of a nuisance than a brother when we were growing up."

I scratched Ragtooth's chin. I could certainly understand that.

"I was desperate to win their approval," River went on. "I followed them everywhere, particularly Sky. He was the most tolerant of me. To a point."

"Did you fight often?"

"My brothers fought. They still do, though it's not so innocent anymore. They are great men, but they care for little other than power."

I tried to make out his expression in the darkness. It seemed to be a vague sort of grimace. Tem's words came back to me. "And you don't? Care about power, I mean."

He gazed at me. "As a means to an end, it's useful. But power for the sake of power is meaningless—empty air. I've never understood the appeal."

We were quiet again. The falling snow tapped against the oilcloth like a visitor requesting entrance. My eyelids felt very heavy. I hovered at the edge of sleep, unwilling or unable to let it take me.

"I'm worried about Lusha," I said quietly.

River shifted position. "Well, Mara's never been the determined sort, though he'd claim otherwise. My guess is they encountered some difficulty and turned around."

"That's what Tem said."

"Tem is probably right."

"Aimo—" I faltered. "It was so quick. I can't stop thinking about that. One minute she was behind me, and then—" I swallowed. "What if something like that happened to Lusha? What if she's gone, and I never even had a chance to say good-bye?"

"It's possible," River said. "But either way, there's nothing you can do now."

Somehow, his calm acknowledgment brought me comfort, more than if he had denied my fears.

"Is there something else?" he said.

"I don't know." I couldn't put my feelings into words. I only knew that, when I thought of Lusha, I felt fear, and worry, and anger at myself. There was something I was missing, I was sure of it.

River moved again. I couldn't see him—it was too dark now, beneath our blanket of snow. Then he pressed his palm against the back of my hand, and we threaded our fingers together. My heart sped up, but I was tired, so tired. I turned on my side, trying to make out his outline in the darkness, even as my eyes drifted shut. As I fell asleep, my last memory was of a warm feeling of safety, the likes of which I hadn't felt since leaving Azmiri.

NINETEEN

MY BREATH ROSE around me in billowing clouds, and my nose ran constantly. My hands were like claws clutching at my tools. I couldn't feel my face.

River and I had just started up the ice wall. It was painfully slow going. I didn't like using ropes, which I viewed as unnecessary interruptions to the rhythm of climbing, but River had insisted on it. I had to admit, grudgingly, that I was relieved. The Ngadi face wasn't like anything I had faced before. I was beginning to wonder if it had an end—if so, I couldn't see it through the clouds. Perhaps River and I would keep climbing until we hit the moon.

The weather was not much better than yesterday. It had stopped snowing, but the wind had lessened only slightly, and the clouds were low and threatening. River and I had debated waiting an hour or two to see if conditions improved, but had eventually decided to push on. When we set off, I shoved Ragtooth in my pack, despite his desire to stay wrapped around my shoulders like a smelly shawl—I couldn't be distracted by him. Azar-at we left at the bottom, gazing up at us.

"He'll meet us at the top," was all River said.

We had decided to use a running belay—not the safest technique, but certainly the fastest. River and I were tied securely to either end of a long rope attached to fixed anchors along the way. I went first, to hammer the anchors into the ice, and River followed, retrieving them as he climbed. I was not pleased to be going first—not because it was more strenuous work, but because the best climber never went first using this method. River, however, had been unyielding, and despite my misgivings, I now found myself fifty feet above him, hammering pitons into the ice.

I hauled myself up another foot, kicking my toes against the wall until the iron crampons I had attached to my boots found purchase, then stopped to secure another anchor with the hammer end of my ice ax. My axes were sturdy but light, attached to each wrist with a loop of rope to reduce the odds of dropping them. The piton would only go in partway—that would have to do. Carefully, mindful of my aching fingers, I threaded a spring hook through the hole in the piton, then attached it to our rope. I looked down, and River, yards below, gave me a thumbs-up. His face was flushed and speckled with frost, but he did not seem distressed. On the contrary, he seemed to be whistling. I caught snatches of it on the wind, twisted and intermingled with its wild howl. Strangely, the sounds seemed to complement each other, to match in some indefinable way.

Time passed. I couldn't have said how much—all I knew was the steady pattern of motion. Reach up with my ax, pound away until I found a good hold, step up, stab the toe of my boot into the wall, then do the same with the other foot. Reach, pound, step, step, reach. Below me, I could hear River doing the same, matching my movements and speed. Ragtooth poked his snout out every once in a while, sniffing the air, but stopped as the wind picked up and the chill deepened. I heard him snuffling around in my pack, turning in circles as he always did before settling in for a nap.

Sometimes, I envied Ragtooth.

As we climbed, I kept watch on the clouds. A thick mass gathered above us, though it was hard to tell precisely how far away in this world of soft grays and whites.

The wind gusted, and this time it brought with it a dusting of snow. I looked up again. The clouds were closer now—much closer. We were not only moving toward them—they were moving toward us. Fast.

"River!" I shouted. He glanced up, a question forming on his lips. I didn't get to hear it, because at that moment, the squall descended. An icy wind struck me with the force of a hammer, and it was only by chance that I managed to keep my hold on my axes. I pressed my face into the ice, hoping it would let up. After a few breathless minutes, it did, but only slightly.

"River!"

There was no answer. Most likely, he couldn't hear me over the gale. Snow was falling—or rather, *striking*, sharp crystals pummeling every exposed inch of my skin.

I knew there was nothing to do but carry on. Surely—surely—we would reach the top soon. I could continue; at least I thought I could—it wouldn't be my first time climbing blind in bad weather. But would River be all right?

I gave the rope three sharp tugs. After a long, agonizing moment, I felt three tugs in reply.

Setting my jaw, I kept climbing. Despite my thick sheepskin gloves, my fingers were stiff with cold. I was having a hard time managing the ropes and the anchors, and was beginning to wish again that I could climb without them. I felt certain I could be at the top in half the time.

I couldn't tell how much time passed—perhaps five minutes, perhaps an hour. Finally, the clouds parted, revealing the top of the ice wall, only a few dozen yards away.

I let out a cry of relief. The clouds swallowed the view again, but they were thinning now, and the snow had all but stopped. I looked down. River was too far away—at some point during the squall, he had fallen behind.

"We're almost there," I called.

He glanced up. His face was pinched, and he looked exhausted. Still, he managed a weary wave of acknowledgment. Turning my face back to the wall, I took another step.

A tremendous *crack* split the air. I whipped around, just in time to see the section of ice supporting River give way.

I screamed. River was falling—and he was no longer attached to anything. As he fell, for some unfathomable reason, he reached out and drove the blade of his ax into the rope, severing it instantly.

He cut the rope.

Somehow, just before he disappeared into the cloud below, River managed to ram his ax into the lip of an overhang. He hung suspended, his legs dangling over a void. His second ax went spinning into the clouds below and was swallowed up. The clouds billowed over him, swallowing him too.

"River!" I shouted. I didn't even think. I just started descending as fast as I could. But would I get there in time?

I made a decision. An awful, stupid decision I knew I would regret, even as I made it. I shuffled across the ice, glancing down to judge my positioning. Then, gritting my teeth, my heart hammering in my throat, I sank the smaller ax I carried into the ice—a shallow thrust, with none of my usual force. Then I lifted my other ax free of the ice, and kicked my feet out from the wall.

Immediately, I began to fall. Or rather, to slide—fast, much faster than I had anticipated. I dug my feet back into the ice, but this did little to arrest my descent. My crampons made a terrible grinding, squealing noise as they skidded down the ice. I choked on a scream. At the last minute, as I neared River's position, I rammed my second ax back into the ice wall.

Not deep enough. The ax stuck for a bare second before the ice gave way. A shower of ice rained down on my face, a chunk the size of my fist striking me on the chin.

Again, a small, desperate voice in my head commanded. *Do it again.*

Gathering all my strength, I drew my arm back and pounded the ax into the ice. It stuck this time, and I was wrenched to a painful halt. Shaking, I dug my crampons deep into the ice, securing myself properly. I had come to a stop above River, but only just. It was the work of a few seconds to reach him.

"Kamzin!" he shouted. His expression was dazed. "How did you—"

"Shut up," I said shortly. "I'm going to get you out of this." He said something in reply, but I couldn't hear it over the wind. He seemed to be laughing, though it was not his usual laugh. It was an eerie, broken sound that sent a shiver down my spine. Had he well and truly lost his mind?

"Ragtooth," I said. The fox was certainly not sleeping now. He emerged from my pack, the spare ax already clutched in his teeth. He clambered across my shoulders and hopped down onto River's head. River took the ax, though he seemed to have trouble maintaining his hold on it. Finally, he pounded it into the ice, and managed to haul himself up to a place where his feet could grip. He leaned against the ice, still laughing. Tears slid down his cheeks.

"Stop that," I said. "We have to keep going, River."

Still the laughter went on, even as I clipped him back into the rope. Even as the clouds floated around us again, even as the ice gave another ominous, groaning creak.

"All right, that's it," I said. "Ragtooth?"

The fox gazed at me with glittering eyes. Then he leaped back onto River's shoulder. Once there, he sank his teeth into his ear.

River shouted in pain. He flailed at Ragtooth, but the fox was already in my pack again. To River's credit, he soon calmed down, and pressed his forehead against the ice. He seemed to be breathing hard.

"Are you going to be all right?" I said.

He looked at me. His face was pale, but he seemed mostly sane again. "Yes."

"Let's go, then."

I helped him retrieve the spare ax in his pack, and then attached the now-shortened rope to his harness again with a crow's-eye knot. We reached the top of the Ngadi face soon after, having made exceptional time over the remaining distance. It was as if the wind was pushing us up, we were so eager to be off the ice. As I hauled myself over the edge, I found myself facing a narrow ridge of snowy ground, too narrow for two people to stand abreast. Ahead was a small indentation in the rock face that would provide some shelter against the wind. River and I dragged ourselves there, and collapsed. Ragtooth emerged from my pack and huddled against my chest. I folded him into my *chuba*, grateful for the warmth and the steady beat of his little heart. River lay on his back, his arm folded over his eyes.

I rummaged around in my pack until I found my canteen. I took a long drink, then handed it to River. He drew himself up and leaned against the rock.

"Let me see that bite," I said.

River was motionless and quiet as I examined his ear. Ragtooth had bitten clean through the lobe, and blood stained his neck and the collar of his *chuba*. But it seemed to have stopped. I pressed a piece of snow against it so that the melting would clean the wound while it reduced any swelling.

We sat in silence. The clouds below us parted briefly, revealing the valley far, far below. They drifted together again slowly, like a door swinging shut.

"I couldn't think," River said. His gaze was unfocused. "It didn't even occur to me to use magic. I was about to die, that was all I knew."

"It's normal to feel that way, in that situation," I murmured. "You must have had close calls before."

"Never that close." He laughed. I watched him warily, wondering if I would have to summon Ragtooth again, but he soon stopped.

"I don't think there's another person in the world who could do what you did," he said. "I don't think *I* could have done it."

I shrugged. I couldn't meet his eyes. "I don't know about that."

He gazed at me. "I wouldn't have made it without you, Kamzin."

"That's true enough," I said, smiling as I heard the echo in his words. He had said the same thing when I led him to Winding Pass, breaking the spell that had hidden it from his eyes. "Without me, you'd still be wandering the Samyar Plains right now."

He laughed at that. Before I even realized what was happening, he leaned forward and kissed me. His lips were cold and dotted with snowflakes that melted as we came together.

By the time he drew back, my heart was hammering again. He leaned against the mountain and closed his eyes.

"Give me a few minutes," he said. "Then we can set up the tent. I've had enough for now."

"Me too," I said, trying to keep my voice even. I was indeed exhausted, my body one large ache, and I was relieved that I would not have to travel farther today. But part of me wished we could simply keep going, to use movement as a way of shaking off this new awkwardness I felt. The wind eddied over the mountain, its voice a distant howl. We were protected from it here in our little pocket of rock.

"You cut the rope," I said quietly.

River didn't open his eyes. After a moment, he said, "I guess I must have. I barely remember. It's all a blur."

I didn't reply. I was still having difficulty comprehending it. A fall while climbing with a running belay was dangerous—but one scenario was far more dangerous than the other. If the first climber fell, the consequences were usually minor—the second climber's weight would stop the first from going far. But if the second climber fell, he pulled his partner down with him, and the force of that pull could be deadly. By cutting the rope, River may have saved my life. At the same time, I thought, stunned by the realization, he had almost thrown his away. It would have been a split-second decision based more on instinct than anything else.

Why?

But the question felt too big to ask, so I didn't ask it. The adrenaline was wearing off, and I felt drained. Finally, River declared that he thought he could stand again without falling over, and we began setting up camp.

TWENTY

WE WOKE THE next morning to a sky of liquid blue, scoured and scrubbed by the winds to such purity that it almost hurt to look at it. The mountains gleamed in the early sunlight. Raksha's peak loomed overhead, as if it too was yearning toward the distilled sky. Everything was stark, and keen, and glistening.

River and I had entered uncharted territory. Mingma's map did not detail the terrain past the Ngadi face. The air seemed to crackle with anticipation.

The vague unease that had plagued me since the icefall was not dispelled by the fine weather—if anything, it had only intensified, dogging my every step like a living creature. I didn't like the pattern that was emerging. First I had been nearly crushed by the seracs, and then River had been cast off the mountain—both of us brushing against almost certain death within the space of a day. What future calamities did the mountain have in store for us? Could we count on being so lucky next time?

River, by contrast, was merry again, almost as if yesterday did not exist. I recalled what he said about finding it difficult to hold on to feelings. I made a point of mentioning his fall several times, just to see his brow furrow and his expression darken slightly. It was important, I thought, for him to remember what it was like to feel things like an ordinary person, even if those things were unpleasant. Even if I wished for the ability to so easily abandon my own fears and worries.

The *kinnika* were in my pack. The black bell had sounded briefly that morning, as had the burned one beside it. River, no doubt noting the anxiety this caused me, had encouraged me to put them away. I couldn't see any reason to argue with him. They were as useful, in my hands, as a lump of rock. Less—I could do more damage with a lump of rock.

Azar-at trotted ahead of us, his bushy tail wagging. The mountain sloped almost gently here, and we were slowed only by deep snowdrifts—some as high as my chest. A rock face loomed ahead, curving around the mountainside. It was hard to tell at this distance, but it looked taller even than the Ngadi face, with few good places to fix ropes.

I clenched my jaw, trying to ignore the now omnipresent pain in my knee. The episode yesterday had not helped it, and now that pain was accompanied by an even worse throb in my shoulder, from my wrenching arrest with the ice ax. I rubbed it gently, praying it wasn't dislocated.

River stopped suddenly, interrupting my thoughts.

"What?" I came to stand beside him. And froze.

Against the boulder ahead of us, covered in a thin layer of snow, was a body. It lay on its side, facing away from us, arms and legs folded. It was as still as the rocks themselves.

"Who is that?" I murmured, my ears ringing. *Please, no. Please, please, no.*

River bent over the body. After what felt like an eternity, he replied, "I don't know. Whoever he is, he's been here awhile."

My knees wobbled with relief. "He has? Are you sure?"

"Oh yes. Years and years. He must have been trying to take shelter here, poor fellow." River surveyed the terrain, his expression thoughtful. The discovery of the body did not seem to disturb him at all. "Perhaps a storm caught him unawares, and he grew senseless from the cold."

"Could it be Mingma?" I didn't like to consider the possibility, which stirred up both sadness and dread.

"Perhaps, or a member of his expedition." River stood, dusting his hands. "We should keep going." He moved on but stopped when I didn't follow. "Kamzin?"

"Right." I shook myself. It was difficult to stop staring. The dead man's arms curled toward his head, as if, in his last moments, he had pressed his face into his hands. It was not that I had forgotten that twenty men and women had died trying to reach the summit of the very mountain I was challenging. But after days of pouring over Mingma's map, reading his notes, I had begun to see him almost as another companion on the journey. And now, this stark reminder.

The fear seemed to lengthen and grow.

We reached the rock face that afternoon and began exploring the terrain. It was not an easy task. As the winds tossed snow against the mountainside, much of it settled here, creating drifts that extended far above my head. River and I roped ourselves together as we walked, keeping a safe distance so that if one of us fell through the snow, the other would be able to haul them out. While we slogged through the drifts, Azar-at glided over the surface like a puff of cloud.

"What do you think?" River shouted as the sun dipped behind the mountain, plunging the world into shadow. Clouds billowed over us in cold sheets, and the winds grew ever more ferocious.

I kicked at the snow in frustration, nearly falling over in the process. We were over halfway up the mountain, but how we would make the final ascent was a mystery. We had spent hours traversing the uneven bench that bisected the upper third of Raksha from its lower slopes, searching for a way up the rock face. It was possible that a path lay ahead, beyond the curve of the mountainside, but we were not likely to find it in the dark.

I rubbed my hands over my face. I was exhausted—so exhausted that the world seemed enveloped in a heavy fog, separating me from the mountain, from River, from everything. I was moving my feet, and yet moments would pass during which I was aware of nothing, not even the snow crunching beneath my boots. Despite my annoyance, I was relieved that River wanted to stop too.

The rock face was scarred with innumerable pockets and caves.

River had discovered a large one earlier that day that he declared would serve as a perfect shelter—flat and deep, and almost high enough to stand in. Returning to it as the shadows deepened over the landscape, I felt a shiver of apprehension. There was something about the mountainside here—its nakedness perhaps, or the caves that riddled the rock like the holes of burrowing insects, that made me uneasy. I would have sooner chosen to sleep outside in the tent than turn to Raksha for shelter.

Still, once we were settled in the cave with a small fire burning—our first since leaving Tem and Dargye three days ago—and River had piled snow in front of the cave entrance to block the howling wind, I began to feel more comfortable. It was warm enough to remove my *chuba* and heavy boots. After a hot meal, I felt almost like my old self again.

"What are you doing?" I asked River. The fire was dying down. I was wrapped in my blankets in the corner of the cave, watching him.

He looked up from the bundle of string he was weaving with his fingers, forming intricate shapes between his open palms. "It's a trick for divining the weather. If you can read the patterns, you can see what the winds have in store for you." He loosened several strings and rubbed his hands together. When he drew the string taut again, it showed an entirely different image. He peered at it closely. "Hmm."

"I've never seen anyone do that," I said. "Not even Chirri."

"It's very old magic."

"Like astronomy?"

"Not really. Astronomy is a messy way of seeing the future. There are too many variables. I've never had much use for variables."

We fell silent. I was warm, almost too warm, though it was far from hot in the cave. It was as if my body was becoming so accustomed to the snow and the ferocious chill that it had begun to believe that was its element now.

"Tell me about your family," River said suddenly.

I dragged my eyes open. "What?"

"Your family." His voice was quiet, musing. "Tell me about them. I never had a normal family—you have no idea how fascinating you are to me."

"My family isn't all that fascinating." I yawned. "You've met my sister; you know what she's like."

"I know she's nothing like you."

"That's true enough. We've spent most our lives arguing about something or other. When we were little, and I did something she didn't like, she used to threaten that when she was Elder, she would have me exiled to the barbarian lands, or tied to a yak and dragged down the mountain."

River laughed. "She sounds vicious."

I shook my head. "She hated that I wasn't afraid of her, the way everyone else was. I used to follow her everywhere. Sometimes I think she started hanging around the seer's observatory to get rid of me. I always found astronomy terribly boring."

"And your father?"

Elder's face rose before me, and I felt a pang. I missed him badly—I hadn't realized how much. "My father is a busy man. He didn't always have time for us growing up. I know he loves me, though. Even if I am a disappointment and a stain on the family honor."

"How do you know?" River's head was bent over the strings. I couldn't see his expression. "How do you know he loves you?"

I thought. "I don't know. How do you ever know someone loves you? You just know."

River seemed to ponder this. "Tell me more," he said.

So I did. I told him about my mother—her frequent absences, her laughter, her ability to rivet the attention of a room with one of her stories. I told him about Father's desire for me to be a great shaman, my years of miserable lessons with Chirri. I told him about Tem, and how I was always dragging him along on my adventures.

River, in turn, told me stories about life in the emperor's court. He told me about a dinner at the palace, when the emperor's niece had mistaken a carelessly placed dish of dragon treats—dried beetles and kitchen scraps—for an appetizer, and no one had the courage to correct her. I was soon snorting into my pillow as he described the looks on the courtiers' faces when they realized they would have to go along with the mistake. He told me about the strangest expeditions he had undertaken, such as his visit to the Ajnia Lakes, ringed by mountains, where the villagers lived in floating huts and rarely set foot on land. I asked him question after question, and he answered them all.

We talked for hours. Eventually, we fell silent again. The gentle rustle of the string against his hands formed a soothing backdrop to the crackle of the fire. I closed my eyes, intending to rest only briefly. But when I opened them again, the fire was out, and River was gone.

I sat up, rubbing my eyes. "River?"

The snow we had packed over the door to the cave was still in place, apart from a narrow gap just wide enough for a body to slip through. I looked around. Azar-at was gone too. River's pack was still there, leaning against the cave wall.

A strange sensation passed over me—a sort of echoed foreboding, as if something I had been dreading had at last come to pass. I clambered to my feet, my injured knee protesting the unexpected effort.

Something had woken me, I was sure of it. I listened hard, but all I could hear was the wind sweeping over the mountainside. But then there came another sound—faint, almost impossible to distinguish.

Whispering.

I woke Ragtooth, who protested sleepily, burrowed down among my blankets. Once he saw me pull my boots on, however, he stirred and stretched. He hopped onto my shoulder as I stood up and nestled himself in his customary place between my hood and neck.

The whispering came again. It was definitely coming from outside, but whether it was beside the cave, or halfway down the mountainside, I couldn't tell. The wind carried sound over long distances sometimes. I wasn't afraid—River and I were the only ones on the mountain, so what was there to be afraid of? I was only curious.

With Ragtooth secure around my shoulders, I stepped out into the night.

It was cold, so cold. The winds had died down, but even a gentle breeze was fierce at that altitude—it funneled through me, draining away the warmth that clung to me from the cave. The pale slope of the mountain stretched before me like a gray canvas, and snow gleamed dully on the nearby peaks. The sky was thick with stars, their cold light blazing more brightly than I had ever seen. The Winter Tree constellation hung directly in front of me, its many branches reaching up to ensnare the Dancing Dragons. Nothing moved, apart from the loose snow sweeping over the mountain like fog.

"River?" I called. I could just make out his tracks in the snow, leading off to the right. The whispering came again—from the opposite direction.

I wandered toward it. The wind was against me, whipping my hair back from my face. I called River's name again, and thought I heard someone reply.

I stopped in my tracks. A figure stood before me. A young man—tall and broad-shouldered, with an imperious tilt to his head. His skin glowed with a sheen like fish scales, and he wore a long *chuba* edged in gold thread and cut in an old-fashioned style. It rippled around him in a way that seemed oddly familiar.

I stared, openmouthed. Ragtooth let out a long, low hiss. He leaped to the ground, placing himself between me and the stranger, his fur standing on end.

"Who are you?" I said when I finally found my voice.

"Never mind that." The young man's voice was cold and strange. It reminded me of chimes moving in the wind. "You must come with us."

"What?" Something moved out of the corner of my eye. I screamed.

A head—a *head*—floated through the air toward me. Its cheeks were sallow and sunken, giving it a skull-like appearance, and its eyes were wide and staring.

I staggered back, still screaming, and collided with the man— who was not a man at all, judging by the iciness of his skin and the strange softness of his body, which felt like a wall made of wind.

"Take her," the ghost said, and suddenly I was surrounded. Ghosts stretched their pale arms toward me, gaped their hideous mouths. Cold hands closed around my arms and legs, and I was borne away, screaming all the while.

TWENTY-ONE

I SCREAMED UNTIL my throat was raw. The ghosts traveled terribly fast, leaping over chasms and snowdrifts as if they were nothing. As they moved, they swirled together to become indistinguishable, so that I felt as if I were being transported by a chill fog with many viselike hands. I did not touch the ground, and no matter how much I struggled and screamed, I couldn't loose myself from their grasp.

A rock wall loomed before us, craggy and thick with shadow. We seemed to be heading right for it. I squeezed my eyes shut, but rather than striking hard stone, we passed into a cave, much larger than the one River and I had sheltered in. The faint glow of the ghosts illuminated a tunnel of sorts, broad enough for several men to walk abreast, sloping down toward the heart of the mountain. The ghost cloud bore me along, not taking any care to prevent me from bumping against the rubbly boulders that lined the tunnel, evidence of previous cave-ins. These obstacles did not hinder the ghosts—they raced on, whispering together too quietly for me to interpret what they were saying. I caught only the occasional word. *Girl. Others. City. Witch. Demon. Stardust. Coming.* It was a meaningless jumble.

Finally, the ghosts slowed and began to drift apart again. We had come to a vast cavern—at least, I guessed it was vast; the roof was hidden in shadow. Dark holes in the rock wall hinted at passages leading to yet more rooms of stone. I barely had a chance to look around, however, because suddenly the ghosts released me, and to my horror, I was falling.

I hit the ground hard, my arm bent painfully beneath me. The ghosts moved away, all but the terrible, drifting head, which leaned over me, baring its teeth. I rolled away from the thing desperately, overwhelmed by terror and repugnance.

"What's the matter, girl?" the ghost said, widening its bloodshot eyes. "Not regretting your decision to come to our mountain, are you? To sneak around like a thief in places you don't belong?"

"Quiet, Orti," said the first ghost. He was young, or had been when he died. His large eyes gave him an almost girlish look, or would have, if not for his dark, brooding brow. He had an aristocratic bearing, his back unnaturally straight and his head held high, as if there was a hook in his scalp drawing him up. I couldn't help thinking that he looked familiar somehow, but the memory darted away like a silverfish. He appeared to be wearing a tahrskin *chuba*.

"Why have you brought me here?" I rasped. I drew myself to my feet. "How dare you—"

"How dare we?" the ghost said. "How dare *you*—trespassing on the forbidden mountain."

"*Forbidden*," the ghosts whispered.

"Nobody gets away with that," the bodiless head said, with a snort of mad laughter. "We certainly didn't."

I was baffled, even through my terror. "Forbidden? By who?"

"What shall we do with her?" Orti demanded. "Shall we play with her before we kill her? Or watch her starve to death?"

The ghosts began clamoring at that. But the young man waved his hand.

"No one will hurt her. Not before we've determined her purpose here, and located the others."

"I don't mean any harm," I said. "And I'm sorry if I disturbed your rest. I'm here to find the sky city."

A hush descended. Goose bumps spread over my body as the dead gazed at me in silence, their stillness more disconcerting than a threat.

"Luta, Penzing," the leader said at last, motioning to two ghosts, "find her some accommodation."

I was lifted into the air again and borne down another passageway. This time I didn't scream or flail about—I tried to focus on my surroundings, to commit the path to memory. But after numerous twists and turns, I was no longer certain of anything, even which way was up or down. The end of the passage had caved in, revealing a gaping, open pit. Into this pit the ghosts half dragged, half dropped me. I barely had time to take in the terrifying sight of bones piled in the corner, and the towering, featureless walls, before my head struck the ground and the world dissolved.

I fought against unconsciousness, willing my vision to steady and my head to stop pounding. The darkness was absolute—the ghosts had gone, taking their lights with them. The only sound was that of my own breathing, and my pounding heart. I would have given anything to hear the murmur of the wind or patter of snow—something, anything to prove that there was a world somewhere beyond the black place I had fallen into.

After two failed attempts, I managed to push myself onto my hands and knees. My head swam, and I had to lean against the wall, which was cold and damp, and smelled like a grave.

What did the ghosts want with me?

Where was River? Had he been captured too? He must have been—I pictured the ghosts dragging him away as I slept, as surely as they had dragged me. I thought about shouting his name, but I didn't want to draw the ghosts' attention.

I put my hand to my head. Despite the pain, it wasn't bleeding. I held my hand in front of my face and waved it. I felt the motion stir the air, but that was all. I could see nothing.

A sob escaped me. Where was I? The ghosts had carried me some distance, but precisely how far I had traveled off my course was a mystery. River and I had come so far—we had only a few thousand feet of distance between us and the summit. And now—

Now I was lost. And for the first time since leaving Azmiri, I was alone.

Forcing back another sob, I pulled myself to my feet, using the wall for support. My balance was shaky, but I was able to take several tentative steps. Something crunched beneath my boot.

I knelt, fumbling around in the darkness. My fingers brushed against what was, unmistakably, a thin, curved bone, possibly a rib. I jerked my hand back as if burned.

Whose bones were these? Did they belong to the ghosts? Had they kidnapped other explorers and left them here until they starved?

I was shivering. The silence was spiteful; it played tricks with my ears, making me hear bumps, groans, and mysterious rustlings. I knew the pit was empty, apart from the bones; I had seen that. So why did I sometimes catch a flickering movement out of the corner of my eye?

I gave my head a hard shake. No. I would not start doubting my sanity now.

The rustling came again, louder this time, a *pat-pat-pat* as of tiny feet against bare earth. I was certain now that there was something in the pit with me. The something brushed my leg and let out a low growl—a familiar growl.

"Ragtooth!" I almost passed out with relief. Faintly, ever-so-faintly, I could make out the green glow of the fox's eyes, which even in this dark place found a little light to reflect. "You followed me."

The fox nipped my hand and darted away. Now that my eyes had adjusted, I could just make out the blur of movement in the darkness. His claws scrabbled up the side of the pit.

I ran my fingers over the wall—it was solid rock, much of it loose and crumbling. And it was high—thirty feet at least. It would be an impossible obstacle for most people, particularly in total darkness.

But not for me.

I set my jaw. Wherever River was, I knew that he wouldn't simply give up—it wasn't in his nature, no matter how terrifying the situation. So I wasn't going to give up either.

I braced my foot against a tiny crevice, lifting myself cautiously onto the wall. But the rock was softer than I had expected, and it collapsed beneath me with a shattering crash.

I fell with it, rolling onto my back, my injured shoulder spasming in protest. The crash seemed to echo endlessly, reverberating through the empty caverns of the mountain.

I lay there, motionless, suddenly fearing the return of the light—for it would mean the return of the ghosts. My heart thundered in my chest.

All was quiet and still.

I drew myself to my feet. Ragtooth had already reached the top. He made a questioning sound, a low squeak that emanated from the darkness above me. I couldn't see him.

All right, I thought. *First things first.* I removed my boots and hurled them, one after the other, over the top of the wall. It took several tries, but I finally succeeded. Then, balancing carefully on the sides of my feet to spread my weight evenly over the rock, I started climbing.

It was an uneasy balancing act. I had to move slowly to find the strongest holds, but not so slowly that the weak rock gave way beneath my weight. When I slipped, I sent showers of rubble to the floor of the pit. Each time I froze, holding my breath. I focused on moving as silently as possible. I pictured a mouse scurrying up a tree, a spider clinging to a wall—River could move that silently, when he wanted to.

My foot slipped, sending another rock tumbling to the bottom of the pit. I put River out of my mind, forcing myself to concentrate on rock, hands, feet.

Finally, I felt fresher air against my face—I was almost there, mere feet from the top. Conscious of the distance between myself and the ground, I slowed still further, testing each hand- and foothold. My feet, by this time, were scratched and bruised, and so cold I could barely feel them. My hands too were battered by the jagged rock, my nails broken and bloody.

When at last I clambered over the edge of the pit, I collapsed. I felt as spent as I had when I reached the top of the Ngadi face, though the distances were not even close.

Ragtooth pressed his cold, wet nose against my temple and let out another squeak.

"I'm all right," I said. "I think."

It was only slightly less shadowed in the passageway than it had been in the pit, but to my light-starved eyes, that was enough. I could make out the walls, and Ragtooth's small body. The fox darted off to retrieve my boots, dragging them one by one in his mouth.

Once I was dressed, I picked him up and we set off together.

"Which way?" I murmured when we came to a fork in the corridor. Despite my efforts to pay attention to the route the ghosts took, I was hopelessly lost. Ragtooth sniffed the right-hand path, then the left. He growled low in his throat. I took the way he indicated.

"Who built these?" I couldn't help musing, running a hand along the smooth wall of the tunnel. It certainly wasn't the ghosts. I splashed through a frigid stream—there was runoff here, meltwater from the snow blanketing the surface. Patches of the tunnel were covered in ice.

I was soon convinced that Ragtooth was leading me in the wrong direction. The ground was rubbly, and the tunnel now was much narrower than I remembered. I hesitated, wondering if I should turn back.

The fox bit me.

"Ouch!" I rubbed my arm. "All right, all right. But if we end up right back where we started, making friends with a pile of old bones, I'm blaming you."

We turned another corner, and I stifled a gasp. Ragtooth had led me to the cavern—not to the threshold I had crossed with the ghosts, but to another, narrow opening concealed behind a pillar of rock. The air was almost fresh here, with a hint of snow. Water dripped somewhere nearby. We were close, so close, to the broad tunnel that led to the surface of the mountain. I stood still for a moment, weighing whether it would be better to make a dash for it and risk immediate detection, or sneak carefully through the shadows along the edge of the cavern. But as I was making up my mind, Ragtooth let out a growl.

I turned slowly. The light should have alerted me sooner—I found myself facing the ghost I had first met, the dark-eyed leader. He stood with his arms crossed, watching me.

"Well," he said drily, "this is inconvenient."

Something in his voice made me freeze. I gazed at the tahrskin *chuba* he wore, at his strong, long-fingered hands. Artist's hands. And then at his face.

It can't be.

And yet I knew, as I gazed at him with mingled terror and awe, that it was.

The ghost shrugged, seeming to take no notice of my reaction. "I suppose I shouldn't be surprised. You made it up the Ngadi face, didn't you?"

"Please." My voice was barely above a whisper. "Please let me go."

He snorted. "Why would I do that? I'm the one who brought you here, you stupid girl."

"Because I know who you are." I swallowed. "You're Mingma."

The ghost stared at me. His expression softened slightly, some of the bitterness leeching away. "I didn't think anyone still spoke of me."

"You're one of the greatest explorers who ever lived," I said. "I—I have your map of Raksha."

"The map." The ghost looked stunned. "It survived?"

I knew, in some distant corner of my mind, that I should have been planning my escape. The other ghosts hadn't noticed me yet, and if I could get past him before he sounded the alarm . . . But I couldn't tear my gaze away.

Mingma.

Looking at him, I thought I could see hints of the man who had helped guide me this far—in the wry tilt of his mouth, the focused intelligence in his gaze. He was Mingma, but what else had he become, in the long decades he had endured in this lonely place? And why had he brought me here?

"Did you look through it?" There was a wistful note in his voice. "I ran out of ink near the end."

"Look *through* it?" I frowned, confused.

He shook his head slightly, dismissing the question. "How did you recognize me?"

"I know your face," I said. "There's a statue of you in the square of your village—it's a good likeness. The Elder has it cleaned every day, in sunshine or snow."

Mingma's expression was distant now. Something in his bearing had altered, and the unearthly glow of his skin diminished. He looked almost alive. A young man in old-fashioned clothes. "Is the tree still there? The old fir next to Elder's house that all the children used to climb?"

I frowned. It had been several years since I had visited Mingma's village, a tiny place deep in the Southern Aryas. "I don't remember. I'm sorry."

The ghost seemed to shake himself. "No matter. I barely remember it myself. I've been here for so long."

"What about the other ghosts?" I said. "Who are they?"

"The members of my expedition," he said. "We came here, and we died here, without ever reaching our goal."

"And this is what you've become," I said softly.

"Not by choice," Mingma said. "We were trapped on our way to the next world by a powerful spell."

"What spell?" I started. "The witches? They trapped you here?"

He gazed up at the distant ceiling of the cavern. "These tunnels are ancient. They lead in all directions—some to the summit, others to the base of the mountain. You could not use them—no human could, unless they had wings, or were more shadow than substance." Mingma's gaze sharpened on me. "When the witches abandoned Raksha, they left more than their city behind. To protect it from thieves and explorers, they set a spell upon the mountain that would prevent any who died here from escaping its shadow, binding them to this world and stopping them from moving on."

I felt cold. "Why? To punish trespassers?"

"More than that." A shadow crossed his face. "You see, we are not merely bound to this place—we are bound to protect it against invaders. We are the guardians of Raksha."

I swallowed, unable to look away from him. "Why? Why would you—"

"I have no choice." Mingma's hand went to his neck, as if remembering an old pain. "I didn't die a natural death. I was killed—murdered by my own men. By the ghosts of those who died during a storm halfway up the mountain. They didn't want to take my life."

A sickening horror rose within me. "You can't mean—"

"I have no choice," the ghost repeated. "The spell is too strong."

"Fight it. *Please.*" On an impulse, I reached out to seize his *chuba*, or perhaps his hand. I remembered myself a heartbeat too late, as my fingers drifted through him.

The dead explorer only looked at me.

Get out of here, a small voice urged. *Go. Now.*

I took a step back, and then another. I turned to run, but found myself face-to-face with the bodiless ghost, bug-eyed and gaping. I screamed. The ghost swooped toward me, but Ragtooth let out a hiss, and lunged at it, claws out. The ghost screeched as Ragtooth clawed and bit, raking its hideous face over and over again. The ghost finally shook him off, and the fox landed lightly on his paws. The ghost darted away, howling. The other ghosts who had gathered, drawn by the noise, made no move to approach me.

"Ragtooth!" I was astonished—how had he hurt a creature that had no substance? "How did you do that?"

The fox gave me an almost pitying look. He leaped lightly into my arms again, and took up his usual post on my shoulder, his teeth bared.

Mingma's eyes narrowed. He looked as he had when I first saw him—any trace of regret was washed away, as if it had never been. All that remained was bitterness, raw as a wound.

I made a run for it, but one of the ghosts reached out with its ice-fog hand and tripped me. I landed hard, my hands scraping against the rock. The fox tumbled tail over snout until he collided with a rock and was still.

"Ragtooth!" I cried. I lurched toward him, but the ghosts were in the way, a swirling, whispering mass.

"Where are your companions?" Mingma's voice was calm, as if I did not lie bleeding at his feet. "How many were you traveling with?"

"I have no idea where they are," I spat. Let him think there were others besides River—let him think there was an army. "And if I did, I wouldn't tell you."

"We'll find them," Mingma said, nodding to the jeering ghosts. "As for you, Kamzin, I'm afraid we can't have you escaping again."

I drew myself to my feet. The ghosts surrounded me, blocking my path to the tunnel.

"How should we do it?" one of the ghosts demanded. "Throw her over the cliff?"

Mingma face darkened. "That's an unpleasant end."

"That's the whole *point*," the ghost said, but Mingma held up his hand, and they fell silent.

Mingma made another motion, and before I could even open my mouth, I was lifted in the air and borne to the back of the cave.

"Mingma!" I shouted. "Don't do this, please—"

The sound of water grew louder. What was this? Did they intend to drown me? No sooner did I have the thought than I was falling onto a sheet of ice that cracked under my weight.

The cold hit me like a boulder, and I was breathless, gasping. Water flooded my lungs. I couldn't breathe. I was choking. Dying.

I pushed at the ice that closed over me—it was thin, and my fist punched through it. But the ghosts were all around, drifting through the water, pulling me down as I fought to rise.

Forbidden, they whispered. *Forbidden*.

After what felt like an age, my head broke the surface. I choked on the air as if it too were a foreign element. Tremors wracked my body.

They had dropped me in a shallow pool, fed by some unseen stream that trickled out of the rocks. But I was clumsy, as if I had suddenly become twice my normal weight, pulled down by my boots, now filled with ice water, and my sodden clothing.

I tried to swim, each breath rattling in my lungs. The ghosts swirled through the water like luminous ink, tugging at my *chuba*, pulling me under again. I fought my way to the surface, choking on a scream.

Mingma stood by the edge of the pool, watching. Other ghosts hovered in the air, whispering together.

"Don't do this," I croaked.

"Don't worry," Mingma said. "This way isn't so bad, really. Soon you won't feel anything. And then, before you know it, you'll be one of us." He almost seemed to smile, and I saw a hint of the man I had glimpsed before. "I think I'll enjoy the change of company."

The cold burrowed inside me. It was as if my very bones had frozen. Even if I could drag myself out of the water, I was doomed without a blazing fire and dry clothes. The only question now was how long it would take for the cold to defeat me—to slow my limbs, and then my breath. My mind flashed to the story of what River had done to an enemy—taken his cloak and left him bound in the snow. That sort of death was slow, but as sure as an arrow to the heart. The cold was death itself—this had been drilled into me, and all the village children, since we could speak.

A look of understanding passed over Mingma's face. "It's all right, Kamzin. You don't need to be afraid."

Anger made my sluggish blood quicken. "No, but you do," I forced out through my teeth. "When River finds you—"

"No one will come for you," he said. He knelt beside me, his voice a hiss. "You think I enjoy this? You think I want to watch you die? I'm trapped, Kamzin. As trapped as you are."

"I think you don't even try," I snapped. Each word caught in my throat, but I forced them out anyway. "I think you're bitter because you're stuck here—and now you want me to suffer the way you have."

Mingma drew himself up, his expression hard. "You don't understand. But you will, soon enough."

"Kamzin?"

I was seized by a desperate relief. "River!" My voice broke, barely above a whisper. "I'm here!"

A light trembled along the tunnel, growing stronger and stronger, and then River burst into view, one hand cupped beneath a hovering flame. He halted, seeming to take in the scene before him—the ghosts, the dark cave, the pool of ice.

"Hello, River," the dead explorer said. "Nice of you to stop by and save us the effort of capturing you."

"Mingma, I presume?" River transferred the flame to his other hand. "I wish I could say it was a pleasure to meet you."

The two explorers gazed at each other like contorted mirror images in their tahrskin *chubas*. Both wore the pale side, so that they seemed like two smudges of light against the darkness.

"Let her go," River said, his voice quiet but carrying.

The ghosts made no reply. Slowly, they drifted closer to River, keeping to the shadows. They were all eyeing the flame in his hand—ghosts hated light, it was true, but was that hatred strong enough to protect him? He did not flinch as they surrounded him.

Mingma let out a short, harsh laugh. "You can't be the Royal Explorer, surely? How ridiculous. Is the emperor hiring children now? Things were much different in my day."

"Your day is long gone," River replied. "It's time you moved on."

"Past time." The bitterness entered Mingma's tone again. "What difference does it make?"

Something like regret crossed River's face. He raised his hand, and the flame burned brighter. The ghosts stopped their advance—some even took a step back. The flame rose into the air, a sphere of white light. It struck the ceiling of the cavern, where it grew and grew, hovering like a massive chandelier, sending small flames cascading down.

The ghosts shrieked, diving for the shadows. Mingma let out a cry of anger as he too retreated to the edge of the cavern.

River flashed me a smile, and then he was gone, darting down one of the tunnels, away from the light. The ghosts poured after him.

I hauled myself out of the ice-water, my fingers so numb it took three tries before I could maintain my hold. I tried to stand, but my body wouldn't cooperate. I couldn't feel my feet; they clung to my legs like stone blocks.

"Kamzin."

I started. A hand touched my shoulder; mismatched eyes peered into mine. "River, how—"

"Azar-at is leading the ghosts on a chase," he said. "A distraction—we don't have much time. Can you move?"

He took hold of my chin, his thumb brushing my cheek, and examined me. "You're like ice." He wrapped his arm around my waist and hauled me up.

"I'm fine." I took a step, and immediately, my legs buckled. I was shaking so hard I felt as if I could come apart. River looped his arm around me and helped me walk.

"Wait—Ragtooth!" I cried, spying his limp body. Grimacing slightly, River lifted the fox by the scruff of his neck and stuffed him in his pack. Ragtooth stirred, and I felt a wave of relief. River pulled me close again, and we limped on.

Distant crashes shook the ground, and shouts echoed through the mountain. "What's going on?"

"Azar-at is sealing the cavern," River said, "melting the rock with fire and weaving it with a spell the ghosts won't be able to penetrate. They won't trouble us again." I gazed at him, startled by the barely contained fury in his voice. His arm tightened around me, his hand gripping my hip as if at any moment he expected me to be torn from his side.

"You're—you're sealing them in?" I breathed. "Can't you set them free?"

"The spell that prevents them from crossing over is ancient, and as strong as the mountain itself. It's possible that I could break it, but it would cost more than I'm willing to sacrifice."

Water sloshed around my boots. We were wading through a stream that had not been there before. It was growing, spreading across the cavern floor.

River dragged me through the water, which began to lap around my ankles. "The fire," he muttered. "Azar-at's spell. It's melting the snow above the tunnels."

"What?" How could he not have considered that?

"I was in a hurry," River said. "I'm not sure I fully thought this plan through—"

"Do you ever?" Fear brought some of the feeling back to my limbs. The water rose rapidly, swirling around us in powerful currents. We plunged into the tunnel that led to the surface, gaining elevation with every step. Still the water surged, lapping almost to my waist. It lifted me off my feet, but River kept his grip on me, and finally we broke free of the torrent. I bit down on a scream as I looked back. The cavern was now completely flooded.

And rising through the flood was Mingma, one hand outstretched, eyes wide with some terrible combination of horror, hatred, fear. River yanked me back around, and we sprinted the final distance, bursting out of the mountain and into the light of a gray sunrise. River let out a wordless shout as we fell forward onto the snow, throwing his hand out. The rock behind us seemed to glow and melt. It crumbled, sealing the shadowy entrance with a surprisingly soft sound like a sigh, and it was as if the tunnel had never been.

TWENTY-TWO

CLOUDS GATHERED ALONG the horizon, their gray backs brushed with pink and gold. The sunlight was already spilling over the mountain, igniting the snow. After being so long in darkness, the sight made my eyes ache. I lay still, overwhelmed.

"Hey." River lifted me upright, his voice low and urgent. "Kamzin. Stay with me."

Stay with him? Where else was I going to go? Then it occurred to me that he had interpreted my stillness as a sign of dire health. I made no move to discourage the notion—I felt breathless and bloodless, as if I were suspended in ice.

"Let's get this off." River unbuttoned my sodden, ice-crusted *chuba*, drawing it over my shoulders. He stopped suddenly, as if realizing what he was doing, and an unfamiliar color entered his cheeks.

He was *blushing*. I blinked. I had never seen River blush before—it wasn't something I had thought he was even capable of.

"Azar-at," he called. I couldn't see the fire demon—it was beyond my range of vision—but I felt it when River's hands on my arms grew warm, a warmth that spread across my body. The moisture rose from my clothes and skin in a cloud that was borne away by the wind. I began to shiver again as I dried. The warmth remained when River removed his hands.

I stood slowly. I felt strange. River had never used his magic on me before, and the sensation was . . . befuddling. It felt different from Chirri's magic, or Tem's. Was that because it came from a fire demon?

The power is Azar-at's, he had said, *but the magic is mine.*

The warmth lingered on my skin, on every inch of me. He returned my gaze, and I realized that he could feel the spell too. I looked away, color spreading across my own face. As I did, my gaze fell on the tunnel, or the place where the tunnel had been. And I felt the chill of water like knives burrowing into my bones, and saw Mingma's remorseless face looming over me.

I pulled myself to my feet, stumbling only slightly. Then I began to march away, very fast, not looking back.

"Kamzin?" River had to jog to catch up with me. "Slow down; you don't have your strength back—"

"This is the way back to camp?" I said, not slowing.

"Yes, but—"

"Good." I clambered over a boulder, banging my knee. That didn't slow me either. "We'll gather up our things and set out for

315

the Ngadi face. If we move fast we can reach it by nightfall."

River grabbed my arm, but I threw him off. "You want to give up?"

"I'm not giving up," I snapped, my tone so ferocious that River took a step back. "You can't give up when you had no hope of succeeding."

"Kamzin—"

"They'll win, River."

"Who will?"

"The witches." I stopped and faced him. "This is their mountain. They have the power—they trapped Mingma and his men, turned them into evil things, just like they are." I saw Mingma's face again, rising toward me out of the water, saw him trapped there in the darkness as minutes turned to days, and days to years—I shoved the image back, because it was too much. "Do you know who Mingma was?"

He gazed at me, silent, his mouth a thin line.

"He was a great man. My father's library is filled with scrolls about his heroism. He drew half the maps of the Empire. He was fearless, brave. And the witches defeated him without even raising a finger."

River rubbed his eyes. He was still soaked, I noticed, though the cold didn't seem to trouble him.

"This is their world," I went on, "and it doesn't want us here. What will happen when we reach the summit? When we find their city?" I shook my head. "Tem was right. This expedition is madness—we're much better off returning to base camp and figuring out another way to defeat them."

I watched him, waiting for him to argue with me. To say that we couldn't return, that there *was* no other way to defeat the witches. To talk me out of leaving.

"I'm sorry," he said.

I started. "What?"

"I should never have agreed to this," he said, seeming to speak half to himself. "I shouldn't have brought you this far. You should have stayed back at camp, where you were safe."

Something was rising in me, something darker than anger. I could have hit him. My desire to get off the mountain as quickly as possible was all but forgotten.

"You should have left me where I was *safe*?" I said. "As if I'm some frightened child? Where would you be if you had left me back at base camp? Dead, that's where. Have you forgotten how I saved your life? Your recklessness would have—"

"*My* recklessness?" Suddenly, River seemed as furious as I was. "You're the one who decided to go for a late-night stroll, right into an army of ghosts! Why on earth did you leave the cave and the protection of the warding spells?"

"I was looking for you!" I snapped. "Why did *you* leave the cave?"

"To chase the ghosts away, of course. How do you think I felt when I returned and found you gone? When I realized they had taken you, that you could already be dead?"

I stared. "I don't know."

River glowered at me. "You're an idiot, Kamzin."

317

We glared at each other, and I felt as if I *would* hit him. That infuriatingly handsome face wouldn't be so perfect with a black eye or a missing tooth. My entire body seemed to pulse, as if the warmth he had pressed into my skin had turned to fire and was consuming me. Then, suddenly, he pulled me into his arms, pressing his hand against the back of my head so that my face was buried in his shoulder.

I folded myself into his embrace, as if I were not holding him but melting against his body. As wondrous as it felt, it was also strange, because he was River Shara, and the Royal Explorer, and the most powerful shaman I had ever met, and I knew I shouldn't be doing this. And yet he was also just River, who had become my friend and who I now trusted with my life. He ran his fingers through my hair, brushing it off my face. He was gripping me so tightly that I could barely breathe. I didn't mind. I lifted my face to his and kissed him.

River's magic still brushed my skin, but the warmth that overwhelmed me didn't come from that. This kiss was different than the half-drunken kiss we had shared on the cliff. That kiss had set my heart pounding, but this one was as heady as a barrel of *raksi*. Kissing River reminded me of dark forests and night skies. It was nothing like kissing Tem, or any of the village boys I had kissed because someone dared me. As different as night from day.

It lasted only a moment, and then River drew back. His hand was still pressed against my face, his thumb and forefinger framing my eye.

"What?" I murmured.

River stepped away, a familiar veil dropping over his expression. "We need to get you back to camp. Make sure that water didn't give you frostbite—it can set in without you noticing."

I stared at him. He turned to walk away, but I grabbed his arm. "Why do you keep doing that?"

"Doing what?"

"Pretending you don't care about me. That I'm just some assistant you hired to carry your bags or cook your dinner."

"I do care about you, Kamzin," he said, a knife edge in his voice. "That isn't why we can't do this."

"Why, then?" Anger rose within me again, and I had to grip the sleeves of my *chuba* to keep from lashing out. I had almost died. And somehow that had broken something, some reluctance or fear that had prevented me from voicing what I felt. I was frightened, and exhausted, and *furious*. I would make him talk to me. I would make him admit what I knew to be true—that he felt the same about me as I did about him.

"Is it because you're of noble blood, and I'm not?" I demanded. "Because after this is over, I'll go back to my village, and you'll go back to some palace in the Three Cities?"

"No. If you were someone else, any other girl, I wouldn't think twice."

I made an exasperated sound. "So the reason you won't kiss me is because you care about me?"

River let out a sigh of relief. "Yes! That's it exactly. I'm glad you understand."

319

"I understand that you're a lunatic," I growled. "But I already knew that."

My hand was still on his arm, and his face was only a foot from mine. The veil had slipped, and his expression was an odd combination of confusion, anger, and longing. So I pulled him closer and kissed him again.

He hesitated at first, but then suddenly he was kissing me back, with a forcefulness that took me by surprise. I was lifted off my feet and propelled backward until I was pressed against the rock face. I wrapped my arms around him, tightening my hold, heedless of the uneven rocks pressing into my back. River ran his hand over me until I found myself cursing the layers of clothing that separated us. It was as if the feeling that had been building between us all this time had exploded, and we were both giddy with it. I wanted him to kiss me until the snow melted, until Raksha was worn to nothing by the ice and the winds.

"Would you like me to give you two a moment?" said a voice.

River pulled away sharply, and I slid down the rock, landing with a soft *oof* in the snow. Standing behind us, framed against the distant peaks and valleys, was Mara.

TWENTY-THREE

THE CHRONICLER'S FACE was creased with fatigue and shadowed with an unkempt beard. His *chuba* was torn and stained with mud at the hem. He seemed thinner, or perhaps it was only weariness that bent his shoulders and made him a less imposing figure than I remembered. His gaze, though, was clear, and he seemed unhurt.

"Mara!" For a moment, I could get no other words out, I was so astonished. Was he a ghost himself, to have appeared like this in our midst? Then I was on my feet and racing to his side. I grabbed his arm—he was flesh and blood.

"Where is Lusha?" I demanded. "Is she with you? Is she all right? How did you get here? *When* did you get here? How did you find us?"

He shook off my hand. "Your sister is fine. We noticed your

tracks last night, and followed them to your camp in the cave. I volunteered to set out at first light to search for you."

"But how?" I stared at him, happier to see his haughty profile than I ever could have imagined. "I thought you must have turned back. I thought you could be—could be—"

Could be dead, I wanted to say, but couldn't. Mara took no notice of my hesitation—he had barely glanced at me. His gaze was fixed on River.

"Mara," River said, in a quiet voice that nonetheless carried over the wind. "You've exceeded my expectations. I doubted you would make it this far."

"Hello, River." Mara's disdainful expression slipped slightly. He raised his chin, as if to compensate. "I'm glad I'm able to surprise you once in a while."

"You know I don't like surprises," River said. His expression was calm, but a darkness lurked beneath it.

"I can see you're angry—" Mara began.

"Why would I be angry?" River said. "You only stole my supplies, my assistant. You've attempted to steal my title."

I felt a twinge of surprise, and a hurt sort of irritation. Was River still upset about Lusha choosing Mara over him?

"And after this," he continued, his voice low but eerily carrying, "you have the audacity to survive long enough to find yourself in my presence again."

Though Mara's mouth was set in a hard line, I saw it tremble slightly before he mastered himself.

He's afraid. And with good reason. I recalled the stories of what

River did to those who betrayed him. And I didn't doubt that Mara had seen demonstrations of River's power.

"You talk of betrayal?" Mara said. "Of loyalty? How am I to remain loyal to someone who has deceived me for so long?"

I stared at him, baffled. River took a step forward, his expression stormy. "How have I deceived you?"

Mara didn't reply. He watched River as one might watch a dangerous animal. I looked from one to the other. This was ridiculous. They were going to come to blows, here, after all that had happened. After I had just learned that Lusha was safe.

"River," I said, touching his arm. "I want to see my sister."

He blinked, and something within him seemed to recede. "Yes. Of course you do. Lead the way, Mara."

The chronicler gave him a long look. He walked past us, giving River a wide berth. I could have run after him, but River grabbed my arm.

"Are you all right?"

"Yes," I said. I felt perfectly warm, and though his magic still hummed distractingly against my skin, the sensation was fading. "Your spell—"

"That's not what I mean."

Something in his tone made me think again of the ghosts, and the chill water wrapping me in its deathly embrace. Somehow that chill still burrowed inside me, though I felt warm enough on the surface. I looked away.

"I think so."

River shook his head, dismissing my words. He took my chin

gently in his hand, sending a shiver down my spine. Then, just as gently, he brushed my lips with his.

Some of the ice melted.

River turned. "Come, Azar-at."

I started. I had almost forgotten the fire demon was there, perched by the mouth of the cave, gazing at us. It had surely been watching as River and I kissed, as we almost—what? I shivered, despite River's spell. Azar-at's fiery gaze was calm, patient. So like a wolf, and yet so unlike. Even when I turned away, I knew that its eyes were still on me.

"What?" River's pack was *moving*. He wrenched it from his back and dropped it in the snow. A horrible growling emanated from somewhere within its depths.

I laughed with surprise. I knew that growl. "Ragtooth! We forgot all about you."

The pack continued to emit menacing sounds. The fox had woken up in an unfamiliar place, and he was not happy about it. The pack began to roll down the slope, writhing, until I caught it and yanked the creature out. Ragtooth leaped up my back and wound himself around my shoulders, nipping my ear.

River looked into his pack, letting out a cry of dismay. He lifted what looked like a handful of ribbons. "That rabid beast shredded my spare shirt."

"Sorry," I said. Ragtooth made a sound that was almost a snort.

By the time we arrived back at the cave, it was full morning. In front of it, someone had built a fire, which silhouetted a hunched figure. The sound of our boots made him turn.

He was pale, with a faint sheen of sweat upon his brow. When our eyes met, his face lit up with such unbridled relief and joy that I let out a cry.

"Tem!" I ran to him and threw my arms around his neck. "What are you doing here?" The dragons fluttered out of the cave, wheeling in a circle around us as if they too were delighted by our reunion.

Tem hugged me back, so tightly I could barely breathe. "Kamzin. You're all right."

"Why wouldn't I be?" I drew back, half laughing, wiping the tears from my eyes.

He touched my face, then drew back, frowning. "Your hair is wet."

"It's a long story. Tem, how did you—"

"Lusha and Mara found us," Tem said. "They were camped on the far side of the glacier. They saw our fire and hiked over. Showed up only a few hours after you left. Dargye just about fell over, he was so startled."

"Where is Dargye?"

"Back at camp with the yak." Tem shook his head. "He was in no shape to go any farther, with his injured arm. Lusha, Mara, and I followed your tracks in the snow to the Ngadi face, and I used my magic to help us up."

"You used your magic." I gazed at him, amazed yet again by the evidence of my unassuming best friend's power. "Tem—"

"I know, I know," he said. "You wanted me to stay behind. But

I couldn't, no matter what it cost me. Not after what Lusha told me."

"What?" I said. Something flitted by overhead, momentarily blotting out the sun. "What did she say? Where is she?"

Tem's gaze drifted. The shadow flitted by again, and then a sharp cry shattered the air—

A raven's call.

"What—" I began, before something black and flapping descended on my head. I waved my arm, stumbling away from Tem, as the raven skimmed my hair with its talons.

"Biter!"

I recognized the raven instantly. The creature darted away from me as a second dark shape floated into view—Lurker, her wings tucked against her body as she dove toward the snow. Toward River.

He was crouched at Azar-at's side, murmuring something to the fire demon. Lurker let out a sharp call a second before she struck, and when she did, it was no ordinary feint. Her talons raked the side of River's face, speckling the snow with small drops of blood.

River swore, pressing his hand to his head. A second later, Biter joined the attack, coming away with a strand of River's hair. River raised his arm to protect his face, and in response, Lurker sank her talons into his hand, spilling more blood.

"Stop it!" I started forward. "Biter, stop!"

But the birds paid me no heed. Again they dove, and again, the snow was dotted with blood. The ravens were large birds, but

326

I had never feared them before. They were quick and merciless, with an eerie focus.

"Enough."

As Lurker circled back for another dive, River made a motion with his hand. The raven abruptly paused in midattack. Her body shuddered, and she dropped to the ground. She lay there in the snow, one wing half-raised, and was still.

"No," I whispered. River's gaze turned to Biter, and I grabbed his shoulder. "No! River, don't."

"To me," a voice cried.

Biter wheeled around with another echoing *crrrk*. He drifted over the snow, wingbeats scattering the loose flakes, and settled on Lusha's shoulder.

Lusha.

She strode toward us, her head bent against the chill breeze, her eyes full of fury. She walked with a slight limp that did little to lessen the imposing aura that surrounded her. Like Mara's, her face was pinched with weariness, her *chuba* torn. Her normally glossy, flowing hair was a tangle. But somehow, with her height, and the darkness in her gaze, her disheveled appearance only made her more intimidating. She could have been an avenging spirit. I had imagined running to her, and hugging her as I had hugged Tem, but I now had to suppress the urge to run away.

Though the drifts were knee-high in places, Lusha plowed her way through them as if she were made of fire. A few paces from where River and I crouched, she stopped.

"Kamzin, get away from him." She didn't look at Lurker's

motionless body. Her voice was quiet, so quiet you almost had to strain to hear it. Lusha didn't yell when she was truly angry. Her anger condensed inside her to a silent, glittering heat, like a cloud brewing with lightning. "Now."

I was still holding River's arm. "What are you talking about?"

Tem went to stand behind her. Mara lurked by the cave, his eyes darting from one person to another.

"Please listen to her," Tem said. He was holding the *kinnika*—he must have retrieved them from my pack, which I had left in the cave last night. He held them before him now, as if to be ready to sound them at any moment. The scorched bell rang faintly, for no apparent reason.

I let out a disbelieving laugh. "Have you all gone insane? Tem, are you going to cast a spell on *River*?"

"Only if I have to." His face was grim.

"You really don't have to," River muttered, his expression a grimace of pain. I turned away from the others to examine him. His hand was bleeding freely, as were the three deep scratches that had just missed his eye. His ear was bleeding again too, the one that Ragtooth had bitten. I scooped up a chunk of snow and pressed it against his forehead. The blood had already trickled onto his *chuba*.

"Kamzin." Tem's voice had a plea in it.

"Mara, I have some bandages in my pack," I said, pressing more snow against the wound. "Can you fetch them?"

"If you'd just listen to me," Lusha snapped, "for once in your life."

"You've gone mad, Lusha," River said. He drew himself to his full height. "You may be in the habit of setting your ridiculous pets on people you don't like, but you've gone too far this time. You know who I am."

"That's the problem," Lusha said. "I don't."

"What are you talking about?" I said. I took the bundle of cloth Mara handed me, and used it to bind River's hand.

"There is no River Shara," Lusha said. "He doesn't exist."

I stared at her. Then I let out a sharp laugh.

"He's right here," I said. "Are you saying he's a ghost?"

"No," she said calmly. "I'm saying there is no River Shara. Not according to the stars."

"Spirits," I muttered. River was right. She *had* gone mad.

"She may need more of an explanation than that," Mara said. He moved closer to the fire—which also happened to be farther from River—and rubbed his hands over the flames.

Lusha sighed, rubbing her eyes. The weariness I had seen in her face seemed, for a moment, to overtake her. But then she straightened, forcing her shoulders back. "As you know, Kamzin, or you should know, the stars can't predict every event. Not everyone's birth can be read in the patterns of the constellations and the paths of shooting stars. But many can—the Sharas, for example, are an ancient and powerful family. Their births are always foretold—you can see them. It isn't easy to read the past in the stars, much harder than it is to read the future, but I managed it. I found the story of every Shara since the Empire's founding—their births, their lives, and in many cases, their deaths. All but one.

River. He simply isn't there."

Biter croaked, and Lusha, in an absent gesture, touched her finger to his beak. "I don't know who he is," she said, "but he isn't the emperor's cousin. I puzzled over it for days before River came to Azmiri, but it wasn't until I met Mara that I knew I had to take matters into my own hands."

"Mara?" I stared at him. "What does he have to do with this?"

"Once I realized that there was something strange about River, I began searching the stars for those who I knew were close to him," she said. She paced before us—three steps one way, three steps the other. "Mara, for example. I studied the events of his life. After speaking with him, I discovered that he had no memory of things that are written about him in the stars."

"Like what?"

"The time he drowned in Nageni Lake, for one. And another occasion, when he was taken prisoner by witches in the Night-wood."

My head was spinning. "Why would he have lost his memories?"

"The only explanation I could come up with," Lusha said, "is that someone took them. Someone with an extraordinary magical gift."

Everyone, suddenly, was staring at River. He gave a short laugh.

"I can assure you that Azar-at and I have better things to do than muddle around in Mara's head."

"Lusha." My voice was low. "You're wrong. You read the stars wrong."

"No."

"Of *course* you did." My anger was rising. "Did that possibility never occur to you?"

"Yonden verified my findings," she snapped. "I'm not wrong."

"No," I muttered. "You never are, are you?"

Lusha's expression closed, but not before I saw a flash of pain. My words echoed with an old argument, sharp and bitter as bile. I had shouted something similar at her after our mother died. When I had been angry at everyone, but especially Lusha. For she should have known. She could read the future in the stars. How could she not have known? How could she not have prevented what had happened?

But the simple truth, as I had finally realized when my anger faded and was replaced by cold grief, was that Lusha could not see everything. The messages woven in the stars were imperfect, flawed.

And so was my sister.

I turned to Tem. "And you believe this?"

"Some of Mara's memories have been stolen," Tem said quietly. "At some point, he was enspelled. I used the finder's incantation—there are traces of magic all over him, like cobwebs. I don't know the spell that was used, but I'm trying to find out."

I threw my hands up. "And you assume it was River?"

River touched my shoulder. "It's all right."

"No, it's not," I said, shaking him off. "How can you say that?"

"I don't see the point in arguing with them."

"Of course he doesn't," Lusha snapped. "He wants us to step

aside and let him continue to the summit. That isn't going to happen."

River's expression became flat and cold. "Isn't it?"

"No."

They stared at each other, and I was surprised that the snow-drifts surrounding us didn't melt into vapor. Hastily, I stepped between them. I wasn't certain whose safety I was more concerned for, but it didn't matter. This was ridiculous.

"Lusha," I said, "why did you come here with Mara? What do you want?"

"The witches' talisman, of course," she said. "Or rather, to stop River from taking it. Whoever he is, I can't allow something so powerful to fall into his hands. It was Yonden who worked it out—when River wrote to me, asking my help in guiding him to Raksha, but refusing to reveal any details about his intentions, we decided to search the stars for the truth. Many of the signs surrounding the expedition were strange and contradictory, but there was enough for Yonden to make the connection between Raksha and the tales of the witches' sky city, and the power hidden there. At first I planned to lead River's expedition to Raksha, as I promised, and then steal the talisman once we located it—destroy it, if I could. But once I discovered how River had altered Mara's memories, I knew that course was too risky—he is too powerful. I decided I would beat him to the talisman, to prevent him from ever touching it. It was then that I enlisted Mara's help—he may not be the Royal Explorer, but he has led many expeditions in his lifetime. I also hoped to break the spell on his memories, to unlock the secret of who River is, and what he wants."

"Lusha, Lusha," River said, "this is ludicrous. Think about what you're doing. You know that by threatening me, you're threatening the emperor himself."

"Then I am threatening the emperor himself." Lusha's voice was ice.

"Lusha—" I said, horrified.

River exhaled slowly. "You have no idea what you're saying."

"I know exactly what I'm saying."

"Stop, please," I said, as fire crackled between them again. "Both of you."

There was a painful silence. Lusha and River looked daggers at each other. Tem's eyes flicked back and forth, his hand clenched tight around the *kinnika*. Mara leaned against the rock, his face pale. Azar-at moved quietly to River's side.

River's laugh cut through the silence. I drew a small sigh of relief, though the others did not seem comforted by the sound. They watched River with wary expressions.

"All right," he said, waving a hand wearily. "You can stand down, Tem. I won't fight you. Nor will I argue with the stars— there are far too many of them. But a thousand voices can be as wrong as one, and if I were you, Lusha, I wouldn't put so much faith in the stories they tell." He yawned. "I'm going to get some sleep. I had a very tiring night, and this certainly hasn't helped. Azar-at, come."

The fire demon slid across the snow toward River, following him into the cave. Mara leaped out of their way as quickly as if something had bitten him.

"What are you doing?" I said to Lusha. "Did you just threaten the emperor? I thought you cared about Azmiri's safety."

Lusha shook her head. Now that River was gone, she seemed to have deflated, as if he had taken some of her energy with him. She reached down to rub her calf, wincing. "That's *all* I care about. If you'd only open your eyes, you'd see that."

My eyes narrowed. "What's wrong with your ankle?"

"Nothing. I tripped back in the icefall. Tem healed me."

"It doesn't look healed. Why don't you let River—"

"No." Lusha's voice was like a lash. "I'll be fine."

"I think you'd refuse help if you were dying. Let me see it, then."

"I'd have to *be* dead before I let you use your unfortunate magic on me, Kamzin. Leave me alone."

"I did what I could," Tem said, coming to Lusha's side. He looked relieved to have a reason to join the conversation. "But I'm not at full strength, and the healing charm wore off too quickly. I may have done more harm than good."

"You did fine," Lusha said. "I just need to rest it for an hour or so, then I'll be as good as new."

I rolled my eyes. "Oh, right. Like you were 'good as new' after a cup of Aunt Behe's tea the night you fell asleep stargazing. You lost a toe to frostbite, all because you were too proud to complain."

Lusha gave me a look of dignified disdain. "I won't get into old arguments with you."

"Let's take another look at Mingma's maps," Mara said,

touching her arm. "He hinted there might be an easier route to the summit beyond that ridge." As he watched my sister, his gaze was filled with concern. Concern—and something more than that. I had to suppress a bitter laugh. I had seen enough men direct similar gazes at Lusha to know what they meant. He was in love with her—or at least, he thought he was.

Lusha nodded to Mara. "Fine. Kamzin, you're not going any farther along this path. Get some rest, and then head back to base camp."

I stared at her. "You can't just order me—"

"If I have to get Tem to knock you unconscious and float your body down the mountain, I'll do it."

"Tem would never agree to that," I snapped, though I was only half-convinced of this.

"Then I'll have to resort to nonmagical means of knocking you unconscious. I can't say I would mind the challenge."

I stomped off, neither knowing nor caring which direction I was headed in. Tem called after me, but I ignored him. I knew that I was exhausted, given what I had been through, but I couldn't feel it. Perhaps it was that I was still charged from the battle with the ghosts, or perhaps it was my anger at Lusha—her infuriating self-assurance, even when it flew in the face of all logic; her ability to bend everyone around her to her will—that drove me on. Either way, I walked for at least a quarter hour, wading through knee-deep snow, heedless of the danger I could be placing myself in by venturing out alone. I finally came to a precarious ledge that faced south, overlooking the undulating, dragonish spine of the Arya mountains. If it weren't for the haze that still clung to the land, I could have followed with my gaze the route we had taken to reach Raksha, at least from Winding Pass. Mount Azmiri was hidden from view, but it was there, somewhere. I could feel it.

I lowered myself onto the ledge, swinging my legs over the vast expanse. My head whirled with a hundred different thoughts. Most of all, though, I felt lost.

How could Lusha believe what she had seen in the stars? How could she be so convinced—always so convinced—that she was incapable of making a mistake? Perhaps someone had tampered with Mara's memory—perhaps it had even been River, despite his protests. But that didn't mean River had some dark plot in mind. He was the Royal Explorer, the emperor's trusted confidant. He had been sent on a mission to retrieve a talisman that could save the Empire from ruin, and Azmiri with it.

I learned my head against the rock, letting the sunlight soothe my painfully exhausted body. I had been so worried about Lusha, so desperate to see her again. And yet now I wanted only the last few days back, when River and I were alone and everything was simpler.

I must have dozed off, for suddenly I was jolted back to alertness by a dragon landing on my lap. It sniffed at my hands, then turned to regard me hopefully with its luminous golden eyes. I turned my head and found Tem seated behind me, several feet back from the edge.

"Sorry," he said. "I asked him to wake you. You have no idea how scary that looks."

I blinked at my surroundings. I was balanced on a narrow ledge thousands of feet above the ground. It would be an odd place for most people to sleep, I supposed.

I glared at him. "Lusha sent you to keep an eye on me, didn't she?"

Tem's silence was reply enough. I turned away from him, leaning my head against the rock and pointedly closing my eyes. He let out a small sigh that turned into a cough.

"I know you're angry," he said. "But Lusha only wants to protect you."

"Maybe I don't want to be protected," I muttered. "You're taking her side, just like everyone else always does."

"I'm not—"

"I almost died," I said. "River saved my life."

I saw Mingma's face again, felt the hungry chill of the water. It would haunt my dreams for many nights to come.

"I didn't know," Tem said quietly. He made a sound as if to speak again, but I turned my face away.

There was a long silence. Tem made no move to leave, though he did call the dragon back to his side. I knew I wouldn't be able to fall asleep again, but I kept my eyes closed nevertheless.

It wasn't long, though, before I began to notice how the rock was digging uncomfortably into my back, and that my stomach was rumbling for breakfast. I snuck a glance at Tem, and was surprised to find that he was leaning his head against his hand, seemingly asleep. As I shifted position, his eyes opened, settling on me. I noticed for the first time how dark the circles under his eyes were. There was a heaviness about his movements, as if his weariness were an invisible pack he carried with him.

"Your cough is worse, isn't it?" I said.

He rubbed his eyes, which only increased their pinkish hue. "Yes, but that isn't the problem. I've been using magic too often. It's taking a toll."

I felt a stab of anxiety. Too many spells wore a shaman thin, to the point where ordinary methods of restoration—sleep, food, a warm fire—were rendered almost useless. It was as if the magic ate away at the shaman's ability to protect himself from its effects. Shamans who overused magic were in danger of all sorts of ailments, or even death if they were of sufficient age.

"I helped us reach the top of the ice wall," he said, rubbing his head as if the memory pained him. "That was a tricky bit of magic, what with Lusha's ankle and my poor climbing skills. I ended up choosing an incantation I've used before with the calves, when I want them to herd together. I modified it from a herding spell to a pushing spell, to help propel us up, step by step."

I stared at him. "You invented a new spell?"

"I don't know about 'invented.' It was the same spell, at the root. Anyway, that wasn't what tired me, not really. It was trying to undo the spell that was placed on Mara's memories. I worked at it for an hour last night, and I'm not sure I made any progress. It's a strange spell, and *strong*. And it's as if it was designed to fight against any shaman that tried to break it."

"Hmm." I considered this. Chirri had taught me about memory spells once—she had even placed one on me, causing me to forget what I had eaten for breakfast that morning. She had wanted me to break the spell myself, but, true to form, I only made it worse, and eventually forgot what I had eaten for the past month. "Did you try the wayfarer's incantation?"

"What's that?"

"It's something Chirri recommended for spells of the mind— to retrieve memories, or rescue someone from madness. The shaman forms a connection with the afflicted and helps them recover what they've lost."

Tem looked interested. "Could you teach it to me?"

"I'm not sure." I bit my lip. "I don't remember it all."

Tem gave me a small, tired smile. "That's all right. Don't worry about it."

I shook my head. "I owe you an apology. I'm the reason you're here, caught up in this mess."

He shrugged. A faint smile spread across his face. "It's my own fault for inviting myself along."

"Yes. Next time, keep in mind how crazy I am before you decide to join in my adventures."

Tem laughed. I felt myself smiling too. I had missed him. Tem and I might argue, but he was always there for me. It wasn't something I could say about anyone else.

The *kinnika* tinkled faintly, making me start. Tem, though, barely seemed to notice.

"They're still doing that," I said.

He nodded. "I wish I knew what it meant."

"Maybe nothing," I said, even as I felt a familiar shiver of unease. "Maybe it's just an echo."

Tem unlooped the string of bells from his neck. He grasped the bell that had sounded, which I recognized—the small, singed one next to the black bell.

"I've been trying to work out the character at the base," he said. "It's not easy—the metal is warped. But I think it's 'shadow-kin.'"

It was an old-fashioned term for witch. I gazed at the bell. It seemed so small, so ordinary. "So what does it mean? Are there witches nearby?" I suppressed the urge to glance over my shoulder—it felt wrong even to speak of witches in a place as unearthly as Raksha.

"If so, it seems odd that we haven't seen any sign of them."

"We've been lucky." My voice was more hopeful than I felt.

"Yes," Tem said. "Almost too lucky. We've been in witch territory for days now. Don't you think it's strange?"

"What are you saying?" A cold weight settled in my stomach. "Do you think they've been . . . stalking us? Why wouldn't they have attacked by now?"

"I don't know." He rubbed his eyes. "I don't know. I'm so tired, Kamzin. Sometimes I—I feel like I can't separate what I'm afraid of from what's right in front of me."

I stretched my arm toward him. My fingertips could just barely reach his knee, but he caught my hand and held it tight.

Back at the cave, I rooted through the remaining supplies, scrounging a cheerless breakfast of *churpi*, a rock-hard yak cheese, and dried lentils. Lusha and Mara hovered around the fire just outside the cave, debating whether Mara should go ahead to scout out the ridge they had identified, leaving Lusha behind to rest her ankle. Lusha, unsurprisingly, was not happy with this idea, and as their argument went around in circles, I stopped listening. I was past exhausted and probably could have slept in a snowdrift—instead, I retreated into the cave, grateful for the shelter it provided. I would rest for a few minutes, that was it.

River lay on his stomach, his blankets forming a haphazard cocoon around him. He muttered something as I settled beside him, a crease forming between his eyes. Something was troubling him—a fragment of a dream, perhaps. The blood from the ravens' talons had run down the side of his face before it dried. He flinched as I wiped it off, gently. Given the depth of the marks, there was little doubt he would have a scar there. Shaking my head, I lay down and was soon fast asleep.

When I opened my eyes, all was quiet. River breathed softly a few feet away. The wind moaned over the mountainside. Something had woken me—but what?

My dreams had been filled with ghosts—or rather, ghostly hands, seizing at my *chuba* and dragging me toward the brink of an abyss. Mingma was there, watching from a distance, the remorse on his face as sharp as broken glass.

I rubbed my eyes. Now I had new monsters to haunt my sleep, as if the *fiangul* weren't enough.

Ragtooth stood near the mouth of the cave, his back to me, fur standing on end. Tension was written in every line of his body. I called to him, but he didn't move a muscle. The back of my neck prickled.

Then the rumbling started. The entire cave shook, bits of loose rock twitching across the ground like insects. River started, his head jerking up.

"Where is it?" he said nonsensically. His cheek showed the imprint of his blanket.

The rumbling began to subside. I loosened my grip on my knees. I had been squeezing them so tight my fingernails would have left marks.

"That was an avalanche," I said faintly. "And it was close."

"Too close." River was fully alert now. He tossed his blankets back and yanked on his boots.

I followed him outside. A towering cloud of ice crystals had descended on our little camp, dusting the tent Mara and Lusha had erected against the rock face. Lusha was only half-visible, standing at the edge of the camp and squinting out into the chaos.

"Lusha!" I shouted. There came another rumble, quieter than the last. Lusha saw me, and came hurrying back.

"Mara went to scout out the route to the north face," she said. A net of snow covered her hair, and her expression was stern, pinched. It was a look I had seen only rarely—Lusha was frightened.

I felt cold. "Mara is out there?"

"Yes. He took Tem with him."

"*What?*" I started forward, but River grabbed my arm.

"Hold on," he said, turning back to Lusha. "How long have they been gone?"

"Half an hour—maybe more. They were heading for the ridge."

"This should clear quickly, with the wind." River squinted up at the mountain's peak, which was invisible through the cloud. "But there may be another one coming."

Tem. Panic rose inside me like a clawed thing. "We have to go after them."

"We will," Lusha said, her tone reassuring. Her expression, though, was still pinched, pale.

River whistled. "Azar-at, bring my pack."

Lusha opened her mouth as if to protest, but I grabbed her shoulder and shook her. "Lusha, there's no time! We need his help."

Her mouth closed in a tight line. She glanced up at the mountain, seeming to fight with something inside herself. After a moment, narrowing her eyes at River, she gave a jerky nod.

"We'll have to use snowshoes," River said. "It won't be—"

Another distant rumble. The panic that had been rising overwhelmed me—I could hardly think. I threw off River's arm and ran. The ice crystals hanging in the air stung my face, my throat, my eyes. I didn't care—I ran on.

Up ahead, the snow cloud was beginning to settle. I could see now that the avalanche had slid right past us, tumbling down the snowy slope beside the rock face and down the mountain. It was probably still falling toward the valley floor.

Suddenly, I stumbled over something warm and soft, with the texture of dandelion seeds. I landed facedown in a snowdrift and surfaced coughing on a lungful of ice.

You must wait, brave one, Azar-at said. The fire demon's ears were pricked, alert. *Not safe to wander alone.*

"I don't care." I stumbled to my feet, ready to set off again. But suddenly, River and Lusha were there, roped together, both wearing snowshoes.

"Rope," River said. Lusha handed him a coil unquestioningly. He looped it around my waist and secured it to the rope he wore. Lusha, meanwhile, attached a pair of snowshoes to my feet, her hands moving so quickly I could barely distinguish each motion. Within seconds, they were both done.

"Lead," Lusha said, and River nodded. She set out first, followed by River and Azar-at. I was left to trot along behind them like an obedient child.

"Why can't I lead?" I demanded. They both ignored me.

We strode on at a punishing pace in our heavy snowshoes. I was soon panting, and only through sheer force of will was I able to leave any slack between myself and River. The last few days had taken a toll on me, and lack of sleep didn't help. We trekked up a steep snowbank River and I had investigated the day before, and along the ridge Lusha had indicated. The land fell away on our left, breathtakingly steep. With every minute that passed I felt my panic increase.

It doesn't matter, I told myself over and over. *He could still be alive.* I had been buried by an avalanche once, spending several long minutes in an air pocket beneath the snow before Lusha found me. Tem could be in the same situation. He could even now be counting each breath he took, rationing the air in the hopes that someone would find him in time.

I clung to that image, shoved the terror down until it was a heavy weight at the pit of my stomach, and focused on putting one foot in front of the other.

One breath. Another.

The snow was treacherous—loose and slippery, clinging precariously to the slope of the mountain. I wasn't afraid of heights, but even I tried to avoid looking down more than was necessary. The slope here was sharp, and if anyone put a foot wrong, there was absolutely nothing to stop them from tumbling down and down the mountainside, except the ground. This was far enough away to be separated from us by wispy clouds.

Lusha and River paused several times to confer about the route. They didn't bother to include me in the conversation, and as much as I resented it, I couldn't blame them. I had little experience with avalanches, at least on this side of them. Lusha, on the other hand, had taken part in several rescue missions on Azmiri with Father—as the future elder, she needed to know how to respond to emergencies.

"Hurry up," I nearly screamed as they paused for what felt like the hundredth time. Every moment was precious. Didn't they understand that?

River glanced my way. He muttered something to Lusha, and they set off again, moving faster despite the risk.

Azar-at trotted ahead of us, nosing the ground. He paused suddenly, burying his entire head in the snow.

"What is it?" I demanded. "Does he sense something?"

River gazed at the snow, his lips pursed. He cocked his head to one side, as if listening to something. The seconds went by. The sight of our breath, rising in clouds, was a torment to me.

"River!" I grabbed his arm.

"This way," he said. Azar-at was already moving, uphill this time. The incline was punishing, and we leaned forward onto our hands to maintain our hold on the mountainside. Occasionally, there were rocks and boulders mixed in with the snow. I tried not to focus on these.

Another breath. Then another.

Abruptly, Azar-at came to a halt. He nosed at the loose snow next to a boulder, only the tip of which was visible. The fire demon's tail wagged frantically.

"Is it Tem?" I surged forward. Wordlessly, Lusha unslung the small shovel from her back and began to dig. River was already digging. I didn't have a shovel, but I knelt anyway, trying to shift the snow with my hands. Lusha grabbed me by the shoulder and shoved me away.

"That's not helping," she said shortly, lifting the chunk of snow I had been scrabbling at with her shovel. "Stay out of the way."

I sat there, helpless and ragged. Lusha and River did not speak a word. Their shovels slicing through the snow was the only sound. My breaths rose in the air, vanishing one after the other.

Suddenly, a hand poked up through the snow.

River tossed his shovel aside. He and Lusha reached out as one and dragged the hand's owner out into the light.

It was Mara. I suppressed a sob as the explorer fell forward onto the ground. With my disappointment came guilt, but I barely noticed it. Where was Tem?

The chronicler doubled over, coughing. Lusha handed him a flask. "Here." Mara took a sip, and the coughing subsided somewhat.

"Thank the spirits," he said, his voice a tremor. "I had just about given up—"

"Where's Tem?" I demanded. "Was he ahead of you?"

Mara blinked repeatedly. His expression was dazed, and he seemed to make an effort to focus. "Last I saw. Perhaps twenty yards."

River motioned to the fire demon, who darted forward, snout to the ground. I watched, frantic, as the seconds passed. Azar-at paced back and forth, his nostrils snuffling against the snow. But still he did not give any sign.

"He may be buried too deep for Azar-at to smell him out," River said, his brow furrowed.

"Can't you do anything?" I said, desperate.

"That's not a good idea." Lusha gave River a dark look. "The slope isn't stable. If he uses magic—"

"We'll have to deal with the consequences," River said. It had the air of an announcement. "Lusha, take Mara back to camp."

Scowling, Lusha knelt over Mara, helping him to his feet. She supported him as they made their way back along the path of our footprints. Even through my panic, I couldn't help feeling a grudging admiration for my sister. She knew what to do in the face of danger, knew that pausing to argue—even if you were in the right—could make the difference between life and death. She wasn't going to sway River. So she didn't bother to try.

"Thank you," I said.

River only shook his head, giving me a faint smile. Then he turned away.

"All right, Azar-at," he said. "Let's find our shaman."

He raised his hand, and it was as if the air began to hum. My teeth chattered; my skin tingled. I was suddenly very aware of my heartbeat, the feeling of my breath in my throat. And another sound—a strange, distant thudding. Slow but steady. It was a *heartbeat*. From beneath the snow, some yards upslope.

"Tem," I breathed. "Is that him?"

River made no reply. He closed his eyes briefly.

A crack appeared in the snow. It widened into a crevasse that branched outward, splitting enormous chunks of snow and rock. The crevasse was deep—I couldn't even see the bottom. Startled, I took a step back, though I was in no danger—the crevasse did not extend to where we were standing. River raised his hand again, his brow furrowed in concentration. The heartbeat grew louder as a limp figure rose out of the tear in the mountainside. It was Tem.

He floated toward us before coming to rest gently at my feet. I knelt beside him, checking to see if he was breathing. His eyes fluttered as I touched his face.

"Tem!" I dashed away the tears that trickled down my cheeks. "Tem, can you hear me?"

He opened his eyes. They wandered for a few seconds before focusing on my face. His mouth moved. *Kamzin.*

"We have to get him back to camp," I said. "Lusha will know a healing charm."

River made no reply. He had fallen onto the snow, and sat with his head bowed and his hand over his eyes. Azar-at, standing at his side, licked his arm.

"River?"

"I'm all right." His voice was distant. "Just give me a minute."

But as if in response, the mountain gave an ominous rumble. It was even louder than the first. The ground shook so violently I stumbled and almost fell. Tem moaned, muttering something that sounded like *not again*.

I looked up and choked on a scream.

A wall of snow swept toward us—so fast, faster than anything I had ever seen, monstrous in size and utterly unforgiving.

River dragged himself to his feet, and stepped forward to meet it.

"River!" I screamed.

River stopped, raising his hands toward the wall of snow. I stood frozen, unable to speak or even breathe. I was about to die. We were all about to die.

Then the avalanche struck . . . *something*. It seemed to collide with an invisible place just beyond River's outstretched hands, as if we were a rock in a stream—the snow surged past on either side. The sound was that of a ferocious wave pounding against solid rock—a terrible roaring, as if the mountain were placing its will against River's. He staggered back a step, but did not fall. Azar-at stood still as a stone at his side. I sensed, rather than saw, the connection between them—like a rope stretched taught. I stared at the snow pouring past, only a scant few yards from where I knelt next to Tem. It was like the landscape was being pulled out from underneath me, while I sat motionless, a mere observer. Even after the mountain grew still again, I could only sit there, staring, as the snow cloud swirled and settled around us in thin sheets.

We were still there when Lusha returned. Tem was awake, though dazed and groaning in pain. I was certain his leg was broken, and possibly several ribs. River, who had collapsed once the mountain had fallen silent again, was alive, though he didn't wake no matter how loudly I called his name. Azar-at was silent, watchful, thinking his impenetrable thoughts. He alone was not dusted with snow—anything that touched his fur melted almost immediately.

Lusha lifted Tem, staggering slightly under the weight, and hurried away, leaving me to drag River along. When we finally staggered back to camp, we found that Mara already had a fire going. Apart from a reddish bruise darkening the side of his face, he seemed to be the most mobile of all of us. Lusha collapsed next to the fire, holding her ankle, her face a grimace of pain.

I chafed River's arms and hands. His face was pale; the scattering of freckles across his nose stood out in stark relief. He seemed to be barely breathing.

"Mara, help me bring him closer to the fire," I said.

He is unhurt, Azar-at said. *He requires only rest.*

I glared at it. "Unhurt? How can you say that, after all you've done to him?"

His choice. Always his choice.

I turned my back on Azar-at. "River? Can you hear me?"

But River neither moved nor opened his eyes. In the end, Mara dragged him into the cave, where I removed his boots and covered him with blankets. I didn't like leaving him alone, so still and pale he resembled a corpse more than a living person, but I had no choice.

Outside, Lusha, her face pinched with pain, was preparing a concoction of healing herbs and berries in a pot over the fire. Though she knew the basic healing spells, she was by no means as talented as Tem, and it took us the better part of the day to make him comfortable. Mara assisted when he could, holding Tem's shoulders while Lusha set and bound his broken leg, melting snow to clean the cuts on his face. Even Ragtooth seemed inclined to be helpful, curling himself up against Tem's head to warm him.

As the sunlight faded, I remembered that I hadn't eaten all day. Mara was preparing a stew, which was more broth than substance, but about as good as we could expect given our meager supplies. I helped Tem prop himself up so that he could drink.

Lusha sat beside me. "How are you, Tem?"

"Better, I think." His voice was faint. He blinked a few times before focusing on Lusha. We had given him herbs for the pain, and a side effect was disorientation. "Kamzin, are you there? You keep fading."

"I'm here," I said, taking his hand. "You're going to be all right."

"He won't be, without a proper shaman," Mara muttered.

"That's not helpful," Lusha said. Our eyes met. There was no need for me to ask if my sister was thinking what I was—I already knew it. Mara was right—Tem wouldn't soon recover from such injuries without the attention of a healer. But we were stranded. Lusha's injury alone would make descending the mountain a hazardous feat—Tem's condition made it impossible. Both our firewood and food were low, and we wouldn't be able to stay where we were for much longer. To add to our predicament, clouds were massing against the peak of Raksha, and thickening and swirling their way toward us. The chill wind warned of a brewing storm.

Our prospects were suddenly very grim.

The others took shelter in the tent that night, but I wanted to be close to River. He was still asleep, still barely breathing, but at least he no longer seemed as pale as death. There was nothing I could do except make sure that he was warm. I adjusted the blankets around him and brushed the damp hair gently off his forehead.

I turned my attention to my feet. They had been aching for days, on and off, but something had changed after that day's frantic trek in my heavy, cumbersome snowshoes. I drew my boots and socks off carefully, wincing.

The blisters on my heels had burst, and blood stained my socks. Two of my toenails were blackened and broken, and would surely fall away soon. But what worried me most were my toes—the two smallest ones were bent oddly and had a grayish tinge. Could it be frostbite? I massaged my feet. It was as if they were swathed in thick blankets, diminishing their ability to feel anything.

Next I examined my knee. The swelling had gone down somewhat, though my recent exertions and lack of rest had prevented it from healing properly. Even now, whenever I took a step, a shard of pain stabbed into the bone.

I lay down, forcing my thoughts away from my injuries. Ragtooth nestled against my head, his tail folded over my neck. Sleep took me as soon as I closed my eyes.

Some time later, I was jolted awake by crashing thunder and pounding hail. I lay there, listening, for what could have been a minute or an hour. I felt even more the strangeness of being there, stranded in the sky so far from home. As the storm crashed and the wind raged, it was easy to imagine that the mountain was trying to shake us off, as a yak would shake off a mosquito. I wished that I could hear River's steady breathing in the darkness, but such sounds were lost among the clamor of the storm. I gathered my blankets around myself, shivering, praying that morning wasn't far off.

TWENTY-FOUR

WHEN I OPENED my eyes, a faint gray light was spilling into the cave. I could hear voices outside—Mara's and possibly Tem's. I propped myself up on my elbows, blinking. Judging by the light, it was perhaps an hour after dawn, and the storm seemed to have broken.

I looked over at River. But instead of a mound of blankets with a tousled head sticking out of them, I saw only bare rock.

River was gone. So were his blankets and pack.

A shiver traveled slowly down my spine. I pulled on my boots, ignoring the accompanying wave of pain, and hurried out into the light.

The clouds gathering along the mountain peak were ragged, but the thick cluster lurking to the east warned that the storm was not entirely past. I could not see the sweep of the landscape;

a blanket of fog covered all below us. The sun shone only inter-mittently through the clouds, like a tired eye opening and closing.

The tent flaps were tied back, exposing Tem to the heat from the campfire that burned low among the rocks. He lay asleep in a nest of blankets. Lusha sat beside him, murmuring a healing charm while she waved a bone talisman. Mara bent over a pot of melting snow.

"River's gone," I said as soon as I reached Lusha's side.

She didn't look up. "I'm not surprised."

I stared. "He wouldn't just leave. Not without saying some-thing."

Lusha gave me a dark look. "Why? If River Shara makes his mind up to do something, I doubt he pauses to inform anyone else. All he cares about is reaching the summit." She threw down the rag she had been using to wipe Tem's face. "And now we have no way to stop him."

"He would have told me," I insisted. "Something's happened to him. I know it." My mind was filled with images of the ghosts. Could they have returned for River? Or had he been so unwell that he had, in a daze, staggered off into the storm?

Lusha made an impatient noise. "What could happen to him, with that creature at his side?"

"When did you notice he was gone?" Mara said. To my sur-prise, he actually appeared to be listening to me.

"Just now," I said. "But I don't see his tracks in the snow."

"The storm could have buried them," Lusha pointed out.

"Only if he left when it was still raging. Why would he have done that?"

"I'll go have a look around," Mara said. "Before these clouds close up again." He rose and was gone before I could even thank him. Lusha turned back to Tem, her lips pursed.

"Well done, Kamzin," she said. "Now I'll have another person to rescue if Mara gets himself lost."

"He won't."

Lusha settled back onto the tent floor, massaging her leg. "I couldn't sleep last night. What we went through yesterday more than undid Tem's healing spells. If anything, the pain is worse. My ankle is broken."

I stared at her. "You should have told me."

Lusha gave me a look. "I'm telling you now. There are other people here who need your help more than River Shara."

I bit my lip and did not argue. I melted another flask of snow, then took over watching Tem while Lusha lay down, her arm pressed over her eyes and her face pale. Tem stirred when I touched his face, but did not wake. Sadly, I put the healing herbs aside, not trusting my abilities even with them.

Mara returned an hour later, his expression dark. Fat snowflakes clung to his hair and beard. "I saw no sign of his trail," he said. "I climbed onto a boulder to try to sight him, but I couldn't make out any human shapes either above or below us. The visibility was deteriorating, so I turned back."

I felt a surge of panic. "What about the ridge? I could—"

"There's nothing more we can do in this weather," Lusha said. "You and Mara can search again once this lets up. Until then, please help me with the fire."

I bit back a retort. It would do no good to quarrel with Lusha. Yet I was certain something was wrong. As I stirred the ashes of the fire, trying to rouse the few remaining embers enough to melt one last pot of snow, I gazed up at the peak of the mountain. It was hidden from sight, but every once in a while I caught a glimpse of its jagged outline through the cloud.

As the storm worsened, Lusha and I took shelter in the cave. Mara stayed with Tem—his injuries were too raw to risk moving him. I shivered in my blankets, hungry and exhausted and out of sorts, as well as sick with worry. The snow fell in thick, roiling curtains from the dark cloud that surrounded us. The wind howled dully, rising every few moments to tremendous gusts that pummeled the mountain until it shook. I wished my sister would speak, but Lusha's eyes were half-closed, her face pale; she seemed occupied with her pain.

I shifted position restlessly. My feet still ached, a dull, wearying throb, and something was digging into my neck. I reached beneath the blanket, expecting to find a rock. Instead, I discovered the bundle of string River had been preoccupied with.

My lower lip trembled as I unfolded the bundle on the cave floor. It wasn't the ratty mess River had been peering into; he had somehow shaped the strings into an intricate looping pattern. Against the dark cave floor, the pale bundle reminded me of the lillies and orchids he had summoned out of the darkness as we sat together toasting his nineteenth birthday. It seemed like so long ago now.

My eyes stung with tears. River had placed this in my bed last night—he must have. What did it mean? And where was he now?

Why had he left me?

The wind rose again. Suddenly, the air was split by a tremendous crash, followed by muffled shouting.

It was coming from the tent.

"Tem!" Tossing my blankets back, I dashed out of the cave.

Tem lay exposed to the storm, his arms raised as if to push it back. The tent was in tatters around him, having been torn off the bamboo poles. Part of the fabric, still buffeted by the wind, was wrapped around his injured leg, and he was yelling in pain. Mara, in his socks in the blowing snow, was attempting to unwind the fabric.

I raced to Mara's side. Together, we freed Tem from the remains of the tent. The scraps floated away like monstrous bats. We lifted Tem, blankets and all, and carried him into the cave. I tried to be careful of his broken ribs, but to no avail. His body went limp in my arms—he had fainted from the pain. Lusha helped me settle Tem on the floor, and then Mara dashed back into the storm in search of the supplies that had been in the tent. He returned with only two satchels.

"We lost the rest of the blankets," Mara said.

"What about the other tents?" I demanded. "Are you saying you only brought one?"

"We left most of our supplies with Dargye," Lusha said. "We didn't think we'd be on the mountain for long."

"You might be right about that," I said grimly. Being stranded without food was one thing—a person would be fine for a few days, if they were fit and strong. But lacking reliable shelter was something else entirely, in an environment where even one night of exposure to the cold meant frostbite or worse.

How would we survive now? How had everything fallen apart so utterly and completely?

No one spoke for a long time. With four people in the cave, not to mention two sleeping dragons, it was warm, almost too warm. I shrugged my *chuba* off and tucked it under Tem's head. I was fighting back tears. I stroked his head, praying for him to wake up soon. It was a selfish hope—Tem was much better off asleep, in his condition—but I couldn't help it.

Lusha leaned against Mara, who seemed to be occupying himself with a longing examination of the top of her head. She fiddled with something, moving it back and forth between the palms of her hands.

Our mother's statue. She had carried it all this way. I swallowed as tears blurred my vision.

Our eyes met. For a moment, I didn't think she was going to speak, but then she said, "Would you like to hold it? It's strange, but I find it helps somehow. At times when everything around you seems dark."

I took the little statue gingerly. It was barely the length of my palm. It looked nothing like my mother, of course—my mother, with her broad shoulders and callused hands, and a laugh that seemed to shake the very ground.

I thought about what Lusha had said, about the statue bringing her comfort. But it was cold against my hand, cold and heavy and unyielding. I could find no comfort in it.

Mara leaned forward suddenly, his hand pressed to his eyes.

"Are you all right?" I said.

"Yes," the chronicler said tersely. Lusha touched his shoulder.

"He gets these headaches sometimes," she said tiredly. "Tem thinks they're connected to the memory spell. They've been worse since Tem tried to fix him."

The memory spell. My mind drifted back to Chirri's lessons. Oddly, I had paid more attention than usual to her lecture on these spells and their counterspells, perhaps because I had felt so resentful toward the old woman for laughing at my attempts to retrieve my own memories.

"When did Tem last try?" I said.

"This morning," Mara said, rubbing his eyes. "Felt like a hammer against my skull."

I heard Chirri's voice in my mind. "We should try again."

"Why?" Mara said. "Tem couldn't—"

"I know an incantation," I said. "Tem might be able to use it to get Mara's memories back."

Lusha sighed. "What does it matter now? We have more important things to worry about. Like staying alive."

"I know," I said. "But we should at least try."

"I thought you believed River."

I felt a sharp pain. "River's gone. He left. I don't know what I believe anymore. If Mara's memories can help make sense of all this, we need to get them back."

"Kamzin." Lusha pressed her chapped lips together. "Tem's in no condition—"

"I'll try it," said a wan voice.

"Tem!" I knelt at his side. "How are you feeling?"

"Like I've been run over by a yak," he murmured, accepting the sip of water I offered him. He coughed, grimacing. "Make that a herd."

"Do you think you're up to this?"

"I don't know," he said. "But you're right, Kamzin. Mara's memories could help us work out River's intentions. I don't want to rely on a guess."

"A guess?" I stared at him. "Do you know what River's planning?"

Tem seemed to be having trouble looking at me. "I have a theory," he said quietly.

"A theory?"

"It would explain what Lusha read in the stars about River." Tem seemed to speak half to himself. "Or rather, what she didn't read. I can't think of any other reason why River's life, given all he's accomplished as Royal Explorer, wouldn't be written there. And I just have this feeling that I can't shake—"

"If you know something, now's the time," Lusha said.

Tem flushed. "I—I don't." Again, he seemed to be avoiding my eyes. "Not for certain. Let's just focus on the spell."

"Let's," Mara said, rubbing his brow. "I'd rather not have these headaches anymore."

Tem took my hand. "Kamzin?"

I recited the incantation, as much of it as I could remember. Tem grew thoughtful as he listened.

"Of course," he murmured. "It's not a healing spell at all— that's where I went wrong before. It's a curse spell, at the root."

"A *curse* spell?" Mara's face paled.

"Not all curses are bad," Tem said. "Sometimes they're the only way to break through another, more powerful spell. They attack the magic, not the person. How fascinating. Why didn't I think of it?"

"Tem?" I said.

"Right, sorry." He pulled himself upright, his face a grimace. "Where are the bells?"

I handed him the *kinnika*. "Can you do this? I don't remember all the words."

"It doesn't matter," Tem said. "I can work out the rest."

I fell silent. Tem's other persona was in charge now—calm, confident, decisive. He brushed his hand across the bells, sounding them gently.

"Are you sure about this?" Mara said. "I don't like the sound of curses, particularly when they're directed at my head."

"Don't talk," Tem said, not even looking at him. He closed his eyes and began to mutter the incantation, much more fluently than I had, weaving it into another spell I didn't recognize. He sounded the bells again, then two in alternation—one plain and smaller than my thumbnail, the other broad and inlaid with intricate carvings. The sound seemed to rise to a crescendo, and then, abruptly, the bells fell silent.

Mara blinked. "Is that it?"

"It may take a moment," Tem said. Sweat stood out on his forehead. "Unless I didn't use the correct bell."

"Or the incantation is wrong," I said, feeling a stab of guilt.

Mara eyed the *kinnika* warily. "It's good to know you're all so confident about this."

"Let me try again." Tem shook the *kinnika*, tilting his head like a musician tuning his instrument. He removed several from the chain, then sounded the remaining bells. He began the incantation again, matching his voice to the cadence of the *kinnika*. I held his arm, but it was as if Tem was no longer fully there—part of him was lost in the spell he was weaving in that tiny cave, as the wind raged outside. It made me uneasy, and I fought back an urge to shake him, to anchor him back to Earth, and to me.

After another minute or so, Tem stopped abruptly. He opened his eyes, blinking, as if uncertain of his surroundings.

"Are you all right?" I said.

"Think so." He blinked again. "Did it work?"

Mara's brow was furrowed. He hadn't moved since Tem started chanting, and his eyes had a glazed appearance. "No, I—Spirits protect us!"

"Mara?" Lusha touched him.

The man lurched forward, pressing his hands against the side of his head. He let out a cry of pain that reverberated through the cave, guttural and chilling.

"Tem!" Lusha said, grabbing Mara's shoulders as he spasmed back. "What's happening?"

Tem had fallen back against the cave wall, looking gray. "It will pass—he just has to endure it. Memory spells are never pleasant when broken."

"I remember," Mara muttered, his eyes still shut tight. "I *remember*." He repeated it again and again, as if it were a chant.

363

"You remember what?" Lusha shook him. "Mara, tell us."

The chronicler didn't reply. His mouth moved silently, still repeating the words. I wanted to edge away from him—Mara's expression was wild, and he pressed his fingers so hard against his head that I saw tiny drops of blood form under the nails. The blood was dark, almost black, and seemed to disperse into the air like shadow. I blinked, and the illusion—had it been an illusion?—vanished.

"Mara," Lusha said, raising her voice. "What do you remember?"

Mara finally opened his eyes. "The expedition. The witches. I *remember*."

"What expedition—" I began, but Mara rambled on.

"Everything that he tried to hide from me, it's all back."

My heart was pounding now, in slow, heavy thuds. "So River *did* alter your memories?"

"Yes, him and that creature. And they had good reason to do it—Spirits protect us!" He pressed his head into his hands again.

Lusha's brow was furrowed. "Why did River do it? What was he trying to hide?"

"He's—" Mara's face contorted, and he let out a groan. Lusha motioned to me, and I brought him a flask of water.

"Thank you." Mara sipped from the flask. As he did, his expression cleared. "The pain is lessening."

"It will take time," Tem said. "It was a powerful spell, cleverly cast."

"Mara," Lusha said slowly, "what was River hiding?"

"He's not human, Lusha." His face was blank with shock. "He's a witch."

TWENTY-FIVE

I COULDN'T MOVE, or think. Shock enveloped me like layers of snow. I felt buried, trapped. Lusha said something, but I couldn't hear it. It was several moments before my senses returned.

"—explains the contradictory portents," Lusha was saying. "A witch's plans can't be read in the stars—they're shaped by wild magic, chaos itself. The stars can't make sense of witches; that's what Yonden once told me."

"River is not a witch," I said. Why was she even entertaining this? "It's not possible."

"It's the truth," Mara said. "I don't know how he did it, or what his true name might be."

This is madness. The spell had destroyed Mara's reasoning. "How can you—"

"Be quiet, Kamzin," Lusha said. I fell into a mutinous silence, my mind whirling. Lusha touched Mara's shoulder. "Why don't you start at the beginning?"

Mara scrubbed his hand over his face. His face was dark, furrowed with pain. "Where is the beginning? I feel I can't trust my own mind—it's as if my thoughts have been woven with falsehoods."

"Tell us about the expedition to the Nightwood," Lusha said. "The witches' forest. What did River want you to forget?"

Mara nodded slightly. "Yes—the Nightwood. It's becoming clearer every minute. This was two years ago, not long after River was named Royal Explorer. The emperor had sent him to investigate some disturbing rumors—that the witches were gathering on the other side of the Amarin Valley, possibly preparing for an attack on the southern villages."

"Were the rumors true?" Lusha said.

"No." Mara's expression darkened. "The truth was far worse."

"Go on."

Mara knitted his fingers together, seeming to arrange his thoughts. "Norbu and I were nervous from the beginning," he said. "We were the first explorers to enter the Nightwood in decades, and we had little idea what we would find. River, to my surprise, seemed to have as little enthusiasm as we did. Usually it seemed that the more dangerous the mission, the more he relished it.

"To cross the Amarin Valley from the south, you must use a series of rotting suspension bridges built over a century ago. Each crossing felt like a lifetime. Not merely because the bridges were old, but because we knew that every step brought us closer to the

Nightwood. I fell behind the others, pausing to take notes. I took a single careless step, and a board gave way. The bridge sagged to the side, and then I was falling into darkness."

Mara stopped, a troubled look on his face. In spite of myself, I was rapt. Even shadowed by pain, Mara's voice had the cadence and resonance of a born storyteller.

"What is it?" Lusha said.

"This is where River made me forget," Mara said. "My memory isn't quite right in places—it's like looking into a muddy pool. I must have hit branches as I fell, or I would not have survived. All I know is that they surrounded me as I lay bruised and bleeding on the forest floor.

"They were six in number, but they may as well have been sixty. They were both like and unlike their descriptions in the stories. They moved with a grace that was as far from human as a leopard's prowl, and seemed to melt in and out of the shadows, as if they were shaped from them. Their hair was tangled with leaves and needles, and they stood barefoot in the snow. Their leader—for he was clearly the leader—had a feral look, his hair patchy and his eyes rimmed red. His mouth was twisted, cruel, and despite his broad shoulders he was half a skeleton. He was the most terrifying creature I have ever beheld. The others circled like hungry specters. One said I looked like a noble and might be worth ransoming. Another wanted to torture me until I revealed my purpose. They argued until the leader silenced them with a gesture. They would take me to the empress, he declared, and she would decide my fate."

"The shadow empress?" Lusha said, her eyes widening. "Father said he'd heard rumors of her death."

"Every few years there are rumors of her death," Mara said. "Little is known about what goes on in the Nightwood."

"Did you see her?" Lusha murmured. I found myself leaning forward. The witch empress was a monster commonly invoked to terrify children in the mountain villages, often described as an animate shadow, lacking flesh and bone. *Don't stray too far after dark, or the shadow empress will get you.*

"Thankfully, no," Mara said, "for it became clear that the leader of the group was her son, and I would not care to see the creature who bore him."

"How did you escape?"

Mara swallowed. His hand went to the scar across his forehead. "I nearly didn't. Once they made their decision, one of the witches lifted me and tossed me over his shoulder as if I weighed as much as a doll. Then they were running, leaping through the tree-choked ravine with a nimbleness and speed no human could match.

"We must have traveled for hours. You cannot imagine what it was like. I knew we were moving far too quickly for River and Norbu to follow, if they had even found my trail. I was bounced around carelessly, my face slapped by branches and grazed by boulders. And then we were no longer in the pass—we had left the Empire behind.

"The Nightwood is a strange place, desolate and dark, as if a permanent shadow lingers over the land. The trees are evil, dead-looking things, their limbs twisted together overhead in strange patterns. The farther north we traveled, the more barren the earth became, apart from the trees, which increasingly came to resemble misshapen skeletons rising out of the soil. The air was rimed with a thin, dry smoke, which seemed to rise out of the ground from subterranean fires.

"When finally the leader called for a halt, the witch dropped me to the ground. I lay there, sick and dizzy and in pain, while the witches set about making camp. When I say that, I don't mean they built a fire or erected shelter. For the cold didn't seem to trouble them—in their rags and bare feet, they seemed less conscious of it than I, in my layers and heavy *chuba*. When they slept, they simply chose a place on the ground and lay down in a tangle like a pack of wolves. Before doing so, one of the witches lashed me to a tree."

He paused, his lips pressed together in a tight line. Though I had little affection for Mara, I couldn't help feeling a stab of sympathy.

"The night deepened. I was cold and bloody, with no prospect of relief. The witches set no watch upon me—there was no reason to, in that desolate maze. Tears ran down my face as I contemplated the end in store for me. Then, from the darkness, came a low hiss.

"I saw nothing but shadow at first, until River materialized, tapping his finger against his lips. He moved as silently as the witches had. Without a word, he removed a knife from his *chuba* and began cutting the ropes.

"I was astonished. How had he found our trail? How had he

caught up to us so quickly? These questions, though, dissolved in the face of my overwhelming relief.

"River helped me stand. We managed to stagger away from the sleeping witches and plunge back into the forest. Once we were out of earshot, I opened my mouth to speak, but River again pressed his finger to his mouth. I tried, and failed, to make my footsteps as quiet as his.

"At one point, River stopped and seemed to listen for something. He repeated this several times, though I could hear nothing but the wind brushing through the skeletal branches, which chattered together like teeth.

"Then, suddenly, they were upon us. Hands gripped me, clawed hands that scraped at my skin as I wrenched away." Mara brushed his scar, as if remembering. "One of the witches leaped onto River, rolling him over in the snow, while another seized me, locking my arms behind me so painfully that I sank to my knees. River and the witch were indistinguishable for a moment, and then, to my amazement, he threw the witch off.

"The witches circled. They were only three, and their terrifying leader was not among them. They must have split into two search parties when they noticed I was missing. River met the gaze of a white-haired witch, who stopped suddenly in her tracks.

"'My lord prince!' she said. 'Is it you?'"

Tem let out a stifled gasp.

"*Prince?*" Lusha repeated. Her face against the shadows was very pale. "You're certain that's what she called him?"

Mara gave a grim nod. "I couldn't move—I could only stare,

370

my gaze drifting from River to the witch. He seemed changed—
something in his bearing, or the way he moved, or perhaps I was
merely seeing him truly for the first time. There was an aura of
sinuous power about him that put me in mind of a cobra. He
ordered the witches to release me, and they did so without hesitation. He told them he had been sent by the emperor to spy on
them, and they laughed together, the sound echoing through that
evil place.

"The white-haired witch embraced him as if they were family.
River spoke something low in her ear, and suddenly, the witches
were gone, and I was alone with him.

"I staggered back. My voice returned at last, and I shouted at
him, calling him a traitor and a monster and worse. He watched
me expressionlessly. He seemed to be considering something,
though I could not comprehend what. I knew he meant to kill
me, now that I had learned his secret. He raised his hand."

Mara fell silent again. My heart pounded dully. I felt sick.
Faint.

"Well?" Lusha said. "What happened?"

"I don't know." Mara swallowed. He swiped his hand across
his eyes, as if to clear his vision. "Everything went dark. When I
awoke, I was back in the ravine, and River was beside me. He said
that I had fallen, that he had sent the others ahead to make camp
while he searched for me. There was nothing in his face that belied
his words, and I didn't question him. I recalled nothing beyond
the fall from the bridge."

TWENTY-SIX

WE WERE SILENT for a long moment.

"He's a spy," Tem said, his voice quiet. "All along, a spy."

I felt myself come out of the daze I had been trapped in. Something cold and heavy had settled in my stomach.

"We have to find him," I said. My voice came out too quiet. "Maybe there's another explanation—"

"Don't be mad, Kamzin," Lusha said. "He'll only try to deceive us again. He's a witch. There is no innocence in their hearts, only malice and treachery."

"He rescued Mara," I argued, but my words sounded feeble to my own ears. "Where was the malice there? He could have left him to die, but he didn't."

Mara shook his head. "Perhaps he thought I was useful somehow."

"Kamzin." Tem's voice wavered as he met my gaze. "The witches were banished for a reason. They're murderers and thieves—their power comes from a place of darkness."

"Does the emperor know?" Lusha said. "Could he be part of this?"

"The witches will destroy everything he's built, if they get their powers back," Tem said. His voice was hoarse. "I doubt he even suspects."

"He's won the respect and trust of the court," Mara said. "He will have learned many of the emperor's secrets."

Lusha gazed at the blank wall of the cave. "Including what the emperor has been seeking. The witches' talisman. River will see that the emperor and his shamans never touch it."

"There's more to it than that," Tem said. "The talisman is an object of great power—all the ancient shamans' accounts say so. *A power to remake the world*—that's how one described it. I think it's likely River means to use it to break the binding spell."

For a long moment, no one spoke. The wind howling outside somehow only magnified the silence.

"But that would mean . . ." Lusha's face was pale as death. "Azmiri."

At that word, I felt something break inside me. Azmiri, perched on its mountain overlooking the Southern Aryas—and the Nightwood. Azmiri, its neat, terraced farms stretching to the Amarin Valley, the very route the witches would take if they decided to invade the Empire.

They had once tried to burn the village to the ground, and

had very nearly succeeded. What would they do this time, their powers unleashed and a two-hundred-year-old vengeance in their hearts?

"We won't even have a chance to warn them," Tem murmured.

I lowered my face onto my hand. Spots flitted across my vision, as if I was about to faint. I would have welcomed the darkness, but after a minute, it parted like a curtain.

Lusha was gazing at me with an unfamiliar expression on her face—something akin to pity. It made me want to shout at her or hit her—or bury my face in her neck and sob.

"Kamzin—" she began.

"Stop," I said. "Just stop."

I felt ill, and *hot*. Too hot. The storm was still raging outside, but I didn't care. I walked out of the cave. No one called after me.

Stepping outside into the wind and blowing snow was like being struck by a charging animal. I staggered a few steps, only barely managing to maintain my balance. Then I stumbled headlong into the wind.

I didn't know where I was going. I didn't care. At one point, I tripped and fell, sliding down a small ridge. By chance, I found myself in a depression partially sheltered from the icy wind. I didn't move. I merely lay where I had fallen and cried. Around me the wind howled and the snow pounded its tiny, insignificant fists against the mountain.

How could he do this? How could he lie to me?

On some level, I knew that it was a nonsensical question—if River was truly a witch, asking his reasons for betrayal would be akin to asking why the winter nights brought frost. I pictured all the things he had done—rescuing us from the *fiangul*, plucking me away from the ghosts, sacrificing part of his soul to save my best friend's life. Cutting the rope on the ice wall. What had been the reason for it? Had he merely wanted to keep me at his side, to keep me loyal, so that I would help him? None of it made any sense. And now he was gone, and I could not ask him. He was gone, and I could not rage at him, or kiss him. I loved him and I hated him, but I couldn't tell him.

Lusha found me a few moments later, still in the same position. She didn't say a word, but merely helped me to my feet and led me back into the cave, her arm a gentle weight around my shoulders.

Something tickled my face in the darkness. My eyes opened, my hand reaching automatically to brush at—whatever it was. Something nipped me on the ear, and I caught the glow of tiny green eyes.

Ragtooth. He had been gone since River left. I pulled him to my chest, relieved that he had returned. The fox bore this for only a moment before struggling for freedom. He went to the mouth of the cave—I could see his small outline silhouetted against the night. He glanced over his shoulder, as if waiting for me to follow.

My heart began to pound. Lusha, sleeping next to me, murmured something as I sat up, but did not wake. Silently, I rolled my blanket up and gathered my pack. Then I slipped out of the cave.

I blinked at the view. It was the clearest night I had ever seen.

The clouds were gone, chased away by the wind that scraped its chilly fingers over the mountain. The stars were so bright and so close I felt as if I were standing among them. I could reach out and catch one, trapping it between my palms like a firefly.

Ragtooth growled quietly. As soon as I had emerged from the cave, he had trotted down the slope, heading north. He was stopped now, looking over his shoulder at me.

I followed him.

But I had only traveled a short distance when I heard someone clear their throat. I started, whirling around. Lusha stood only a few steps behind me.

"Where are you going?" she said.

"I don't know." Lusha was a dark, ominous figure above me, her arms crossed and her long hair entwined with the breeze. "Ragtooth wants to show me something."

"And you thought you'd bring your pack?" Lusha limped forward into the starlight. Her expression was almost wry.

My startled brain tried to come up with a response. "I—"

"You think he's going to lead you to River, don't you?"

I said nothing. I looked away, glad that the darkness would hide the flush creeping up my face.

"I can't stop you," she said quietly. "And I can't follow you. None of us can. Do you know what that means? If you keep going, you'll be on your own."

I swallowed. "I know."

She gazed at me. "You might think you know what it's like to be alone in a place like this, but you don't. There will be no one around to fix your mistakes. You'll have to stop making them."

I stared at her. "So you're not going to argue with me?"

She let out a long sigh. "I'm tired of arguing. Aren't you?"

I didn't trust myself to reply. Instead, I simply stepped forward and wrapped Lusha in a hug.

She stiffened at first, likely out of surprise more than anything. Lusha and I did not hug—the last time had probably been when we were both too young to remember it, and no doubt at Father's urging. But, after a little pause, she hugged me back, patting me awkwardly.

She pulled back and lifted her hand. A ribbon of darkness fluttered toward us—Biter. Lusha transferred him onto my shoulder. The raven gave her finger a gentle peck.

"He'll go with you," she said. "At the very least, if you lose your way and want to come back, he'll lead you right."

"Thank you," I murmured.

Lusha paused. "You can't stop River. He's powerful, and he's determined to get his way."

"I know." I shook my head. "But I have to try. This is my responsibility. I brought him here, didn't I? If it wasn't for me, he never would have come this far. If the Empire falls, if Azmiri—" I couldn't finish the sentence.

I wouldn't have made it without you, Kamzin. For a moment I felt like screaming, or collapsing again into sobs. But I forced it down, down, until the fury and pain condensed into a weight deep inside me, small but impossibly heavy.

Lusha touched my face briefly. "None of this is your fault."

She stepped back. "Good luck."

My eyes stung, but I nodded and turned to follow Ragtooth. Biter took to the air, weaving back and forth through the wind like a dark needle.

I turned back only once. Lusha was still standing where I had left her, arms folded, watching me. I could not make out her expression. She looked small from that distance. A childlike figure suspended between the immensities of sky and mountain. I turned away and hurried after Ragtooth.

TWENTY-SEVEN

THE NIGHT WAS eerily quiet.

After enduring the wrath of the wind for so many days, it was liberating to be free of it, at least temporarily—though the still air was heavy with foreboding. It was as if the great mountain had drawn a deep breath, and this was the moment before the exhalation. The sound of my feet crunching through the dry snow was all there was.

Ragtooth, ahead of me, was silent as a ghost. He did not slow or pause, but led me along the ridge Lusha, River, and I had traversed the previous day. I felt a shiver of fear as I spied the disturbed ground. With all the snow that had fallen since, it was difficult to make out the exact path of the avalanche that had trapped Tem and Mara.

"Are you sure this is right?" I said. Ragtooth, of course, made no reply, nor did he pause even to glance back at me. Gritting my teeth, I followed him. I was limping now; the pain radiating up my legs intensified with each step. The simple act of breaking a path through the loose snow seemed to demand more energy than I had left. In spite of everything, I couldn't help fantasizing about the warm cave I had left behind, the feel of blankets piled around me. There was a small noise behind me, and I jumped, my thoughts immediately leaping to Mingma and the other ghosts. But it was only the snow settling. We were moving up the mountain now, away from their tunnels. That, at least, was some small comfort.

Past the ridge was a rocky outcropping that melted into the upper spine of the mountain. Ragtooth led me alongside it for a while, beside a ledge that narrowed and narrowed until I was hugging the rock, and then he stopped.

"What?" I stared. "He went *this* way?"

The fox lifted his leg and begin licking his foot.

The rock face staring back at me was pale, brittle limestone, perhaps two hundred feet high. Past the halfway point, it seemed oddly free of snow and ice. It was not the snow or ice, however, that concerned me—it was the gradual backward arch of the rock, which continued toward a bulge where the snow disappeared altogether. From this bulge I would be suspended, nearly horizontal to the ground thousands of feet below, and travel perhaps fifteen feet in that position until the rock bent back again, after which it seemed to be a reasonable climb to the top of the face.

I sat down, hard.

Ragtooth placed his front paws on my knee, nosing my *chuba*. I barely noticed. I stared at the rock—ordinary rock, grainy and fragmented. I removed my glove and ran my hand over it to feel its texture. I tilted my head back, back, gazing up at the mountainside.

"This is ridiculous," I finally muttered. Sitting there wasn't going to solve anything. I stood up, ready to launch my attempt—

Then promptly fell to my knees and threw up.

This pattern repeated itself over the course of an hour, until I had nothing left in my stomach. I leaned against the rock, gazing at the clouds sweeping over the landscape below, while I swished a lump of snow around in my mouth. Ragtooth had barely moved throughout my convulsions—he merely crouched on a ledge, his tail folded under his chin. Waiting.

I had two options—continue or turn back. The thought of continuing made my stomach churn again. But turning back?

Everything in me recoiled as I imagined walking back down the slope, back to camp, and telling Lusha and Tem that all was lost. Returning to Azmiri with the shapeless, inevitable threat of the witches and their dark powers hanging over the fate of the village. No matter what Lusha said, what had happened with River, and what he would do when he achieved his goal, was my fault. I had led him to Raksha, I had risked my life time and time again to help him. And for what?

Guilt, heavy and cloying, overwhelmed me as I looked back on the days since I had left Azmiri. I had been so consumed with my own success, with impressing River and the emperor, making a name for myself as a great explorer.

How meaningless that seemed now. People had already died because of my choices—how many more lives would be lost?

My mother, I remembered, had once compared guilt to a dagger. *You can let it defeat you*, she had said, *cut you, strike you down. Or you can take it and use it as a weapon against the world.*

I drew myself to my feet. Nausea rose again, but I forced it down.

"All right, River," I said to the wind, "if you made it to the top, I can too."

Not that this statement made sense. River, for all I knew, had turned himself into a cloud shaped like a mountain goat and floated up the rock. I chewed my lip, tilting my head back. Which route should I take? There were several possibilities. If I chose wrong—

I glanced down at the earth, as distant as a star. Well. I would have a long time to regret it.

As I paced, I tripped over a lump in the snow. I kicked at it, expecting to dislodge a rock. Instead, the lump snapped back, dislodging the snow that covered it. I blinked, my mind failing, for a moment, to understand what my eyes were telling it.

It was a boot.

I stumbled back, tripping over Ragtooth in the process. The scream in my throat died as the fall knocked the wind out of me.

Breathe, I told myself. *Breathe. It's just a body. It can't hurt you.*

My mind worked frantically. The boot was old-fashioned, the leather stitched together in a crosshatch pattern that was rarely used anymore. It was weathered, some of the stitches broken by years of exposure to sun and ice. It was another member of Mingma's expedition, still here after fifty years on this lonely slope. I was astonished—I hadn't known that any of those long-ago explorers had made it this far.

The wind rustled over the broken snow, revealing the hem of a familiar, gold-stitched tahrskin *chuba*.

Mingma's.

A tear spilled down my cheek. The explorer's face rose before me—not consumed with bitterness, but the way he had looked when he spoke of his village, lost in a sadness so old it had etched itself across his face like a tracery of scars. He had been young, and brave, and he hadn't deserved what had happened to him.

I wiped my eyes. I had little time for this—I had to catch up to River. But as I turned from Mingma's body, I remembered something.

Did you look through it? I ran out of ink, near the end.

I started. The memory was so vivid it was as if the ghost had spoken in my ear. I wrenched open my pack and pulled out Mingma's maps. With shaking fingers I found the panel that showed the slope I was standing on, then held the thin paper up to the sky. The starlight shone through it.

There. Etched into the malleable parchment, as if with the edge of a fingernail, was a thin, looping scratch. A line—a route, up the side of the mountain.

My vision blurred again. Mingma, like a true explorer, had recorded even his last moments. A character indicating a waypoint was etched onto a ledge above the rock face—he had made it to the top. And then, judging by the position of his body, he had fallen.

Had he been alone? One of his companions had found the body, that was certain—one of the only two survivors, who had retrieved the map and a few of his belongings and fled. But had he been alone when he died?

My hands shaking slightly, I unwrapped Lusha's scarf from my neck. I placed it over the explorer's face, which was only faintly visible through the snow, weighted it with rocks and then covered it with more snow. I felt as if I should say something, but I couldn't find any words. I turned back to the mountain.

I stuffed Ragtooth into my pack and set about arranging my harness. I considered climbing without it, which would have been faster and less fiddly, but Lusha's cautions still rang in my ears, and with Biter circling above, it felt as if my sister were still watching me. I attached two loops of rope to the harness, wrapping them over my shoulders to keep them out of the way. Then I started to climb.

Almost immediately, my mind cleared. My worries about what was ahead quieted to background noise—all I could see was the mountain. Following Mingma's route as closely as I could, I reached the overhang. There I hammered an anchor into a crevice in the rock, and attached one of the rope loops to it with a spring hook. I attached the other loop to a second piton a few feet higher, unclipped from the first, and then repeated the process, moving slowly but surely. Now I was surrounded by stars; I could almost feel the night sky pressing into my back. I did not look down. I tried not to think. One wrong move, just one—

I shoved the terror back, over and over, as I moved through the thin, hungry air.

Ten minutes later, my nails cracked and bleeding from gripping the rock, I had cleared the overhang. Biter squawked at me, his wings beating frantically. He settled into nooks and crannies in the rock above, croaking encouragement. Once I reached him, he would take flight again before positioning himself upon an even higher ledge.

An inhuman moan cut through the regular sound of my footfalls. I pressed my body against the rock as a blast of icy wind engulfed me, nearly knocking me off the mountain. It subsided, but I could hear another howl picking up, speeding in my direction. My chest clenched as I realized why this part of the mountain was free of snow—it was battered daily by vicious winds that beat against this side of Raksha like a turbulent river against a stone.

I had to get off this rock face, fast. I was too exhausted to withstand prolonged attacks by the wind. Another gust struck me, swinging my body sideways like a door. The impact knocked the breath out of me, but I held on. Somehow, I forced myself to pick up the pace. Each time the wind struck, I braced myself until it passed, then climbed another few feet. It was exhausting. I barely noticed the passage of time, or the ache in my arms. All I knew was the feeling of the rock against my hands and the sound of my breathing. I was almost startled when I looked up and found that I had almost reached the crest of the rock face. A few moments later,

I was hoisting myself onto flat ground, and crawling to the shelter provided by a small boulder.

I sat there for a moment, breathing heavily, my legs dangling over the side of the cliff I had just scaled. The sun would rise within the hour; the horizon was lightening and the stars were beginning to fade. The view was immense, too much for my exhausted brain to take in. I took a drink from my canteen and ate a few bites of dried yak meat. Ragtooth hopped onto my lap and accepted a small piece of cheese. Biter settled next to me, his feathers puffed out against the wind. He turned up his beak at my breakfast, but accepted a drink from the water I poured into the palm of my hand.

Once we had finished our meager meal, I tucked myself against the boulder on that barren ledge, drew my hood over my face, and was instantly asleep.

I woke to sunlight spilling over the horizon. For one disoriented moment, I was convinced I had sleepwalked out of my bed and up to the snowy heights above Azmiri village. Then I blinked, remembered, and started upright so quickly I hit my head.

It was several minutes before I was able to force down my involuntary panic and think clearly. How long had it been since I had left Azmiri? I thought about three weeks, but my muddled brain couldn't be more specific. The days blended together like farmers' fields under a carpet of snow.

Rubbing my temple, I took stock. My hands, which I had stupidly failed to tuck inside my *chuba* before I fell asleep, were

386

cramped with cold, the blood from my cracked nails frozen and crusted. My arms were so tired I could barely feel them, and there was an ache in my side—the side that had slammed into the mountain—that was worryingly sharp, and could mean a broken rib. My throat ached from the cold and the ice crystals I couldn't help inhaling; every breath felt like swallowing sandpaper. I had no food left, and very little water, and I was no less exhausted for having slept for an hour—it was too cold, the air too thin, for rest to properly revive me. I had slept not because I had wanted to, but because I had been incapable of maintaining consciousness.

All things considered, my chances of making it to the summit of Raksha were not good. The chances of me making it down the mountain again, however, were almost nonexistent. Descending a mountain was always more dangerous than climbing it, and this had never been more true than it was for me now. I couldn't even imagine tackling the punishing rock face and its violent weather in my current state.

A wave of sadness welled up in me. It wasn't sadness for myself. It was sadness for Tem and Lusha, who would have to accept, as the hours passed and I didn't return to camp, that I was never going to return.

Ragtooth nudged my knee, letting out a squeak.

"You're right," I said, wiping my eyes. "Let's not think about it."

The fox shook himself, stretching. He was shivering with cold, and moved more slowly than usual, but he trotted ahead before I could put him in my pack, thereby lightening my load.

I followed the ledge cautiously, the path underfoot uneven with ice and pebbles. Looming ahead of me was a long, snowy slope, treacherously steep but still walkable. I readied my ax just in case.

Once I had reached the brow of the slope, however, I froze. The ax slipped from my hand, impaling itself in the snow.

"What is that?" I murmured.

Before me lay a long, jagged ridge of spiny rock that punched up through the snow, which misted off the mountainside in the fierce gale. The entire ridge was barely wide enough for a single person to walk along, and in places, it did not even appear wide enough for that. The ground fell away in a miles-long, snowy arc toward the valley on one side, and the lower slopes of Raksha, pierced with boulders that could have been grains of sand, on the other.

I sank to my knees. I could not stop staring at the ridge; I felt as if I could blink and it would be gone, merely a figment of my imagination. After what I had just endured, I had come to this? The mountain was no less than a series of nightmares, each darker than the last.

I looked at Ragtooth. The fox looked back at me. I groaned, my head sinking into my hands.

"How is it possible?" But even as I said it, I began to notice the telltale signs of another person's presence. The snow along the ridge was rippled in places, as if by footsteps that had not yet been worn by the wind. Close to where I sat, a few threads of rope fiber were caught on the sharp edge of a rock. Someone had traversed the ridge, perhaps only a few hours ago.

"Thanks a lot," I muttered, following this with a string of curses that I wished with all my heart River could hear.

Gritting my teeth, I lowered myself onto the ridge. Ragtooth was already creeping along ahead of me, his back hunched, his bushy tail flicking back and forth. The wind was even stronger here than on the rock face, pummeling my body as if its sole desire was to push me to my death. My *chuba* flapped madly, and my hair loosened from its knot and floated around my face, making my vision flicker.

The first few steps were more terrifying than anything I had experienced. I had no fear of heights, but this was not simply a matter of heights. The terrain was treacherous; mounds of snow concealed slippery, uneven rock, or sometimes nothing but crevices and empty air. Each step required calculation and testing—not an easy thing, in my exhausted state. Biter flew ahead, or rather, tried to—the wind buffeted so fiercely that he was often forced to fly far to the side of the ridge.

As furious as I was with River, I couldn't help marveling at his gumption in even attempting a route like this. River had Azar-at, though. I had nothing but a fox and a raven.

The sun rose higher, and the shadows shrank. As I walked, I didn't look ahead. I didn't want to be discouraged by how far I had to go. In some places, the ridge was so thin that it was like walking along a branch. I had to wait for a break between gusts before even attempting these sections, and then dash across them as quickly as I could. This took time—not because of the wind, but because I kept losing my nerve at the last moment, and having to spend several minutes sitting in the snow with my head between my knees.

I had just crossed one of these rock branches, and stood breathing heavily on the other side, when the snow gave way beneath me.

I fell with it—over the side of the ridge.

I swung my ice ax desperately and somehow, somehow, managed to wedge it into a crevice. I hung there, my feet scrabbling uselessly at the snow-blanketed wall of the ridge, as far below me clouds drifted over the landscape.

I found my voice and screamed. I gripped the ax with both hands, my entire body shaking. I dared not look down again. I could not breathe or think. I could *feel* the distance below me, the skeletal nature of the air at this height.

The wind whistled past my ears. In my delirium, it sounded like Lusha's voice, low and disapproving. *There will be no one around to fix your mistakes*, she had said. *You'll have to stop making them.*

Somehow, the memory brought me back to my senses. Ragtooth poked his head over the side of the ridge, staring down at me. He was close, so close. I unhooked the smaller ax from my pack, and swung it up over the edge of the ridge. It caught, and I hauled myself up a foot. Enough to dig my hand into the rock, and hook my leg up over the side. I pulled myself back onto the ridge and lay there, facedown, my feet dangling off either side. Ragtooth licked the top of my head, but I did not move. My breath hissed against the snow, and my forehead began to numb. I stayed there for perhaps a quarter hour before I trusted myself to sit up. Biter settled on my shoulder, croaking softly in my ear.

As much as I wanted to remain there, to simply sit reveling in the sound of my heartbeat pounding in my ears, I knew I could not. After a few deep breaths and a sip from my lightening flask of water, I set off again.

The sun was sinking below the horizon by the time I finally reached the end of the ridge and set foot on solid ground again. I squinted at the darkening sky, dazed. I hadn't even noticed the hours passing, so focused had I been on each step I took.

I thought about continuing, but the terrain was treacherous here—steep and still uncomfortably narrow in places. I didn't trust myself in the darkness, given the state I was in. As I carried no shelter with me, I had only one option: to make a snow cave.

I chose a spot behind a low ridge of rock and began to pile the snow up against it. Once the pile was large enough, I hollowed it out and clambered inside with my blanket. I didn't have the energy to build a proper cave, and this one was big enough to accommodate me only if I curled my legs up. I didn't mind this, however. It was a relief to be sheltered from the vengeful wind and the great and terrible distances, and I was asleep as soon as my eyes closed.

Ragtooth woke me at moonrise. I gazed up at the low roof of my shelter, icy from the melting caused by my breath. I didn't want to move. My head throbbed. Every inch of my body hurt.

I forced myself to leave the cave. I was so tired that the thought of donning my pack made me want to cry. I placed the *kinnika* around my neck and tucked them into my *chuba*. I didn't know why I bothered. I just knew I couldn't leave them behind.

Though sunrise was a long way off, the moon was near half-full, and provided enough light for me to see my way. Even the darkest stars shone here, so far from the earth, and their brighter cousins gleamed like tiny suns. I did not hurry. I was too weary for that, so weary that I no longer felt the pain in my feet or the chill in the wind. Biter, balanced on my shoulder now, nipped at my ear whenever I took a careless step or let my focus drift. Finally, I reached the edge of the ridge, with its jagged projections and pitted mounds, and I could *see* the summit before me. The slope that led to it was gentle, broad, and snowy. Compared to what had preceded it, it was almost a joke. I stepped forward warily, half expecting a chasm to open beneath my feet.

Where was the witch city?

I wondered if it would simply appear in my midst, the world parting like a sheet of fog. I forced my feet to keep moving. I felt half in a dream.

It was a strange feeling, setting off on the last leg of my journey. I had doubted I could come this far under any circumstances, let alone the strange ones I found myself entangled in. I walked on, my boots slicing easily through the dry snow, as the horizon turned from black to indigo to gray. And then I came to a place where the mountain stopped. Where there was nowhere else to go.

I had reached the summit of Raksha.

TWENTY-EIGHT

I BLINKED. STANDING there, I thought I would have felt joy, or astonishment, or even terror, gazing down at the world so far away. Instead I felt a weary relief, like that which followed putting your feet up after a long day, or completing a chore. I was left with only the feeling that something had ended.

The world was still dark, save for the first pale sunbeams that spilled over the horizon. Mountains unfolded across the landscape—the Arya range to the south and west, and the mysterious Ashes to the north. I could see everything in every direction. It was too much to take in, as if I were gazing into a spirit realm that had been shaped by beings far greater and wiser than myself. The summit was a ghost floating in midair, deep shadows beneath it. I gazed around me, taking in the uneven terrain, which dipped toward a lower ridge that was jagged and worn like old teeth. Suddenly, I froze.

The ridge below, which sloped gradually toward the shadowed west, was lined with strangely formed pagodas and towers of what must have been stone, though they had a formless, shifting quality. Some had steps leading up them, while others, perched on precarious outcroppings, seemed made for creatures who could leap great distances or sprout wings and fly. The stone was dark, almost black, and the structures were guarded by tall, carved figures of animals rendered indistinct by the constant buffeting of the wind. Their position allowed for sweeping views to the north and west, while a narrow path—I could make out the line of it through the snow—led to the summit, where I stood.

I had found it—the witches' sky city.

I gazed at it, transfixed by awe and fear. How was it possible that something like this could exist? I closed my eyes, wondering if I had stumbled into a dream. But when I opened them, the city was still there, as incomprehensible as it had been at first sight.

Swallowing, I began making my way cautiously down the stone path. It was steep, each stone uneven and several times the height of an ordinary stair. It was as if the witches had hewn the steps out of the mountainside itself.

I didn't see any sign of River as I approached—the shadows were too thick. Nor was there any trace of his footsteps in the snow. With the high winds, though, I was not surprised. I had to crouch to the ground every few steps, gripping the stone, to avoid being buffeted over the side of the mountain. Biter didn't attempt to fly—he burrowed into my hood, making himself as small as possible. Ragtooth, lower to the ground, did not appear bothered by the wind, though the tufts on his ears flapped madly.

As we approached the city, the first rays of the rising sun struck the towers. I gasped. Small crystals in the stone seemed to catch fire, and the entire city shone like a dark river against the snowy mountain. It was beautiful, though not an inviting sort of beauty. In that land of sky and fading stars, with its strange, enchanted stone, the city was forbidding. More than forbidding—I had an overpowering sense of being unwanted, as if a thousand pairs of angry eyes were boring into my back. The feeling was so strong I swayed, almost losing balance.

Ragtooth, oblivious to my distress, charged ahead, nose to the ground. Gritting my teeth, I stepped off the uneven stairs and followed. My boots crunched through the snow, deafeningly loud, it seemed, in that empty place. The snow was crusted and hard, the wind having swept away any loose powder. I thought—I *thought*—I could just make out the suggestion of someone else's trail.

I surveyed the landscape, the scoured pinnacles and craggy ridges, the city tucked against a half-moon-shaped hollow in the mountainside. I had a strange urge to shout River's name. A ludicrous instinct—River was my enemy. He had used me, and when I was no longer of value to him, he had tossed me aside.

I fought back the swell of fury and grief. I couldn't lose control, not now, after coming so far. I squinted into the brightening sunlight. Where was he?

It doesn't matter, a small voice inside me said. If River had already found the talisman, all was lost. But if he hadn't—

Then I might.

"Biter," I called. Lusha's raven settled on my outstretched arm. "Do you know what we have to do?"

The bird gazed at me with emotionless black eyes. I had never cared for Lusha's ravens, and they, for all I could tell, had never cared for me. But now I felt a strange kinship, as if the creature carried part of my sister inside itself. Biter croaked softly, cocking his head. Then he took off, soaring above the towers of the witch city, where he was lost to sight.

"All right, Ragtooth," I said. "Biter will search from the skies. That leaves us to search from the ground."

We set off, Ragtooth leaping through the drifts, his tail flicking back and forth. My tired, aching body protested as I forced it up a small rise, toward a squat tower with windows but no visible door. It was still hidden from the sun by the shadow of the land.

Something about the strange black stone mesmerized me. It was like no material I had ever seen—the smoothness of obsidian and the density of coal. Everything about it said *stay away*. The tower was not for human eyes. I was not meant to be here. And yet, in spite of this, or perhaps because of it, I felt compelled to touch it. I reached out.

My fingers passed through the stone.

I leaped back as if stung. The tower shuddered, wavering slightly before settling back into shape. There were four windows now, where before there had been five.

A slow shudder traveled from my neck to the base of my spine. The tower was made of shadow. It was impossible. Apparently, that didn't matter in this impossible place.

I took a step back as another shudder raised the hair on my neck. The entire city was like this, its tiered pagodas and open-walled observatories, and unidentifiable beasts guarding it all. Was it truly a shadow city, or were my human eyes unable to comprehend the truth of it—like a monster in a dream that lurked always at the edge of sight? Every instinct screamed at me to turn back. *Stay away.* The angry eyes seemed to bore deeper.

Ragtooth let out a fierce growl. I whirled, following his gaze.

Standing on a raised promontory, his tahrskin *chuba* streaming behind him like a dark banner, was River.

TWENTY-NINE

I DOVE BEHIND the tower before I realized how ridiculous that was—taking shelter behind an apparition. Nevertheless, I poked my head around cautiously. River had not seen me—he stood with his back to me, gazing over the city. I could make out only a sliver of his profile. His arms were crossed, his chin propped in one hand, as if lost in thought.

My mind worked frantically. What did I do now? I couldn't very well search the mountain with River standing guard. Besides that, I had no idea what I was looking for. River had—purposely, no doubt—refused to give any of us even the most basic description of the talisman.

An idea blossomed.

Slowly, I stood up, ignoring Ragtooth's growls. The fox tangled himself in my legs as I walked, trying to trip me.

"Stop that," I hissed. "Trust me, Ragtooth. I have a plan."

The fox gave my boot a spiteful nip, but he allowed me to pass.

River could see me now, if he turned his head. Every instinct in my body screamed at me to hide. I silenced those instincts, focusing on putting one foot in front of the other, on taking calm, even strides. I could have been out for a stroll in Aunt Behe's goji patch. Only the shaking of my hands belied my act.

No big deal, I thought. *I just climbed the world's tallest mountain on a mission to stop you from destroying the Empire. What's new with you, River?*

A mad giggle threatened to escape me. I scanned the area for Azar-at, but to my infinite relief, the fire demon was nowhere to be seen. As I drew near, River cocked his head, as if listening to something. His hearing had always been unnaturally sensitive—why had I never wondered at that? Or any of the other small things that hinted that he was something more—or less—than human? He turned, and his gaze met mine.

"Kamzin!"

Even at a distance, I could see the shock on his face. He stood there a moment, staring. Then he leaped from the rock—a drop of perhaps twenty feet—and strode toward me without pausing. I forced myself to stand still, unflinching.

"Kamzin, how did you—"

"I know what you are," I said. "We broke the memory spell. Mara told us everything."

River's expression faded from stunned to wary. For the first time since I had known him, he seemed at a loss for words.

Then his eyes narrowed.

"So," he said, "you know what I am. But you don't know everything, Kamzin."

"I know that you lied to me." A tear rolled down my face, and I brushed it away angrily.

"I had to. I needed your help."

"How?" I shook my head, lost. "How did you do it, River? Is that even your name?"

"Yes." He took another step toward me, but stopped when he saw me flinch. "It is my name. Though *Shara* is borrowed."

I searched his eyes. Part of me wanted to take another step back, to put more distance between us. But another, stronger part held me in place.

"How did you deceive the emperor and his court?" I demanded. "Whatever you are, whatever you've done, you owe me an explanation, after all we've been through."

"I know." He ran his hand through his hair, as if pondering how to begin. The gesture, absent and unaffected, was so familiar that I found myself faltering. I had expected to confront a witch, a dark creature who had deceived me since our first meeting. Instead, I had found only River.

"Gaining a place at court wasn't difficult," he said. He had to raise his voice to be heard over the wind. "I chose to assume the Shara name for good reason—they are an ancient line, with as many branches as a willow. The family I chose were shy, modest people with few acquaintances at court. With Azar-at's help, I altered their memories so they would recognize me as their brother and son. It wasn't difficult, from there, to insert myself into the emperor's inner circle."

"And no one guessed what you are? Not even the emperor, not his shamans?"

A faint smile crossed his face. "The emperor is clever, Kamzin, but unless given a good reason, he pays little attention to anyone other than himself. He is an obsessive man—obsessed with his youth, his reputation. I gave him no reason to question me."

I shook my head. "Why did you do it? To spy on him?"

"Initially. With the binding spell weakening, we knew that the emperor would be searching for a way to repair it."

"The talisman." I laughed humorlessly. River's plan had been flawless. Not only had he learned the entirety of the emperor's plan, but he had ensured that *he* would be the one to carry it out. It was as clever as it was chilling.

"Yes. Which is not really a talisman at all, but the bones of an ancient king, my ancestor. The most powerful witch who ever lived."

I felt a surge of triumph. Now I knew what I was looking for. "Are you're sure they're here?"

River closed his eyes briefly. "Yes. I feel something—I think it's him."

"But you haven't found anything yet."

"I reached the summit last night," he said. "I had to wait for sunrise to begin my search. After dark, the city has no shape."

Another shiver traveled through me.

"Kamzin." He touched me. I shook him off, hating what I still felt when his hand met mine. Hating him.

"I'm not stupid," I spat. "I know I can't stop you. But I'm going to try. I'll die trying, if I have to. Because I can't let you do this. If the witches get their powers back, they will destroy everything that belongs to the emperor. They'll destroy Azmiri."

"You don't understand." River ran his hand across his face. I noticed, for the first time, how tired he looked. It was subtle, but it was there—in the shadows under his eyes, the tension in his mouth. He was still beautiful, still the same indomitable River. But even he was weary, after all that had happened. "How could you?"

"Why don't you explain it, then?" I said, my voice rising. "Stop lying to me, River. I'm so tired of your lies, I can't—"

"All right." He grabbed my arm, and this time, I didn't draw back. He pulled me close; our faces were only inches apart. "You want to know the truth? The real reason that Emperor Lozong took our powers?"

"I already know," I snapped. "The witches terrorized the Empire. They couldn't be reasoned with. The emperor wanted to protect us. It was the only right thing to do."

"Right?" River laughed, but there was little amusement in it. "The emperor stole from us! Took all but the most rudimentary of our magics away. Trapped us in our human forms and banished us to a nightmarish place. Is *that* right?"

"Then you deny that the witches ever hurt anyone?" I gazed at him incredulously. "You deny that they attacked Azmiri, that they nearly razed it to the ground?"

He made a frustrated sound. "I don't know. It's true that some of my kind are brutal, thoughtless creatures, delighting in cruelty and trickery. I understand that better than most—after the time I spent among humans, I can see my family, myself even, more clearly than they're able to see themselves."

I shook my head. "And yet you still wonder why the emperor bound the witches' powers?"

"He didn't bind them. As I said—he stole them."

I blinked, uncomprehending. "What are you talking about?"

River's gaze drifted over me. "Where are your bells?"

I was momentarily thrown. "I don't have them," I lied, even as I felt one rustle traitorously against my collarbone. "There was no point."

River smiled sadly at that. "Yes. You are as hopeless at magic, Kamzin, as you are spectacularly adept at other things. A fact for which I'm grateful—I'm glad I don't have to fight you."

I swallowed against a lump in my throat. "What do the *kinnika* have to do with stolen magic?"

"Everything," he said. "They *are* stolen magic. So is every other talisman used by shamans."

I stared.

"You're mad," I said finally. "The shamans have their own power."

River gave a short laugh. "Some do—a trivial, rudimentary power, nothing compared to ours. In the old days, the shamans would heal animals, tame dragons, brew potions to ward off illness—small magics, the extent of their abilities. Now that they've come to rely on talismans, their power is much greater. But not because their own gifts have grown."

I shook my head. I couldn't comprehend it. "Magic needs talismans to harness and direct the flow of power from the shaman. That's always been true. Chirri called them 'the cardinal links.'"

"Forget about what you learned from Chirri. What I'm telling you is the truth: the emperor stole our powers and trapped them within commonplace objects. Objects that could be sold, or traded, or distributed at his discretion. These are the talismans you speak of so highly. It's true that talismans existed, in some form, before they were imbued with our magic, but these were mere objects of superstition peddled by charlatans. The emperor attacked the witches not because of our supposedly evil deeds, but because he wanted our power. As his empire grew, he became increasingly fearful of us. He had his armies, his powerful weaponry, his great cities, but we had an ancient magic he could not understand. And so he stole it."

I did step back then, because it was too much. I couldn't process it. I thought of the talismans I had used—fumbling, unsure—in my lessons with Chirri. I thought of the *kinnika*. Could this be true? Could they be vessels of dark magic, and not mere tools to channel a shaman's own power? I had certainly never felt any power stir within me, but then I had always assumed that was because I had as much talent for magic as a badger had for flight.

"I'm not asking you to believe me," River said. "Because I know you will, eventually. But do you understand?"

"But does this mean—" I couldn't speak. "It means the

emperor's shamans will be defenseless if the spell breaks? We'll all be defenseless?"

River gazed at me for a long moment.

"I'm sorry, Kamzin," he said.

"River, please." I was close to tears now. "I don't understand this, or what the emperor did all those years ago. But let me help you. Tem can give you your powers back—I'm sure he could, if he tried. Just you—not the others. I know that you don't want to hurt anyone. Please, let me help you."

He brushed a strand of hair back from my face. "I wish you could. But there is only one way for me to be free."

I shook my head, unable to look away from him. "Please don't do this."

His expression was dark. The amusement was gone, replaced by something flat and cold. "You shouldn't have followed me here, Kamzin."

A sharp cry overhead. Biter fluttered into view, his wings beating madly at the thin air. River and I both looked up as the raven circled, then darted away, flying toward a wind-scoured cliff just below the summit of the mountain.

"Biter!" I shouted, horrified. He was going to show River where the talisman was. "To me, to me!"

But the wind snatched my voice from my lips. Biter flapped up the cliff and came to rest on a narrow ridge crowned by a single tower, which tilted to one side. The light hadn't hit it yet—a pillar of shadow, even blacker than the blackness that surrounded it.

"Well." River gazed at me, a calculating look on his face. "It seems these pets of yours do have their uses."

I stared back, uncertain, as the seconds stretched out. River knew where the dead king's remains were now. Why didn't he do something? Use his power to cut a path through the snow, or split the mountainside open and retrieve the witch's bones. But he only stood there, watching me, as if trying to glean my thoughts.

That was when it hit me.

I may have destabilized something. River had said it in Winding Pass, after his spell had defeated the *fiangul*. I remembered the second avalanche that had been triggered when he rescued Tem. River would be afraid to use Azar-at's magic here—if he did, there could be consequences. Consequences that could destroy the witch king's grave. A fierce hope rose within me.

I met River's eyes, narrowed now, and realized we were having the same thought.

Perhaps all was not lost after all.

"Kamzin—" he began.

I didn't hear the rest. I was running, faster than I ever had run before.

If I can get there first, I thought. *If I can get my hands on even one of those bones, if I can give it to Biter, if he can take it to Tem—*

I couldn't hear River pursuing me. I had no idea if I had outpaced him, or if he was there, drifting like a dark cloud at my heels. I ran, exhaustion making the motion feel dreamlike—my feet, churning up the snows, could have belonged to someone else. I reached the cliff, which was bracketed by a pointed ridge that formed a small canyon. Snow piled in deep drifts at its base. I stumbled, letting out a shout that echoed oddly off the rock. Every sound was amplified in the canyon—the clatter of loose rock as it slipped under my feet, the rasp of my breath. It was as if the mountain mocked my efforts.

I began to climb, my hands trembling against the icy stone. My fingers, chafed by the climb up the rock face where Mingma had died, burned from the effort, the skin tearing again. Still I forced myself up. I could make it. I had strength left.

But then—

A strong hand wrapped around my boot, and I was airborne. I landed in a drift of snow with an *oof*, the wind knocked out of me. I lay still, too surprised to move, one leg folded awkwardly beneath me. River, barely pausing, began to climb, moving as smoothly up the rock as a shadow. Ragtooth scrabbled after him with a ferocious growl.

"Ragtooth, no!" I remembered all too well what River had done to Lurker. But River only glanced once at Ragtooth, then kept going, and the fox soon slipped down the rock. Already River was almost halfway up the cliff, his *chuba* whipped by the wind.

I stood, and a red-hot bolt of pain darted up my leg. I sagged against the rock as spots flickered across my vision. My ankle was twisted—badly.

I took a slow, deep breath, counting silently to three. *It's nothing*, I told myself, as the pain seared and pulsed. *It's nothing. You're fine.* I forced those thoughts to flood my mind, forced back the pain.

I started climbing again.

River was well ahead of me, but I moved like a possessed thing, and soon closed the distance. It was a twisted version of our old game—the memory of it, of the laughter we had shared, made me burn with fury. He glanced down, an amazed look on his face.

"It's no use," he called, and the mountain echoed his words, twisted strangely by the wind. "You won't make it, Kamzin."

"Maybe not." I met his gaze, knowing my face was contorted with pain and fury. "But neither will you." I reached into my *chuba* and drew the *kinnika* out. They were warm from pressing against my skin, or perhaps from the magic that ran through the metal.

River stared at me. Then he began to laugh, so hard he had to lean into the rock for support. The mountain echoed the sound, sharing his amusement.

"Kamzin, Kamzin," he said, "you couldn't bespell a mouse, let alone a witch."

I flushed. It was true: my gesture had been an empty threat, a distraction. But as I glared at him, the pain raging in my leg, one of the bells twitched.

Not the black one—that was still, quiescent. The one beside it, the scorched bell carved with the symbol for "witch." It had sounded before, many times, for no apparent reason.

But always, I realized with a chilling certainty, when River was near.

I looked back at River—almost too slowly to catch the grimace that flickered across his face. It was gone in a heartbeat. If I hadn't been looking for it, I never would have noticed.

"It hurts you," I breathed.

"Kamzin." River's voice was low, warning. Its echo was a whisper, thin as thread. "Don't—"

I yanked on the bell, and it broke from the chain. Gripping the tiny thing in my palm, I sounded it as hard as I could.

There was no mockery in the mountain's voice now. The bell's ringing flooded the canyon, notes clashing with their own echoes, a terrible cacophony that hurt my ears. The wind howled as the sound spilled across the mountainside, as if it too was in pain.

River pressed his forehead against the rock face, his shoulders shaking. I couldn't make out his expression, but it seemed like every muscle in his body had grown taut, as if he fought an invisible attacker.

He turned to me, his face a grimace of pain, and for one heart-wrenching second, I faltered.

What was I doing? This was *River*—I had saved his life. He had saved mine. We had faced death so many times, relying on each other with that pure and total trust that was fundamental to survival in a place like this, and in that moment, some animal instinct rebelled against hurting him.

Father. Aunt Behe. Chirri.

Their faces crowded my mind, along with those of every aunt and uncle, cousin and acquaintance in Azmiri. I saw my home, its tidy, whitewashed walls hung with the familiar tapestries. The well that Tem and I used to race to, the orchard where we stole apples every fall—those apples would be almost ripe now, the farmers pacing among the trees at dawn, tallying the harvest. I saw black flame consuming them, consuming everything I had ever known.

I sounded the bell again.

The wind howled. River slipped another foot as the bell's piercing tongue sang out, and the echoes answered tenfold. It was as if the entire mountain was keening. My head pounded and my eyes watered. I rang the bell again, and River slipped another foot.

"Kamzin," River murmured. He was almost level with me. Our eyes met, and his gaze was not cold anymore—it was desperate, a desperation tinged with sorrow. He was terribly pale, the freckles standing out in stark relief. For one agonizing second, I felt my heart stop.

No.

I sounded the bell with all my strength.

River fell. He struck an overhang, which broke free with a terrible *crack*. And then he was gone, tumbling into shadow and out of sight.

THIRTY

A SOB ESCAPED me. I pressed my face into the mountain. My cheeks were wet with tears that dripped from my chin and onto the rock, where they froze instantly, glistening.

Keep going, some small part of me said. *You're not finished.* But I couldn't keep going. I could barely breathe.

My foot slipped, and the pain in my ankle wrenched me back to myself. I remembered where I was—at the summit of Mount Raksha, in a city of shadow.

Stay calm, the voice said. *Just a little longer. Then you can fall apart. Then you can rest.*

The tears didn't stop, but they slowed—enough for me to see my way. Because of my ankle, I was forced to climb with a sort of hopping motion, as dangerous as it was tiring. The rock was nowhere near as high as anything I had recently climbed—if it had been back in Azmiri, I would have laughed at it. But by the time I reached the top, I was so exhausted I could barely stand.

I wiped my face—the tears had partially frozen, covering my cheeks in a lacework of ice. I reattached the witch bell to the string of *kinnika* and dropped them in the snow. I couldn't look at them—I couldn't think about what I had done.

River was gone, but that didn't mean the danger was past. The binding spell would break, if not today, then tomorrow, or a year from now. It made no difference. When it broke, the Empire would surely fall, and Azmiri with it.

I had to find the witch king's bones.

The shadow tower loomed before me, wavering ever so slightly in the breeze. It was hard to believe it had ever had a practical function, even when it wasn't terrifyingly shapeless—it was windowless, and barely broad enough for a person to stand in. Perhaps a monument?

But a monument to what? I scanned the ledge. In front of me, it sloped down, toward a sheer drop of thousands of feet. I could see Raksha's neighboring mountain, which River and I had named Aimo, ensconced in cloud—it was higher than Azmiri, but below where I stood now. The land fell away, crumbling, its decay hastened by endless cycles of wind and snow. Jutting out from the rocky earth was the edge of a box.

A coffin.

I staggered forward, ignoring the dangerous slope and the expanse beyond it. I tried to pull on it—the wood was so ancient that it seemed to splinter in my hands, and the box remained stubbornly stuck in the mountainside. Changing tacks, I scrabbled at the frozen ground, managing to pry up a sheet of ice that held the box locked in place. Finally, the soil shifted, and I pulled the coffin free.

I stared at it, hardly daring to move. Inside were the bones of an ancient witch king. How could I think about touching them? How could I even think about opening his coffin?

As I sat there, the wind seemed to whisper in my ears. The shadow tower—had it moved? Was it closer to me now?

I shook off my fears. I was here, at long last, and I had to do this. Still, a strange sorrow tugged at me, at the notion of disturbing the rest of an ancient king, witch or no. River's ancestor.

"Forgive me," I whispered, and wrenched the heavy lid back.

It skidded sideways, landing in the snow with a dull *thud*. Swallowing, I gazed down at the skeleton.

It was paler than moonlight, and so fragile it looked liable to turn to dust if touched. Any clothes it had worn had long since disintegrated. The bones had a faint sheen, a glow that seemed to emanate from within.

Apart from this, there was nothing to identify it as a witch. The skeleton could have belonged to an ordinary man, if ordinary men received burials in shadow cities thousands of feet in the sky.

I was pondering what to do next when I heard the black bell sound. I turned slowly, my heart heavy with dread.

Behind me, close enough I could reach out to touch its smoke fur, stood Azar-at, tail wagging, a doggish grin on its face. Clutched in its jaws was the string of *kinnika*. The black bell swayed back and forth, though there was no wind to move it.

Ching, ching, ching.

"Azar-at," I said hoarsely, "give those to me."

Should not abandon power, brave one, the fire demon said. *Should keep it close, keep it safe, or others will come and claim.*

I lunged after the creature, but it retreated toward the mountainside—with every step, just out of my reach. I finally stopped, gasping, my ankle throbbing.

Suddenly, Ragtooth was there, a growling, spitting bundle of fur. He launched himself at the fire demon. Azar-at, startled by his ferocity, fell back a step, dropping the *kinnika* in the snow. The fox nipped at the creature's toes, forcing it back another step.

"Ragtooth!" I shouted. "Get back!"

But Ragtooth was impervious to my commands. And Azar-at, to my horror, seemed to be quite over its surprise at the attack. Its form wavered, dissolving, and for a moment it became a smoke cloud with only the hint of a hideous, grinning face.

Ragtooth darted toward the *kinnika*, ignoring my shouts. They were inches from his grasp when the fire demon shifted position again, appearing at the fox's side. Ragtooth reared, teeth bared, but Azar-at was faster. The creature snatched Ragtooth in its mouth, shaking him from side to side like a ragdoll. Then it threw him against the mountainside, so hard a piece of rock shattered into a cloud of dust. The fox tumbled into the snow, his back bent at a strange angle, and was still.

Ragtooth.

It was impossible to comprehend it. I fell to my knees. Any

moment now, Ragtooth would sit up and shake himself. He was hurt, that was all. He would rise again, and everything would be fine.

But he didn't move.

A guttural sound tore from my throat. Something was choking me, something inside me that clawed its way to my chest. I couldn't look away from Ragtooth's motionless form. In some distant corner of my awareness, I knew that Azar-at had taken up the *kinnika* again, and was gliding away, toward some dark shape that appeared at the edge of my sight.

"We'll take it from here, Kamzin," River said.

I whirled around and screamed.

River was an image from a nightmare. Blood soaked one side of his head, running in rivulets down his face. His right arm was angled oddly. The bone stuck out above his elbow, piercing his *chuba*. I felt sick.

"River—" I choked out.

"Concerned?" Despite his state, his expression was still eerily cold. "Don't worry, I'll heal soon enough. As soon as I have my rightful powers—which won't be long now. Ah—thank you, Azar-at."

The fire demon dropped the *kinnika* into his hand. Wincing as the witch bell sang out, River turned and flung them over the side of the mountain.

I let out a wordless cry. River didn't even pause. He bent over the bones of the witch king.

Shakily, my ankle screaming in protest, I took a step. Then

another. Then, suddenly, I was running headlong across the ground, which sloped downward, toward the terrifying drop. I plowed into him, knocking him over.

We rolled together. I knew that the empty air was close, so close, but I was heedless of the danger. I had to stop him. Somehow, I had to. When finally the motion ceased, I was on top of him, pressing his shoulders to the ground.

"Kamzin," he said.

I realized I was crying again. I couldn't look at him. I fell sideways, and he rose, his fingers brushing my hair. I couldn't stop him—I couldn't even lift my head.

"For what it's worth," he murmured in my ear, "I'm sorry."

"River, please—" But he was already turning away. He bent over the bones and seemed to run his hand over the skull without touching it. Something unreadable flitted across his face. Then he turned to Azar-at.

"Let's end this." He raised a hand over the bones and closed his eyes.

The bones seemed to flicker, small shadows flitting over them like birds. Then, to my horror, they began to move. The dead king seemed to raise himself into a half-sitting position, one arm darting out as if for balance. River raised his hand again, and the flickering, rippling apparition intensified. The shadow spread over River and the king, then spilled up into the sky, where it pooled and pulsed like a spreading wound.

The world shattered.

The ground heaved, pitching me sideways. I would have

tumbled right off the cliff if my instincts hadn't kicked in, causing me to slam my hand into the earth like the blade of an ax. The lid of the coffin slid down the slope and into the abyss of sky. The rumbling grew. Boulders shook loose from the mountain and tumbled into the sky, or rolled through the witch city, tearing its towers apart. My vision flickered; shadows darted everywhere, or perhaps the world had turned to shadow, I didn't know. There came the distant roar of avalanche after avalanche. It was as if the mountain was tearing itself apart, and all I could do was wait for it to fall out from beneath me, and leave me adrift in the clouds.

Then, after what could have been seconds or hours, the mountain stopped roiling, and the shadows cleared enough for me to see. River was crouched on the snow, his hands pressed against his head.

He seemed to be muttering something, but the words were garbled and unintelligible. The air rippled around him, as if the shadows were descending upon his body, consuming him. He let out a cry of agony, and then another. I pressed my hands against my ears—even after the mountain's terrible roar, this sound was so raw, so agonized, that I could not bear it.

Finally, River was silent, his breath hissing against the snow. Azar-at approached him and sniffed his head. He sat up slowly.

Are you all right?

"Yes." River sounded dazed. The strange rippling was gone. He stared down at his hands, as if seeing them for the first time. He began to laugh. It was his old laugh—and yet it was different, a darker version of the same color.

You smell of the wilds now, Azar-at said. *Of forests and lakes and open skies. Of rock and earth and valley.*

"Thank you, my friend." Though River sounded exhausted, he was smiling. I could no longer see any sign of injury—no blood or broken bone. He stroked the fire demon's muzzle. "According to the terms we agreed to, our contract is dissolved. I have my rightful powers now. And so do the others."

Azar-at nuzzled his hand. *I will miss you.*

"Strangely enough, given how you have gnawed away at my soul, I feel the same." He gave the fire demon's ears one last scratch. "Good-bye."

Good-bye, my friend.

River stood. He seemed to have changed in a way that was impossible for me to describe. There was a *lightness* about him—a grace and otherness. Though he still looked the same, it was somehow starkly clear, in a way that had not been quite visible before, that he was not human.

"River?" The tears were drying on my face. I felt hollowed out, a frozen, empty vessel.

He looked at me only once. Then his gaze drifted past, and his eyes closed, his expression flooded with what could only be described as joy, pure as sunlight or rain. It happened suddenly, too sudden for human eyes to follow. One moment, River was there; the next, a black leopard stood in his place, its long fur ruffled in the wind, half shadow and half flesh.

The leopard shook itself. The sunlight made its coat gleam with fire and copper. It stretched, then set off at a run, heading toward the cliff's edge. As if delighted by the sensation, it ran even faster. It leaped down the side of the mountain, its claws gripping effortlessly at the nearly sheer slopes. I followed it as far as I could, until it rounded the curve of the mountainside. Then, in a moment shorter than a breath, it was gone.

THIRTY-ONE

I SCRAMBLED BACK down the rock below the witch king's grave, my knees wobbly, my breathing uneven. I was traveling too quickly; as I lifted my foot, my boot caught, and I lost my grip. I slid down the last few feet, scraping my palms, not even bothering to arrest my fall. I came to a stop finally, and lay there on my side. I had no desire to get up again. I turned my face into the snow, my shoulders heaving with my sobs.

I had gathered Ragtooth's small body into my pack, unable to bear the thought of leaving him in that forsaken place. Now I clutched the pack to my chest, howling. My tears were for Ragtooth, but they were also for Lusha. For Tem. For my father. For myself. I had failed. And now we were all lost.

Finally, there were no tears left. My breath came in ragged pants as I stared blindly at the sky. I felt as if I could lie there until the snow and ice covered me, as it had covered Mingma's broken body. Biter alighted on a rock nearby, croaking, but I paid him no notice.

Then something warm brushed the top of my head. Something with a long snout that seemed to exhale pure heat, almost too hot to bear. Slowly, I sat up and turned to face Azar-at.

The fire demon cocked its head at me. *No help for sorrow, brave one*, it said. *Best to carry on. This is not a place for lingering.*

I recoiled, my disgust so strong it was like a living thing twisting in my stomach. "Go away."

It is over, the fire demon murmured. *Nothing more to do here. Best to leave, help friends. Friends are waiting for you—*

"Go away!" I screamed. My voice echoed off the mountainside, and came back to me in broken fragments.

Azar-at fell silent, but it did not leave my side. Warmth radiated from its body. I felt myself shivering as the feeling returned to my hands and face. I hadn't noticed how chilled I was.

"Why are you here?" I said, every inch of me despising the creature. I wasn't afraid anymore—let it kill me, see if I cared. Let it snatch me up in its jaws and break me as it had broken Ragtooth. "Did you stay to gloat?"

Gloat?

"The spell is broken," I said. "The witches are free. Free to destroy the Empire, and everything in their path. Your plan worked."

Not my plan. The fire demon tilted its snout back to sniff the air. *River's plan. I care nothing for spells and schemes. I merely help my friends.*

I laughed, a cold, empty sound. "Yes, I've seen where your help leads. People will die because of what you've done. Does that make you happy?"

Death is a human notion, Azar-at said. *I do not understand your question.*

I made a frustrated noise. "Of course not. Fire demons don't answer questions, do they? They share power, not wisdom. That's what the stories say."

Azar-at only cocked its head at me, tail wagging gently, looking for all the world like a dog eager to please. I shoved my fingers into my hair, digging them into my scalp so hard I could feel the strands tear. Think, I commanded. *Think.*

What's wrong, brave one?

"What's wrong?" I let out another dead laugh. "What's wrong is that I have to do something. But I can't. I can't even get myself off this mountain, let alone—"

Let alone? What must you do?

"I don't know," I cried. "I have to stop this somehow. What if the witches attack Azmiri? What if they hurt my family?"

Azar-at whined. *That would be sad. Witches must not harm them.*

My eyes narrowed. "Why do you care? In case you don't remember, you've already murdered someone I love."

For River. To help my friend. I care about you. You are my friend too.

At those words, Yonden's warning echoed through my thoughts. A cold shiver traced its way down my back.

"I would rather die." My voice was flat.

You need me. Something changed in the fire demon's tone. It became low, soft. *You need a friend, Kamzin.*

I turned away, wishing I could block that strange, silken voice from my mind. "No."

Think about it. I could grant you power—power greater, perhaps, than what I granted River. For even though we forged a mighty partnership, he is a witch, and fire demons clash with witches as smoke does with shadow. But you—you could be great. You could save your friends down below. You could fight witches, protect your village, protect the emperor himself. You could do whatever you wished.

"And you would help me?" I gazed at Azar-at, disbelief mingling with my disgust. "Even if what I asked went against what River would want? We're not on the same side, you know."

The fire demon's tail stopped wagging briefly, then started again.

I do not understand sides, it said. *I help my friends.*

"I can't believe I'm even talking about this." I rubbed my hands over my face and stood. "I will not make a contract with a fire demon. I'm not as mad as River. Biter—come."

I limped off, moving only slightly more steadily than before. My muscles were straw, my head ached with pain and dehydration, my ankle was a red-hot mass. I had no food, no water, no medicine. There was no way, the logical part of my brain knew, that I could make it back down the mountain, no way I could rescue Lusha and Tem.

But the logical part of my brain was not in control now. I kept walking, feeling as if I had been hollowed out.

The fire demon fell into step beside me. *You saw how my contract with River ended,* it said. *It is not a trick. We could end our agreement at any time. You would have only to say the words, and I will be gone.*

I forced a dismissive laugh. It sounded false to my own ears. My heart was thudding again, and my thoughts had begun to race.

What Azar-at said was true. River had ended the contract when he no longer needed it. Was it truly that easy?

How will you help your friends, Kamzin?

Tem's face rose in my mind, creased with weariness and pain. I saw Lusha hunched over her broken ankle. I shivered and stopped walking. Biter croaked softly.

"I've never been good at anything," I murmured. I wasn't sure if I was speaking to Azar-at or myself. "Except *this.* Climbing. Mapping. Exploring. But I have to be good at more than that, if I'm going to be any use to Lusha or Tem. Or anyone."

The fire demon's tail wagged faster. *Then you agree to the contract.*

"I haven't agreed to anything," I snapped. "If I was even going to consider this, you would have to accept my conditions. You might not want anything to do with me, after you hear them."

Please, Azar-at said, *tell me.*

"One, you will not lie to me," I said. "If I ask you a question— any question—you will answer honestly. Is that clear?"

I would never lie to my friends.

"Is that clear?" I said, emphasizing each word.

The fire demon paused. *Yes.*

"Two, you will leave when I ask you to," I said. "No matter when that happens. No matter how it happens. Our contract will end when I wish it to end."

I said that—

"I know what you said, and I also know that you like to twist words," I said. "So I'm straightening them out for you. Do you agree?"

Yes, Kamzin.

"Three," I went on, "you must not hurt anyone I care about. Not even if I ask you to."

You would never hurt your friends.

"I might." I swallowed, recalling how River had looked, the chill in his gaze. "If I give you enough of my soul, I might stop caring about the things I care about now. I don't know for certain. But I won't let you turn me into a monster. That will never happen."

The fire demon was silent for a long moment. *I agree to your conditions.*

I glanced at Biter. The raven croaked, his tail feathers twitching. "I know," I said to him. "But I can't think of anything else to do." Hopelessness threatened to overwhelm me. But it was a reckless sort of hopelessness, a feeling that skittered inside me like a captive insect, and made the blood thrum in my veins. "I won't be powerless. I won't feel the way I felt back there with River, not ever again."

The raven cocked his head, regarding me.

I began to pace. If I accepted Azar-at's power, I could save Lusha and Tem. Not only that—I could return to Azmiri, and battle the witches myself. For I didn't doubt there would be a battle. Even if the witches didn't strike Azmiri, Father would never allow them to pass through the Amarin Valley into the Empire. He would stand between them and their path to the Three Cities. Without great power on his side, he would die.

And as for my soul—

I saw black fire sweeping the village, heard the anguished screams. What use would I have for a soul, if everyone I loved was dead?

I turned back to the fire demon. "Azar-at, I accept your offer."

Immediately, I felt a strange tugging sensation somewhere around my navel. Or heart—it was hard to be certain. I gasped, stumbling forward. In the same moment, the fire demon disappeared, melting into a column of liquid flame that crackled and sparked. I bit back a cry as the cloud drifted toward me. Little bolts shivered off, striking the snow, which melted with a sizzle. I thought, for a moment, that I saw a terrible, grinning face at the center of the column, with a gaping mouth of fangs and eyes as black as emptiness. But then it was gone, and the cloud had enveloped me. The tugging sensation dissolved into wrenching pain—but before I could even draw breath to scream, it was gone, leaving me half in doubt that it had ever been. When the light faded, I found myself hunched over in the snow, my hand pressed against my chest. Azar-at sat in the same place, tail still wagging, as if nothing had happened.

But I knew it had.

I stood slowly, trying to judge where this new feeling of strangeness, of *imbalance*, emanated from. But I couldn't place it. Biter croaked softly.

"I'm all right," I said, "I think." I turned to Azar-at. "I don't want the others to know."

Azar-at seemed to ponder this. *As you wish, Kamzin.*

I took a deep breath, gazing at the landscape before me, the snowy slopes touched with fire from the newly risen sun. Somewhere, in the still-shadowed curve of Mount Raksha, Lusha and Tem waited for me. And somewhere in the distance, in an equally shadowy and terrible corner of the land, the witches were awakening to a new day. A new world.

"All right," I said, setting my jaw. "Let's go home."

ACKNOWLEDGMENTS

THANKS TO MY brilliant agent, Brianne Johnson, who is the best possible champion an author could have, and to my equally brilliant editor, Kristin Rens, for her insights, questions, and encouragement. Thanks to Jeff Huang, the artist behind the amazing cover, and to the rest of the team at Balzer + Bray (I couldn't imagine a better publishing home), including Bess Braswell, Tyler Breitfeller, Laura Kaplan, Sarah Kaufman, Kelsey Murphy, Emily Rader, and copy editor Janet Robbins Rosenberg.

Thanks also to those who read the book and provided enormously helpful feedback at various stages, including Amy Chen, Stephanie Li, Jordan Rai, and Wendy Xu. Thanks to Dr. Lauran Hartley, for her many insights on Tibetan culture and language, and to Shannon Grant, for reading it twice. Any flaws remaining are, of course, mine alone.

I also want to acknowledge the incredible female mountaineers who helped inspire this story, particularly Lhakpa Sherpa and Junko Tabei. And finally, thanks to my family and friends, for their encouragement and support, particularly my parents and my sister, and to you, for picking this book up and joining Kamzin's expedition into the unknown.